Ascension
A *Tangled Axon* Novel

Ascension
A *Tangled Axon* Novel

Jacqueline Koyanagi

MASQUE

ASCENSION
A *TANGLED AXON* NOVEL

Copyright © 2013 by Jacqueline Koyanagi.

Cover art by Scott Grimando.
Cover design by Sherin Nicole.

Masque Books
www.masque-books.com

Masque Books is an imprint of Prime Books
www.prime-books.com

For more information, contact Masque Books.
publisher@masque-books.com

Print ISBN: 978-1-60701-401-0
Ebook ISBN: 978-1-60701-400-3

Printed in Canada

For all those who were born to be in the sky.

Chapter One

Heat buffeted my face, whipping my locs behind me. Sweat and dirt stung my eyes as I held my breath.

Please let their waveguides hold. We can't lose another ship.

Aunt Lai and I watched the Series IV Greenbelt disappear into the atmosphere, carrying a team of biosynths with it. They couldn't even think about seeding the universe with new species without a working ship, and that's where we came in, the engineers: stitching together humanity's lifeline out in the Big Quiet.

The biosynths could only cover half the labor costs for repairing their damaged waveguides, but we took the work anyway. Money was money in this economy. Even when it wasn't *enough* money.

The team had cast impatient glances toward the sky while we worked, as if those naked planets might bioform without them. I knew that look. That craving to break free of the ground. Dirt doesn't feel right on the heels of someone born to be in the sky.

I'd had my hands in the entrails of so many ships I'd lost count, but even after over thirty system-years of life on Orpim, I'd never set foot off-planet. An entire universe carried on without me out there in the silence while I kept everyone else flying. I couldn't tell you how many nights I lost sleep imagining tendrils of electromagnetism arcing through the cosmos, holding together the galaxies and planets our biosynths ignited with life. And there I was, a woman who yearned so hard for the sky there had to be stars in my blood, yet I was stuck in Heliodor City, missing it all.

Neither Lai nor I said the obvious as we stood with dust in our hair and mouths, watching the place in the sky where the Greenbelt had disappeared into the upper atmosphere.

Our last pending job.

Maybe solar winds would blow in another one tomorrow, but we never knew, and debt didn't pay itself back. When the economy tanked twelve years ago, the freelance shipping industry took the biggest hit. Ships and pilots alike fell into disrepair when manufacturers and medical facilities started outsourcing to Transliminal Solutions in a desperate attempt to save their businesses. Starship surgeons like Lai and me? We struggled along behind everyone else, taking whatever repairs folks could afford to throw at us. Half the ships out there probably floated along in the silence on a spirit guide's prayer, hoping their sails and waveguides and thrusters held for just one more month, one more year, instead of coming in for the tune-ups that could save their engines when it counted.

During times of need, it was always the people with the least to give who ended up sacrificing the most. Hardly a building remained in our sector that wasn't a palimpsest of closed businesses.

"Well," Lai said with one heavy slap on my back, mouth forced into a smile. "That's that."

I twisted a copper wire around one finger, coiling and uncoiling it needlessly. A leather tool belt hung heavy at my waist, like old hope gone slack. "Yeah. That's that."

She winked at me, gripping my shoulder with a rough hand. Despite her smile, the tension in her muscles betrayed her true feelings. I'd been watching her grow more frightened with every launched vessel. Seemed like the time between jobs got bigger by the day.

"Supposed to get warmer overnight," she said, heading to the entrance of the shop and inputting the security code. Her hands shook: age and disease catching up with her faster than it should have.

"Mm-hmm."

There was so much we weren't saying as we stepped inside, door whispering closed behind us. So much about our empty shipyard. About the chronic meds we couldn't afford. About the gear we needed to replace. About the back rent we still owed my sister Nova, and the magnanimously offered debt forgiveness she continued to hold over my head.

"I heard Bran closed shop yesterday," Lai said. "Took a job at Translim."

"Yeah, she told me that was coming." I sat on the counter at the front of the shop, picking at the grime under my nails. Did we have to talk about this? What good did it do to be reminded?

Lai dropped her tool belt onto the rusted table and dabbed the sweat from her face with a towel. "At least they're paying her decent. Got the shift supervisor position."

Tension drew the air drum-tight between us at the mention of Transliminal. Quietly, Lai tied back her locs, avoiding my gaze. She traded her cargos and boots for slacks and a tie, and called a transport to take her to her second job at the call center. I wanted to tell her to quit, to have more faith in her work. If all the fringe folk folded, there'd be no one left to hold up our cities.

No point in saying it again. As much as the sight of Lai in that damned costume gnawed at me, I just let her put it on without comment. Old arguments tasted sour, anyway.

Within five minutes the shuttle arrived, the letters "TS" slicing across its black hull in sharp, iridescent white. As the transport attendant grabbed Lai's hand and helped her up, I caught a glimpse of the face below the pilot's helmet. My heart stuttered before I could ice it over.

Kugler, my friend-turned-girlfriend-turned-ex-wife. The girl I grew up chasing around the Adul research station on our school breaks, three planets away, while our parents worked on translating an alien language. The woman I'd thought I'd fallen for until I realized the difference between love and nostalgia.

I leaned on the shuttle and shoved my hands in my pockets. "I didn't think you worked this shift anymore."

Kugler was quiet for a beat, eyes darting over my hair, my work-worn clothes. The crisp lines of her pristine uniform looked alien out here on the fringe. Even more so on her.

A memory flashed through my mind—an image of her face pressed against a viewport on the station, making goofy expressions at the Adulan giants floating outside. She'd painted a stolen dermal layer over her cheeks; it shimmered in cascades of white and blue as it translated our message into the Adulan color-language. White, blue, white, followed by a complex ripple.

Do you dream?

Or at least that's what we were trying to ask. We knew it was probably gibberish to the Adulans, and that we'd never understand the response even if we got one.

Today, Kugler ignored me while Lai settled herself into the nearest transport seat, making no effort to conceal her eavesdropping.

"I thought you hated nights," I said.

"Yeah, well," Kugler said. "Third shift pays better. I bet you're still barely scraping by just so you can flirt with old ships."

I clenched my teeth.

"Thought so," she said, then turned toward the navigational controls. I wanted to retort with some nasty comment about roping women into long-term relationships with grand promises of metal and flight, only to tell them to give it all up for babies and real estate. Our final argument—a year ago—happened when she tried to get me to leave the shop to work for

Transliminal Solutions like her. "Stability is more important than playing with dying vessels," she'd said, clutching one of my medical bills.

I felt lied to. With her rakish hair and quick wit, it was as if she'd promised me someone more independent and left-of-center than she ultimately was. Seeing her there now, wearing her cool posture like a mask, she couldn't fool me—she still hated me for choosing my work, just like I hated her because I lost her friendship in the divorce.

Whether it was dignity or pride that kept me from saying anything while standing in front of the transport doorway, I don't know. Maybe it was the lines around her mouth that were now much deeper than when we'd met. Heliodoran life wasn't kind to anyone.

A light pressure landed on my arm. Lai crouched in the shuttle to reach down and touch me, jogging me out of my bitterness. Her soft-but-stern expression said everything: Be the bigger person.

"You take care of yourself, Kugler," I said, then turned to my aunt without giving Kugler room to respond. "Do you have your medication?"

Kugler rolled her eyes and threw herself into the pilot's seat, passive-aggressively checking the time display embedded in the sleeve of her jacket. She tossed me a final glance—one I couldn't quite parse—and activated the anti-glare lenses over her retinas, darkening her eyes.

Lai held up a bright blue bottle, then raised her eyebrows to ask me whether I had my medication too. I held up my own: *Yep, I've got it.*

We popped the lids, fished out a pill each, did a mock toast over the short distance between us, and tossed them back. We were pros; no need for a chaser.

I backed away as the shuttle took off toward downtown Heliodor, kicking up a small vortex of dirt. Every time Lai left, I worried about her. She didn't fit into the city center's culture,

Translim tech coating it to a high sheen. Out here, we were all old stone and rotting wood, with a grotesque touch of high-tech gloss here and there where someone had dumped their savings into one last push, one last effort to not be left behind.

But let's face it. We were dirt to flick from the shoulder of the city, nothing more.

As I went back to cleaning up the mess we'd made working on the Greenbelt, I fell into a natural rhythm that helped me think about something other than money. I recalled the distinct sounds of the Greenbelt's engine, its song stuck in my head. Metal and coil resonating quietly around a heart of fire. Every piece of scrap felt good in my hands, and the heft of my tools was as natural to me as my own skin. Nothing that provided this much purpose and joy could ever be in vain, no matter what Kugler said.

The sun set on the city while I worked, orange light glinting off the opalescent albacite exterior of its central buildings. Heliodor's eyelids grew heavy, but out here we never really went to bed, just in case a job showed up. You slept in your office, your shipyard, your bar. Some of us even figured out how to nap on our feet. The trick was to stand with your feet shoulder-width apart, hips in front of something solid in case you leaned forward. And to make sure your neural interface's notification settings were on if you had one; nothing woke me up like a screech in the ear when someone walked into the shop.

As if reading my thoughts, a notification buzzed in my right ear, followed by a sonorous voice: *Monthly check-in with Doctor Shrike, due within the hour.* My fourth reminder today.

Ugh. Fine.

I dropped the scrap and looked at my empty hands to determine how bad the tremors were today—hands that should have been learning the curves of a ship instead of reaching for prescriptions. Hands that would become unreliable without medication, weak and gnarled. I didn't feel sorry for myself.

I knew I could accomplish amazing feats with these hands, given the right tools and a ship to love. It's just that, well, I got frustrated that my ability to function—to do the one thing I'd loved since childhood—was entirely dependent on synthesized chemicals.

No use dwelling on it. Besides, after three years of saving, my bank account said I was halfway to the Transliminal Solutions remedy that would fix both me and Lai—our system's medicine could only treat, not heal. Transliminal would cure.

I washed my hands and turned on the comm panel at the back of the shop. An old model left over from when this place was a dentist's office, before my sister bought it. I beeped Dr. Shrike, and her face soon appeared on the screen.

I barely recognized her. In lieu of her usual short blond hair, she'd grown parrot feathers. Her aged skin was now smooth and youthful, while storms of shifting color undulated in her eyes.

Transliminal mods. Envy surged in my gut.

"Doctor," I said, leaning back into my chair and resting my hands on my stomach. "You've had work done. Going on vacation?"

She laughed and looked away, nervously touching her feathers —the anxiety of the privileged. "How are you feeling, Alana? Any pain today?"

"Some. Just the usual."

"Hands? Back? Neck?"

"Yes."

"Legs?" Each time she blinked, it drew my attention to the auroras in her eyes.

"Yes."

She took notes on the implant along her inner arm. "We can try anti-inflammatories to—"

"No, that's okay. I can't afford it."

"We have payment plans for meds. I really wish you'd consider one and upgrade your pain management. Doing these check-ins is already a stretch. What I really need is for you to come in every month and let me examine—"

"I have the Dexitek. I'm good."

She sighed and shook her head a little, then continued with her litany of questions. She tried the same thing every month, and every month I refused. People like Shrike had no idea what it meant to have to choose between paying bills and paying for food. How *could* she understand? And if I paid for a new cocktail of pain management meds now, I wouldn't be able to afford the real treatment later.

The one that would mean saving myself.

"Any lameness, numbness?" she said. "Loss of motor function?"

"A little tingling in the fingers of my left hand about a week ago."

She nodded and tapped in my answer, feathers bobbing. "Nothing to be too alarmed about. Loss of visual or aural acuity?"

"Come again?"

"Very funny. Loss of appetite?"

"Definitely not."

"Heart palpitations?"

"Only when I beep you, Doctor." I bounced my eyebrows at her and laughed when she tried ignoring my flirting. Though I did get a tiny grin out of her.

"Any reactions to the medication or other concerns to report?"

"All systems functioning within normal parameters, Captain."

"Okay, okay." Shrike swept a finger along her implant and its light went dim. She clasped her hands together and leaned closer to the screen. "Alana. This," she said, gesturing to her modifications, "feels incredible. I don't even experience *light* the same way now—"

"How nice for you."

Shrike raised her hands defensively. "I'm getting to a point here. I had no idea how easily Transliminal could manipulate the body until I experienced it myself. This has real promise. I know you're saving for the treatment, but I'm sending you a free Translim sample."

"Of what? Feathers?"

"A slow-acting cure."

I sat up. "What do you mean?"

"This is a viable alternative to the one-time treatment. It's a proven cure to Metak's Disease, PTSD, agoraphobia, drug addiction, even Holme's—"

"And Mel's Disorder?" I nearly whispered.

"Yes, Alana." Shrike smiled in that condescending way doctors had when they believed they could save you. "Mel's too."

A small light flickered near the bottom of the screen, and the distribution panel next to it flicked open. Inside the compartment was a small, clear package vacuum-sealed around a tiny purple pill with a "P" engraved on it. I took it between my fingers.

"Stands for Panacea," she said. "Appropriately."

"How does it work?"

She flushed. "That, I'm not sure. Transliminal is playing its cards as close to its chest as it can. We do know the Nulan government has sanctioned it, and that it's a genetic treatment that comes in a series, but I couldn't get more than one sample dose per month. They may be doing a lot to help the people on our side of the breach, but profit is still the bottom line, and they want you to know what you're missing after you've taken just one. You'll develop a temporary dependency after one dose. Take it, but only when you're absolutely sure you want to. After the first treatment, you will either need to take it the rest of your life or suffer a . . . very uncomfortable week of withdrawal. Your condition might even worsen. Be careful."

"How much?" I said, weighing the package in my palm.

"Alana, we can figure out—"

"Doctor Shrike, how much?"

"Three-thousand credits a month."

I sighed, examining the unassuming little thing that could supposedly give me a small taste of healing. Take the pill, and I'd know what it meant to be in a state of *no-pain* for four weeks, but to stay that way, I'd have to come up with more than I usually made in a month. Translim sure knew how to rope us in.

"Transliminal does offer payment plans, Alana," Shrike said quietly.

Great. I knew all about their "payment plans." More like indentured servitude. They'd own not just my city, but my body. My suffering and its relief. My life. Not sure how I felt about this so-called panacea.

She avoided looking directly at me. "I still think asking your sister to help you would be a good idea."

"I told you. She doesn't support Transliminal's technology. She won't even take clients who work for them."

"Well . . . " Shrike fidgeted. "As I said, they do have payment plans."

"Don't you have to work for Transliminal to qualify?"

She was quiet for a beat. "I think they could use someone with your experience in their outreach department—"

"No." Make that hell no. Not if I had to hang up my tool belt.

"Alana—"

"See you next month."

I cut off the transmission.

I couldn't think about it anymore. I shoved the Panacea sample into my pocket where it snuggled up to the familiar vial of Dexitek that would keep me going until I could afford something else, whatever that ended up being.

Exhaustion chewed at my muscles, so I grabbed a plumberry from the kitchen, cut it up, climbed up to the roof, and lay down on my sweat-soaked back. Spasms twitched across my neck to my arm, nerves firing with referred pain. The inevitable consequence of physical labor when you lived in a body like mine.

Every part of me that wasn't hurting melted into the albacite tile Nova had installed when she bought the place. An unfortunate reminder that she'd gentrify the whole fringe if she could, but I still loved it up there. It was the closest I could come to the Big Quiet. On the roof, I could set aside all the financial woes and the nerve pain and just let myself *be* for a while.

I held a slice of the fruit up to the full moon, pale light shining through it, turning it into a jewel. Juice dripped down my fingers and mingled with the dirt beneath my nails, trailing in syrupy rivulets down my arm.

A gift from my sister. Every time she finished leading a new client into a deluded, mindless stupor—what she called "raising their vibrations"—my sister sent me something from the planet's biocatalog to celebrate completing another guide contract, another notch on her belt. Sometimes it was something nasty, like the wrong end of a sea creature masquerading as a local delicacy, but this? Heaven. It's like my whole childhood burst on my tongue, all the sweet and sour of it, the sunbaked possibility I'd lost somewhere on the way to adulthood.

I licked the juice from my arm, relishing in the sugar mixed with a metal tang that was practically seared into my skin from a lifetime of making love to machines. A thrill shivered up from the soles of my feet to my legs, my hips, my chest. Fringe folk learned how to take pleasure in small things.

In that moment, I could forget about Dr. Shrike and my disease, forget about making decisions about treatments. I could forget that Lai was being scrutinized by Transliminal Solutions while cold-calling failing businesses to solicit tech upgrades. I could forget about the money we owed the hospital, or about the power my sister had over our shop. I could even still the ache in my chest where my parents lived—parents I hadn't seen in over three years because none of us could afford interplanetary travel anymore. And they didn't want Nova's charity any more than I did. Not when it came packaged with lectures about the pointlessness of scientific research in a universe where "real magic could be found within." Or something like that.

Now, between the fruit and the moon, there was only me. I relaxed my sore body, weary from work and illness. The stabbing along my right arm was almost welcome, a reminder that I was alive despite it all, and that I was working as hard as I had to if I wanted to get out of this pretentious hole of a city, disease or no.

I looked up at the gradient of atmosphere and space, with me at one end and *everything* at the other. Maybe gravity is more will than physics, and all it takes is a lapse of faith to float away. Lying there, juice-soaked and tired, I could believe it. The roof seemed to lift away from the building in a swell of vertigo, my brain convincing my body it was actually floating into the black by sheer force of desire. I opened my arms to the Big Quiet beyond and imagined I was falling up into the oil-dark blood of the universe.

Lost in the magnetic upward pull, I started fantasizing a ship descending toward me, belly open as if it would swallow me right there on the roof and carry me into the silence. She'd come a long way, I imagined, for the chance to be heard by someone who knew how to listen to her song. For someone to heal her—a sky surgeon. Me.

Don't you worry, sweet thing, I thought to the ship. *I hear you. I'll hear you even when I've gone deaf with age. I'll hear you through my skin if I have to, and I'll help you live forever.*

Yeah, I know. I talked to ships the way other folks might talk to a lover who haunted their dreams. But me, I wasn't waiting for someone to rescue me. I waited for vessels *I* could rescue from death by chop shop. Beauty didn't deserve to go out like that. All that metal wrapped around a beating plasma heart, an engine full of fire. No human could compare; people fell dim in the shadows of the ships I touched.

When my imaginary ship kept descending toward the repair lot, stirring the Orpim dirt into a frenzy, I sat up. The air around me bent and rippled with heat from the ship's secondary thrusters as they blasted the land. Bands of plasma illuminated the yard, zapping the rods we'd set up around the landing area. Dust whipped around the vessel, grit stinging my eyes despite my high vantage point.

This was no fantasy. It was a job.

The transport ship seemed to stare at me with its bridge windows like two unblinking eyes, challenging me to diagnose it, heal it, send it back into the Big Quiet. And in return, I'd be a small percentage closer to the treatment.

"You got it, gorgeous," I mumbled with a grin. I didn't care how tired I was or how nauseated the Dexitek left me. My hands itched at the sight of her. I scrambled to my feet and almost slipped off the slick white tile.

A small figure disembarked from the vessel's cargo bay and headed for the shop below, but I couldn't make out their features in the dark. I tried shouting at them, telling them I'd be there in a minute, but the engine noise drowned out my words. I braced myself on my way back to the ladder, careful not to slip again.

Moments later, an urgent voice came via neural interface. "Hello? We're looking for Ms. Quick."

I flipped the tiny transmit switch behind my ear with the tip of my nail, connecting my voice to the intercom in the shop. "I'm coming! Hang on a second."

"It's important," the voice barked.

"I hear you, I'll be right there. I'm coming down."

At first I took the ladder to the stairwell one rung at a time, but I couldn't get down there fast enough—I bypassed the last dozen rungs by sliding down while lightly gripping the banisters. Taking two steps at a time, I banged my way down the metal stairwell to the office, wiping my hands on my pants to rid them of juice and grease.

A voluptuous woman stood in the doorway of the shop, her dark hair pulled back in a high ponytail, toes of her shoes barely crossing the threshold. She bounced in place, eyes darting around the lobby as if she were looking for something specific.

"What can I do for you?" I said, nodding my chin at her. "How's your drive—"

She strode forward and placed a hand on my shoulder. Her nails were short like mine, but not anywhere near as dirty. Between her joyless face and the tension in her hand, I figured there must be something seriously wrong with her vessel. Bad for them, good for me.

I peeked around her to determine whether I could diagnose the ship at a distance, but everything I could see from that angle looked fine. I'd need to examine her hands-on, and believe me, I wasn't complaining. My blood raced just thinking about working on an old Gartik transport. They didn't make those anymore, not since Central bought up the Gartik Shipyard fifty years ago and turned it into a pharmaceutical distribution warehouse. So where'd this one come from? Someone had done some serious mod work on her, from the look of it. An extra structure bubbled up out of the starboard side, shimmering each time a tendril of plasma discharged from the electric rings around her engine. Just gorgeous. Whoever owned her clearly loved her hard enough to treat her like a lady even in this crap economy.

"You're Ms. Quick, right?" the woman said, jerking my attention back to her. "Marshall and Thia's daughter?"

She still gripped my shoulder, but I held out a hand in the hope that a little courtesy could calm her split nerves. "I sure am, where did you hear about us?"

Ignoring my hand, she pulled me out the door by the shoulder. "We're going for a ride."

I stumbled along with her. "Who are you?"

"We're contracting you for a month or so," the woman said, hurrying me toward the ship. "Already put the request through your agent. Straightforward guide work."

"Whoa." I twisted away from her and held my hands up in front of me. "Guide work? I'm an engineer, not a spirit guide. Where'd you get that idea?"

She sighed. "Nova Quick?"

"Alana. Nova's my sister."

She paused, eyes flicking to the side while obviously listening to someone over comm. Her movements were harried but professional. I tried not to betray my eagerness while I waited.

"She's gone," I said at length. "Nova hasn't been back here for about six months now. But where are you headed to? If you need some work done—"

The corner of her mouth twitched downward and she looked at me again. "We didn't know about you. Where is she? Your sister."

"I don't know," I lied. Nova would kill me if I told anyone how to contact her while she was on vacation. I wasn't about to bite the hand that feeds.

"Seriously?" She raised her eyebrows as if I were just being difficult.

A passing Transliminal transport's light illuminated us from above, the overwhelming whir from its engine joining the Gartik's song in a cacophony of sound, prolonging the silence between us. Our eyes remained locked, but I couldn't think of anything to say that would placate her. How could I work this to my advantage? There was an opportunity here; I could feel it.

"You have no idea where she is?" she said, wrestling with her obvious impatience.

I shrugged and put on my best nonchalant expression. "There are a few possibilities, but I'm her sister, not her assistant."

"She owns this place, doesn't she?"

I straightened my back. "The building. Not the business."

Again her eyes flicked to the side as someone stole her attention over comm, while I was equally distracted by the metal lady behind her. The slick curves of the vessel glinted under the moon and yard lights, even while covered in the wounds of a long life. There was grace left in her yet. They'd kept the drive on a low cycle; I swore I could hear music in the plasma arcs dancing around her thrusters. My heart cracked open and peeled apart, desperate for a chance to let her in, to learn the rhythm of her.

Nothing was ever enough. I always craved one more ship, one more surgery. Kugler didn't leave me because I didn't want to be tied down. That was just easier to digest than the truth. Every woman I'd ever been with had left me for the same reason, just variations on a theme: I'd never put them before my work.

Could you blame me? Look at the old girl, all power and freedom dressed in light. I could never give up the dream of wiping the dirt off my heels and living in the black.

Now I wondered why I had to open my fool mouth about Nova. I could have pretended to be her long enough to get on the ship. Not that I looked anything like a spirit guide—my surgeon locs alone should have given that away—but it would have been worth a shot.

"Hey," I said, but the woman held up her hand to tell me to be quiet while she listened to whoever was on the other end of her comm connection. Her captain? What kind of captain buys and mods an old Gartik like that? I felt like a little kid waiting for the right time to interrupt her parents to ask for a new toy. My hands shook, I was so anxious for the chance to change my life. Or maybe it was the medication. Never could tell.

I readied myself, preparing a speech. Lai told me sometimes you have to be rude to effect change since the people with power have no reason to listen.

"I hate to interrupt your call, but I can tell you're in need of a new engineer. Fresh eyes, fresh hands. And mine know what they're doing. I've been working with ships since my fingers were too small to fit around—"

"Never mind," the woman said to me, cutting off her comm connection. "Sorry to have bothered you."

She was already heading back to the ship before I could gather my wits. I jogged to catch up and hurried along next to her, locs bouncing down my back. "Wait! Please. If you bring me with you, you won't ever worry about drifting in the silence without a working engine. I guarantee it."

"We have an engineer and two shuttles for emergencies," she said, still walking.

"Okay. But what if something happens to your chief engineer? Couldn't you use a second?"

The electricity grew louder and more dangerous the closer we got to the ship, but I wasn't afraid. No one who belonged in the black feared the ships that delivered us there. If anything, the power of it thrilled me.

"You need me," I shouted over the noise as she hurried and I scrambled to keep up. "You need a second—"

"What we need is your sister."

Story of my damn life.

"I don't understand," I said. "Why don't you just ask her agent where she is if you want her so badly?"

She didn't answer, but came to a halt and looked straight at me. There was a flicker of tension across her face.

"Please, just let me talk to the cap—"

She cut me off. "Sweetheart, we hear the same thing in every city. Everyone's looking for a job. Everyone's a damned expert who can change your life. What makes you so special?"

"I've been doing surgery since I was old enough to—"

"Save it; that's an old story. It's not up to me. Sorry." She started back to the ship.

I kept following her, so she paused again, and put a hand on my chest. Beautiful though she was, she was also a formidable human barrier between me and the craft, all black hair and fierce eyes. "If you're such a great sky surgeon, you'll know to stand back."

"And if you need my sister so badly, you'd recognize I'm the only one who can help you."

She stepped closer to me and jabbed me in the chest with her finger. "You do know where she is, don't you." It wasn't a question.

I shrugged one shoulder, then slowly pushed her hand away from me. "Mind not touching? As for my sister, that depends."

She clicked off her comm link, scrutinizing me. "How much do you want?"

"A job."

"Look, you're deluding yourself if you think you can just bargain your way onto a ship's crew, especially this one. Anyway, the captain heard our conversation and I told you, she said no." She leaned in, voice barely wavering. "Please. We really need your sister."

I picked at my fingernails and shrugged again. Desperate or not, I wasn't about to hand over my leverage. When I looked up, I stood alone. I just watched as the woman walked swiftly toward the ship and disappeared into it without wasting a single glance back.

I sat on an old crate and stared at the cargo hold, watching crew members move in and out of the ship. A large man examined the thrusters on both the port and starboard sides of the vessel for their pre-takeoff checks, while the woman I'd met dropped off a few crates in our yard. Sweat darkened her shirt beneath the arms and along her back.

Eventually, she glanced at me, making eye contact. She looked angry when she saw me see her.

Let her see you. Let her be reminded of what you can offer. Be patient.

If they wanted my sister badly enough, I'd let them come to

me. I had something they wanted, and more importantly, they had something I needed. Money. Opportunity. I could make at least five times as much on a crew than I did on-planet. Sure, the income wasn't reliable, but neither was the work down here. Better to try something new than keep bashing your head against the same wall.

At least out there, I'd be worth something. Engineers were insurance against a dead vessel. I could do a lot more for me and Lai if I could land a position on a crew. Send money back to her. Get us out of debt, get her up there with me. Get our treatments from Transliminal.

See my parents again.

I'd been trying for years. Asking around. Seeing if any crews were looking for a surgeon, but they never were. Either they already had one or they were saving to upgrade to a ship that ran on Transliminal's "dark energy." Whatever that was. Crews came to us for minor repairs to major damage until they could shed an old skin for a new one. Perfectly good old skin that just needed a little help to stay healthy.

Even in the dark, Heliodor wrapped its heavy, hot arms around me and squeezed the water from my pores. I wiped the back of my hand across my forehead, smearing sweat and desert dirt across my skin. I was used to it, but I could tell the crew wasn't. The engineer wiped his broad face with his shirt while he worked, and the woman looked more agitated with every passing minute.

Finally, she approached me again, makeup now smeared around her eyes from the heat, black strands of hair plastered against the side of her face.

"Sorry," I said, grinning. "Bathrooms are for paying customers only."

"Look." She scraped her teeth over her bottom lip and looked as if she wanted to punch me. Instead, she patted the air and looked away for a moment, as if calming herself down. "This is ridiculous. You can't expect—"

"I don't expect anything. You have needs, and so do I. Didn't your mother ever tell you no one gives you anything for free?"

"Will you just listen for a second?" She glanced at the ship, looking nervous. "You can't expect me to reverse the captain's decision. She has good reason to be paranoid about extra folks milling around our ship, no matter who they happen to be related to. But it seems to me if a ship has its external comm systems offline, then its sensors are offline too. Seems pretty easy for cargo to make it on board without anyone noticing."

"I don't need to transport cargo. I need—"

"Seems to me," she said, stepping closer, "that if the cargo were discovered once said ship were well out of orbit, there'd be no sense in wasting fuel just to turn around and drop the cargo back off. Especially when the cargo turns out to be *useful.*"

She raised her eyebrows at me, then took a few steps back, shrugging. "Not that a medical officer would be able to do anything to help the cargo once it's discovered, because what does a medical officer know about cargo, anyway? We take off in five minutes." She gave me a pointed look, then turned around, and headed back to the ship.

So that was it. Stow away for a chance to change everything, or go back inside. Go back to the debt and the illness and the thin strand of hope that tethered me to Heliodor.

I waited. The shaking in my hands grew worse, so I shoved them in my pockets and grabbed the Dexitek bottle with my right, fingers brushing the free Panacea sample from Dr. Shrike. If I left, there'd be no time to beep Lai first. No time to take anything with me. If I wanted this, I had to do it now.

The engineer came back outside and did the pre-takeoff checks. I couldn't help wondering why it was him, and not the pilot. Everything about this felt strange. Why was the medical officer the one doing all the talking? Why didn't the pilot come outside?

Why did my bones ache at the sight of this ship?

At least a few minutes had to have passed. *Make up your mind, Alana.*

I waited until another minute passed without anyone emerging from the cargo hold, then I moved forward and hid behind an old hull panel closer to the vessel. When I still didn't see anyone come out, I moved from the panel to the other side of the ship in a low crouch, trying my best to hide behind molded crates and metal scrap.

The ship's mouth yawned in front of me. Inside, stacks of sturdy crates were belted to the hold floor. Not a crew member in sight.

If you had dogs at your heels and all the galaxy's glittering possibility in front of you, where do you think you'd go? Backward or forward?

Electricity zapped one of the yard's dissipator rods, sparks raining down on the ship, and I swore I felt her sizzle in my own veins, twining electromagnetic fingers inside me. She was calling, this ship. More than any of the other vessels I'd met, *she* wanted me. I felt it. All her heat and light pulsed like blood, scorching my body, urging my feet onward, toward the mouth, whether I wanted them to move or not. Seeing her close-up like this made me come unbound; my old life peeled away like shed skin, making room for her. I felt like a new soul, naïve and open.

The ship was connecting to me through her song. Welding us together. Heat like that was bound to leave a mark.

Only part of me was aware of my movements. The rest of my consciousness was lodged deep inside the metal of the Gartik transport, beckoned by the mind of the ship. One step after another, I headed into the cargo hold, tucked myself into an empty crate, and held my breath.

Minutes later, the cargo door screeched and slammed shut. Hunger growled inside that sound—a crunching and gnashing of metal teeth. I couldn't help feeling like the vessel was digesting me and turning me into a new organ, a pacemaker stitched into her heart.

Vibrations from the takeoff threatened to shatter bone and tear ligament as I braced myself against the flat walls of the crate. My body rattled as badly as my heart while I crouched there, sweaty and scared, barely dodging a panic attack. I guess in light of my situation—and by situation, I mean crime—I figured I was doing pretty well.

My thick locs hung heavy over my shoulders and back, rendering the heat in the crate all the more oppressive. Pills rattled in my pocket, a chattering of tiny white teeth reminding me of what was at stake if this went as badly as it could. *If you run out of Dexitek . . .*

I tried ignoring the sound of the pills, focusing on the ship's rhythm. Her engine's pulse. Her voice. Letting her inside just as I insinuated myself into her.

What's your name, beautiful?

Every ship I worked on, I got to know by learning her song. I imagined each one stringing wires through me like new arteries, connecting us until I could feel what ailed her reflected in the pain patterns of my own flesh. It was the only hint of spirit guide-like talent that had seeped its way into me. The rest had gone to my sister. When I worked, I imagined shrugging into each ship's hull like a second skin and feeling her ailments inside myself. Getting the scent of her on me until we were more a gradient than two distinct bodies. Each job made me feel alive.

Now, thinking about the vessel peeling up out of the atmosphere and into the silence, the last bits of Heliodor's dirt shaking from the soles of my boots, I felt a little like I was dying. I was in a box, after all. Curled up and hurled into the Big Quiet.

A smile crept along my lips and I pressed my fingers harder against the walls.

I'd take it. I'd take death for a new life.

Chapter Two

All quiet. We were out of Orpim's atmosphere.

The tension that had crept into my muscles traveled into my stomach, seething there like a threat.

I'm in the silence!

For the first time in years, no chunk of rock hugged me to it, and the only city stink to speak of was the smell that still clung to me. Outside—beyond the box, beyond the hull—was the black.

The sheer magnitude of what I'd done hit me. I felt dizzy.

A new thought chewed at the edge of my mind, plucking at my nerves: Lai. I had to at least try to tell her where I was. The last thing I needed was to become a missing person, another flash on the crime ticker. You know, the one no one paid attention to except grieving parents and lovers.

I relaxed my body against one corner of the crate—"relaxed" being relative to my previously inelegant attempt not to break my nose against the surrounding metal. My stomach still churned badly enough that I had to make a conscious effort not to throw up, but I'd manage.

Clicking the transmit switch behind my ear, I oriented my mind toward my aunt and said her name, hoping their disabled comm system wouldn't interfere. While I waited for the connection to take, I kept half my awareness tuned into my surroundings, listening for footfalls. Waiting for someone to find me and grab my arm, my neck, a fistful of my locs, to throw me into the brig—

A click in my ear.

"User offline. Send message?"

They must have kept her late at the call center again.

"Yes."

A beep.

"Hey. Lai." I lowered my voice. "It's me. Look, something came up and if everything works out, I won't be around for . . . a little while. I can't tell you where I am, but I need you to trust me. Everything's fine. Or it will be, if this works. Just don't worry too much. I'll beep you when I can."

Panic ebbed in my gut. Either I would succeed and give us a chance to start over, or else I'd just make life far, far worse. Living in a penal colony wouldn't exactly be conducive to contributing to a household income. They'd probably butcher my head when they removed my neural comm implant, too. Who knew if they'd bother with the Mel's meds; I'd be a useless bag of tremors in no time. Not to mention I was leaving Lai to run the shop alone, banking everything on instinct. Here I was trying to be adventurous while she rotted in the dust and plastic debris of a planet that outgrew us by the minute.

Stop thinking about it. Calm down and listen.

Other than my heartbeat, everything was quiet. I'd been in the crate, breathing hot air on myself for—how long had it been? Ten minutes? An hour? I couldn't know for sure. The stale warmth grew more oppressive by the minute and my legs were cramping. I'd have given almost anything for a glass of water and a bathroom.

I hadn't thought this through. How would I know we were far enough away from the planet to reveal myself? Timing was everything. That medical officer had a good point; I needed to wait long enough that they'd be foolish to turn around and waste fuel. If she was willing to give me that information, they must have really needed my sister.

Still, what was I going to say when they found me? Just rattle off my qualifications again? "I'm sorry, Captain, for stowing away on your vessel. Please don't torture me for information. Let me show you all my surgeon tricks—I can sit, roll over, beg, and even balance a wrench on my nose. Aren't I adorable? Don't you just have to keep me?"

Maybe I should take a nap and see how long I could stand it inside the cramped space. That had to be better than agonizing over what would happen if this didn't work out the way the medical officer had implied. And I was so exhausted my eyes burned.

There was enough air coming in through the wide seams, discomfort aside. If I bent my neck to the left, it didn't hurt quite so much. Sure, I'd pay for it later, but being calm enough to fall asleep might save my ass. Now if I could just get my foot out from under—

What was that sound?

A low rumble, soft but menacing.

Growling?

A shadow moved somewhere outside. Shuffling. Footsteps. More growling, and from the sound, it was coming from deep inside a thick, muscular body. Who keeps an animal in their cargo bay? Was the animal part of the cargo? I didn't remember seeing any cages, but then I wasn't exactly sightseeing. Still, you'd think I'd remember something like that.

The shadow moved, looming larger. Heavy-booted footfalls drew nearer. These were unmistakably human.

An enormous figure dwarfed my pitiful crate. Bracing myself for the inevitable confrontation, I tried ignoring the cramp pinching harder at my stomach with every step the person took.

More growling, right next to the crate. A person—a human—was growling at me. In a ship.

Then came the barking.

At that point I was sure I'd slipped into a dream state,

or maybe I'd overdosed on my meds. Could I even do that? Probably. Maybe I wasn't even in a ship at all. Maybe my body was curled up in bed, sore with illness like a giant bruise, and I was hallucinating to escape from the pain. It had happened before. Surely I'd wake up when a job flew into our yard and poked me in the implant.

"Ovie?"

The medical officer. This time her voice lacked the hurried edge I'd heard in the shop.

"Is something there?" she said.

Oh, come on, I thought. *Make it at least a little easy on me.*

More growling, even closer this time.

Before I could organize myself into something other than a pile of soreness, the lid disappeared and two faces glared at me from above: the medical officer, and a man who was all hard muscle, like he'd tried to press himself into a planet but had to settle for human instead. It was the engineer I'd seen outside. Locs fell over his shoulders and into the crate, draping a strong face—bone-solid and leather-tough. Bared teeth snarled at me from between full lips. Unmistakably Heliodoran, like me. Except for the growling.

His eyes darted to my locs, the grease on my cheeks, the dark skin we shared.

"You?" she said, eyebrows raised in an approximation of surprise. She groaned and ran her hands through her hair as she walked away, cursing. Decent acting.

Only the growling Heliodoran remained. Just as I was about to say something—what, I didn't know—he dropped the lid back down onto the crate with a loud metallic crash, the sound ringing in my ears.

Not really the reaction I'd expected. My heart hammered away at my ribs.

"It's Nova Quick's sister," the woman said. Her shadow moved back and forth as she paced. "Tev is going to kill us."

"She could be leverage." His voice was more growl than

speech, words rumbling like gravel in his throat. What kind of man *was* he?

"Excuse me," I said, tapping on the lid. "I'm sorry for—"

The man peered at me through the slats on the side of the crate, growling and narrowing his eyes.

"Um," I said, stupidly. "I was just hoping maybe I could stand up—"

"I don't think you're in a position to make requests," he grumbled, voice so low it vibrated through me.

"I agree." A new voice. Sonorous, female, and heavy with authority. "Open it."

"Don't you think we should call an enforcement team to pick her up?" the engineer said.

"No."

To me it sounded more like *no-y* or *noer*; I could never quite mimic a Wooleran accent, but the beauty of it distracted me momentarily. It was an accent that glided across the ear, rolling like Wooleran farmlands, wide like their ranches. I could hear the sun in their mouths, bronzing their words. I'd never been there, seeing as it was on the other side of Orpim, but my aunt's first husband was Wooleran and he used to talk to me about burt-cattle droving at the dinner table on holidays. I bathed in every word, soaking in his stories until I could hear the burts' hooves beating against packed dirt.

The crate's lid came off and I stood, not wanting to get caught inside again. Instantly, the engineer grabbed my arms and twisted them behind me, pinning me tight against his solid frame. A wave of pain snaked up my left arm and into my neck.

"Hey," I said, putting up no resistance. "Easy. Where am I going to run off to?"

"Know your place on my ship, surgeon," came that gorgeous, accented voice from behind. The engineer twisted around to face her, turning me with him.

The woman sizzled in front of me—all blond hair, boots,

and confidence. She tilted her head at an angle of self-important disdain, hip cocked to match. Cargo pants hung below her waist and a white tank top bared her toned arms. A metal necklace circled her neck, not quite a choker. A necklace similar to one the engineer wore, I realized.

We locked eyes. Her barbed expression pricked at me from beneath her bangs, as if I were a spot of rust on her ship that had the audacity to sprout up when she wasn't looking. Muscles pulled at the corner of her mouth.

She took two steps closer. "I should throw you out the airlock. Explain yourself."

"I'm Alana Quick."

I sounded ridiculous.

"Yes. Nova's sister. That's the only reason we're even having this conversation. But it's her I want, and my medic tells me you refuse to talk. So what exactly am I supposed to do with you? You're not even worth keeping as a hostage. All I see is one more mouth to feed and a whole mess of liability." Her green eyes looked me up and down, her authority unquestionable. I could feel the current of her stare energizing my nerves just like the ship, and it took all my willpower not to look away.

The pain from my arm was making its way to my head, seeding the beginnings of a migraine. My wrists throbbed under the engineer's tight grip.

"Please." I glanced at the medical officer. She shook her head just enough for me to notice. I'd get no help there.

"I'm sorry about stowing away," I said to the captain, "but I'm desperate. I'll make myself useful. I'm an engineer, and I'm damn good. Give me a chance in exchange for the information you want. What's your name?"

The medical officer laughed and shifted her weight, shaking her head. The captain ground her jaw to the side, clenching her teeth.

We stared at each other. While she presumably thought about what to do with me, I fought the urge to say anything else.

Her eyes scanned me, jumping from my locs to my clothes and back to my eyes, while I searched her expression for anything that might be useful. All I could see was the cold intensity of her eyes, the subtle dark circles beneath them. Between that and their urgent need for my sister, I knew they had bigger problems than a stowaway.

"Captain?" A young female voice came over the ship's intercom.

The captain pushed aside her hair and switched on a transmit connection behind her ear, keeping her eyes fixed on me. "Go."

"We're running low on helium-3. Permission to alter course to Ouyang Outpost?"

My heart fluttered. Ouyang Outpost orbited Adul opposite the station where my parents lived.

"Do it," she said.

"If you give me a chance," I said as soon as she switched off the transmission, "I can increase the efficiency of your propulsion system. You won't make as many of those refueling stops. You'll have at least a twenty-percent decrease of burn off—"

"You don't seriously mean to tell me you've trespassed onto a private vessel so you can beg for work?" She stepped closer, until her face was mere centimeters away from mine. The scent of rosemary and ozone haloed her, at once soothing and enticing. "Don't tell me. You just want to save up some money for medicine for your dying mother. Son? Grandparent? . . . Dog?"

The engineer barked a laugh and the captain bounced her eyebrow at him over my shoulder, a lopsided smile twitching at the corner of her mouth. But only for a moment. She locked eyes with me again, close enough that I could feel her breath on my face.

"So what is it, *surgeon*?" She sneered the last word, then lowered her voice. "What sob story can you give me that I haven't heard already? What makes you entitled to a place on my ship? Why should I take money from my crew, who've earned the right to be here, and give it to you?"

Embarrassment and rage flushed my cheeks. I had nothing to say, nothing more to offer than my word. Now that I stood in front of this flame of a woman, well outside the atmosphere of my home planet, the whole situation just seemed ridiculous and childish. Groveling for a free ride home—or at least a safe drop-off at the Adul station—might be the best I could do at this point, but even that seemed impossible.

The captain's scorn rendered her otherwise soft features menacing.

"Ovie," she said, still lacerating me with her eyes.

"Captain," the engineer growled.

"Put her in the brig."

The engineer—Ovie, evidently—shoved me forward. With me in his custody, he walked toward the fore of the ship, and I took in everything I could while the medical officer followed us. Observations came in flashes I would later remember. I took note of the rooms we passed and where they were in relation to each other and to the cargo bay, even if I had no idea what was behind each door. A faint, pleasantly industrial smell slithered through the hallway to greet me. Boots clanged up metal stairs, across metal floors.

The ship—whose name I had yet to learn—hummed quietly beneath it all, singing softly to herself as she sailed through the black. The one bright spot in the middle of all this fear, this beautiful vessel protected us from the dangers of the Big Quiet. I imagined her slicing through darkness with grace while the interplanetary medium glittered invisibly around her hull.

Tell me your story, I thought to her, my fingertips aching, longing to trail along her metal as we walked. *Tell me what you've seen. Tell me why you called to me.*

I had to find a way to stay on this ship long enough to find out.

We had arrived in the crew's dormitory, where Ovie shoved

me into the "brig"—nothing more than an unoccupied quarters. Departing without comment, he left me with the medic.

"So this is the brig?" I said, taking in the crisp sheets and extra blanket folded at the foot of the bed. A built-in desk and a lamp occupied the opposite corner of the room. Empty shelves lined the wall, and a couple of silver charms consisting of interlinked rings hung from a stud in the ceiling. Rings like those comprising the crew members' jewelry.

The medic sat on the bed and leaned back on one elbow. I noticed she wore a bracelet made of the same metal rings. "Where's Nova?"

"Why do you need her so badly?"

She laughed, but it wasn't kind. "Why is it you keep asking questions as if you're not the stowaway here? We ask, you answer. That's how this works."

I sat down next to her and whispered. "I thought we had a deal."

"I have no idea what you're talking about."

"Will you at least tell me your name? The name of the ship? Anything?"

She smirked. "I'm Doctor Helen Vasquez. As far as you're concerned, I'm the bitch keeping an eye on you until the captain decides what to do about our dirtheel infestation. You realize there are plenty of captains out there who would've shoved you out the airlock without a second thought. You're lucky ours has a soft spot for strays."

"Why are you acting like you don't know anything?"

She sucked her teeth at me and clicked off the intercrew comm link behind her ear. "What, you think you have a right to be here?"

Heat rose to my neck. "If you want my sister, your captain will have to be a little more accommodating than throwing me into the . . . " I looked around and laughed. "Brig."

"I'd be careful about making demands, stowaway."

"I'd be careful too, accomplice. Tell me why you want Nova,

or I'll just disembark at Adul and you won't be any closer to finding her."

She laughed. "I only put my ass on the line for you because you have information we need, girl. Don't make me regret it."

"If you have nothing to offer me, I don't see why I should help you."

Dr. Vasquez sighed and tilted her head, staring at me as if she couldn't quite decide how to reprimand me. "Oh yeah, I get it. We all want to fly. We all have the same sad story, the same debt collectors chasing us, but no one's entitled to be here. What makes you special enough that we should make room for you on our ship? You think the world owes you something? We don't even know you."

"I don't think the world owes me—"

She waved her hand dismissively. "Save it. I don't want to hear anything else unless it has to do with Nova Quick."

Maybe I was being stupid, but I couldn't lead them to my sister in good conscience until I knew why they wanted to talk to her. I rested my head in my hands, face against my palms. Now that the adrenaline was wearing off, the pain from my arm had amplified and migrated to my shoulders, neck, and head. Migraine territory, ahoy. Soreness crept along the tendons in my hands, throbbing with every pulse.

The Panacea sample loomed larger in my awareness than such a tiny object should. I touched my fingers to the outside of the pocket, feeling the bulge of the familiar Dexitek bottle and the smaller, more ominous shape beside it. A shape that contained all the power to relieve my symptoms in one capsule, albeit temporarily. Power to heal me in exchange for creating some kind of chemical dependency I wouldn't be able to feed.

No. Not yet. You need your wits.

I drew my hand away from the pill.

When the silence persisted, I just listened to the ship to distract myself. That electric hum, ever-present and soothing. Pops and creaks in the hull. Someone's voice on another part of the deck, muffled by the walls between us. It sounded like Lai, though I knew it wasn't. Maybe the captain.

I took in the musty scent of the room, so similar to the Adul station. Something familiar to cling to. At least if this didn't work out, I'd soon see my parents. Shuttles ferried folks between Ouyang Outpost and the research station all the time.

"Why don't you just tell us where Nova is?" the doctor finally said. "Why'd you bother stowing away if you didn't plan to give us anything?"

I lifted my head and looked at Vasquez, who leaned back on her elbows like she had all the time in the world. Legs crossed, thick hair spilling from her ponytail.

"What do you want with her? Does the captain need spiritual counsel? Someone to serve as guide during a mystical journey?" I couldn't keep the sneer out of my questions.

"Not exactly. Why we want her is irrelevant, anyway. If you help us find her, the captain might see you as valuable. Or at least worth a little more than a stop at a penal colony."

"I don't think trespassing merits incarceration. A fine at the most—"

"You'd be surprised how little the authorities want to deal with us fringe folk these days. Penal colonies are convenient."

"You're just trying to scare me."

"Is it working?"

"Maybe a little."

"Well." She shrugged, a grin perking up her face. "There you go."

"Why you want my sister isn't irrelevant to me, you know."

"Either way, I'm not authorized to tell you."

I bit down on my frustration. "I know what I look like." I bunched my locs between my hands and tossed them back over my shoulder, a nervous habit that I knew made me seem even smaller, emphasizing the fountain of hair that dwarfed me. "I look younger than I am. I bet you think I'm fresh out of some internship, but I'm not. I'm thirty-two central years old—"

"Great. You're an old bag like the rest of us."

I refused to take the bait. "You're missing my point. I'm saying you're right. About all of it. About me being no different from anyone else. I'm getting older and I have no money and no real future in Heliodor. I'm desperate, but desperate people are powerful, Vasquez! I really can make your ship more efficient if you just—"

"Yeah. You said that. What we want is your sister." She lowered her voice. "I made that clear at the ship yard."

"I can hear it." I pointed up, as if that's where the ship was. "In her, the vessel. You hear the hum, right?"

"The buzzing noise?"

I couldn't help smiling, and shook my head. "Not exactly. There's a broken thread in her that needs mending. I feel it."

I meant, it too. I felt the ship's discomfort deep inside my forearms, layered underneath my own cramping muscles. Meant there was something that needed adjusting in her thrusters.

"It's not like she's ailing, really," I continued, "but just not operating at full capacity. I can help."

"That sounds more like mysticism than ship doctoring. Maybe your sister has rubbed off on you."

I bristled. "Look, I'm not asking for a lot. Just a chance."

She sucked her teeth at me again. "You really don't get it, do you? That *is* asking for a lot. How do you plan to feed yourself, dirtheel? We're already going to have to waste rations on you as it is. If you don't have information for us, we don't have anything for you."

"I do have information. I just want to know why you want a member of my family first."

"This isn't a debate. Tell us how to reach your sister or you're useless to us."

Staring at Dr. Vasquez's anxious face—the way her body periodically shifted out of eagerness—I could see what was going on: I had the real power here. Or at least *some* power. They were trying to get what they needed from me without helping me realize how much influence I really held, as Nova's sister. Their silence on the matter made me all the more determined to find out why.

"Let me talk to the captain," I said, straightening my back.

She stood up, towering over me, her wavy hair falling over her shoulder like a storm cloud.

"I've been beyond patient with you," she said. "Let's try this instead. You sit in here and hope the captain keeps feeling generous. Accidents happen in the black all the time. Getting rid of you quietly would be a lot less paperwork than turning you in, believe me, and we wouldn't have to waste time docking somewhere while we press charges. So you just keep that in mind and think real hard about your situation, about what's smart here. We'll talk tomorrow. See if you're feeling more cooperative."

"Your threats are empty." I hoped they were, anyway. "Without me, you've got nothing. I'm not telling you a damn thing unless you tell me why you want her."

She shrugged and opened the door, its metallic complaint punctuating her anger. "Your choice."

I swallowed. "Wait."

Her grip tightened on the door handle and her shoulders tensed. "Yes?"

"I have Mel's Disorder. It's an autoimmune disease. My digestive system is wonky, so if you end up bringing me anything to eat—"

"Do you think this is a passenger ship? Is there a menu in your room? Do you see me carrying drinks or tapping out orders? Do you—"

"I get it." I massaged the center of my palm, trying to get the pain to ease up for a second. "I just figured . . . you know, you're a doctor. I figured you'd want to help."

Dr. Vasquez stared directly at me, the lines of her face hard. She seemed to be debating something; her silence gave me a glimmer of hope.

"You figured wrong," she said at length. "Use the time to think. Hunger sharpens the mind."

She stepped out, closed the door, and locked it. The metal clang reverberated in my ears.

I was alone.

"Go to sleep."

My body wouldn't listen. Every time I closed my eyes, hoping sleep might pass the time, I homed in on the sounds of the ship instead. The minute flexing and stretching of her hull. The occasional voices of the crew. Bootfalls down the hallway. Eventually I gave up fighting the urge and placed my hand on the wall to see if I could feel the sky in the ship's skin. Humming tickled my palm, soft and low. She was warmer than expected; I imagined it was her blood rising to the surface, all plasma and light.

I thought about Nova carrying inspiration and comfort to patrons on distant planets, and I was both envious and full of admiration for what she had accomplished, as much as I hated admitting it. I might have been no fan of mysticism, but she'd been out here in the Big Quiet for over six years now, trading in magic. All her innate talent for shaping belief and weaving reality-patterns into shiny new futures for her clients had granted her an easy life. There wasn't a spirit guide enthusiast in the system who didn't know her name. Meanwhile, I woke up every day and struggled just to find work.

But now I was out here too. In the black. On a ship.

As much as I longed to see my parents again, I wouldn't be able to stay with them on the outpost. There was no way I could give this up. I'd sacrifice almost anything to look inside this vessel's engine, see the plasma moving through the heart of her, slide my fingers through her wires like a lover's hair. Listen to the thrum of her reactor while my hands learned her every curve.

I needed to know her name.

After being surrounded by othersider tech for so long, it felt good to be inside a solid old ship. A piece of the technology from our side of the breach. As miraculous as Transliminal's advances seemed, they still scared me. Just like the pill sitting in my pocket scared me. We didn't understand their technology because they wouldn't let us, and as desperately as I wanted a cure to Mel's, I was frightened of letting them mess with my body when I didn't understand what it would mean.

This vessel reminded me the world I belonged to was still out here, that our science still meant something, and that the whole system hadn't already been handed over to the othersiders. To folks from *over there*. This vessel? She was real, solid, and true. Part of our universe. She made sense, unlike the terrifying ships that made up the Transliminal armada.

Not that I'd ever seen them, mind—I'd just heard stories of light twisting out of the dark folds of reality, ribbons shivering in impossible shapes. Vessels that ran on "dark energy." A vague name for something they refused to explain to us, and we just accepted our ignorance because they had the cures and advances we'd failed to find on our own.

Why had they succeeded where we failed? I thought. *Why do they scare me? Just because they come from another universe?*

Ugh, I hated being stuck in here with nothing but my thoughts. At least they could've left me some metal to play with. Being off the grid, I couldn't even access shows or books through the net.

It occurred to me then: Had Lai gotten my message? My implant had probably bounced the transmission through Orpim's net instead of the ship's, but how reliable was the connection during takeoff?

Stop thinking about it.

I turned over on the bed and picked out patterns in the discolored spots on the floor. My pill bottle dug into my hip, reminding me of how little time I had, which in turn stretched each minute out like taffy while I lay there with absolutely nothing to occupy my time. Forty-eight pills. Twenty-four days. And then, if I couldn't get more, I had to either get home or watch my motor functions deteriorate until I couldn't walk, much less operate on engines.

Unless I wanted to take Transliminal's appetizer and become dependent on them long before I could afford to be.

I had to give them Nova's location. There just wasn't any other way.

Suddenly, a pair of small, bare feet appeared in my field of vision. I sat up to face the young woman who'd somehow come into the room without making a sound, barefooted and wearing a white shirt over shorts.

Any words I might have conjured fell away as I took her in. She didn't look a day over eighteen or nineteen, but I felt the unmistakable gaze of time staring back at me from behind her dark eyes. Sleek, straight black hair draped over her shoulders like liquid, falling almost to her waist, and her skin was so white I could almost see through it. Her left upper-arm was covered in a tattoo sleeve of a honeycomb—an arresting look on someone with such a young face. The phantom taste of honey coated my tongue, its scent surrounding me. Surrounding *her*.

She said nothing, but hollowed me out with her stare. Any hope I had of forming coherent thoughts slipped away. I felt her inside me, disturbing me, rocking my reality sideways. Like a negative picture with white spaces in all the wrong spots. Inside my head, I felt her awareness probing me—a lightning-bright mind with a hole where her heart should have been.

"You are on my ship," she said, tone flat, voice soft. She tilted her head to the side, her movements languid. "Are you paying attention?"

When she spoke, a buzzing sound hovered somewhere between my ears, between the music of the ship and the rush of my blood and the awful disturbance that was her mind. Buzzing like summer insects.

A faint movement flitted across her face. At first I thought it was a muscle twitch, some indication of emotion, but then it happened again, and . . . I saw. There could be no mistaking the patch of translucence that rippled across her left cheek, shivered down her neck. Muscle, tooth, tendon, and bone: a shimmer of anatomy beneath the invisible sheath of her skin.

She wasn't just pale; she was translucent, in a constant state of fading and rematerializing.

I tried to answer her, to ask the half-formed questions eddying in my mind—*Who are you? What are you? Paying attention to what? Why are you here? Can you help me?*—but nothing came out. The taste of honey slid down my throat. Buzzing drowned out any hope of translating thought to speech. Hollowness pulled at me, an ache behind my eyes. Somewhere in the back of my mind, I was aware of the ship's anticipation.

As quickly as it appeared, the window into the girl's body vanished. She was whole again, if only for a moment. Then another shimmer, and her right leg was missing. Her shorts remained filled out as if it were there, but there was no muscle or bone to be seen—only empty space where flesh should have been.

My mind grappled for purchase.

Gradually, the bone, muscle, fat, and skin reappeared, though unevenly at first. My world shifted, groaned, stretched. I struggled to make room for something that shouldn't be, but was. Tears welled in my eyes, not from sadness, but from my ever-loosening grip on reality.

"You are distressed," she said. "Go to sleep."

Immediately, I lost consciousness.

That night I dreamed I lost my hands while working inside the ship's engine. I grew new fingers full of metal and electricity, and their fire licked away what remained of my bones.

Chapter Three

Morning came with a bang and a shake.

As the world rocked around me, bits of reality trickled in, my thoughts mere fragments: *Dizzy. Muscle aches. Stiff neck, cramping hands. Starship. Stowed away. Pills? Pocket. Hunger.*

When my mind settled into something more closely resembling coherence, I realized I wasn't alone. The shaking came from Dr. Vasquez, who had pulled me into a sitting position on the bed.

The captain stood in front of me. She put her hands on my cheeks and forced me to look at her, blond hair curtaining her face like a veil of silk, and all I could think through my bleary-eyed half-consciousness was, *her hands are warm.*

Something beeped at the site of my implant.

"She's fine," Vasquez said, pulling her medical monitor away from my head. "Her Mel's is flaring, but blood pressure is normal."

"Good!" The captain patted my cheek a little too hard, then let go. "Morning, love. It's time to talk to us about your sister."

Excruciating pain pummeled my lower back and hands—my price for curling up in that box. Mel's didn't take kindly to cramped spaces. It took a fair amount of concentration not to let it show. Weakness wouldn't help my case.

"Can I have something to eat?" I said, pinching the bridge of my nose to steady my head. Memories from the previous night flashed into my awareness. The girl. Her disappearing skin. The phantom sensations of buzzing and honey and that uncanny sense of unreality she seemed to carry with her.

The captain stepped back and put her hands in the pockets of her cargo pants. Her movements kicked up the faint scent of rosemary again. "I don't think food should be your primary concern."

"Who was the girl?" I said, still trying to wipe away the last vestiges of sleep and disorientation.

"I'll be outside," Vasquez said, giving me a strange look before stepping into the hallway.

"No questions until you give me what I want," the captain said.

"Okay, what do you want?" I grabbed the strip of fabric I kept tied to the belt loop of my pants and secured it haphazardly around my locs to get them out of the way. Dryness filled my mouth and I had to work hard to focus on her face. Even talking hurt.

The captain remained silent, watching my movements carefully.

"I don't even know your name," I said.

"Tev Helix. And what I want is your cooperation."

"In exchange for what, exactly?"

An unconcerned shrug. "For not throwing you into the silence."

"You won't do that."

She smiled, bouncing an eyebrow. "We can find out."

My body boiled with a mixture of attraction and fear, which I attempted to shove aside in the interest of reason. I leaned back on my elbows. "Why do you want Nova?"

"I want to buy one of her contracts."

"Why don't I believe you?"

Every muscle in Captain Helix's face tightened, and a flush of pink colored her cheeks. "This is exactly why I don't pick up dirtheels. You're all insubordinate and entitled. You're the criminal here, not me."

"Why does everyone keep calling me *dirtheel*?" I said. "How do you know I've never been off-planet? Maybe I grew up on a starship. Maybe my parents owned one and I was born in zero-g."

She laughed. "Vasquez told me how you looked at our ship. Like you'd never actually walked the corridors of a vessel before."

She leaned closer, purring in that gorgeous accent. "Hands all tangled up in engines, love? I can tell. I reckon you're so trapped in the coils that you've never even flown. But you talk like you think you belong up here."

I didn't flinch. "Maybe I do. I can hear your lady; she's been talking to me ever since I set foot in your cargo bay. I can make her more efficient. You haven't given me a chance to show you."

"You don't know this ship," she hissed. "Don't act like you do. This is my vessel and you'll do as I say if you don't want to see what she looks like from the black."

I said nothing. Just sat there, challenging her with my stare. No easy feat with that aura of intensity sizzling around her like her own ship's plasma arcs.

"I know your type," she said. "You think this is all so romantic, don't you? An escape from whatever drab existence you've got going on back home. We run into people like you all the time. Folks with something to prove. I don't hire amateurs." She sneered and talked with her hands, throwing them around to punctuate nearly every word. I actually found it all a bit charming despite my situation. I liked fiery women, but I didn't think she'd take well to me saying so.

I stood, but Captain Helix refused to acquiesce any space to me. Despite the eight or so centimeters she had on me, I was a lot curvier than she was; my sturdy body helped me own the territory I claimed. "If you think you're looking at an amateur, then you're right about one thing: I'm on the wrong ship."

She shifted her weight, and something made a clicking

sound at her knee. A prosthesis? One of my aunt's friends had one that made the same noise.

"Insubordinate *and* melodramatic," she said. "Charming."

"What do you want with Nova?"

She kept her gaze locked on me like a leash. "Maybe I just need a spirit guide to tell me whether it's a good time to invest. See if the stars are aligned in my favor. Cultivate that portfolio with the help of a little divination for auspicious timing—"

"If you're going to be sarcastic, forget it," I said. "I don't know where she is. I lied to your medical officer about it because I just wanted a job."

"Marre," Captain Helix said. Even the ship seemed to stand at attention at the sound of that throaty voice snapping.

"Yes, Captain."

My blood froze. The voice. It was the girl from the brig.

"Is our trespasser lying?" the captain asked.

"There is an increase of noradrenergic activity in her locus ceruleus, with increased levels of norepinephrine. While that's not enough to be certain, she's definitely in a compromised state of mind. This may or may not be indicative of deception. She is at least anxious."

I looked around. "How did she—"

"That's good enough for me," the captain said, grabbing my arm. "Let's go. We're making a call."

When I arrived on the bridge with the captain, there was no time to appreciate my surroundings. She said something as she joined Dr. Vasquez and Ovie at the starboard side of the bridge, but I didn't make it out. Chills rolled over me in relentless waves as reality narrowed to a point. The girl from the brig, Marre, sat in the pilot's seat, her bare legs folded so that her chin rested on her knees, a thick jacket wrapped around her. Our flight path to Ouyang Outpost flickered on the view screen, which she adjusted to account for traffic through this sector of the system. As her hands moved, I noticed a woven metal cuff around her wrist similar to the jewelry worn by Vasquez and Helix, only this one consisted of rings in dappled, aurora-like rainbows.

That same buzzing from the night before returned, loud and unforgiving. Endless sound reverberated against my skull.

"Are you staring at me?" she said, her voice appearing at once from without and within. She just continued working without looking at me, arms reaching around her thin legs. Translucence rippled up her calf, revealing striations of muscle beneath.

I tried answering but the buzzing drilled through my thoughts, shattering them before I could come up with anything coherent.

"You *are* staring at me," she whispered. Then, over the intercom, her small voice exploded through us all like thunder: "That's rude."

Captain Helix, Vasquez, and Ovie turned to us. Helix raised an eyebrow.

The disappearing girl pulled the jacket's hood over her head and removed the flight path from the screen, defaulting to a view into the silence.

Even while submerged in the buzzing and disorientation, the sight of the brilliant black twined through me, bathing me in wonder. I decided then, with my dirtheel past peeling away from me like old skin, that you'll never know true awe until you stand on the bridge of a starship. The view from the shuttles to Adul, or even from the station itself, was nothing like this. A million pinpricks of light burned through the velvet black—rivets in the hull of the universe. I swore I could feel the ship around us singing louder, her song filling up my veins, threatening to burst out of me in a fit of ecstasy, scattering my body's matter across the cosmos. The buzzing, Marre's haunting presence, the crew lingering in the bridge's shadows, the pinch of hunger twisting in my belly, my ever-present anxiety over the impulsive decision that led me here—each registered as a distant trifle in the presence of the silence, vast and heaven-black. I'm sure I stood in a silent stupor for no more than ten seconds, but I felt suspended in eternity.

Beyond the vessel was *everything*. Do you know what that feels like? To have the enormity of creation stretched out before you and know you're still only seeing a minuscule fraction of what's out there? To know you're utterly insignificant and powerful all at once, simply by virtue of being part of something so limitless?

Desire stirred in my chest as the ship's song still echoed inside me, eclipsing all other sound, wending its way through my heart.

"Close your mouth," the captain said, suddenly behind me. Reality snapped back into place as she shoved me toward the comm panel harder than necessary. "We've reconfigured our connection. Make the call."

"I'm sorry," I said automatically, though it sounded distant behind the buzzing that now returned, filling up my brain. Then, just as quickly as it had begun, the noise stopped.

"Whatever," Marre muttered at the same time the captain said, "Just make your call."

"For the last time, I'm not cooperating until you tell me why you want Nova," I said, shrugging and turning back to the viewer. I tried recapturing that feeling of connectedness to the ship, but it was gone.

A crackling noise came from just behind me, then a shock to the back of my neck. My teeth clenched, muscles tensed. Energy surged through me for a brief instant. Lights exploded behind my eyes. Blinding pain, as if someone ripped my soul up through my skin.

When it was over, I grabbed onto the comm panel to steady myself, breathing heavily and trying not to cry out from the sensations throbbing through my already sick body. I didn't need to see it to know what the captain had used.

A biter. Illegal for citizens to possess these days—approved for enforcers only. Its teeth felt like a million little mouths gnawing at your nervous system at anything but the mildest setting. At its most intense, there wouldn't be much of your body left to throw into the Big Quiet. And the captain had barely touched me with it. Not enough to be considered anything but a warning.

"Make the call or pray you have a strong heart." Captain Helix grabbed my wrist, twisted it behind my back, and shoved me into the comm panel so its edge dug into my hip bones. Her voice was low next to my ear, making my breath catch. "I'm not telling you again, love."

Vasquez stepped toward us. "Tev—"

"I don't want to hear it, Slip."

"Captain, her joints—"

"*Doctor Vasquez*, that's enough." She didn't move her face a centimeter before addressing me again. "You don't seem to have many choices here. We're just talking about a little beep across the system to wherever your pretty sister is hiding so we can have a chat. We're not going to hurt anyone, you included, unless you refuse to cooperate. In which case . . . " She dug the biter into my neck, where a metal prong jabbed a trigger point and shot referred pain up the back of my skull.

I glanced at the other crew members from the corner of my eye. Vasquez nodded almost imperceptibly at me. Ovie didn't seem to be paying attention, instead fixated on the back of his forearm. A faint light glowed against his skin as he moved his finger across a dermal comm implant much like Dr. Shrike's.

Marre wouldn't look at me. The hood shadowed her face.

"Time's up," the captain said, and she clicked the intensity setting on the biter. Fear percolated down my body, running cold.

"Okay!" I shouted, my legs weak. "I'll call her."

"Marre, pull up the comm interface."

"Just get that thing away from my neck." My skin twitched beneath the device. "Please."

"We're staying cozy until the call is over, love." She tightened her grip on my wrist and pressed closer to me. The scent of rosemary, everywhere. Her warm body against mine. Just like that, heat rushed in to mix with the fear. My head buzzed on its own now, and it just made me angrier. I'd learned a long time ago that bodies can't be trusted, but now was not the time for mine to betray me. I didn't want to want the woman who'd just tested a biter on me.

She dug the weapon into my neck and released my hand. "Make the call."

I clicked the switch behind my ear, then placed my palm on the projected touchscreen on the panel. It instantly synced to my biometric signature, connecting me to the ship's comm system through the implant. "Nova Quick," I said, and the screen flickered.

I waited five seconds. Ten. Thirty.

Then, my sister's face and shoulders appeared. Her curly hair was dyed orange in lieu of our family's natural near-black brown. Bright blue contacts rendered her wide, panic-stricken eyes even more striking than usual.

"Alana! Are Mom and Dad okay? Who's that with you?"

"They're fine—"

Captain Helix urged me to the side, but kept the biter firmly affixed to my neck. "I'm Captain Tev Helix of the *Tangled Axon*. Nova Quick?"

The ship's name clicked into place in my heart: *Tangled Axon*.

My sister's apparent concern was short-lived. "Alana. I told you not to call me unless someone was on their death bed."

I glanced at Tev, then back to my sister. "Well, it's not that, but—"

"You're so selfish sometimes. You know I need my vacations. Not all of us get to luxuriate in silly hobbies on Orpim. I work hard and I'm tired! How difficult is it to just not beep me for a while?"

Anger slashed through me. "It's not like I just want to gossip. Something's come up."

"Who's that blonde with you?"

"I told you," Tev said. "I'm—"

Nova gasped, then laughed. "Is my little sister seducing a captain? I didn't give you enough credit. Wait until I tell Mom and Dad. They'll be so glad you're dating again. She's cute, too!"

"What!" Tev shouted, jamming the biter into me inadvertently. "No. I have to discuss some things with you. In person."

"Don't you think my sister's cute? You can't tell me you don't get lonely out there in the black. It's all over your aura."

Tev's neck turned pink. "Are you listening? I need to talk to you off-net. We can offer you the biggest contract you've—"

"Excuse me," Nova said, straightening her posture. "I'm flattered, but I never forget a client's face, and I know I don't have you on my roster. You'll just have to talk to my agent and wait for an opening like everyone else. Or find another spirit guide to smooth out your energy. There are plenty of us. Do you need a specialist? I can get you a list. Past life access, divination, creative inspiration, guides to help you on mystic journeys—"

"We need you," Tev said. "Specifically."

"Please, listen to Captain Helix," I said, widening my eyes at Nova.

"Alana, really. I'm hurt you'd bother me with something like this. You know how busy I am. Do you realize I just finished a contract last week where I had to act as creative inspiration for a writers retreat on Gira? Exhausting! Creative types are never satisfied. I need this vacation. I should project over there and have my spirit give yours an ass-kicking."

"Nova!" I shouted, leaning forward over the console in the hope that I might reach her ego-clotted brain. "Please, *listen* to me for five seconds. I need your help."

Nova sighed and shifted her weight, gold eyeshadow glittering as she moved. "How much?"

"What?" Tev and I said.

"Don't lie. I know my sister, and I can see financial anxiety all over her aura. Little white splotchy spots around her neck and head. Let me guess what happened: you careened into her shipyard with just the right amount of swagger, and now you're pretending to hold her for ransom so you two can collect the money and run off to do whatever it is you do in the silence. Other than the obvious. So, let's get this over with. How much money?"

"I'm not calling you for money!" I shouted. "They've threatened me if you don't cooperate!"

Nova just sighed again. "Don't be dramatic."

"Shut up, both of you." Tev shoved the biter into my back and held me tighter. "Since you don't seem to be getting it, I'll make this clear. Meet us at the Ouyang Outpost at Adul or your sister dies."

Nova's face hardened. She tilted her chin up ever so slightly. "You wouldn't. The punishment for murdering a guide's family member—"

"Ow!" A dull pressure struck me in the neck, I knew I was being injected with something. The pressure stopped, and Ovie walked back to his position in the corner, holding a pharm-injector.

"What the hell!" I felt the spot where he stuck me. "What was that?"

"Alana?" Nova sounded genuinely concerned, and if she was worried, it meant she saw something in Tev's intentions only spirit guides could detect. Something that meant I really was in trouble. "Are you okay?"

Dr. Vasquez stood where she'd been the entire time, silent and impassive, eyes locked on me.

"Some doctor," I spat. "Where's your medical integrity? What did he do to me?"

"Yes, what did you do to her?" Nova said, her voice now regal, self-assured. "Tell me, or I'll disable your ship's engines and take her with me."

"Mel's Revenge," Vasquez said as she took the injector from Ovie. She placed the instrument in her pocket. "A poison that will destroy your sister's nerve cells. Essentially, it will accelerate her disease until she succumbs to it. Painfully."

Images flashed through my mind in quick succession. Video shots of Mel's Disorder patients who couldn't afford treatment. Their words indecipherable as the disease stole their voices. Tremor-ridden hands and heads. After I was diagnosed at age twelve, I pulled up net records and watched interview after interview of patients and loved ones. I was obsessed with the genetic disease that could—and very well might—claim my life, as well as Aunt Lai's. But not before robbing me of control over my own body. Mel's might as well have been a slow descent back into infancy while your mind remained trapped.

"I'm still me," I remember one of the recorded patients saying, my implant translating and dubbing his slow, slurred speech. "I'm still the same guy in my mind."

I found the bottle and sample in my pocket and gripped them tightly, affirming my lifeline as I grew dizzy with dread. I wondered if I could take the Panacea sample to offset the effects of the poison.

"You want to do what we're asking." Tev's voice snapped me back to the present. She crossed her arms, stance wide, just as sure of herself as Nova. "The poison is already inside her. Unless you want a pile of quivering muscle for a sister . . . "

I struggled to discern whether she was bluffing. Could these people be so nonchalant about destroying someone? They were desperate, but I hadn't gotten the impression they were genuinely dangerous. Had I read them wrong? If Nova was worried, maybe I should be too. She was telempathic and would sense their intentions.

Fear crept up my throat and I forced it back down.

"Give her an antidote." Nova banged on something for emphasis, practically baring her teeth. "Now."

"We'll be at Ouyang in fifteen hours," Tev said, then nodded briefly at Marre to give a silent order. "At the refueling station. Orbital coordinates are being transmitted to you now. If you show up, your sister lives. If not, she'll be trapped inside her dying body, and we'll find you anyway and get what we need. Your choice."

"Please, don't—"

Tev flicked a switch on the comm panel and cut off the transmission. "Don't fuck with me."

Chapter Four

"We'll be at the outpost in a little over ten hours," Tev said as Marre disabled the ship's external comm link. "That gives us plenty of time to grab the helium-3 before they meet us."

The crew ignored me, casually discussing ship functions as if they hadn't just threatened my life. How could they be so callous while I could do nothing but stand there with my hand on my neck, visualizing the poison insinuating itself into my body? My fingers shook.

Tremors. It was already starting. Or was I just that afraid?

No one seemed concerned about me being fifteen hours out from death—not even Vasquez, who you'd think would be bound by the healers oath to at least pretend to care. Why had she been worried about Tev tweaking my joints if she was content to let me die? How dare they exploit my disease? They had no idea how deep that cut.

Rage surged up inside me.

I lost it.

Gritting my teeth and rushing Vasquez, I slammed her into the wall by the neck. Ovie leapt on me, peeling me away, but I thrashed at the doctor, determined to flay at least one of them for what they'd done. I probably should have targeted Tev or Ovie, but it was the doctor who knew enough about my illness to exploit it. It was the doctor who had convinced me to stow away. I'd tear her apart.

Maybe it was stupid, but I felt betrayed by these people I barely knew. Vasquez's face flashed between her own and Dr. Shrike's and Tev's in my mind while I thrashed and punched until I realized it wasn't working, that my upper body was pinioned against Ovie, and I kicked at Vasquez instead, knocking Ovie off-balance momentarily. My boot barely nicked her hand, doing little more than making her bracelet jingle. She stepped backward out of my reach and looked at me like I was a wild animal.

"I'll kill you! I'll take you out with me!" I shouted, trying to pry myself free. I heard the hysteria in my voice, but didn't care. I'd spent a lifetime fighting this illness and now she was going to kill me with it just like that. My rational mind tucked itself away and watched the whole thing, more than willing to let my anger take the helm. Every movement seemed to come from someone else. It was easier to detach from my body than feel it shut down on me. Parts of me could almost feel calm that way, watching my limbs bear the burden of my emotions.

"We're not doing anything to you," Ovie growled in my ear, thick arms secured around mine. "You're fine. It was saline. We're not murderers."

"What?" Surprise diluted my anger. I stopped kicking but still struggled to wrench myself free. Slowly, I stepped back into myself and stopped fighting, panting from the exertion. My muscles ached from the tension of being restrained.

When I remained calm for a few long beats, Ovie let me go, but Vasquez immediately grabbed my arm. I was getting damn tired of everyone manhandling me.

I tried swinging at her again with my free arm, but she caught that wrist too. Strong for a medical officer.

"Hey," she said. "You need to work on your hook if you're going to try to hit people. And he's right. That was saline. I mean, come on. 'Mel's Revenge?' Have you ever heard of anything so ridiculous? Relax. You're fine. We're not going to poison you, and we're not going to use the biter on you. It was an act. I wouldn't let anyone on this crew hurt someone for personal gain."

She relaxed her grip and I jerked away.

I clamped down on all the terror and rage, releasing only a fraction of what I felt through my words. "You're still monsters. You exploited my disease to get my sister to cooperate. You have no idea what it's like—"

"Don't tell us what we know," Tev said from right behind me, startling me. I'd forgotten about her, she'd been so quiet during my outburst. When I turned around to lash out at her, I was met by sadness flickering across her face, the expression delicate as a trembling leaf. It caught me off-guard. I forgot what I was going to say.

When she spoke, her voice came softly.

"You do what you have to do when your ass is on the line, so I'm not sorry, love." Something in her expression told me otherwise. "Be grateful you stowed away on this ship and not another one, or you'd have been long-frozen out there." She nodded at the black. "You're not dying. You're fine."

"I'm supposed to thank you for not killing me?"

"Did I say that?" She raised her eyebrows, but the hard edge to her voice from earlier had yet to return.

I shoved my hand into my pocket and fingered the Dexitek bottle. "If you're not planning on hurting me, why was Nova worried? What was she sensing in your intentions that made her so concerned? How do I know you're not lying now?"

"We have ways around a guide's empathy."

Anger still bubbled in my chest, tugging at me in an old, familiar way. Chafing at the knowledge that my body could break down on me if I didn't keep it in check. It felt like I'd let out five years worth of steam when I attacked Vasquez; I wanted to collapse and sleep for a year. So much time spent holding all that emotion in. It was a constant battle not to let the disease curdle my personality. People like being around those who make them feel good, not someone who brings them down; I was well-schooled in the art of hiding my resentment.

But I'd never been so close to my fate as I had on that bridge, breaking under the weight of mere saline.

"I think I've earned the right to know why you want my sister."

"Fair enough." Tev glanced at Vasquez and Ovie. "Leave us. I'll fill her in."

Ovie wandered out, scratching the back of his head in a vaguely canine fashion. Vasquez gave Tev a look I couldn't decipher, but Tev said nothing. The doctor shrugged and left us alone on the bridge with Marre, whose left hand now lacked skin on half its fingers.

I did my best not to stare. I just focused on calming down.

"I heard you met our pilot last night," Tev said, plopping into the copilot's seat and kicking her legs up onto the console, crossing her boots at the ankle.

Skin re-grew across Marre's fingers in a cross-hatched pattern, filling in over the tendons beneath. She said nothing in response to Tev talking about her as if she weren't there.

"With all due respect," I said, trying to appeal to her ego, "what does that have to do with Nova?"

"The CEO of Transliminal Solutions wants to buy out all your sister's contracts."

"Birke?" I laughed. Birke was the single-named woman who headed the powerhouse from another reality, the woman whose influence was slowly replacing all our own industries. "That's not happening. Nova won't do business with othersiders."

"I know. Your sister's reputation precedes her."

"She has a talent for that. So let me guess—Transliminal wants Nova, and you want something from Transliminal."

Tev pulled her legs off the console and sat forward in the chair, jerking her head to get her bangs out of her eyes. "Marre."

The pilot continued monitoring the navigational controls. "Yes, Captain."

"How long have you been on my crew?"

"Seven years, Captain."

"But you're so young!" I blurted out, and immediately regretted it when Marre's fingers tensed.

"I'm older than you are, young lady," Marre said, eyes fixed on the view screen.

"It was her ship," Tev said, "and she sold it to me with the stipulation that she be given the chance to stay on and pilot. She's been with me longer than anyone else. My most loyal crew member. And surely you've noticed her condition. She's dying."

Although her body was now mostly covered by her hooded jacket, images of Marre's disappearing skin flashed through my mind. The velvet-red muscle beneath. The buzzing, the phantom smell of honey. The way Marre's eyes seemed to contain all the forbidden, dangerous things children whispered about at night, long after their parents had gone to bed. Worst of all, the distinct feeling that she could sense my fear and that it pricked her, cut her, in subtle but damaging ways.

"What happened to you?" I said.

Marre finally looked at Tev, and nodded at the captain before turning back to her work. Marre's hands paled, then seemed to disappear into the console. I couldn't even imagine how it must feel to lose pieces of yourself like that, over and over again.

"She was a spirit guide," Tev said. "She'd finished her undergraduate work at the guild and was preparing to enter the graduate program for spirit possession when something happened. An accident. It left her struggling to hang onto herself. That's all I'm telling you, surgeon, and don't you dare push her on the matter."

Marre tugged her hood around her face, burying herself deeper into the fabric, bracelet glinting in the light from the console. I thought about the stories Nova brought home from guild training and couldn't figure out what might have done that to her. What kind of accident could have possibly loosened her hold on her own flesh?

"We want to help her, and the only people who can do that—"

"Transliminal Solutions."

Tev shrugged. "I don't like it, but we've run out of options—"

"What about the guild?"

"How about you interrupt me again?"

"Sorry."

Tev cracked her neck, then continued talking. "I've been trying to help her for years. Slip—Doctor Vasquez—can't figure anything out. Marre tried getting help from the Spiritual Advisory Guild when it first happened, but they couldn't do anything for her. We've tried contacting them again since she became my pilot, but they still can't help her. They're saying initiates sign waivers that absolve them of responsibility in situations like this." Tev made a skeptical face, gritting her teeth. "Some policy. Where I come from, we take care of our own. Anyway, Transliminal is the only option we have left. We don't have the kind of money they're asking for in exchange for specialized medical care, so we needed to find out what else we could barter."

The word "barter" ignited my anger again. "My sister isn't a piece of merchandise."

"Sorry," Tev said, showing her palms in a placating gesture. "Bad choice of words. But you understand what I'm saying, surely?"

I flinched under the sharp, repetitive slicing of a growing headache. "Why does Birke, of all people, want Nova?"

Tev shrugged. "Wants what she can't have? How should I know? I'm sure we'll find out when we get there. We just know our reconnaissance contacts have been intercepting her transmissions to the Spiritual Advisory Guild for months. There are multiple offers from Birke to Nova's agent in the pipeline.

To the point that she's offering to buy out her contracts for life and employ her as her personal spiritual advisor."

Something wasn't right here. I couldn't shake the feeling there was something more to Birke's need for my sister than Nova's skill or her rejection of Transliminal Solutions. Besides, Nova was good at what she did, but there were other, more experienced, more accomplished people in her field. People with more specialized skills that would be better suited to serving a CEO from another universe. And why hadn't Nova crowed to me about Birke's persistent attempts to hire her? She may have hated Transliminal Solutions, but she loved any opportunity to revel in her glowing reputation. Preferably within earshot.

I leaned against the console. "So you came to my shop to find her because you're delivering her to Birke in exchange for Marre's medical care?"

"Something like that. We were hoping Nova would be willing to help us convince Birke to help Marre. Use her spirit guide enchantments." Tev wiggled her fingers in imitation of these *enchantments*. "Or at least function as leverage."

Laughter bubbled up in my chest at the thought of Nova helping anyone do anything that wasn't her own idea, but I held it back. "How exactly did you plan to convince her to cooperate?"

"We have you. You're dying, remember?"

I had to respect someone so determined, even if she was using me. I guess I sort of invited it by stowing away on someone's private vessel.

"And when she realizes I'm not in danger?" I said. "Then what? You don't want her as an enemy. With all those high-profile clients, she can blacklist you from a dozen industries with just a few comm beeps."

Tev stood, accompanied by a few clicks. Her boots fell heavily as she stepped closer to me, her face pure control. Blood thundered inside my head as my nerves grew anxious, and I heard the ship humming somewhere deep inside her engine, growing louder with each step Tev took. I felt both Tev and the ship prickling under my skin. When Tev looked me up and down, her posture all authority, some long-dormant part of me fluttered to life.

"We have the same interests," she said. "You and me. This crew. You'd be well-advised to make sure Nova does cooperate."

A shiver worked its way from my head to my hands, but I concealed it from her. "More threats?"

"No, I don't need to threaten you. Those meds you keep cradling in your pocket are a far cry from what Transliminal could do for you if we exploit Birke's desire to contract your sister. We think Marre's condition would be easy for them to treat. They have more resources than they know what to do with. Convince your sister to help us, and we'll make sure you're taken care of too. Why not dangle that in front of her as motivation?"

I was about to answer, but Marre made a small, startling sound somewhere between a grunt and a groan. She doubled over on herself, folding into a small ball on the chair, gripping at her stomach and crying out. Translucence rippled over her entire body in waves, as if she were made of liquid instead of flesh. Every centimeter of her struggled to maintain visible cohesion. The pain of it distorted her features into a grimace. My heart broke. I knew that kind of suffering, even if for different reasons. Watching someone else endure it—Lai, Marre, anyone—made me feel utterly helpless.

Crouching down in front of her, Tev gently turned the pilot's seat toward herself and placed her hands on Marre's shoulders. "Breathe," she said, her low voice soft as clouds. "Slowly."

Marre tried complying, but I recognized the pain-induced fear in her dark eyes. Buzzing sounds filled the room, as if a swarm of insects had invaded the bridge. Marre tore off her jacket and threw it to the floor. Tev recaptured her before her panic could wind up out of control, placing soft hands on Marre's bare arms. As soon as they touched, the buzzing receded to a distant murmur.

"In, and out." Tev demonstrated, inhaling slowly, exhaling slowly. Every word and breath was patient, loving. Gentle. "In . . . out."

Mimicking Tev's breathing, Marre slowly calmed down, tears spilling from her cheeks when she let out a trembling exhalation, then disappearing halfway down her face. Her body gradually regained its normal level of cohesiveness. Small patches of invisibility afflicted her arms and legs, occasionally shifting to other parts of her body—face, fingers, neck—but it no longer threatened to consume her completely. The more Marre breathed and focused, the more cohesion she regained.

"Breathe," Tev said again, stroking Marre's hair. "You're okay. You're here. I feel you—you're solid and real."

Marre nodded, again exhaling deliberately and slowly. "Thank you, Captain."

Tev leaned forward placed a lingering kiss on Marre's forehead, and Marre closed her eyes, placing her hands on Tev's cheeks. I felt like a voyeur, but I was drawn to both of them, warmed and moved by Tev's kindness and Marre's strength.

"So are you going to help us, or not?" Tev said eventually, pulling away from Marre and turning back to me.

I forced myself to refrain from looking at Marre any longer; I didn't want her to mistake my concern for gawking. "I want to, but I don't know about gambling entirely on my flighty sister. You don't know how stubborn she can be."

"Exactly. I don't know her. You do. You want to stay on this ship? Prove your worth to us. Be useful. Get her to cooperate."

"I'm an engineer; that's where my worth lies. My sister and I don't even get along. I want to help, but—"

She stepped closer, hands on her hips, looking down at me with those bright green eyes. Just like that, she'd transformed from nurturing to intimidating. Standing near Tev felt seductively dangerous, like waving my bare palm over a flame. "Try harder."

Heat licked up my spine.

"Your sister is the only lead we have, the only thing we know Birke wants badly enough that we can use as leverage. I'll be damned if I'm not helping my pilot. She's suffering. If you have a better idea, let's hear it."

"You're underestimating how little Nova might care."

Tev tilted her head a bit, as if she wanted to say something but refrained. "You'll just have to think of a way to convince her it's in her best interest to work with us, then. You know her. Find a bruise and poke it."

"She doesn't bruise easily."

"But she *does* bruise. Spirit guide or not, she's still human."

We stared at each other. She was just as rough around the edges as me, and it was the first time in awhile I'd met anyone who could keep me on my toes other than my own aunt. Unless you counted Nova, but that wasn't the same. She kept me on my toes like an insect bite on the bottom of my foot.

Tev Helix, on the other hand, intrigued me. Her abrasive personality went way beyond her protectiveness over Marre. Who *was* she? What kind of person mods a Gartik transport vessel, employs a disappearing pilot and a man who acts like a canine, and fancies herself capable of manipulating a powerful othersider with nothing more than one spirit guide?

"So," I said. "If I'm helping you, are we still calling that room I slept in the brig, or my quarters?"

Tev looked unimpressed. "Don't push your luck."

I spent the afternoon taking a shower, stretching my sore body, taking the dose of Dexitek that would take the edge off my symptoms for a little while, and trying to come up with a way to convince Nova she wanted to help the crew. It was better than obsessing about whether Lai would be fretting over my absence, whether she'd gotten my message, whether she'd secured any jobs for the day, whether her meds would keep her illness at bay well enough for her to work one more day. Ruminating about my aunt would do nothing to help anyone. Convincing Nova to help Tev, would.

We still had six hours until we arrived at the outpost, and if I were honest with myself, I was as excited to see Nova as I was dreading it. Some part of me always hoped each time we saw each other that this time we'd reconnect, find some common ground, if only I could figure out the right way to reach her. Maybe this was an opportunity that went beyond helping Marre, or even healing my own body.

I had plenty of sore spots where my sister was concerned. Our every interaction ended up an acidic reminder of what we *weren't* to each other. We tried to understand each other, but our efforts were always short-lived, tempered by our fundamental differences in values. Frankly, I wasn't sure if she cared enough about our relationship to try anymore; she was too busy fawning over her own accomplishments.

Just as I was about to try to leave thoughts of Nova behind in favor of a nap, someone knocked on the now-unguarded door of my former "brig," and stepped inside. Dr. Vasquez held two small, brown boxes and a water bottle. She seemed warmer now, her face relaxed and open. Apologetic, even.

And with good reason. No matter how noble their intentions, I'd probably be bitter about that stunt with the injection for a while. Still, I was glad for the company. She made her way to the bed and sat down next to me, offering one of the boxes. "Hungry?"

"Oh, for love of the black," I sighed, tearing open the box with no shame. I hadn't eaten since that plumberry on Heliodor. "Yes. Oh, yes."

Vasquez laughed, reminding me of the kind of woman I wished my sister had been—all the grace but none of the pretense or vanity. Her black hair bobbed just above her shoulders in waves as she shook her head. "Sorry about the whole not-feeding-you thing. Tev feels bad about it. She's the one who sent me here with the food, but don't tell her I told you."

Too busy chewing to answer, I just waved her off. Spiced, dried meat filled my stomach with such a welcome heaviness and warmth that I didn't care what animal it came from. Or what part of said animal, for that matter. A caramel-flavored nutrient block sat next to the meat. I procrastinated reaching for it; we ate them regularly back in Heliodor. They were cheap, easy to find, and kept you healthy, but they tasted more like expired ass than the advertised flavors. Still, I was grateful for the nutrition and for the growing ache of a full belly.

"So why aren't you eating with the rest of the crew?" I said. "Drew the short straw? Stuck with the stowaway?"

"We grab meals when we can. Not always together. There's too much to do on a ship and not enough hands to go around. Like keeping an eye on the criminals that wander on board in our crates."

Anxiety fluttered in my chest, but she winked at me and I relaxed.

She tilted her chin at my dinner packet. "Sorry we don't have anything better. It's not all glamour in the Big Quiet."

"Heh, it's not glamorous on Orpim either, trust me. Not in my part of Heliodor. And even the nice neighborhoods are built on the bones of industry."

"Have you always lived there?"

"Yeah."

"You sound thrilled."

"That's because it's so thrilling," I said flatly.

I slowed my chewing and relaxed into the meal. No one was going to burst into the room and take this food away. No need to rush.

"Ovie hated it too." Her voice was soft. "Hasn't been back in about ten years."

"He's not missing anything. Fringe folk are all but crowded out now," I said. "Even the families who were there a long time before othersiders gentrified the damn place. Now they look at us like we don't belong there, like it wasn't our town before it became their playground."

It was easy to hate the lie Heliodor had become.

"Not like I remember it ever being any other way," I said, "but my aunt does. Now the city doesn't think we're worth anything unless we cover our houses in albacite. I guess at least it's imported from a planet on our side of the breach. At least it's *real*. That's something."

Vasquez made a disgusted face. "Don't even get me started on that blood mineral."

"They try to hide poverty in my city with layer after layer of it, like you can just cover folks with gloss. Why do you think I wanted out?"

She set her packet down on the blanket and leaned back against the wall. "Same reason we all do, I'd guess. You're running for the sky, or something sappy like that." She smiled. I heard the fringe in her voice too, though her accent wasn't Heliodoran. Didn't matter. There were folks like me everywhere. Probably back in the othersiders' own universe, too.

"You're not so bad, Doctor Vasquez."

"Call me Slip. No one here uses my title except Tev, and that's only when she's pissed."

"Why Slip?"

She took a swig of water from the bottle and handed it off to me. "I don't know you well enough."

"Okay." I held my hands up in mock surrender. "How about telling me something about everyone else, then? Only seems fair to know who's sticking me with fake poison."

"They'd kill me."

I grinned. "And? You've proved those threats are empty."

She just shook her head and smiled. "You're not that bad either, surgeon. I hope you don't disappoint us."

"I wanted to ask about the other engineer." I didn't meet her eyes as I set aside the food, saving a little for later. "Ovie."

She laughed, a mischievous look creeping into her eyes—almost a challenge. "What about him?"

"He barked at me."

"Of course he did. You were a stranger stowing away in our cargo hold. He could smell you the second he stepped in there."

"Smell me?"

"Yeah?"

"And he barked at me."

"That he did."

Between Marre and this, I was starting to feel a bit crazy. Shards of my sanity dropped away and shattered on the floor with each new conversation. Why was I the only one who found it unsettling to watch a grown human growl like an animal?

"What do you see when you look at him?" Slip said, leaning back against the wall.

"A big, *human* being. No tail, no fur. Sky surgeon locs." I gestured at my own. "Sweat and grease. Reminds me of my aunt, only harder. Bigger. Healthier."

"Half the time, I see that too," she said. "Minus the part about your auntie. But sometimes, I see something between a wolf and a dog. Black fur, long tail, tongue hanging out the side of his mouth when he sleeps upside-down. Ears pricked up when he's interested in something." Her face grew softer as she spoke of him, her eyes glazing over as she recalled the images. "Grease on his paws instead of his hands. Sometimes he flickers between the two. He's no small canine, that's for sure, just like he's no small man."

"I don't get it."

She patted my leg. "You don't have to. People don't exist for us to get."

Evidently that was the only explanation I'd receive, at least for now. I shoved another piece of nutrient bar into my mouth, pretending it was a piece of fruit instead of a nasty compressed morsel of whatever. Ever since setting foot on the *Tangled Axon*, I'd found myself more frequently at a loss for words. There's not a lot to say in response to being told that a person is, in fact, sometimes a wolf, and you're the odd person out if you can't see it. Nothing coherent, anyway.

"Don't worry so much about it," Slip said. "You'll get to know him the way you get to know anyone."

"Okay." I kept eating. Getting to know him is exactly what I intended to do if I wanted to work in his engine room. What do you do to get on a wolf-man's good side? Bring him a ball? A tug toy? A herbivore?

"What about you?"

"What?"

"You think this is a one-way thing? Tell us something about you."

I shrugged. "Like what?"

"Pick a story."

"A story." I thought about my life, which I saw stretching back in time as a series of love affairs with ships. "What kind of story?"

"You're the one who'll tell it." She shrugged. "Not me."

"I don't know what you want."

"I told you." Slip laughed. "A story about you."

One memory floated to the surface, so I plucked it out of my brain and started talking.

"My sister hated my hobby growing up—building miniature working ships. Baby ships, my parents called them."

"Cute."

"Nova thought they were dirty and noisy and not becoming for the sister of a spirit-guide-to-be. My aunt even came over and helped me make better vessels. I didn't think about it then, but she taught me the art of ship doctoring through hobby shipmaking, knowing I'd grow up and want to play with the real thing. Absolutely no one was surprised about the sky surgeon I grew into; I probably came screaming into the world with engines in my eyes."

Her soft smile warmed me. "I bet you had little sky surgeon braids in your hair and everything."

"Oh, no. You kidding? Nova would've cut my hair off in my sleep. Especially after the baby Series II Greenbelt I made—I think that was the last straw for her. That little ship was beautiful, let me tell you. But I wired the thrusters wrong. When I turned her on, she worked fine at first, gliding up into the sky and scaring off a flock of red-winged blithes. But when I maneuvered her back down, she took on a mind of her own and went tearing through the neighborhood. Shot straight through a neighbor's workshop and started a fire that jumped across the trees on his property burned down the back of his house. The Greenbelt stopped when she cut a trench through someone else's yard. I remember chasing the damn thing down and laughing the whole time, which just made my sister even more furious. 'You think this is so funny, don't you?'" I mimicked her over-enunciation, then laughed to myself. "And yeah, I did. At least until my parents knew they had to do something to teach me not to tear up the neighborhood with my ships. Banned me from my aunt's shop for three months, much to Nova's smug pleasure. I was a lot more careful after that."

I shoved another piece of bar into my mouth and tried not to gag. I really hated those things.

"Why did your sister hate ships so much?"

I shrugged. "It's not ships she hates. She's pretty indifferent to them, same way I'm indifferent to my toothbrush. It serves its purpose. What she hates is the idea that her own sister lacked talent for spiritual guidance. Even worse, I had no interest in trying to expand what little innate ability I had, to become metaphysically useful beyond repairing ships. Just not in my blood to be a spirit guide, I guess. She never understood why I'd choose to be an engineer when there's a whole world of subtlety and magic to tinker with."

Slip was quiet as she seemed to consider this. I just kept eating, suddenly exhausted from stirring the sediment of my childhood.

"So," she said, eventually. "Go ahead."

"What?" I said around the chewed gunk.

"Ask about the captain."

I almost coughed up the bar, but held it in and swallowed. "Where'd that come from?"

"Oh please. You were going to ask."

"I wasn't. She doesn't seem like the type who'd want me to know much about her."

"But you do want to know."

"Of course. She's the captain."

"Uh huh." She smirked, then rested her head against the wall again and closed her eyes. "Well, you're right. She's pretty contained when it comes to her private life. I'm lucky I got as close to her as I did. You think it's hard getting past that granite exterior she's so proud of now? Try dating her."

Jealousy soured the already-disgusting nutrient bars sitting like rocks in my stomach. Dating?

"She seems desperate," I said, shoving the unwelcome emotion down. "I can see that much."

"You'd be desperate too if your whole life were wrapped up in a glowing hunk of metal and the pilot at her helm. We all are. Marre's not just our pilot. She's family."

I grazed my fingers along the wall, again feeling the subtle hum that told me the *Tangled Axon* was listening, breathing, functioning. I imagined Tev doing the same, listening to the metal lady she depended on for survival out here. Wouldn't I do anything to save my family?

"Why doesn't she find another pilot?"

Slip sat up and opened her eyes. "You don't throw family into the silence just because they're sick."

"I just meant—"

"I don't care what you meant. You should know better."

"I meant if she loves her ship and her pilot so much, and Marre is suffering, why not relieve her of her duties?"

"Marre may have an affliction, but she's a damned good pilot, and as long as she's alive she's the only person who's going to touch those controls."

"I'm sorry."

"It's fine."

I could tell it wasn't. My words had come out all wrong. I'd be just as irritated if someone suggested I should put away my passion because of my disease. I thought about how Tev had comforted Marre, soothed her, and how similar it was to the way I felt in the presence of a ship like the *Tangled Axon*. Where the ship intersected with my hand, there was an undeniable charge, a frisson of empathy I couldn't ignore. She had called to me on Orpim, and she called to me now.

I exhaled a breath held too long. "Tell me about *her*, now," I whispered. "Please. The *Tangled Axon*."

Slip brushed her hands on her pants and scooted closer to me. Graciously, she seemed to be shrugging off the offense I'd unintentionally caused. She leaned toward me and smiled broadly. "There's only one thing you need to know about this ship."

"Yes?" My breath caught on my rapidly beating heart. I felt like a teen again, talking about girls. Flushed cheeks and all.

"If she wants you to know her, you will. If she doesn't, not a power in all the silence could help you pry your way in." She patted my back, wiped her mouth, and stood, cutting our conversation short. "I'll let you get some sleep."

I wanted to tell her to stay, keep me company, tell me more. Teach me about everyone. Everything. Give me a doorway into the world I'd only barely glimpsed. But I let her go, hoping I'd made a decent impression despite my comments about Marre.

I slept away the remaining trip to Ouyang Outpost and dreamed of schizophrenic engines gone mad with age, spinning uncontrollably into the dark. At the center of all of them, I was there, a strong and inviolable version of myself, flame-bright like molten steel. A woman of metal and fire.

Chapter Five

Adul's atmosphere filled the bridge view screen, blocking out all the black and void of the silence. We'd docked at Ouyang Outpost about thirty minutes before Slip came to wake me. Now we were just waiting for Nova, who—true to form—had yet to show up. Fashionably late even while my life was on the line, as far as she knew. Slip waited for her on the outpost station while the rest of the crew prepared to refuel.

I did my best to stay out of the way and ignore the fascinating but unsettling people around me. Marre most of all, who I could have sworn was watching me even while plotting our next flight path. Her telepathic buzzing droned on like a specter in my head, whispering psychotically beneath the voices of the crew. Ovie, with his occasional growls and dog-like scratching, became mildly annoying in his stoic incomprehensibility. And Tev—her imposing presence, that silken voice, and the sheer power she represented in my new life—dwarfed everything else on the bridge. A maddening aura of control and sexuality surrounded her no matter what she was doing. And still there was that sadness behind her eyes that softened her when she thought no one was looking.

Really not the kind of distraction I needed at the time. Besides, she was spoken for.

So I focused on the familiar gas giant in front of us in an effort to forget everything else. Vertigo overtook me as I watched

Adul's slow rotation, as if the gravity of the planet tried pulling my soul out through my eyes, through the screen, on into the black. I held onto the comm panel to steady myself, the crew's activities a mere blur in my periphery. Longing pinched at the back of my throat. I'd missed my second home.

Pale bands of atmosphere twisted in ropes around Adul, like shifting sand. Or maybe more like the layers of a cake, but that might have been my renewed hunger talking. Still, the child in me wouldn't have been surprised if a mouthful of Adul tasted of sugar and cream. Smooth and rich, whipped into a froth by its storms.

In school, most kids said they loved the resort planet Gira best. It was fun, exotic. Covered in wildlife preserves and green landscapes—far more romantic than the industrialized Orpim that Heliodor called home. Our planet creaked and groaned and spit sulfur, but Gira's roots were in the far more glamorous field of eco-tourism. A biosynth team refashioned the whole planet decades ago for the sole purpose of making money for the Nulan system's upper class. Even the othersiders were taking notice now, buying up entire swathes of Giran land. An entire world had turned into a holiday delicacy for the decadent rich.

Which meant, of course, I'd never seen it.

That was okay. I wasn't as interested in Gira. Adul was the object of my childhood affections, and it wasn't until I was older and understood the nature of gaseous planets that I let go of my belief that there were entire seas of sweet cream churning beneath its upper atmosphere. During my school breaks, Kugler and I had begged my parents to let us take a shuttle from the research station to travel down through the storms and into the sugar-sweet winds below.

More than twenty years later, I found it no less enchanting. Our people peeled away bits of its ephemeral skin, separated its isotopes at the orbiting low-temperature rectification factories, and distributed the helium-3 to ships that ferried us through the silence. Adul gave our vessels their blood from whorls of her breath, like a mother. A goddess.

Best of all, I loved the gaseous creatures who lived in Adul's upper atmosphere, organic balloons bobbing between bolts of lightning. Beings who gave my mother and father purpose as their linguistic team worked to decipher the Adulan language of color and light. Floating and puffing innocently through the gas, shimmering with bioluminescence, a single entity would have dwarfed my entire neighborhood back in Heliodor.

Unlike most other beings in the system, the Adulans weren't crafted by biosynths. They had evolved on their own on Adul, all the more wondrous to me in their rarity. Only three times had we learned of a natively evolved intelligent species, and two of them weren't in orbit of our Nulan star. Even most human populations had been seeded from other human-occupied planets.

Slip returned to the bridge in a hurry, limping under the weight of the large travel case she carried. "Tev—"

"Alana!" An unmistakable, lilting voice.

Swathed in fabric so gauzy and golden she looked like liquid sunlight, my sister swept onto the bridge from behind Slip. Her hair—naturally coarse and wild like mine—was pushed back into a glitter-laden orange poof that haloed her head. Gold threads dangled from the hair tie, matching her long, gold earrings and the gold necklace sparkling at her dark throat. Just the right amount of skin peeked through her clothes, daring anyone to ask for more.

Before I could move, speak, or think, she wrapped me in a sun-draped hug, sleeves billowing around us. Jasmine wafted over me, as if she carried a glamoured breeze with her.

Actually, she probably did.

Nova pulled back to look at me, hands still on my shoulders, face thinner than usual. I hadn't noticed during our comm link. Had she lost even more weight?

"Are you okay?" Nova said, taking my cheeks into her hands and examining me, tilting my face this way and that.

"Oh yeah," I said. "See if you can crack it to the left."

She sucked her teeth. "This is no time for joking. Are your muscles okay? You can move okay?" She didn't wait for my answer before looking at the crew members, one after another, still holding my face as if I were a child. "Give her the antidote. Now."

Slip, wearing her lab coat for show and holding another saline-filled injector, made as if to move toward me. How were they preventing Nova from detecting their deception?

"Belay that, Doctor Vasquez," Tev said, confronting Nova. "You don't rush onto my bridge and start giving orders. You have to promise to stay. Put it through the guild as a contract. Delay or cancel whatever you had going on for the next couple of months. Alana gets nothing in the meantime."

"I've already done all of that." Nova sighed and tossed her arms in exasperation. "Honestly, I've been doing this job long enough to know how to manage my contracts. I'm a stellar-class graduate of the Advisory Guild's highest level of honor, three-time winner of the Seelig Award, and I've served over two-hundred clients—"

"We don't need the rundown, Nova," I said.

She smiled indulgently and patted my cheek. "The point is, I have accrued a great deal of experience, darling. I know how to tend my own schedule." She let out another hard sigh, muttering to herself. "For spirit's sake. Giving me orders as if I don't know to put it through the guild."

Tev raised an eyebrow, shifting her weight. Again, her leg clicked. "And you'll be staying."

Nova adjusted her dress, fixing some minute flaw only she could perceive. "I'm hardly at the beck-and-call of someone like *you*. You're from Woolera, aren't you." Her voice fell flat. "Leave it to my sister to pick a farmer's daughter over someone who could actually support her."

"What is that supposed to mean?" Ovie growled, fists clenched.

"Down, fella." Nova winked. Then, briefly, her eyes locked onto Marre's back at the navigation console, and a flicker of something unnamed crossed my sister's face. Marre hadn't acknowledged Nova; in fact, she seemed utterly uninterested in anything happening around her.

Nova just turned toward Tev. "So. The antidote?"

"We'll give it to her when we've left orbit. She has plenty of time." Tev gave her a sarcastic grin. "The tremors shouldn't start for another couple of hours."

Slip returned the pharm-injector to her pocket and shrugged, as if my life were inconsequential. "Captain's orders, ladies."

"Heartless lowlifes." Nova said, then turned to me, obviously no longer interested in what anyone had else to say. "Sweetheart, you really need to do something about this hair." She sucked her teeth again and played with a few of my locs, then dropped them. "You look so dark and brooding with it hanging down by your hips. Like some kind of wild thing on Valen. You should let me cut it."

"You know I can't."

She waved her hand. "Really, Alana, still going on about all that sky surgeon nonsense? No one hires you because of your hair, of all things."

"It's tradition."

"Blah, blah, blah. Well?" She opened her arms in a grand, sweeping motion as if to embrace the *Tangled Axon*, landing her gaze on the captain. "Where's my room? I assume I have a room to myself if you're taking up my time with such brash confidence and assaulting my little sister. Knowing my luck, you won't even tip me well. I should at least have comfortable quarters."

Tev took a breath but obviously contained whatever response she'd had in mind, instead glancing at Ovie. "Will you?"

He said nothing, but grunted and gestured for Nova to come with him. She just followed him with her eyes and crossed her arms, gold-tipped nails shining against her skin. "Really, Captain. Employing a wolf?"

Tev didn't even bother looking up from the flight path she now examined. "Who I choose to employ is none of your concern. We're done here. Marre, I want to route us around Sena. Too much traffic since Translim opened that rental ship depot."

"Let's talk!" Nova linked her arm with mine, capturing me in her bubble of jasmine and wafting us out into the corridor like mist. She waved at Ovie. "Go on, show me to my room. And take my travel case; you're bigger than me."

He glared and shoved the case toward her with his foot. "You have arms."

I mouthed *sorry* to Ovie, but he just glared, face stern between a frame of thick locs.

Positively seething with offense, Nova straightened her back. She looked at me, but there was no way in all the silence I was carrying my entitled sister's luggage. She knew as well as I did that an uncoordinated stumble down a corridor with a heavy bag would exacerbate my Mel's pain. I just tied my hair back and raised my eyebrows at her. "No time like the present to start working out."

"Rude." She grabbed a strap hanging from the end and dragged it as we walked, ranting to herself. "No concept of manners on this ship. Haven't they ever worked with a guide before? Oh, of course not. *Look* at them."

"How did you know?" I said, knowing better than to argue with her when she was on a roll. "About the wolf thing."

Nova scoffed. "Alana. Don't be so simple. Canine stench permeates his whole aura. Always been more of a cat person myself. I met the most wonderful panther-person on Valen last year. Gave me a tour of her plumberry winery. Remember that bottle of 2494 I sent you—"

"Nova. Stop. What the hell are you talking about?"

"How did my little sister end up on a *cargo ship*, anyway?"

She said "cargo ship" the way someone else might say "infectious disease" or "low credit score."

"You have to promise not to tell Mom and Dad," I said, rubbing at a knot at the back of my neck.

Nova paused in her lurching attempt to drag her travel case, tilted her chin up a few degrees, and gave me a *you should know better* look. "I make no such guarantee."

"Fine, forget it."

"Oh, don't be like that. You know I can't keep secrets from kin." She fluffed her hair and resumed her pulling, following a silent Ovie. "It's not in my nature. So tell me. What are you doing on this clunker?"

I sighed. "They came looking for you at the shop and I kind of stowed away."

"What!" She wheeled toward me and grabbed my shoulders again. "You didn't!"

"You're right. I didn't. You're hallucinating. It's all that perfume you're wearing."

"Alana Quick, I don't believe you."

"Okay."

"This is unbecoming behavior for a Quick woman. For no other reason than that, I won't tell our parents; it would break their hearts to know you threw away everything to gallivant around between the stars."

I liked the sound of gallivanting around between the stars. I was pretty sure they would too.

"This selfish behavior has to stop," Nova said. "Before you end up hurting someone. Life isn't all about you, you know."

I could pretend to be hurting far worse than I am, I thought. That would get her to stop talking. Capitalize on her belief that I'd been poisoned just to get her to stop nagging me. Tempting, but ultimately I thought better of it. Criminal or not, I did have some integrity. Besides, distracting her now would just make my job harder later, so I bit my already-bruised tongue.

"You've lost weight," I said.

"Have I?" She grinned, fanned her arms open, and looked down at her body, shifting each hip in turn to examine herself. Flawless, dark expanses of skin poked out of her gold garment, legs thin and taut. "Oh, I never know what my weight is doing these days, but you're so sweet to say so."

Of course, she feigned all modesty; the flicker of self-satisfaction across her face told me as much. Never mind that my comment wasn't intended as a compliment. Her flesh had lost more softness than it should have, cheekbones too severe for her face. But what else was I to expect? Guides ate as little as they could, exerted minimal physical energy, and subsisted on the lowest-calorie diet they could manage. The SAG installed biomechanical nutritional applications in their contact displays when students graduated from the guide program. Caloric restriction was simply part of the guide lifestyle.

As Nova babbled about her vacation on our slow march to her quarters, I remembered when she first told me about it. The lifestyle, that is. The caloric restriction and the slow whittling away of the physical self. Nova had come home from guild training on holiday one year and explained everything to me in a flurry of excitement, face bright with new experiences. She'd told me that guides from all over the system were waiting for the first of them to achieve the impossible: to become mere wisps of energy, rid of the bodies that confined them, free of the flesh that insisted on twisting gruesome blood and muscle around their pure spirit forms. "Ascension," she'd whisper, awed. Ever since, I'd watched her waste her healthy body, worry it away with resentment.

It didn't surprise me. The first time I saw Nova injured as a child—a paper cut, nothing more—she screamed and wept for hours, unable to reconcile the visceral, heartbreaking reality of blood and split skin. It was too much, too far removed from her expectations of what little girls should be made of. Surely a tear in her flesh should have leaked purity and rapture into the world. Surely her soul should have escaped in vaporous arabesques, dissipating into the aether.

Each day thereafter was a bitter disappointment to Nova. She felt her embodiment as an unwelcome thing that hung onto her like a demon's shadow, and she told me about it when we fell asleep at night. In her mind, if she could project her spirit-self across the system, if she could inspire greatness in artists and writers, if she could help the dying walk into the next life with grace, then surely she should have been able to free herself of the confines of skin and muscle.

I understood what she refused to acknowledge, and no matter how many times I said it to her, she waved it away in denial: because Nova persisted, her body persisted. There was no difference.

No more than five minutes after settling into her quarters, Nova had opened her small planet of a travel case and draped gold and red silk over one wall. Ever determined to surround herself with color and luxury, even in the belly of a cargo ship. Her impromptu wallhanging caught light from the dim lamp in the corner, softening the room. I had to smile at seeing the *Tangled Axon* draped in something so beautiful. This ship deserved it if anyone did.

"I do hope we leave soon," she said, crossing her endless legs and eyeing me while fanning herself. "Are you feeling okay? Does the poison hurt?"

"About that." I looked around for a place to sit, but I wasn't sure what to do with myself. She'd already established her dominion, claiming every centimeter of space she moved through as if she'd been born to inhabit it. I'd vowed never to tell her how envious of that ability I'd always been, or how badly I wished she'd have taught me how to do it, growing up.

"Oh, just sit there." She wiggled her manicured fingers at

the end of the bed. "Are you going to tell me what's going on, or not?"

"I was going to." I sat, pointlessly smoothing my pants, conscious of her staring at my hair.

"Don't worry," I said. "The injection was saline."

I braced myself for spitfire, but she just sighed and plucked at the end of her sleeve, not meeting my eye. "I know. I'm not stupid. I'm surprised you even bothered lying."

"You know."

"Obviously. You can't lie to me. I knew the instant I saw you; it was all over your energy. I'm just glad you're okay."

"When they injected me, I thought it was real. But how did they convince you?"

Nova remained quiet for a beat. "That girl on the bridge. She blocked my empathic abilities during our comm link. I don't know how. Something is terribly wrong with her."

"That's what they want to talk to you about—"

"You've got to take better care of yourself, sweetheart. Running around with these types is not good for your reputation." She placed a hand on my leg. "It's good to see you anyway, Alana."

"You're not upset with me?"

Nova sighed and idly examined her clothing. "You cut my vacation short. I certainly should be angry, but even guides can't be too picky about the contracts they accept these days. Clients aren't as plentiful as they used to be." Her gaze snapped up to mine. "Not that I'm hurting for money, mind you. It's just not worth getting angry when a job is a job, and I get to see my little sister, make sure she's not getting into too much trouble with these fringe folk."

"These fringe folk are my folk, Nova."

"You're my sister; you're better than that." She yawned. "Anyway, what do they want?"

"Has your agent been getting contract requests from someone named Birke?"

She grabbed my hand, recognition registering on her face. "Yes, I—"

Something almost threw us off the bed. The world upended, spinning and rocking as the ship rumbled, hull groaning. Lights flickered. One corner of Nova's silk hanging came undone, fluttering over us as we were thrown into the wall. My head banged against the metal, tweaking my neck muscles and temporarily blurring my vision before I could grab onto the edge of the bed and situate myself. Clothes, shoes, and crystals launched from Nova's case when the ship rocked again.

Once we'd righted ourselves, we stayed plastered at the corner of the bed and I checked to make sure the pills were still in my pocket. Centrifugal force pressed us to one side as alarms wailed over us. Nova reached for my hand and squeezed it, nails digging into my palm, eyes wide with confusion.

"Are we crashing?" she shouted over the noise, voice almost a squeak. "What's happening?"

The disturbance was brief. The *Axon* stilled.

Tev's voice burst in over the intercom, replacing the alarm. "This is the captain. All hands to the bridge."

"You stay here," I said, hurrying to the door, but Nova grabbed me by the shirt.

"No way. She said all hands."

"I don't think she meant—"

"I doubt you speak for the captain."

Before I could say anything, she ran down the corridor in a flutter of gold, and I hurried to catch up. Once on the bridge, I could see we were well away from Adul. The planet was no longer visible.

"Captain . . . " Ovie clutched Marre's shoulder and her half-fleshless hand rested on his. They both stared out the viewer.

Another crash rocked the ship. Everyone grabbed the nearest thing, be it console or seat or person.

"Is this ship safe?" Nova said, voice pinched, her words

coming rapidly. "Is it going to fall apart on us? I can't stay on a faulty ship! This thing is so old."

"No hull damage," Marre reported.

"The ship is fine," Tev said to Nova, hand and eyes lingering on the wall a moment longer than necessary, as if sensing the *Tangled Axon's* well-being through her skin. "And you'd do well to show some respect."

Nova locked eyes with me, breathing heavily, eyes wide. She fanned herself frantically.

I took one of her hands into mine and rubbed the back of it. "Everything is okay," I said, keeping my voice low. She continued fanning herself with her free hand and nodded slowly. I kept her close and looked at Tev, then the other crew members. "I'm sorry, she's not used to—"

"I don't care what she's not used to," Tev said. "This is a vessel with a chain of command and she will show some respect. And keep herself together." She gestured at the crew with her chin, eyes acid-hot beneath her bangs. "Everyone shut up and stand by. Marre, what's the status of engineering?"

"Stable," she said.

"And the projectile?"

"It wasn't launched from the engine."

"What was that?" Slip asked as she hurried onto the bridge at the same time I said, "What projectile?"

Tev moved toward Slip as she spoke. "Marre, activate comm and pull up imprints from the outpost. Start thirty seconds before the event." She lowered her voice a little and took Slip's hand. "Are you okay?"

Again, such a quick transformation from authority to tenderness sent a wave of longing through me. When Tev caught me staring, I turned away, ears hot with embarrassment.

Marre linked up to the comm system with tiny, deft fingers, and downloaded the 360-degree feed from the outpost's security recordings. The bridge view screen now displayed Adul and Ouyang Outpost's refueling station as seen from the station itself. Marre panned around the outpost until she had the ship's departure in view.

Adul glowed softly in the background in smooth shades of white and caramel. No matter how many times I'd seen it, Adul's beauty always made my whole body ache. In the foreground, the *Tangled Axon* looked like a creature on fire, arcs of electricity igniting around her.

"Wait," Tev said. "Hold the wide shot with the ship and the planet. Go from there."

Marre complied. The crew was a captive audience before the recording. We watched as the ship sailed away from the outpost, business as usual. The others seemed unmoved, but to me, the only thing more incredible than watching the *Axon* sail away from Adul was having watched her descend into my repair lot on Heliodor.

Something bright flashed across the screen, too quick to make out.

My world capsized.

Impossibly, Adul shivered. Starting at the equator, the planet bulged, inflating like a balloon. She almost seemed to be taking a slow inhalation. A glimmer of movement radiated out from the planet's center in a ripple, heading north and south through the same pale, warm bands of cream and caramel I'd loved all my life. Clouds roiled in the planet's atmosphere so deceptively it could have been mistaken for liveliness, but some deeper part of me knew, instantly, that I was witnessing one last gasp. One more flurry of life before my parents and my childhood blinked out of existence. Before the truth crystallized coherently in my mind, I could already feel myself dividing between the *before* and the *after*, a mitosis of grief.

Adul faded slowly, like mist, or a half-remembered dream. Irrationally, I wanted to reach out and grab her atmosphere, cradle it and reposition it and fix her the way I fixed ships, make her whole again, heal her, stop this horrible thing that I couldn't believe I was witnessing. I want to hold the planet in my arms the way Tev had held Marre, tell her to breathe, keep breathing, to hold onto herself, *please*. It was then that I realized I was in a panic, my breath coming in short heaves, palms damp against the console.

We were too far away to see the Adulans in the upper atmosphere while the planet faded, but I felt them out there the same way I'd felt the *Tangled Axon*, only this was awful, like a sickness pulling apart my cells one-by-one. Images of the bright creatures in Adul's atmosphere appeared in my mind, over and over again. Millions of serene, sentient beings floating harmlessly between electrical storms, flashing poetry across the thin membranes of their bodies. All those light-words—graying, dying, lost.

Gradually, holes punched what remained of Adul's atmosphere, honeycombing the planet. Ouyang Outpost and the station were distant flecks in the dark, crushed and devoured and burned by the dying planet. I felt the station and my parents and all those creatures—felt them pulled into the tidal wave of destruction that ate the planet away. Somewhere around me, in some other reality, the crew of the *Axon* was shouting and talking, but it was meaningless to me as I watched, struggling to breathe around my horror. Each second stretched out inside me as I watched my parents crushed inside the gravity well of what was once the most beautiful planet in the system. The space behind Adul began peeking through its shrinking gaseous bands, like night sky through branches. I could think and feel only one thing: *no, no, no . . .*

Piece by piece, puncture by puncture, Adul disappeared. Sixty seconds, and there was nothing left. A bolt of agony struck through the center of me, worse than anything Mel's had delivered. The world yawned open and I fell through into a twisted, ugly place where my parents were dead and Adul had fallen into oblivion.

Sensations I didn't have room for closed in on me: my toes crushed by the then-unbearable pressure of my boots, skin a hot and oppressive casing over my body, heart thundering hard enough to feel in my head and fingers and legs, breath too short to do any good.

It took me awhile to realize Nova was making an awful sound somewhere between a sob and a howl, but like the crew, it sounded wrong and far away, part of some other existence. She grabbed my arm and pulled on me, as if I could do something to stop this thing that had already happened, a thing we would have had to reach through time to reverse. Distantly, I was aware of putting my hands on hers and prying them away from my arm, but all I could see was death, all I could feel were the tremors of nascent grief tearing through my body. All my movements moved as if through water. Even the air was heavy and viscous.

My parents' lifework, the station that brought them together, the station where I'd known my ex-wife as a child—all of it. Gone. Pain compressed my skull until I bit my fist so I wouldn't give voice to it. Memories shot through me like lightning: watching one of the Adulans exchange colors with my mother and the team; helping my father scratch coded love messages for my mother into the metal behind her desk after hours; Kugler and I falling asleep against the observation deck glass while schools of Adulan juveniles floated past.

But Adul was gone, and had taken its entire population and my parents with it. Spots of light floated across my vision. Little suns that spread into the center of my head and carved out pain-furrows until all the voices and images on the bridge with me just magnified the sensation. Objects floated through space in ways they shouldn't.

"They're dead," I whispered. It didn't sound like me. "They're—"

From the point in space that was once the planet's core, a shockwave shot out in all directions, knocking into the *Tangled Axon* and sending us into a temporary tailspin. From our safe vantage point in the future, we watched Marre struggle with the thrusters to right the ship's course. Eventually, the ship stabilized.

"That should have destroyed us," Slip said, her voice distorted in my mind.

Vaguely, I was aware of Tev leaning in and fiddling with the viewer controls. "Apparently not."

"She's right," Ovie said, his low voice a near-echo. "We should have sustained more damage. The ship shouldn't have held together."

I imagined the creatures in Adul's atmosphere being punctured along with the planet. Every last one, disappearing. No resistance. Just a quiet passing into oblivion along with half of my family. Horrible images of my mother and father grappling for purchase flashed through my mind. Images of their bodies crushed under the pressure of a dying planet eating the space station, bloodied and broken between compressed metal walls . . .

Horror slid down my throat and congealed in my stomach.

"They're all dead," I said, gagging on my words.

The screen showed the *Axon* up close.

"What was that flash before the event?" Tev said as Nova's arms enveloped me, her jasmine scent making me sick now. Nova's warm body shook with sobs, her anguish-mangled voice ringing in my ears as Tev continued issuing orders. "Marre, go ahead and play it from just before the light cuts across the screen, but slow it down."

I couldn't keep myself from watching while I held Nova. On the viewer, something moved near the ship, then shot across the screen with a tail of light trailing behind it. Sickness rocked me again, painting a whitewash over my vision, pinging against the physical pain wracking my body. Every few seconds the realization hit me anew: *they're gone. You will never see them again. You will never hear their voices again. They will never fly with you again.*

"Stop." Tev pointed at the object. "It's moving too fast. Go back and replay it. Slow by fifty percent."

There, from the side of the hull near engineering, something detached from the ship. It moved a small distance away from the *Axon*, then fired into Adul.

"That's what did it," Tev said.

"Not possible," Ovie said. "I ran diagnostics already today."

"Shipwide scan confirms a foreign object on the port hull near engineering," Marre said.

"Marre." Tev still stared at the image, white-knuckling the edge of the console. "Get us out of here. Fast."

She seemed unaffected. "Yes, Captain."

Tev didn't move. "Ovie."

"Captain."

"Find out what the hell just happened to my ship."

He left without comment, locs swinging behind him. All my senses snapped back into place, fashioned into a needle-sharp point of determination by some deep, resilient part of myself I didn't know existed. I jogged to catch up with him, fighting to force my feet to carry a weak body down the hallway. Nova shouted after me, but I held my palm up to her behind me to stop her, then turned back to Ovie. My whole body shook. Heat curled up between my fingers, in my palms, at the center of my chest. Fire pumped through my veins.

I knew what I was feeling.

Rage.

"Please." I touched his arm with a shaking hand. He stopped and looked at my hand, then at me. A low growl rolled in his throat.

"Please," I said again, through clenched teeth. I loosened my jaw and closed my eyes briefly before speaking again. Then: "Let me come with you."

"No."

"My parents." I choked. The rest of the words lodged themselves somewhere in my throat. I couldn't say it again. *They're dead. They were on the station.*

"I can't have you getting in the way."

"Please!" I noticed the heat on my cheeks before I registered the tears that blurred my vision. "I have to do something. *I have to.* My parents."

He gave me a hard look with those ice-blue eyes. "Fine. Just stay out of my way."

"Alana . . . " Nova said, having caught up. Her once elegant makeup, now smeared into a mess, made her look alarmingly young and lost. "Where do I go?"

My mind was a mess. I desperately needed to do something to prevent those images from surfacing, all those images of my parents being crushed and killed, their faces stricken with terror, the Adulans flashing in terrified colors, the planet disappearing into an empty point in space. I had to do something useful, had to be somewhere other than the bridge, which was now imbued with death. I had to channel all this trembling emotion into something productive or I would tear myself apart with it.

I couldn't comfort my sister now. I didn't have it in me. Looking at her just made me think about our shared grief—a grief I couldn't yet confront directly, or it would swallow me whole.

I jogged back a few meters to find Slip. "Please, can you take my sister—"

"No." Tev broke her connection to the comm system and took Nova's arm before Slip could respond. Nova tried pulling away, but relented when Tev held her firm. My sister wasn't used to being on the bottom of the hierarchy, but where I would have once relished in her being taken down a few notches, I now only wanted to protect her.

"Our parents were on that goddamned station," I said, unable to keep the vitriol out of my words as I stepped toward them. "Let her go."

"I'd like to go with my sister." Nova said, straightening her back and fixing her face into a mask of regality despite the smudged eyeliner around her eyes, the puffy cheeks, the trembling mouth. She looked like pure emotion barely contained by superficial gloss, and I half expected her to glamour Tev into submission.

"You're not going into my engine room, love." Tev let go of Nova's arm and rested it on her shoulder. "Slip will take you to your quarters. You should rest, and we have to work." She looked at Slip. "Make sure she's going to be okay."

Slip nodded. I watched as she guided a helpless Nova away. My sister didn't glance back at me, or the bridge, or Tev, or the silence beyond where our parents used to be. Her back just disappeared into the dark corridor, enveloped by the ship. As I stared after her, everything leading up to that moment blinked through me in rapid succession: meeting Slip, stowing away, Ovie, Tev, my sister, Adul. The *Tangled Axon* was a thread through the center of it all, tied to my heart, changing me.

Chapter Six

I closed my eyes and placed my hands on either side of the engine room entryway. One step, then another. Deep, shaking breaths. Ozone and metal tinged the air in my lungs.

It felt so damn good to let her course through me and carry all my thoughts away.

The heart of a ship doesn't beat; it thrums in a brilliant, burning plasma cloud above the engine. I wanted to block out all other sensation and feel nothing else but that singed air, the voltaic pulse. The *Tangled Axon*'s song moved through me, louder than ever, her lightning inside my veins. Every centimeter of me was electromagnetically charged, channeled through the ship. I boiled inside her, she inside me. I felt her in my fingertips, my blood, my hair, as if the *Axon* would scorch me straight through to the bone until I were made of pure glass.

This was my prayer. Nova shepherded human souls, but I offered my devotions through copper and coil. My goddess was plasma, and She was fierce. Worthy of worship. I could feel what ailed her, an object like cancer on her hull, piercing my own skin.

"Are you going to meditate or help me?" came Ovie's deep voice.

I kept my eyes closed, shutting away everything inside me that tried rising to the surface. Adul. My parents. Adul. My parents. I shut it all out, that ruminative cycle of horror that wanted to consume me.

Nothing exists but her, this machine, this music.

I'd been in plenty of engines, had my hands inside enough ships that you'd think this would be routine, but it never was. Especially not now. This ship's engine possessed an unparalleled voice—one that sounded to me like sunrise, like falling in love, like seeing divinity. It was so beautiful I mourned how much of my life I'd spent in her absence.

"Hey!" Ovie barked.

"I just need a second," I breathed.

He sighed. "When you're done communing with the door, we'll need to make sure everything's running normally in here before we go outside. It would go faster with two sets of eyes."

My eyes snapped open. "Outside?"

Ovie was hunched over, contorting himself so he could examine the bottom of one of the reactor coils. At my question, he paused, resting his elbow on a knee and raising his eyebrows at me. "That would be where the hull is."

"You're letting me come with you?"

"No. You're standing by while I check it out, but I need to keep you close."

I couldn't help myself. "You just said you could use a second pair of eyes in here. What if the thing out there is more complex than you think?"

He sighed and resumed working. "This ship already has an engineer, and I hear he's decent."

Okay. I knew when to back off, even if it meant fighting every instinct in me. An ailing ship wasn't easy for me to ignore, and it was the only thing that would keep the truth of what had happened from clawing its way to the foreground of my awareness.

Electric webbing sparked and sizzled above our heads, flickering with light. If I weren't worried about lowering Ovie's opinion of me, I would have stretched myself out on the floor right there to stare at the display and take in each note, each sigh between the arcs. I wanted to stop time and listen to the *Axon* until I was fluent in her language.

I made my way over to Ovie and crouched down, still resisting the urge to touch the *Axon*'s coils and wires, like running my fingers through a lover's hair. *There will be time for that*, I thought, though it hurt to wait.

Ovie compacted himself away from me. Clearly, I crowded his space just by being in the engine room. This ship was his girl, after all, and here I was putting the moves on her.

"I'm sorry if you think I want to take your job—"

"Doesn't matter even if you did. You're not going to. Captain Helix is a loyal woman. And you can see how enormous this ship is and how unlimited our supplies are. What makes you think the captain is going to take on the cost of another warm body for no real reason? Once she's sure your sister is staying, she'll drop you off somewhere and give you shuttle money to get home. It ain't personal."

It was the most I'd heard him say since I'd arrived. Evidently, I'd struck a nerve.

"I just want to be part of this," I said.

He huffed, a short growl rolling under it. "The engine?"

"Yes. The engine, the ship, the silence. All of it." I untied my hair and let the locs fall, trying to remind him we were kin, as engineers. "We're not different."

I placed my hand on the coil next to his. Mine looked so small by comparison. "I know you have to hear the songs too, don't you? Her songs? She is so beautiful, Ovie." I lifted my hand and placed it on the coil again for emphasis. "*This* is all I want. I don't want to crowd you out. I just want to be let in."

Cold eyes met mine. Measuring me. His gaze was direct and unsettling, a stare that said, *I dare you to challenge my place here.*

Like a wolf.

Eventually, it was too much. I looked away.

The moment I did, the mood shifted so suddenly even the air seemed lighter. "We don't need to be wasting time talking about it." He stood and offered me his hand. "Everything looks good in here. Time to suit up and play doctor outside."

I grabbed his big, warm hand, and he helped me up with a pat on my back. The kindness was almost too much to bear; it made room for the grief to rush in.

"Do you need my help putting it on?" I said quickly.

"Slip will meet us there. We're both going to need help."

"Both?"

"Yeah, don't get too excited," he said.

"Does the captain know you're letting me onto the hull?"

He huffed another laugh and shook his head, gathering his locs in one hand to toss them over his shoulder. "Do you think anything happens on this ship she doesn't know about?"

"But I thought you didn't want me to—"

"Didn't anyone teach you not to question a good thing? Time to suit up."

He turned around and walked out, and I could have sworn I saw the faint outline of a tail.

"Just step into the boots," Slip said with a mischievous look, like she was asking me to skydive.

Empty footwear awaited my feet in one of three chambers built into the wall. I eyeballed the magnetic boots while I pulled the forest of my hair up into the closest thing to a bun I could hope to get, which was really more like a pile of ropes on my head. I took a deep breath, inexplicably afraid of what awaited me on the hull. I'd never been outside.

"You two don't really need my help, hon." Slip grinned. Her bracelet glittered in the light as she adjusted my hair. "I just wanted to see your oogly eyes when you've got nothing but that thin second skin between you and the silence. Most untrained folks can't handle more than a few seconds, maybe a minute, on the first go. Everyone gets skysick. Universe is too big."

That was enough to urge me into the bio-skin chamber. *Don't tell me what I can and can't handle.* "I'm good. I'll be fine."

She laughed. "We'll see when we record you. First-time spacewalks are fantastic blackmail material. You should see Ovie's—"

A low grumble rolled out of him from the next chamber over. He eyeballed Slip while piling his locs at the back of his head, pinning them in place with an army of clips and bands. A small smile twitched at the corner of his mouth. A thin thread of tension ran taut beneath their easy friendship, making me wonder what more there was to it.

"Well," Slip said, winking at him but still speaking to me. "You get the idea. Everyone freaks out."

"I was born to do this," I said.

"Uh huh. I'm just saying, that's what everyone says." She gestured at my arms and legs. "Don't let it crease. You don't want your elbow to pop out. Not to mention, you'll be just a magnet away from floating away into deep space." She made a popping sound with her mouth to emulate the demise of my elbow, then laughed and closed the door.

I rolled my eyes, though inwardly I was grateful for her easy humor. I know both she and Ovie were helping me avoid my sadness; I'd never forget the kindness. Especially when they had Marre to worry about, let alone the grief of two sisters who were near strangers to them.

I stepped into the boots. They immediately shrank to fit my feet. Keeping my legs locked and my arms straight out to the sides, I waited. The laser scan read my body, and a few seconds later, an electrospinlacer wove the second-skin body suit around me. I imagined the *Tangled Axon* spun gossamer across my body, a thousand tiny spider legs clicking and whirring to produce the barrier that would keep my flesh intact in zero-g.

A plastic smell inundated me. I closed my eyes and let my imagination wander to distract me from that awful popping sound Slip had made with her mouth.

Shimmering fibers clustered together across my body, layer upon layer thickening to create my new skin. I felt the next wave of diamond-strong threads strapping me in like synthetic muscles, strategically placed so I'd still be able to move freely while maintaining the life-sustaining one-third atmospheric pressure and thermal regulation around my body.

I'd read reports about this on the net more times than I could count. Tried imagining what it would feel like. Now here I was, being remade for the Big Quiet. Nothing could have prepared me for the reality of it. Like being wrapped up and reborn.

It occurred to me—and not for the first time—we shouldn't be able to do this. Humans shouldn't be able to walk around on the hull of a metal box in the dead of space. We shouldn't even be in the silence at all; we should all be dirtheels, earthbound and staring skyward. But we aren't. We have ships and suits, and we carry our lives into the void, trusting them to nothing more than the integrity of our ingenuity and craftsmanship.

I didn't care what Nova said about flight: that's real magic.

It was all such a rush that I had to coach myself to calm down so I wouldn't fidget. I knew the second-skin suits were old news, but feeling myself strapped into my own silhouette, snug and safe, was nearly the most exhilarating thing I'd ever experienced—second only to stowing away. All these conflicting emotions made me dizzy and tensed my muscles, provoking Mel's to poke me in the back and remind me that it was still part of me, still creeping along my limbs and fingers, waiting. A familiar, threatening ache had already begun to spread beneath my shoulder blades.

Think about the suit. Think about the here and now.

I marveled at what was happening to me. Sure, maybe the tech was a little outdated, but the beauty of being a newcomer even on an old spacecraft was everything shone as if it were fresh. Everyone else these days wanted to generate those Transliminal Fields for spacewalks, but there was something comforting about relying on the suits. Tech made by *us*, our people, not conjured by the look-alikes from next door. It was daring and human and exquisitely terrifying.

"Arms," Slip said over the chamber's intercom, startling me out of my thoughts. She lifted her arms a couple of times to demonstrate what she was asking me to do.

I raised them higher so the life support system and power supply could be applied over the suit—a thin padding fitted on over the contours of my back. Finally, the visored helmet was lowered over my head and sealed with the skin.

The chamber door opened and I joined Ovie, who waited for me near the airlock door. Even with his enormous body, he looked sleek, sheathed in the same gray material.

"Ready?" he said, voice projecting directly into my helmet.

I gave him a thumbs-up.

"Don't get dizzy," Slip said, still wearing that shit-eating grin.

"Yeah, yeah." I acted annoyed for banter's sake, but excitement burrowed in my chest like a wild animal. *I'm going to walk on the most beautiful spaceship I've ever met. In the silence. Right now.*

I could never tell my parents about it.

No. I shoved the feelings down. *Focus.*

We opened the first airlock door and stepped inside, closed it. Ovie wiggled his fingers at Slip, and she placed her palm on the window. He placed his on hers, on the other side. The doctor's full lips curled into a smile—not sarcastic or teasing, but soft and sincere—and she nodded at him. Ovie nodded back, and before I knew it, the exterior door opened and we were maneuvering around our emergency cables, moving outside.

In the black.

Ovie motioned for me to lock my magnetic soles onto the hull. I complied while fighting the urge to look out beyond the ship. They said you shouldn't do that the first time, that it would make you get sick inside your helmet. But who was I kidding? I knew I'd do it. What if this were my one chance to see the Big Quiet up close? Even with Ovie's and Slip's kindness, nothing guaranteed my place on the ship. Tev could tire of me and hurl me headfirst at the nearest space station.

I looked up along the hull, letting my eyes drift slightly to the side, taking in the darkness.

It took every bit of my self-control not to cry. Here was the universe I had dreamed of since childhood. Here was the source of all the things I cherished, all the life in the cosmos, all the possibility that unfurled from each moment. Here was existence.

So many stars. I imagined the gods of old myth taking turns punching rivets into the universe to hold it together. Nothing about this experience unsettled me the way Slip said it would, except maybe the mild claustrophobia of being inside the helmet. But the expansiveness of the black, the vertigo? I didn't mind. It felt like my soul was ballooning out to meet . . . everything. It reminded me that, failing body or no, I was alive.

They're out there, now. Everywhere. The Adulans. Your parents.

Tears welled up in my eyes. I silently cursed them, unable to wipe them away.

I wished I could see more. The sides of the helmet encroached on the view, limiting how much I could take in from any given angle. Some dark part of me wanted to rip it off and go out in a gasp of awe.

Most beautiful of all was the *Tangled Axon* herself. Ribs of plasma circled her thrusters in bands. It was strange not hearing the buzzing and popping I was so used to from working at the shipyard, but the sight alone was arresting against such perfect darkness, with the stars beyond like drops of mercury. We all grew up knowing there was no sound in space, but until you're surrounded by it, until you're wrapped in that non-noise, there was no way to comprehend it. The absence of sound is a thing unto itself.

"Alana," Ovie said, his voice projected through my helmet. The sound tore through the wall of silence, shattering my nerves. He gestured ahead of us. "There."

I followed where his hand was pointing. A shimmering plateau of green and silver was stuck to the hull, about as large as Ovie's waist—which is to say big, but small enough that we could probably manage to haul it inside on our own.

"How can something so small destroy a planet?" I did my best not to choke on my words, though my eyes kept burning. I was certain I'd dream restlessly for months—all those beings choking, dying, and floating lifeless in a dissipating atmosphere, while my parents screamed inside the crushed space station.

"We'll figure that out when we get it inside."

For an hour, we worked on the device while it shimmered like an oil slick in hues of green. The work was gloriously tedious—exactly what I needed to keep my mind from wandering to places it shouldn't. Tendons burned inside my hands, sore from exhaustion and the disease. The muscles in my back turned to steel cords anchored to my spine. For the first time, I was grateful for the pain. Something physical to focus me away from the dark headspace in which my mind wanted to dwell. I ignored what discomfort I could and channeled every part of myself, all my energy reserves, into the work.

Ovie and I were an impenetrable machine of concentration. Seamless.

Eventually we peeled away the lower layers of the device's architecture, which served largely as a secondary securing mechanism. Once we'd taken care of that, it looked like a squat mushroom or maybe an enormous contact lens connected to a platform. Cables attached the center of it to the hull, but they'd been routed directly through the ship's body and into the engine.

I knew what this was.

"I know this!" I said, tapping Ovie. He waved me off, but I insisted, gesturing as wildly as zero-g would let me. "I know this mechanism! If we take it off, it'll destroy the engine, but—"

"Fuck. Who would do this?"

"I don't know, but don't worry. I used to do this to my sister's shuttle when she'd leave for the guild. Gave her plasma arcs a putrid green tinge she hated. My prank was a lot simpler than this, but I think I can disable it." I paused, swallowing my anxiety. "If you'll give me a chance."

Finally, he turned to look at me, really paying attention now. Scrutiny burned between us. I could almost feel it heat the metal under our boots. His gaze was rough and immutable, challenging me again, and I somehow understood that he knew no other way to look at a person. For Ovie, to look was to see *through*, to dissect, to assess. In this case, to determine whether the risk of allowing me to participate in something so high-stakes was worth it.

Eventually, he gave me a terse nod.

My fingers pushed through the strain and worked like scalpels, rerouting wires and fastening security mechanisms to trick the device into believing it was performing functions it wasn't. Where it connected to the hull, I patched over it with deceptively steady hands. I couldn't tell Ovie that I doubted my ability to pull this off. Don't get me wrong, I was confident *enough* or I wouldn't have suggested it, but insecurity crept into my chest all the same.

They didn't have to know. They couldn't see me steadying my fingers, willing my body not to show signs of fear. Nerves coiling and uncoiling all the while.

A click and a release. The device floated gently above the

hull, placid and thoroughly unmoved by its courtship with the *Tangled Axon*.

When it didn't explode, I exhaled. All the pent-up tension made its way to my hands, shaking them uncontrollably, so I placed my palms flat on the hull and remained crouched. This wasn't just exhaustion; I was late taking my meds. Mel's hated tardiness.

Just let it pass.

Breathe evenly. Ride out the pain wave.

Ovie collected one side of the disengaged object, and I stood and took the other. We nodded at each other before making our way back to the hatch.

At the entryway, I paused. "Wait. Please."

Ovie complied, but I could tell he wanted to get moving.

Gazing out into the black, I could have sworn the universe breathed. I expanded and contracted with it, filling with the light of the stars until my skin grew thin with the tautness of it. I was a pulsar, a red giant, a nebula; I was everything and nothing. Everything I'd lost was swimming inside me. My own mortality seemed irrelevant then, even with Mel's tapping me on the shoulder. All I knew was I didn't want my death to be heralded by a loss of motor function, by garbled speech, by fingers too gnarled with pain to appreciate a ship's contours. That wasn't who I was.

This was me: part of the black. When it was my time, I wanted to be given to the silence. Let her rush in and fill me until I burst into stellar dust. Let me join my parents, the Adulans. Let me be with them.

Before I knew it, Slip opened the inner airlock door, and we moved inside, the device shining between us like an emerald. We set it down and I immediately released the helmet, pulled it off, shook my head. Damn, that thing was claustrophobic.

My hair had to look ridiculous—more cephalopod than locs. My shoulders ached. Hunger gnawed at my stomach. Joints burned. Even the spaces between my fingers throbbed with soreness.

Slip gave me a quick smile. "Good work out there." I felt heroic and couldn't help but grin back.

"Ovie, Slip, Alana," the captain said over the intercom. "You're needed in the infirmary. Now."

"Slip?" Ovie said, eyebrows knitting together. "What happened?"

Her face and shoulders were rigid as she helped us out of our helmets, moving quickly. "Just come on."

My smile and feeling of heroism were short-lived. Something was wrong.

"Nova?" I said.

Ovie touched Slip's arm. "What is it, Helen? Talk to me."

"Let's just get you out of these."

"My sister," I said, pushing my way toward Slip. "Is my sister okay?"

"It's not your sister."

No one said anything as we worked to remove the suits. Heat flushed my face as the Mel's pain began eclipsing everything else; brain fog was taking over. Between the trauma of Adul and having had my concentration twisted to a fine point for so long, the day had taken its toll on my body, and I needed my medication. Combine that with the anxiety I'd felt outside clinging to my spine like a constantly firing electrode, and I was ready to collapse. I dressed as quickly as I could.

Slip had the grace to notice my discomfort; she smiled and thank us for our efforts, patting me on the back. "Tev will be grateful, hon. I'm sure the *Axon* is too. It's just . . . " She shook her head. "Just come with me."

We followed, silent save our boots tromping down the corridor, passing a few charms attached to the bulkheads. We ducked into the infirmary, where Nova paced near the far wall in a flutter of gold gauze, sparing us only a glance. Part of me wanted to go to her, while another knew better than to crowd a grieving Quick woman. Instead, I remained close enough to be there for her if needed, but focused my attention on staying coherent, staying conscious despite the pain.

I'd been so used to the sterile hospitals in Heliodor that the dismal condition of this infirmary shocked me. Frankly, the room looked no different than the corridors or quarters, all metal bulkheads and exposed beds. No Transliminal Fields to quarantine patients here. I'm sure Slip knew what she was doing with what resources she had, but I couldn't help thinking it would be a good idea to not need surgery out here in the black.

Slip was busy drawing up injectables near a row of metal supply cabinets. Two empty exam tables sat parallel in the center of the room. Tev hopped off the one closest to us and patted it, glancing between Ovie and me.

"You two, on the tables."

"Captain, what's happening?" he asked.

Nova finally broke out of her ruminations and hurried to me. "Alana. They're—"

Tev snapped her fingers at Nova to quiet her—frightfully effective, actually—then gestured to Ovie. "Pull up a net news stream."

"What about security?"

"Marre has our comm link riding under a nearby transport's."

"Alana," Nova whispered, skin pallid. "Auntie Lai."

I went dizzy. "What about her?"

"They'll come after her . . . " She clasped her hands together and tucked them under her chin, pleading with me. "You have to fix this."

I approached Tev, trying to get her to look at me. "What's she talking about? Why won't you tell us what's going on? Please."

"Ovie." Tev ignored me. "Now. Any stream, all of them—I don't care."

He looked at her for an extra beat before bending his arm

and using the implanted touchscreen to link up to the ship's comm system. Seconds later, a projected holographic view hovered above his skin. He pinched it with his other hand, then expanded the view window so it was large enough for all of us to see. The screen wobbled slightly when he moved his arm, but otherwise the picture was clear.

System report networks flashed by at ten-second intervals. Some were text-only reports beneath looping recordings of Adul's destruction. Others featured fresh-faced, well-known independent reporters beeped in from political or media outposts, peppered with vids of the planet disappearing, feeds of the *Tangled Axon*, and old photographic imprints of the crew. Words from the feeds buzzed around us, puncturing the tense silence in the infirmary: *Kidnapping of respected spirit guide, Nova Quick. Suspects. Murderers. Terrorists. Genocide.*

There were images of me in there, too, as if I were part of the crew—imprints and recordings taken from old net uploads. Records of my service with Lai's shop. Pix of me with Kugler at a night club in Heliodor. My parents, looking particularly overworked. Every image was a sickening reminder of what had happened. At the end of one of the feeds, they showed a recording of Lai, which then rolled over to the next report in Ovie's queue. Nova gasped and grabbed my arm at the sight of her. "Alana—"

"Wait!" I shouted, putting my hand over Nova's. "Ovie, can you go back to the last one? Please?"

Mercifully, he obliged.

No one spoke.

"—do that," Lai said in the feed, shaking her head. Worry twisted her features, twitching with suppressed sadness as she spoke. "She's a good girl. She loves her family and worked hard growing up. Still does."

The interviewer's voice came from off-screen. "Then what is she doing aboard a terrorist vessel? Why would she help murder her own parents?"

"She's a good girl," she said again. "That's all I know."

"That's enough," Tev said.

Ovie cut the connection. Dread pinched my throat. They were accusing us of genocide. What if the enforcers detained Lai and interrogated her? What if they didn't believe her when she told them she didn't know anything?

"How can they think we did that to our own family?" Nova practically shrieked. "I have nothing to do with it! I don't kill things! I don't even eat anything that wasn't artificially generated!"

"This isn't about you," I said gently, reaching for her flailing arms. "Don't worry. Did you hear them? You're a hostage. They're just after me. The rest of us."

She twisted in my grasp. "Alana, you can't let them do this to us!"

Tev indicated the exam tables again. "Ovie, Alana. On the tables. No one is going to be counted as a hostage or criminal or anything else, because they're not going to find us."

"You can't run!" Nova's eyes were huge. "No, no, no." She shook her head, chanting the word as if it would manifest her desired outcome. "I can't be seen with fugitives! I have clients. I have a reputation! I'm a graduate of—"

"You don't have a say in this," Tev said. "You can't contact anyone without our help, so you might as well relax."

Nova collapsed into a chair near the corner of the room, somehow avoiding any unseemly bunches in the gauze draped around her slim form. Even so, she smoothed the fabric of some imaginary wrinkle violating her appearance, soothing herself compulsively. I could see the genuine distress in her eyes, the sadness breaking over her features, lips trembling with the weight of it. I wanted to comfort her, to rest my head in her lap and be comforted, to take mutual refuge in family.

Part of me was afraid she'd turn us all in out of sheer panic, but Tev was right—there was nothing Nova could do. She couldn't contact anyone without the crew's cooperation. She had no implant with which to contact the outside world, neural or otherwise, because they were thought to interfere with guide work. She relied on older methods of comm linking. The most she could hope for would be an interface contact over her eye, but even those—

Oh, shit.

I clamped my hand over my implant and glanced at Tev, who spoke with Ovie and Slip in hushed tones. His arm was stiff between them, hovering like it didn't belong to his body. Slip's hand gently touched the place on Tev's neck where her own interface lived.

The captain wanted to take our implants.

Even with the external comm link severed, those of us who were implanted posed a threat—a risk we couldn't take when we practically had a price on our heads. I imagined my neural interface conspiring against us, transmitting our location to the system nexus with each heartbeat, the signal surging out from me in invisible waves. Disarmed by something so small.

When they removed it, I'd no longer have access to Lai. Not that I'd been able to get in touch with her since I'd left, but at least the possibility had been there, and that had comforted me. When my body ached under Mel's heavy hand, the implant had persisted—precise and tireless in its inorganic way, connecting me to the world when my muscles refused to cooperate.

I moved toward the closest exam table and threw myself on top of it, closing my eyes against the grief. There was no real choice. Either I let them remove the implant or I'd be off the ship, and then I'd have no chance to see whether Transliminal could help me and Lai when they helped Marre. No matter how hard it was to admit, keeping my implant wouldn't bring my parents back, and it wouldn't save the Adulans. They were already gone.

I pressed the heels of my hands to my eyes. Deep breath.

"I'll go first," I said. "Get it over with."

Even from across the room, I heard Nova sigh and shift her

weight, fabric rustling. "Alana, I don't think you should help these people."

"*These people* are the only way we're getting out of this." I just kept rubbing my eyes, trying to keep my emotions at bay.

Some footsteps and a series of clicks. Tev's low, accented voice. "Trying to be a hero?"

I opened my eyes to find Tev standing next to me, close enough that I could smell the rosemary. Her hair was tucked behind her ears, highlighting her soft features and wide-set eyes.

"No." I swallowed, wiping my palms on my shirt. Suddenly I was acutely aware of how badly I wanted to shower. "It's going to happen one way or the other. Might as well cooperate. I don't want to be arrested any more than the rest of you."

She placed a hand on my upper arm, squeezing gently, startling me.

"You're in good hands. Slip knows what she's doing."

My heart sped up. The warmth of Tev's touch radiated through my arm and shoulder and into my chest, heating me from the inside out. I had to exert great control over my fingers; they wanted to betray me, to touch the back of her hand, to find solace in even that small part of her. Until now, I hadn't realized how badly I craved the comfort of touch.

Instead, I nodded and offered what I hoped was a casual, vaguely friendly smile, but I'm sure I looked more like I was about to piss myself with anxiety. Maybe that was better.

What a mess I was.

Patting my arm, Tev quirked the corner of her mouth into a half-smile—not helping my effort to ignore my attraction— and tilted her chin at Slip. "Okay. You heard her. Let's get this over with. Nova, you're with me."

When she removed her hand, the cold infirmary air rushed in to steal the warmth she'd left behind. Nova complained all the way out the door, citing fines and blacklists and imprisonment and other probable consequences for even having *appeared* to kidnap a spirit guide. Beneath it all, a thread of fear pulled her voice tight.

I heard metal scraping metal as Tev closed the door.

A square device moved into place above me, near the ceiling. A series of dim flashes flickered around us, and we were alone in a box of black. A mobile sterile containment unit. At least there was that.

Momentarily, Slip looked down at me, smiling and patting me with a gloved hand. I felt like a child as she configured the room's settings, glancing at me between tasks.

"Thanks for cooperating."

I laughed. What else could I do?

"Yeah, I know. Not much choice." She eyeballed a pharm-injector, checking the amount of sedative in it. "Ready?"

"Will it hurt? After, I mean."

"About as much as you'd expect. Turn your head to the left."

There was a pinch at the base of the implant. A heady, heavy sensation at the back of my skull. Slip's hands on my arm, motherly.

After the day's exertion, I welcomed unconsciousness.

Chapter Seven

Pain throbbed along the back of my skull. My mouth was dry. A dull chill had taken root in my body. Even the dim light of my quarters hurt my eyes, so I closed them again.

Reality trickled in: no more implant. I tried lifting a hand to touch my neck but my limbs were weak from the anesthesia. Not worth the effort to confirm what I already knew.

Nova and I really were alone now.

I couldn't help imagining there was a gaping hole in reality where the implant used to be—a part of me now resigned to non-existence. I could no longer reach out to the system with a flick of a switch. It may have been synthetic, but part of *me* was gone. A deep sense of loss swept over me, and I struggled not to cry.

Damn drugs, making me oversensitive.

Fabric rustled somewhere to my right. An intake of breath. A yawn. Nova must have stayed with me. Gratitude swelled in my chest, mixing with my grief, and once again my eyes pricked with tears, which just frustrated me, which in turn made me more emotional, which frustrated me more.

How long until the sedation wore off?

The metal legs of a chair screeched slightly. Probably Nova standing up. *Wait. No. That isn't my sister,* I realized. Nova wouldn't click when she moved. Her footsteps wouldn't be heavy with booted soles as she walked the few steps from the chair to the bed.

"How do you feel?" Tev said, voice soft. I could tell she was crouching down next to me but I didn't want to open my eyes.

"Need my meds," I croaked.

She laughed a little. "It's okay. Slip administered them while you were out."

I opened my eyes anyway, but couldn't make out her features through the haze. I just saw a halo of dirty blond hair around the fuzzy image of a face. Backlit by the fixtures above us, low-lit as they were, she looked iconic.

I giggled and batted at the air. "You're no angel."

"What's that you said, love?"

I laughed, waved my hand. Giddy in my insobriety. Every movement hurt my incision, pulling at the skin so delicately held together, and beneath the lazy giggling I could feel anxiety rising. Each pinch at the surgery site was a painful reminder of what I'd lost. I was completely cut off from the outside world now, and it was sinking in. That awareness of my isolation clawed at my mind, sharp and relentless. Isolated, and wanted for genocide.

Tev touched my arm, soft pink lips smiling at me. At least my visual acuity was coming back. "Ovie and Slip moved you to your quarters. You'll have some privacy here. I'll let you rest—"

I put my hand on hers and lifted my head, but it was too heavy and unwieldy to stay up. "Hey, beautiful."

At least the drugs freed me from self-consciousness, pruning my mind of the pesky bits that kept me in line with social mores. Part of me already knew I'd be embarrassed later, but I couldn't bring myself to care.

She didn't say anything, but her eyes flicked toward our hands, then back to my face. I couldn't tell whether she was confused or irritated or both but, well, whatever. There in the dim light of my quarters—*the brig*, I thought, with another lazy laugh—I wasn't intimidated by her. She was too beautiful and I was too high.

"Remember this later." My voice slurred. I patted her hand, nodding as if I'd said something sage and unquestionable.

She laughed. "Okay, you need to get some sleep and I need to get my own implant out."

I closed my eyes and smiled. Yes, sleep was a good idea. My head throbbed. Staying conscious under the weight of the lingering sedatives was a constant struggle. I patted her hand again, then let it go.

"Remember this later," I said again, yawning around the words. I mumbled the rest. "Remember how I let you cut into me so I could be alone with you in the silence."

After stowing away in a crate, being barked at by a man/wolf/dog, watching someone's flesh disappear, witnessing the destruction of an entire planet and its inhabitants—including my parents—going on my first spacewalk, and having a twelve-year-old implant that may as well have been an eye or an ear surgically removed, there was only one cure for the inevitable ache that followed.

A shower.

Never underestimate the sheer ecstasy of hot water—a luxury I'd come to appreciate more than I'd ever imagined now that I was on the lam and homeless in the black. Water, hot and clean, beat against my back, my calves, my stomach, my face. I hoped the heat would sear off all my sweat and sadness, vaporizing it before the water could hit the floor. Every droplet was so exquisite I didn't even care that my arms and legs bumped the walls with each movement in this cramped facility. I didn't care that, despite the water-resistant sealant on my incision, the heat of the shower hurt just as badly as when I turned my head.

Pain meds only did so much. Even breathing moved my skin just enough to pinch at the piece of me that was missing.

I could almost feel its absence tugging at my confused brain:

Where has my implant gone, where is my companion? Where are her wires? Where is her metal? Where is the "we" we have come to know? I was mapped onto her, and she onto me, and now she's gone and I am alone.

The water cut off.

The door flew open and I scrambled for a towel, fingertips missing it by mere centimeters.

"Oh girl, you're going to have to get over that," Slip said, laughing. I looked around to see if anyone else could see me, but she was alone. "Privacy is just about meaningless up here. And get over the idea that you can take those long showers you dirtheels are so used to. You think the *Tangled Axon* carries an ocean in her belly or something?"

"Sorry," I muttered, then nodded at the towel on the metal bar just outside the stall. "Could you?"

She tossed it at my face. I grabbed it and wrung out my hair. Had Tev told her what I'd said about being alone with her in the black? I was high, she couldn't hold that against me—

"Your sister is asking for you. Also, here." She shoved more fabric at me and I grabbed it, feeling ridiculous—cold and naked and dripping pools of water all over the bathroom floor, with laundry in my arms.

"Don't look so pathetic," she said. "They're clothes. To wear. On your body. We figured you'd want something other than the greasy things you've been wearing. The pants are mine, so they'll probably fit. The shirt is Tev's, so don't ruin it by stretching it out."

"Right. Thanks." As if I could tell my body not to stretch out a shirt that fit snug around my curves. I toweled myself off, ignoring the nagging sense of shame in the back of my mind. They might not have been a military crew, but obviously there was a similar no-modesty culture here that I'd just have to get used to. It was never like this on the station. So much room, all those empty corridors. Kugler's laughter sounded infinite up there.

"Nova wants to see me, huh?" I tried focusing on anything other than my memories, made all the more difficult to suppress by the lingering pain meds. Of course, the tiny, cramped shower stall made it a little easier to ignore my thoughts when I was too busy being self-conscious and trying not to fall over while I dried off. If I stepped out to get dressed, I'd probably end up brushing against Slip while I pulled up the pants. That wouldn't be embarrassing or anything.

"Won't say what she wants," Slip said. She leaned against the door. "She's not the most down-to-earth person I've ever met."

"She can be friendly." The cargo pants were a bit baggy, but not so bad they'd fall down. I pulled the tank on and tried not to think about the fact that I was wearing Tev's shirt and her girlfriend's pants. Tried, and failed. "Nova's just been through a lot."

Sliding the bathroom door open, Slip gestured for me to follow her down the corridor. "Yeah, so have you, and you're not acting like you're too good to drink our water."

I wanted to tell her to ease up. I was hard on my sister, but she was my sister, after all. I was allowed to be.

"Anyway," she said, pausing at Nova's door two units down. Just next to the entrance was another of those silver charms. "Tev wants you to talk to her about the othersiders while you're in there. Feel her out, see if she's up for helping us. This whole thing will go a lot smoother with her help. Especially now that we have to fly under the radar."

Fear twisted my stomach into a knot. If the enforcers caught up to us, they'd never believe we weren't guilty of the massacre. We'd spend our lives on a penal colony with no sky in sight.

"I'll do what I can," I said.

"Tev would tell you to do more than that." She looked at me pointedly. "I'll just say 'do your best.'"

I smiled a little, then knocked.

"Come in," Nova sang.

"Oh, and don't wander around the ship," Slip said, then left.

Inside, Nova was curled up on her bed, knitting with what looked like tendrils of light, dress pooled around her in a sapphire lake of silk. Her fragile fingers did the work without the aid of needles. A small diamond of woven brightness, like a mote of starlight, dangled from her moving hands. Instead of the end of the thread disappearing into a skein of yarn, it simply vanished into the air.

"So, sister," she said, not looking at me. "You've thrown yourself over the edge. You're a criminal."

"Nova." I sat on the bed next to her. "It's not that simple."

"Oh, I know." She still wouldn't look at me. She just kept manipulating the light between pinched fingers. Knit, purl. "The captain told me all about their intentions while you were out on the hull. And then those awful news reports . . ."

"It's not their fault that thing attached to the hull. They don't know where it came from. They're just trying to help their pilot. Help us."

She huffed a sarcastic laugh, and her knitting project fluttered under the puff of breath. "Well, if by 'us' you're referring to yourself and the rest of the crew, fine, but don't lump *me* in with that lot."

My sister was as contained as ever, knitting there on her bed. No trace of the grief I knew she had to feel. I worried for her, shoving all that emotion down where she wouldn't have to deal with it. The sound of her wails on the bridge still replayed when the massacre flashed through my mind.

"The people on this crew aren't bad," I said. "If I can sense that, I know you can. What's your deal, anyway?"

Finally, she set her knitting down onto her lap where it illuminated her dress. She looked directly at me. "Shame on you, Alana Quick. Shame on you for leaving Lai the way you did."

"Whoa, hold on a minute. Don't talk to me like I'm a child—"

She pointed at me. "I *will* speak to you as your elder sister when you're being so selfish you can't see past your own wants. You left Heliodor because you couldn't stand it anymore, and you just left Lai there to fend for herself. Now look at you. Running from the authorities. Butchered under some stranger's scalpel."

Anger burned in my throat like bile. It felt good to feel something other than loss. "And you're so magnanimous, aren't you. Turning a profit on the spiritual anxiety of your clients, throwing crumbs Lai's way when it suits you. How is that any better?"

She pointed at me. "I saved your shop. You'd be working for Transliminal if it weren't for me."

"You know I'd never give up my work."

She pressed her lips into a thin line, then sighed and shook her head, tossing her big, beautiful cloud of hair side-to-side. She resumed knitting. "Anyway. I know you want to help that pilot, but—"

"Marre."

"Excuse me?"

"The pilot. Her name is Marre."

"Whatever."

"Why are you so angry at them?" I said, knowing the answer. I just wanted her to admit to her grief out loud. To let it out.

"They blackmailed me and now I'm stuck here because *they're* running from the enforcers. You know that just makes them look guiltier. They're no friends of mine."

"What choice do they have but to run? Do you really think Nulan government would listen to a bunch of fringe folk? Just believe us when we tell them we didn't do it? 'Oh, you say you didn't do it? Well, our mistake! Just be on your way, and here, have some fuel money for your trouble.'"

"Alana, please. That's not necessary."

I sighed. "If you agree to answer Birke's contract requests— if you help convince Birke to help Marre—Transliminal might be able to cure me. I could take the cure to Lai."

Nova put her knitting aside and placed both hands on my leg. "Sweetheart. You should know I'd do almost anything to help you, but I'm not going to let these people manipulate me. At the first opportunity, I'm getting off this thing and taking you with me. We'll go to Transliminal Solutions ourselves and see if they'll help you. We don't need some Wooleran cattle-wrangler to—"

"Seriously? Wooleran cattle-wrangler? Do you forget where *you* came from?"

I could tell she swallowed a nasty retort, fingers stiffening on my leg. The tiniest fluctuations in her face betrayed her effort to rein in her anger before she said something awful. After nearly a lifetime of arguing, you learn another person's expressions, just like she'd learned enough of my weaknesses to exploit them when necessary. She let out a slow, measured breath, then forced a small smile. "I know you love all these romantic sky surgeon ideas, but just because someone pilots a starship doesn't make them a good person."

"Neither does being a spirit guide."

She laughed and let go of me. "I'm a whole lot closer than the rest of you."

"If that's true, then you shouldn't abandon these people. If not for the whole crew, then for Marre. She's a spirit guide too. Or was. I don't know."

Nova resumed her knitting "*That* is not a spirit guide."

"Alana to the cargo hold," Tev said over the intercom. "We have a problem."

"Sorry, Nova," I said, touching her hand one last time before heading for the door. "We'll have to argue about this later."

"It's interesting, you know," Nova said. "Watching you here. Would you be so loyal so quickly if she weren't a woman?"

I stopped at the doorway. "What's that supposed to mean?"

She shrugged and just kept knitting, smiling in a self-satisfied way. I lingered another moment, trying to come up with a response to my sister's implied accusation, but I forced myself to let it go.

I made my way down the corridor and clanged down the metal stairwell leading to the cargo hold, railing cold under my hand as I steadied myself against the Dexitek's side effects. The Panacea sample sounded more tempting by the second. If someone from our own universe could come up with a cheap medication with no nausea or vertigo, I'd make out with them on the spot.

The green eye of the device we'd harvested from the hull stared up at the three crew members surrounding it, so sharp and bright I expected it to blink at me on my way down. A subtle glow from the object illuminated Ovie's arm, which still shone from the antibacterial sealant over the place where his touchscreen used to live. As tired as he seemed, his face was hard with focus as he crouched over the thing, running a hand along its skin. He sniffed at it, then tilted his head as if listening. When he caught my eye, he beckoned me.

"What's wrong?" I called on the way over, checking to make sure Slip's pants were still staying up on my hips without a belt.

"How are you feeling?" Slip asked. Before I could answer, she took my arm without warning. I caught a glimpse of a blood puller for the briefest moment before she stabbed the crook of my elbow, grabbing a sample.

"Ow! Come on, how about asking for permission first?"

"Sorry." She grinned. "Hurts less if you don't expect it. Just be grateful I have this and not a drawer full of catheters."

"We need you to take a look at this," Tev said. "Quickly."

"She needs to rest," Slip said, depositing the sample into a mobile reader. "And so does Ovie."

"This is a shit situation." Tev shifted her weight. "Not much ideal about it. They're the engineers we have, so rest will have to wait."

They're the engineers we have. Was she really grouping me in with Ovie? One of her own?

"Look." Ovie gestured for me to join him, so I crouched down. "The outer section just beneath where it connected to the engine through the hull is a basic Meir configuration." He pointed at a panel he removed from the husk of the object. "But look."

He moved aside the nest of copper wires, revealing a glowing, writhing mass of light.

Reality closed in on me as the truth became clear. My whole existence was reduced to each pulse in my veins, each tendon in my fingers, each breath and heartbeat. No sound. No smell. A white, dead world with Transliminal Solutions at its core.

An othersider had done this. The people I'd believed could save me had killed my family. Somewhere in the distance of the cold, white emptiness surrounding me, Ovie's voice broke through and the rest of the world crashed into me in the wake of his garbled words.

"What is this thing?" I said, trying to keep my voice steady. Trying to pretend I could think of anything but someone from Transliminal massacring my family and pinning it on this crew.

He shrugged. "No idea. Othersider tech. Or however we want to think of it; I don't know if I'd call it science. Marre detected it sending out a signal a few hours ago. The transmission was so hidden by the engine's radiation neutralizer that she almost didn't notice it. It's tracking us. Beeping our location all over the system."

"Shit." I tried to sound alarmed, but I just felt cold, so I'm sure it came out flat.

"If they find us, we're dead. Or as good as, and I can't blame them. All the evidence of the massacre points right to us. This thing is going to be the end of us. We have to figure out how to disable it."

"Throw it out the airlock," I mumbled.

He shook his head and exhaled hard, rubbing his forehead. Exhaustion weighed down every movement. I forced myself to channel all my cold anger into helping Ovie, though I still found it hard to think of anything but glamorously decorated othersiders plotting the demise of my parents. Why? Why would they do this?

"Nope," Ovie said, responding to my blasé suggestion that already seemed so far in the past. "Apparently its function is directly connected to gravity levels. If it hits zero-g?" He punched his palm. "Boom. Besides, we might need it as evidence."

"That doesn't make sense. It was fine out on the hull."

"Must have been activated when we brought it inside." He lowered his voice, glancing briefly at the captain. "I don't know how to fix this. I don't know how it works."

The *Tangled Axon*'s chief engineer was hanging his hope on the possibility that I might know how to fix this and get the enforcers off our tail. Like he said—this didn't even look like technology. I had no idea what to do, but couldn't admit it out loud. Being useful, staying busy, might prevent the grief and rage from eating me alive. If I lost myself to it now, I didn't know if I'd be able to get myself back.

I tied back my locs, bent closer to the exposed section of the device, and examined what little of the light-bramble peeked through the wires. The tangle moved as if it were alive.

Actually, it reminded me of Nova's knitting. I made a mental note to ask her about it.

A few sparks flitted and scattered deep within the device, but were quickly obscured by the undulating strands. This thing was a mess of . . . what? Photons? No one even knew what the othersider ships were made of, or how they worked. No one from our side of the breach anyway. They kept their research under tight control. How could I disable something that wasn't even native to our universe? How could I manipulate a thing that looked more like abstract art than technology?

"Can you disable it?" Tev crouched down on the other side of me, and Slip hovered behind us, penning us in. Not only was I acutely aware of their close proximity, but now the pressure was on. Every word that came out of my mouth, every action I took, would sway their opinion of me in one direction or another, determining whether Tev kept me on the crew beyond my usefulness in persuading my sister. Not to mention our continued freedom depended on me and Ovie figuring this out. How could I think straight with so much riding on my performance? How could I focus when I still felt white anger for what Transliminal had done to us rolling over me in cold waves?

"I'm . . ." I shifted the wires again, trying to see a different angle, as if that might reveal some hidden kill-switch. Nothing, of course. Again my emotions tried encroaching on my concentration, but I pushed them back while ignoring the mild disorientation from the meds.

I'd have to come back later. Take a look at it when I didn't have the entire crew hovering over me. When Tev's body wasn't so close to mine. When I wasn't so aware of the fact that she smelled so damn good. I pretended to further assess the device, but just shut down my thoughts as I got lost in her presence. It was better than the fury, better than the flashbacks. Her long hair brushed my arm, her every movement a charged jolt up my spine. She tucked her hair behind her ear, body turning slightly toward me, and I felt her eyes on my hands as they traced the lines of the object. I sensed the *Tangled Axon*'s energy surrounding Tev like a halo. A thread of need stretched tight inside me, connecting me to her, pulling at my chest.

"Anything?" Slip said.

I tried to focus. *The device. Think about the device.*

The body and electrical panels of the thing were engineered traditionally. It was the innards that confounded me. Maybe if I could disable the connection between the exterior body and the interior, I could disable it completely.

Tev's voice was quiet, as if she didn't want to disturb my thought process. "Can you do something?"

I sighed. "I don't know. I'm sorry. I'm trained in plasma engineering, not . . . whatever this is. I've never seen anything like it."

Ovie sat back, like a dog on its haunches. "I hate to say it, but Alana is right. I don't know any sky surgeon who could work with this."

"Shit," Tev sighed. "We can't do anything to help Marre in the middle of this mess. We need Bell."

Ovie exchanged glances with Slip as he stood up and brushed his hands on his pants, locs dangling.

Okay, I'd ask. "Who's Bell again?"

Tev shook her head, looking at the device as if she'd glean something new from it. She stood and nudged it with her boot. "Weapons dealer on Spin."

Spin was a resort planet owned by Transliminal Solutions: a thick hedonistic crust over a mantle of escapist self-loathing. Each "nation" was devoted to one indulgence or another, empty of anything but pure gluttony and a vile disregard for anything but moment-to-moment indulgence. It was a garish, embarrassing part of our system, full of folks who'd sell their own livers if it would turn a profit. Perfect for someone who brokered deals in illegal tech and weapons.

"You know people like that?" I said.

She gave me an "are you kidding me?" stare. Admittedly, even that looked good on her. "Where do you think I got the biter? A farmer's market?"

"So we're going to the most populated othersider planet to keep the othersiders from finding us?" I said.

Tev took a few steps toward me. She made a face that I'd come to realize was her trying to decide how to respond to me, biting her lip and tilting her head to the side. She never made that face at anyone else. "Okay, surgeon. You got an othersider contact somewhere other than Spin?"

"No, I . . . " I wiped my hand over my face, trying to clear away everything I was feeling. Frustrated. Scared. Bitter.

Longing, more than anything. Longing for my parents. Longing for Adul. For the life I thought I'd have once I got out into the black, where in reality I found only death and the threat of lifelong incarceration. I wanted to feel something good again, to go get lost in the *Tangled Axon*'s engine and not come out.

Too many feelings and too few answers.

"I'm just nervous," I said.

"Psh." Slip made a dismissive gesture. "A place like Spin is lost on y'all. But not me." She grinned mischievously, doing a tight dance next to Ovie, hips undulating to the type of beat you'd find in a hundred different clubs on Spin. He laughed and gyrated with her, syncing to her rhythm, and Tev looked anything but amused.

"Glad you two are having fun while we're running from the enforcers."

They stopped moving and Slip cleared her throat, standing straight. "Sorry, Captain."

Ovie avoided Tev's gaze. He just scratched behind his ear like a canine batting at an itch. I was having a hell of a time trying to figure out the relationships on this vessel.

"We can't inform Bell we're coming," Tev said, letting it go. "No external comm for us, not even briefly. Authorities would be waiting for us if we did. We'll just have to find her on our own."

"What about ol' green eye here?" I leaned my heel against the device. "Won't it tell them where we are?"

"Marre says there's a short lag in the signal, maybe a few hours' worth at most. Probably because of the blended tech, or at least that's what she reckons. It's not much to go on, but it's a risk we have to take. If there really is a lag, it'll give us enough time to at least try to find Bell and ask her how to disable the damned thing. They're going to catch up with us anyway if we don't get help. We can't fly forever without refueling."

I couldn't believe we had to go to Spin. I hated places like that. Reminded me of downtown Heliodor. And it had to be crawling with enforcers.

"Last time I talked to her," Tev said, "Bell told me she's mostly up at night, running the club circuit. We'll start there. Marre's charting a course as we speak; we'll be there in about three weeks."

I stepped forward. "Um."

"Um?"

"Am I staying? I mean, are you going to—"

"Did I say we're dropping off any engineers between here and Spin? Would that even be efficient or sensible?"

I cleared my throat. "No."

She said nothing, just raised her eyebrows at me. The barest hint of a smile teased the corner of her mouth.

Oh. Right. "No, *Captain.*"

Evidently satisfied, she nodded. "There are some rituals on a ship you need to get used to, Quick. There's a chain of command when you're part of a crew."

"Yes, Captain."

When you're part of a crew.

Chapter Eight

Over the next few weeks, I started thinking of the ship as home.

Sure, I knew it was dangerous to let myself get comfortable when I knew all too well they could have a change of heart, but it was hard not to be infatuated with the *Tangled Axon* and everyone inside her. Her song rolled through the corridors, starting in her engine-heart, echoing through her belly and out beyond the hull. That gentle hum may not have erased my grief or the ever-present anxiety that the enforcers would catch up to us, but it turned down the volume—even if only briefly.

I'd stop in the middle of eating, talking, showering, studying the device, and let the *Axon*'s voice cascade through me. Those moments felt delicate and tenuous, as if they might shatter if I breathed too deeply. In their wake, all the sorrow came rushing back in to fill the void, unless I kept busy. Grief makes its home in silence and idleness.

No other crew member seemed to hear the *Axon* the way I did, but I knew she spoke to them all the same. I saw it in the way they paused in their work when she sang, bending their heads toward a sound they felt not with their ears, but their bones. It was the only time real peace came over Tev's face, rendering her achingly sweet. Probably wouldn't have liked me thinking of her as "sweet," but there was no other word for that softness in her eyes, the light sprinkle of freckles across her cheeks, the delicate way she touched the *Tangled Axon*'s controls. She loved this old Gartik. It was evident every time Tev's eyes trailed along the vessel's curves the same way mine did.

It was okay to take quiet comfort in watching the captain, wasn't it? Surely I couldn't be faulted for being soothed by something that did no harm.

I couldn't help imagining what it would be like to watch Tev wake up on some sun-bathed morning on Woolera, her hair spilling over cheek-warmed pillows, face as content as in those fleeting moments of tranquility on the ship. What was she like when she wasn't working?

Daydreams like those made me maintain a conspicuous buffer of empty space between Tev and me. Hyperaware of the self-conscious shifting of our bodies while discussing my research into the device, I'd stammer and flush. My words tangled up in each other. Awkward apologies tumbled out of my mouth when I dared touch her by accident. My hand would disappear into my pocket, curl around the medication. I was *never* like this with women—not even when I was a kid. I just couldn't seem to get it together around her.

The most curious thing about Tev was the room she kept off the port side of the cargo hold. I'd seen her go in and out of it, but she always closed the door behind her, locked tight. When I asked Slip about it, she just shook her head.

"That's Tev's room," she said. "Keeps her grounded. Especially now, when all she can think about is Marre dying, and the Nulan government recycling the *Tangled Axon* when they catch us."

"What's in it?"

"Girl, that's not my place to say. Don't worry about it."

So of course, I did. I imagined all sorts of things, from illegal cargo to an army of trained cats. The room's unknown contents were a constant temptation, mocking me while I studied the device. I stood outside the door of Tev's off-limits room a few times, listening. I passive-aggressively glanced at it while talking to Tev about my ever-fruitless research progress, hoping she'd give me some hint as to what it was. The most I'd gotten was a raised eyebrow.

About three days into our journey toward Spin, Tev loosened my reins, letting me wander around the decks unaccompanied. I split my time between studying the object—gaze periodically flicking toward the closed door of Tev's mysterious room—and memorizing the details of the *Tangled Axon*. The way the decks felt beneath bare feet. The weave and color of each charm hanging in the bridge and corridors, their purpose still unknown to me. The bite of each seam in the bulkheads as I ran my finger along them, learning even that small part of her. The sound of the crew members' footfalls filling her, each distinct enough that I could eventually figure out who was coming long before I saw them. The ship's acoustic signature reverberating against me. Subtle changes in her song when Ovie tweaked some minute setting in the engine room, and the accompanying ache in my fingers as I craved such intimate contact with her.

Being there wasn't just a means to an end anymore. Each sensation, each detail, was something magical gained that I now stood to lose.

Marre occasionally wandered past me with hardly a sound, save her quiet shuffling and the dull buzzing inside my head. Every time, she peered at me but said nothing. She just left in a whisper of black hair and disappearing skin, honeycomb tattoo staring at me like a hundred empty eyes. Part of me wanted to follow her, tempted by the cloud of unease that surrounded her, like chasing a storm. But most of me shuddered at the thought of her skinless face flashing blood and muscle, and I thought better of it.

Sometimes I woke up in the middle of my sleep shift, expecting her to be standing right there in her vibrating, flickering ghost of a body.

Instead of sleeping, I slipped from my quarters and into the cargo bay, where I pressed my ear against Tev's closed door and listened. I slid my hand along the metal and envisioned the oils in my skin sinking into the *Tangled Axon*, inviting her to become part of me, to exchange thoughts with me, that I might know her better—and her captain by proxy.

I learned nothing, felt nothing other than the constant hum of the ship, and an occasional buzzing in my head when Marre haunted the cargo bay stairwell, watching. She always left without a word, the only indication that she'd been there the slight scent of honey she left behind, and the faint echo of her endless noise.

Beyond my connection to the ship, loneliness sank in. Thoughts of my family tugged at me, stealing my concentration. Vivid images of Adul flashed in front of my hands while I tried working. The smallest things would trigger it without warning, paralyzing me. Wires sparking. A piece of metal falling, clanging against the floor. The color beige or cream or orange. When I wasn't thinking of my parents or the Adulans, I thought of Aunt Lai. How much worse off was she, I wondered, stranded on Orpim with both her nieces in trouble? Had the enforcers sought her out? Was she safe?

Even while living in such tight quarters, I'd never felt so alone. I'd have felt completely isolated, if not for the *Tangled Axon* herself.

I didn't reach out to Nova; she rarely came out of her room and didn't want much to do with me when she did. She was still mad at me about leaving Lai, still unwilling to face her grief with me. She just knitted. Knit purl, knit purl, obsessed with that damn thing. Most of our rare conversations primarily consisted of her chastising me for wanting to associate with criminals, her project bobbing beneath her fingers all the while. It looked like a snowflake for a few days, then grew into a small blanket or shawl, glittering and undulating like a flattened star. When I asked her about the apparent similarities between her knitting and the light at the center of the device, she said she didn't know, and changed the subject.

We had little else to say to each other, so I spent less and less time banging my head against that particular wall. Worrying about incarceration was a bit higher on my priority list, anyway. In the end, Nova would or wouldn't help us, and no matter what Tev believed about my relationship to my sister, there was very little I could do to sway her.

But without Nova to talk to, and without making any progress deciphering the device, I needed something to occupy my time when I wasn't working. Anything. I was tired of my mind being so full of grief and memory and anxiety, a cacophony of my parents' deaths, the Adulans' deaths, my own impending, slow death on a penal colony. I wanted to fill myself up with something else, with people whose stories were new to me, untarnished. Fill it up with life.

So I made it my mission to find out something about each crew member, some point of connection that might weave a thread between us and help me find my place there. Maybe they'd regard me as more than just a dirtheel, more than "Nova's sister," more than another deteriorating body—if I could know them well enough to help them see it.

I watched the rest of the crew with as much subtlety as I could manage. Ovie was the toughest to observe. He always noticed me peering at him while I feigned interest in some nearby object. Eventually he called me out on it when he caught me sneaking by engineering.

"Alana."

His huge back curled over a platform at the far end of the engine room. I stopped. Electrical storms raged above us in a latticework of lightning, the *Tangled Axon*'s plasma heart burning hot and bright. Shades of her voice crossed over each other, whispering and singing.

"Just come in," he said. The engine's crackling forced him to speak loudly.

"How do you always know I'm there?" I shoved my hands into my pockets, fingers curling around the medication like a talisman. "Am I really that noisy?"

"Your smell."

"Excuse me?"

He continued working on whatever occupied his attention; I couldn't see around his body. "Your smell. You took a shower this morning and used that awful blue soap. You were talking to the captain before you came here. You're nervous right now. Oh, and you had a nutrient bar for lunch."

"That's a little creepy."

He finally turned to look at me. "What do you want?"

I tilted my chin up at his workstation. "What are you doing there?"

A long moment passed, then he turned back to what he was doing. "Watch if you want."

"You don't mind?"

"What did I just say?"

When I stepped closer and found a spot near the platform where I could wedge myself into the corner and sit, he extended his closed hands to me, then opened them. Metal rings spilled from his fists, falling into small piles on the table, joining hundreds more. Mostly silver, with a splash of color here and there.

"Silver?"

"Aluminum. Some niobium that's been anodized using the ship's plasma arcs."

I watched for a while in silence as he used pliers to open and close them one at a time, weaving them into repeating patterns. Heavy-lidded eyes focused intensely on the growing strand of interconnected rings, as if in meditation. Such large hands had made something so tediously complex; it amazed me. These must have been the charms I'd seen throughout the ship, the jewelry worn by members of the crew.

"You made them. The necklaces and bracelets. You made them for the crew."

He grunted. I took it for a yes.

"And the charms."

"They're good luck," came Slip's voice from behind, startling me. The sound of the ship's heart must have drowned out her footsteps. She joined us and rested a hand on Ovie's back, raising her other wrist, where her bracelet dangled. "We haven't lost a job yet since he made these for us, and no major ship malfunctions. Unless you count the device."

"That wasn't the ship," Ovie growled.

"Do you guys buy that idea? Luck?"

He shrugged. "Can't hurt. Besides, making these helps me forget about the enforcers and Adul. Helps me focus on our family."

My neck and wrists suddenly felt conspicuously bare— another indication I wasn't as at home as I'd have liked.

Slip must have picked up on it. "You've only been on the ship for a little over a week." She dug around in her pocket and pulled out a nutrient bar, unwrapped it, and split it into three pieces. We chewed our compressed crud while talking. "We're family. That's not the kind of thing you can just wake up one day and be part of. It takes time."

Was I so transparent?

"Well in that case," I said, watching the ever-stoic Ovie work. "Impenetrable fortress though this crew may be, how about you let me get to know you a little? I swear you're like a collective brick wall."

She shrugged and half-sat on the platform, chewing. "What's to know?"

"There's always something to know. You could tell me about your nickname."

I avoided looking at Slip as I asked it. I didn't need to see her to know she was making a face at me. When she didn't answer, I glanced up to see Ovie nudging her.

"Fine, whatever." She sat down the remnant of her nutrient bar. "I don't have a medical license."

My hand drifted to my incision, horror rising in my throat. "You're not a doctor?"

"She's a doctor," Ovie barked, dropping his pliers and sending tiny metal rings flying. He turned to Slip. "You *are* a doctor. Rulings don't change that."

She sighed and pushed the wayward rings back into an organized pile for him. "Tell that to the Nulan medical board."

"So why don't you have a license?" I asked.

"Fine, fine." She shifted her weight as if grounding herself. "I did my residency in one of the rural settlements on Gira, near West Lake. When I finished, I decided to stay and teach. They needed someone. You grow up learning about the poverty of the workers there as some vague idea, something to pity, something that serves to throw your life into relief and inspire gratitude for your own blessings. You have no idea until you actually live there. I thought I had it bad as a kid. But this . . . " She shook her head a little. "Anyway, pity was the last thing on my mind. I had a skill, they had a need. But it doesn't matter to the board. Rules are rules."

Ovie let out a small whimper, but continued with his craft.

"I couldn't stand it. Half the time I'd heal wealthy eco-tourists of their mod-induced headaches. Folks from Orpim's Eastern Hemisphere dropped money for high-end painkillers while kids two streets away from the hospital couldn't afford basic medical care."

I felt like my ribs twisted into a knot around my lungs. What she said about the Girans hit too close to home, and it brought to mind the records I'd seen of Mel's Disorder patients and their loved ones. When I discovered those recordings, they made me more determined to always be able to afford treatment. To live. To have the privilege of dying in a vessel accident or a bar fight instead of wasting away, trapped inside a body that wouldn't let me walk, speak, or blink. A body that wouldn't move.

Without treatment, death happened fast. Two years from onset, maybe. People had started showing symptoms at younger and younger ages with no indications why. Treatments worked well enough for us to get by. Most people lived into old age, but the medication, like everything else, has never been free. Life was a privilege, not a right, apparently. Something you had to struggle for when you were unlucky enough to be born at the intersection of poverty and bad genes.

On a penal colony, they probably wouldn't bother with medication for something like Mel's. I might last a whole two years, probably more like six months—most of it incapacitated and in unbearable pain.

Stop it. You'll work yourself into a frenzy. Think about something other than the enforcers roping in the Tangled Axon *like a wounded burt.*

"You okay?" Slip said.

I nodded. "Sorry, please go on."

"When I wasn't treating tourists," Slip said, "I'd see local patients who'd sold something valuable just to bring their children to the hospital." She cleared her throat, tucked her hair behind her ears, and waited a moment before continuing. "Often only one of their children, even if they had more. The strongest, smartest, most promising kids got medical treatment—the ones with the most to offer their family and the community. Maybe two kids in a family would get treatment if they were lucky. Parents hoped they could glean something useful from the visit, something they could take home and apply to the other sick children and to themselves. There was a lot of illegal prescription sharing intra-household, but most of us pretended not to know.

"Of course the hospital administrators refused every proposal for free clinics. One even had the audacity to say they should stop having so many kids—as if birth control were so easy to come by, as if families didn't rely on older kids to help bring in income. Eventually, I couldn't take it anymore. I started smuggling medication out of the facility and became a one-woman underground clinic, offering treatment for free."

My expression must have shifted, because she nodded at me and said, "Yeah, I know. Stupid."

"No," I said. "Brave. You might be my hero."

She half-laughed. "It was great for awhile. Well, as great as something like that can be. I split my off-time from the hospital between dispensing medical advice and treatment, and tutoring some of the local high school kids in math and science with a few other doctors. Those teachers are spread way too thin. We helped the kids apply for scholarships to universities on Orpim. At least the tutoring stuff was legal."

"Someone found out," I said.

"About the illegal medicine? Yeah. A chick vying for my hours at the hospital."

Ovie growled.

"I know it was illegal," Slip said, "but I couldn't help believing she might not turn me in, even after she found out. I know it was stupid of me. I could have done a lot more for them if I'd been more careful, less trusting, or maybe tried to do something through legal channels, inside the system—"

"No," I said. "I get it. Heliodor's not all that different from Gira. Growing up, my dad knew a guy who got into an accident at a mining facility and had to choose between treating his lacerated arm or re-attaching his foot."

"That's just it," Slip said. "I couldn't be like that. I couldn't just let people suffer. We take oaths! How can a doctor just watch and do nothing?"

"So why 'Slip'?" I asked, trying to keep the conversation light. I couldn't handle much more sadness.

"Oh, it's dumb," she laughed. "Like most nicknames. After my board hearing—where they ripped me apart, obviously—I slipped the chairman a note in his back pocket on the way out the door. It detailed his eight-year affair. His girlfriend was one of my roommates during med school, but he'd long since forgotten me. Thought I'd just let that one hover over his head for a while, even though I wouldn't say a word to his wife. I'd never really ruin anyone's marriage by sticking my nose where it didn't belong, but I got a lot of satisfaction out of imagining him sweating it out."

I was laughing. "And that's it? That's where your nickname came from? Some note you slipped to the medical board chairman?"

"Hey, I said it was dumb! During my interview with Tev I told her that story and she loved it so much she's called me Slip ever since. I think she loved what it said about me more than the story itself." She batted a hand at me playfully. "Girl, don't look at me like that—I didn't know it was an interview at the time or I wouldn't have told her about it. We ran into each other at a bar in Heliodor. I was drunk and she had stories of her own. I think she was trying to hit on me until she decided she wanted to hire me. Turned out she could do both." Slip grinned and took another bite of her bar. It was hard to imagine Tev hitting on someone, and just made me all the more curious about her. Which just made me feel guilty, sitting there with her girlfriend.

"Well, you did something good on Gira," I said, still smiling. "I can see why she trusts you."

"Speaking of medication," Slip said, placing a hand on my knee and looking me dead in the eye. "How are you doing on yours?"

I pictured the bottle nestled in my pocket, only thirteen days' worth of pills still knocking around in the plastic container. And that Panacea sample. It seemed toxic now, knowing Transliminal—or at least an othersider—had something to do with my parents' murders and our fugitive status. Still, I held onto it.

If I confessed to being so close to running out of the Dexitek, what good could it do? If they helped me find more, we'd be caught. The symptoms wouldn't get too bad until at least after we'd gotten Bell, and then we could worry about my issues when we helped Marre with hers. Don't get me wrong, I didn't want to be a martyr and I definitely wasn't looking forward to the possibility of watching my body deteriorate, but I shoved all that fear down as far as I could. There was nothing anyone could do. I could always take the sample if things got too bad. I'd deal with the consequences later.

"I'm doing fine," I finally said.

A knock. Tev stood there, tapping the engine room wall with her knuckle, peeking around the corner. A flutter in my stomach.

"Since when does everyone eat in here?" she said.

I stood and tried brushing the crumbs off the platform, but just ended up tossing them—and several rings—around.

"We're just telling stories," Slip said. Ovie kept working.

I plucked at the crumbs, collecting them in one hand. "What can we do for you, Captain?"

"Actually, I'd like you to come with me." She seemed . . . nervous? A smile played on the edges of her lips, her eyes connecting with mine. "There's something I want to show you."

Slip lowered her voice like a news-net narrator. "In a world where hard-assed captains patrol the corridors, many a stowaway heard those words before an untimely trip into the Big Quiet." She wiggled her fingers at me as she got up off the bed, laughing. "I'm going to go make sure your sister isn't knitting a hole into the side of the ship. Have fun."

Ovie got up after her, mumbling something I couldn't quite catch. Tev and I lingered in the crowded engine room as he shifted his big body out between us, giving me a quick smile. Just then, I noticed his unusually sharp canines for the first time. How had I missed those?

"What?" he said when I stared a little too long.

I pointed to my own teeth and stammered something incoherent, but then gave up. "Nothing."

Tev waited until the other two were gone before guiding me out of the engine room and down the corridor toward her quarters, where we stopped at the door. Another stomach flutter. Was she inviting me in?

Stop that. She has Slip, and Slip is your friend.

"I wanted to thank you for cooperating with us. For helping with the device and trying to figure out what it is. Don't think I haven't seen you creeping around the cargo hold when you're supposed to be sleeping."

I opened my mouth to apologize, but she held up a hand. "And for cooperating with the surgery. I wouldn't have asked you to change your body if the circumstances were any less dire." She lifted her hair and turned her head so that I could see an incision at the back of her own ear. I'd almost forgotten she'd had an implant too. "I wouldn't ask anything of my crew I wouldn't do myself. Regardless, you're right about what you said to me; you let us cut into you and isolate you, and the sacrifice hasn't gone unnoticed."

So she'd taken what I said to heart. I was sure I reddened at the memory of my drug-induced comments as I was coming out of the anesthesia. It was just coming back to me that I'd also grabbed her hand. What else had I done to embarrass myself? All those emotions came tumbling back in—attraction, shame, anxiety, grief, loss.

Just pretend, I told myself. Pretend as if I didn't still feel a phantom implant behind my ear. I still slept on one side to avoid hitting the transmit switch even though it wasn't there anymore. I still reached for my neck when I wanted to talk to someone. I still had to remind myself that I now had to seek them out face-to-face. I'd lost a sense almost as integrated as my vision or hearing, and I didn't know if I'd ever not feel a little incomplete. My body missed the metal I'd lost just as badly as if it had been blood or bone.

Tev seemed to search my face for a moment, green eyes capturing mine, gaze working on me in a way that made every part of me shiver. Again, the smell of rosemary lingered around us. Eventually she opened the door to her quarters, then placed a light hand on the small of my back to guide me inside. It was such a gentle gesture for someone who made herself seem rough around the edges. The touch warmed my skin beneath my shirt.

It occurred to me then: why didn't Slip share quarters with Tev?

"After everything you've been through, I think you need this," Tev said. "I only show this to people who feel like part of the crew."

She ushered me to the left just inside her quarters, toward a stairwell leading up. I only caught a brief glimpse of the space she called her own: a shifting imprint display of photos from what I assumed was her childhood, including one of her helping a woman drive cattle. Schematics of the *Tangled Axon*. A few plants in the far corner. A desk with a switched-off holographic projection pad. Magnetic containers haphazardly affixed to the walls. A repeating vid of some Wooleran landscape on the wall opposite her small, unmade bed. Scattered nutrient bar wrappers on the floor.

Before I could take anything else in, she guided me up the stairs.

We emerged into a room that was big for a Gartik transport—so large it had to be one of the mods I'd seen from outside. But there was nothing in it. Just cavernous emptiness surrounded by four black walls and an opening to the stairwell in the corner.

"Do you know what this is?" she said, voice slightly echoing.

We stood in darkness, but the dim glow from the lower deck illuminated her just enough for me to see her face. Her pale skin glowed like freshwater pearl. If we were anywhere else, and she were anyone else but a ship's captain, I would have kissed her a week ago just to see if I could taste the *Axon* on her lips. As it was, all the longing, refraining, and suppressing . . . it burned in my gut like a pile of embers.

I swallowed down my desire. "What, you mean you don't show your quarters to every woman who wanders into your cargo bay?" I laughed, but it came out awkwardly.

She smiled a little and depressed a button on the wall. "Marre."

"Yes, Captain." The pilot's hollow voice echoed in the empty space.

"Open the observation deck window."

The wall opposite the stairwell flickered, along with part of the ceiling and floor, then disappeared.

"Oh!" I clapped my hand over my mouth, not wanting to seem childish.

The whole of the universe seemed to surge before us, around us, and burn right through me. When walking on the hull of the *Tangled Axon*, my vision had been obscured by the helmet's visor, and I'd been under pressure—literally and figuratively. Even the bridge viewer was angled and narrow, affording only a small slice of the sky. But now, here, I stood in the emptiness with Tev, our feet floating above . . . nothing.

"Here." Tev took my wrist. The instant her hand touched me, I snapped my gaze toward it, but I could barely see anything in the pitch black. I was tempted to touch her too, but she pulled me toward the center of the high-temperature quartz glass barrier between us and the Big Quiet. "Look down. Good. Just keep looking at the floor."

Looking at the floor meant staring down into a vertigo of stars. My head spun.

"But I saw already—"

"No, love. You didn't. Trust me."

I knew it was just a Wooleran thing, but every time she said "love," my heart sped up. She moved behind me and placed her hands on my shoulders, nudging me toward a spot she seemed to have in mind. "Don't look up yet." She adjusted me by what seemed to be mere centimeters.

"What—?"

"Just wait."

The temptation was killing me, but I just focused on the pressure of her hands, the scent of her, the closeness. That, and the overwhelming sense that I would float away into the silence.

"Okay. Go ahead."

I lifted my head.

Nothing, *nothing* but a field of endless stars. Stars and us.

She had moved me to a spot where the remaining matte surroundings had disappeared from view, and as long as I looked straight ahead, there seemed to be nothing between me and eternity. There was no edge between the worlds of *inside* and *beyond*. In the life I'd known before, there was always an edge—a doorway, a wall, a horizon—but not now.

No limits, no borders.

I shrank inside myself before the enormity of our galaxy. More than ever I felt the reality of space travel welling in the deepest part of me, in the same way I occasionally became aware of my own mortality. We entrusted the *Tangled Axon* with our fragile bodies out here in the void. Even the strongest metal was still a thin film of hope stretched over us. I imagined the ship's acoustic signature echoing out from herself, surging between each node of light, braiding together with the song of all stars below and above us, racing outward, forever.

"To me, the universe is a mother." Tev's breath grazed my neck. Aching, agonizing desire pulled at me with her every word. "The black is full of her creation. We can't see her face because we live inside her. We just catch glimpses of her in bursts. Light peeks in where her skin grows thin from the pressure of all that creation waiting to burst through."

My eyes burned, as if stinging from the brilliance of so many suns, so many worlds. I couldn't bring myself to speak, and I didn't know if I was more touched by what the captain had shown me, the fact that she was showing it, or what she believed about the universe. Behind all that brittleness and self-control, Tev Helix contained worlds of myth and wonder. Why did she hide it?

I turned to her and, forgetting myself, placed my hands on her cheeks and tilted her forehead down to meet mine, closing my eyes. She stiffened, but I didn't care. This woman—this blond, rosemary-laden captain—gave me everything I'd ever wanted just by letting me be there.

"Thank you, Tev," I whispered, savoring the shape of her name in my mouth. "Thank you."

She relaxed and placed her hands on my arms.

"I haven't done you any favors," she said, breath tickling my mouth. "I've kept you around because that's what's best for my ship and my crew, so don't thank me. Just be a good engineer."

She was so warm. Her breath had quickened, and she hadn't pulled away. I couldn't believe that my engineering skills were all she had in mind when she brought me here. Everything was all mixed up in a haze of confusion and need.

"You can come here anytime, if you ask," she said, pulling back to look at me. "I know captains who would say this place was a waste of resources, a pointless addition at a time of scarcity, but they're blind to what a crew needs."

"And what's that?"

She lifted my hand to the invisible barrier separating us from the void, and pressed my palm against its cold surface, leaving her hand on mine. Again her voice was low and close to my ear in the darkness, her body brushing against my back. "Sometimes they need to wipe the grease from their hands and touch the face of God."

Something in me broke. All I'd been trying to suppress came rushing in.

I was falling in love.

Chapter Nine

Days later, I stood in the cargo bay, staring down at the device's green eye in challenge. This damn piece of othersider tech not only killed my family, but now watched us, beaming our movements back to the system authorities, helping them chase us for a crime we didn't commit. A foreign body in the belly of our metal lady. Hatred for it rose in my throat.

I will ruin this thing.

And when we made it to Transliminal Solutions, I'd expose what they'd done.

When I had detached it from the hull with Ovie, I'd felt exuberant. Limitless. As if I'd accomplished the first task of my real career as a sky surgeon. I tried conjuring the memory of it—the way I'd felt when it clicked, releasing the ship and floating into our hands. When we returned inside, I felt like a hero.

I wanted to feel that way again. To remember I wasn't a dirtheel anymore, and that there was still hope left in the world. To believe that maybe we might not end up rotting in some penal colony, with the whole system's hatred aimed at our heads.

I entangled my hand in the thing's entrails. The silvery web of light was cold around my fingers, slick like oil. Every burst of electricity sent a tiny shock through my nervous system, but it was nothing I couldn't endure. Nothing I wasn't used to; by now, pure plasma coursed through my veins, I was sure of it.

I paused to roll my neck, trying to pop it to relieve the tension that had built from the base of my skull to my shoulder blades. Mel's Disorder and physically grueling work made terrible bedfellows. Still, I pushed through it and folded myself into a knot of pure muscle and mind.

I could feel waveguides between the light-tangle and the heart of the thing, whatever it was made of, which I couldn't quite see but could feel with my fingertips. Occasionally they'd graze something hot and metallic.

Focus on the familiar, Alana. If I could manipulate the tech I understood—the tech from our universe—I hoped it would be enough to disengage the rest. Copper and metal were my home, even when contaminated by whatever this othersider stuff was. Surely I could do this.

My fingers slid along one wire to its point of contact on the waveguides. Something snagged the wire, and before I could assess what I'd done, a thin arc shot out from the open electrical panel and destroyed three cargo crates in an ear-shattering explosion.

"Shit!"

I didn't even know what had happened, only that something caught the wire, and—

Another electric arc snapped across the cargo hold and blasted a hole into the left side of the stairwell leading to the upper deck. A wave of fear rolled through me and I knew the emotion wasn't mine—it was the ship's. Searing pain lacerated my stomach. I was wrecking the *Tangled Axon*'s cargo bay, and she was screaming.

I fumbled with the wire and waveguides, trying to keep my hands from shaking. Sharp twinges pulsed up from my hips, along my sides, down my neck. At this point I couldn't tell which sensations originated in myself versus the ship.

It doesn't matter. Pain isn't real. Pain is electrical signals. Ignore it.

There was something else inside the thing near the

waveguides that had grabbed the wire and wouldn't let go. What was it? Gently but quickly, I tried to disentangle that something from the wire without being able to see it, and I almost had it—almost—but the wire slipped from my fingers. Panic tightened around my throat as I fished around, stretching too-short fingers in a desperate attempt to reach that which I couldn't even see.

Another plasma burst nearly seared my hair off, missing me by less than a meter. My relief was short-lived; it destroyed the door to Tev's private room, and a fire billowed out from inside, flames licking the ceiling and wall, creeping outward. The ship's torment ripped through my body. Every ligament and muscle felt like it was being rent from my bones, and all the while her voice bellowed in my mind like a feral creature.

"No no no no . . . " I had to find that damned wire. I kept glancing at the inferno eating away at the room, but I couldn't do anything about it. I'd started some kind of awful chain reaction that was going to end up setting off this thing's detonator. I would destroy the ship, or at least severely damage her. There would be no way we'd evade the enforcers and— oh, thank the black, the *Axon* doused Tev's room in flame retardant. Maybe whatever was in there could be salvaged. Or some of it. *Shit shit shit. I've really screwed this up. I've turned the* Axon *into a pyre. Please, please hold on, Lady,* I pleaded with the ship. *Please.*

"What the hell is happening down here!" Tev ran down the stairwell, voice carried away by the roaring flames and detonations firing off from the device. I could only spare her a glance as I worked feverishly to stop the reaction. I had to find the—

There! My fingertips pinched the wire; I just had to disconnect it. *Don't drop it. Don't let it slip. Don't destroy the damned vessel.*

Ovie barked, his voice frantic as he banged down the stairs behind Tev, and I thought I could hear Nova shrieking, *Slip* shouting about ruining our chances of getting out of this alive. I closed my eyes and quieted my mind until I could feel nothing but the *Tangled Axon*'s pain instead of mine, think of nothing but the task at hand.

Nothing but me and the ship.

Reality slowed. One breath.

And another.

Slow.

Exhale.

I used my thumb and forefinger to pinch the wire. My right hand slid around the inside panel near an old magnetic-mirror chamber surrounding the object's core, but what was inside it? The only thing I could figure was they used it to confine plasma, but that's not what those undulating lights were. It had to have something to do with what was making this thing lose its shit.

I'm going to fry myself and everyone else along with me. I have no idea what I'm doing.

"No," I muttered, then calmed myself down again with a series of slow breaths, listening to the vessel's pulse beneath my body. Sweat dripped down my forehead and into my eye, burning. I shook my head and carefully bent it to the side to wipe my face against my sleeve, all while maintaining my tenuous grip on the wire. Wild voices and flames stirred into chaos around me.

Connect the wire to the secondary track running behind the far side of the mirror chamber. It would reach, but my palsied, pain-crippled hands were another matter. Tilting one shoulder down, I shifted my body so it was closer to the floor in an effort to angle myself toward the opening. I kept a firm grip on one wire despite my body's distress while reaching around the other side to fish out the one I'd seen earlier.

Every movement was crucial. Every breath. Every minute twitch of my fingers. Every muscle in my body was engaged as my legs and torso held me up, my arms reaching through the device and my hands doing what they were made for, illness be damned. The heat inside the object rose, making me sweat even more. My hands were slick. Moisture dripped down my back.

Endless screaming from the ship throbbed in my head.

I couldn't let myself slip and fall forward. Although I was vaguely aware of frightened human voices, I refused to let them in. The *Axon* kept bellowing, drowning out all other noise.

One wrong move and I could make things far worse.

The two gossamer-thin wires finally caught and twined together behind the waveguides. "Yes!" I shouted. Instantly, the device started to cool and the sparks subsided.

I collapsed forward, resting my forehead on the object, arms limp inside it.

I didn't even care that the metal was hot.

We were safe. The ship was safe.

I let myself breathe.

The quiet in the hold sent a chill up my spine.

I wiped my hands on my pants, leaving behind black streaks, and stood up.

"Alana," Tev said. Quietly, but her low voice still carried, tone flat. "What did you do?"

I didn't want to see the damage, but my feet were moving all the same, betraying my desire to hide. Those feet turned me around, moving me past the warped, blown-off door now lying in the middle of the hold, past the blurry pilot in my peripheral vision, walking me toward the now-open room. My footsteps were an unwelcome noise, loud and clumsy in the dead quiet.

Slip and Ovie checked out the stairwell damage, but they tossed looks at me and Tev. Ovie kept scratching behind his ear with frantic fingers and yawned loudly, like a nervous dog. Nova clutched her white silk robe, watching Tev, who stood with her back to me inside the doorway of her charred room.

The sickness that crept into my stomach felt like a hundred insects clawing at me from the inside out.

Her hands clutched either side of the bulkheads, shoulders hunched. Her sleeveless shirt exposed the rigid muscles of her back and shoulders. Even from here, I could see rage boiling beneath the surface. Every centimeter of my skin felt too heavy and too tight.

"What did you do," she said again. Not a question this time. A command to report.

I was a few steps away, but I couldn't make myself come any closer. I was afraid to see what I'd done, what was in there. "I'm sorry. I—"

"What were you doing, Quick."

My legs and mouth felt weak. "Trying to disable the device."

"But you were aware your orders were to investigate it, not disable it."

"I just—"

"Answer the question, yes or no."

"Yes."

"And you knew it was wired to detonate if—"

"I did, but—"

She slammed her hand against the bulkhead to shut me up, the sound ricocheting through the cargo bay.

I wanted to reach out to her, but I wasn't that stupid. "I'm sorry."

Time stretched out. Quiet murmurs drifted through the cargo hold as Slip and Ovie continued examining the damage.

When she spoke again, her voice was soft. "You could have left us dead in the water."

What could I say? She was right.

"I'm going back to bed. Don't touch the device again, don't look at it, don't even think about it, unless I order you to do so. Just . . . stay out of the cargo hold." She turned around to leave, and as she passed me, I caught a glimpse of eyes red with sadness.

Every part of me ached. I had done this to her ship. To her.

I didn't realize I really *was* reaching out to her until she stopped and looked at my barely outstretched hand with cold resentment.

"Tev. Captain. I . . . "

She continued staring at my hand, which I couldn't seem to pull back. It just hung there in space while failure and shame clung to me like an iron vest.

Eventually, she left, dodging Slip and Ovie on her way up the mutilated staircase, even as Slip reached out to her in comfort. They watched Tev go, then Ovie continued working and Slip looked at me, raising her hands in a *What the hell were you thinking?* gesture.

I shook my head and just turned toward the scorched room. I had to see what I'd done.

Despite the char and ash, I could still see it. Tev's big secret, her tightly guarded space.

A garden.

Suddenly, the ship's hum grew loud between my ears and images flooded my mind, a recording dropped into my head like a datachip: *Tev bends over the soil of a makeshift garden in the center of the room, arranging each plant with careful hands. Fingers trail over the leaves. She speaks in a soft voice as she offers them water. Blond hair brushes the plants, gathering the scent of rosemary between strands. She plucks pieces of it to make infrequent cooked meals feel like home. Dirt lives under her fingernails, rich and earthy and real. She comes here to grow new worlds in the sky. I see flowers emerging from her body. She blinks petals from her eyelids, dusts soil from her arms, and plucks roots from her hair, offering pieces of herself to the garden she carries between planets.*

I wandered through the destroyed room, carrying my shame and guilt with me on a chain, not sure what it was I was looking for until I saw it. Two plants, side-by-side, hidden under a fallen plate of metal. Pitiful stems and leaves bent like injured limbs. The sight of it made me feel monstrous. I didn't know anything about gardening, but I moved the metal aside and promised the little plant I'd do something to make up for this. Salvage what I could, try to give Tev a piece of her garden worth keeping. I didn't want to deliver the plants to her now; if they died, it would be a fresh loss for her to endure. Besides, my face was the last thing she'd want to see. I'd just have to keep them secret and see if they survived.

I breathed deeply to loosen the frustration winding around my stomach, transforming it into determination.

The next sleep shift, I waited even longer than usual to leave my quarters. I swiped two large mixing bowls from the mess hall, wiped them clean of accumulated dust, and hurried to the stairwell leading to the cargo hold. I wondered how long it had been since anyone used real kitchenware.

I made my footsteps as quiet as possible as I headed down the corridor, maneuvered the mangled stairs, and slipped into the torched garden room. I crouched down next to the soil, letting my fingers linger over a patch of unscorched earth. Not knowing the first thing about plants, I almost reached for my comm link to access the net for information. My hand lingered behind my ear for a moment before dropping.

Oh, right. On my own on this one.

Behind me, there was a sound like a spray of water or a hand gliding across paper, and then the buzzing started. I turned to see Marre standing in the doorway, half her jawbone exposed, hands missing, honeycomb tattoo staring at me again. Her voice came in waves of sound—buzzing crashing into me like the ocean, quiet-loud, quiet-loud, words overlapping each other. Even her voice struggled to maintain its form. "You're awake."

I nodded.

"This is Tev's room." Muscle and skin grew over her jaw as her shoulder faded down to bone. "You shouldn't be here."

"Please don't tell her," I whispered, still crouching. White spots encroached on my vision, cold vertigo washing over my head. I closed my eyes and placed a palm on the floor to steady myself, feeling the *Tangled Axon*'s hum underneath me. Grounding the live wire I had become.

When I opened my eyes, it was to Marre's face inches from mine. Her smile reached her eyes as she mimicked my posture, crouching low on the ground with one palm connecting her to the ship, her too-large shirt hanging low over her shorts, her bent, skinny legs making her look much like an insect. Black hair fell over her right shoulder, ripples shimmering through it like light. Like hair made of glass. A crystalline girl.

We *had* to help her.

"What does it feel like?" I said, glancing at a skinless finger on her left hand.

"What does it feel like for you?" she said. "When you disappear into yourself?"

Thoughts dislodged from my unconscious mind. *It feels like I'm looking at life out of the corner of my eye. Like my body doesn't know how to be painless. Like I'm becoming grief and loss, except when I'm with this crew and this ship, when I'm with Tev.*

Marre's fully invisible hand rested on my knee as we crouched there, her uncanny touch interrupting me, bone and muscle exposed at her wrist in a gradient of disappearing pilot. "Me too," she said.

She disappeared.

Not faded, not dissolved, just . . . one moment she was there, touching my knee, and the next, she was gone. Blinked out of the room so suddenly I wondered if my medication was making me hallucinate, or if my grief had pushed me over some edge I hadn't realized I'd been toeing.

Alone in that room with the echo of Marre still prickling my skin, I wanted Aunt Lai. Not Heliodor or even the shop—just Lai. I wanted her to plop down in front of me with that earnest face and tell me I needed to focus on what mattered.

"Pain's not real, girl," she'd said to me, over and over again. The one person in my life who could talk about pain without making me feel erased. "It's all electricity, like everything else. You're what's real. Those ships are real. Our work is real. Pain's not, no matter what it would have you believe."

She'd wipe the sweat off her brow and wink at me, face blotchy with dirt and grease. "Pain is just the world wanting us to pay attention to it because we're so damned beautiful, it can't stand being ignored."

Thinking of her sharpened the edges of my loss.

I exhaled to push out all the memories that tried to surface. I turned back to the garden and collected enough soil to fill each bowl, thinking about plants instead of my family or incarceration. How much soil did they need? I figured too much was better than not enough and hoped I was right. Then I looked around and gathered anything that seemed helpful, hoping I'd be able to wing it if I had the right supplies. A spade, for one. A bottle of fertilizer. Both were charred, but the bottle was still at least half-full and the spade would work just fine.

Kneeling down in front of the surviving plants, I took a deep breath. *I really, really hope I don't kill them trying to save them.* One of the rosemary plants had survived, but I didn't even know what the others were, much less how to take care of them. I'd just have to hope water and fertilizer was enough. And talking to them. You were supposed to talk to plants, right?

If pilots could disappear, and engineers could be wolves, then surely plants could thrive on words.

Carrying them back to my quarters, I passed the device that had caused all this destruction. The eye stared at me, threatening. Black hatred for what the othersiders had done to us bubbled up in me. Fire scorched my heart at the thought of Adul crushing my parents along with the native Adulans, all at the hands of the people who had ripped apart reality and shoved their way through the breach.

Staring at the object, I stoked my anger, kept it alive.

We'd go to Spin and take care of this damned device. We'd find a way to help Marre and Lai, find a way to clear our names, and then I'd burn Transliminal to the ground.

Chapter Ten

I ran out of my medication.

Each hour dragged its heavy feet through the ship in the wake of the cargo bay disaster. One day passed, then another, until almost the entire three weeks had gone by and we were only half a day out from Spin, still without any clear sign of the enforcers. Occasionally we'd hear a creak in the hull or a snap of electricity that made everyone stop in their tracks, afraid it was the sound of weapons fire.

They were out there, though. Searching for us. All it would take would be charting the wrong course through the wrong space, crossing paths with a single patrol.

As Dexitek's side effects started wearing off, in some ways it was an unexpected blessing. Less nausea, more presence of mind. Sometimes I could even stomach the nutrient bars without wanting to gag. That was a first.

But I knew it was a brief reprieve. The real pain would wake up soon enough; Mel's was a long-hibernating hunter that would be eager to make up for lost time. With so much thick, immutable silence between me and Tev, I almost welcomed the oncoming symptoms. At least they'd be a distraction. Can't think about caring for a woman who hates you when your body is busy lighting itself on fire.

Her only words to me were an order here, a quick engineering-related question there—and only if Ovie was unavailable.

When we passed in the corridor, the memory of our time on the observation deck sat heavy between us. Her eyes flicked toward me a few times, but I never could read her expression. She just looked away and walked on. Each silent, inscrutable exchange was a knife in my heart. This chilly disregard was worse than watching her with Slip.

So I spent our trip to Spin nursing the pitiful plants hiding in my quarters. Taking care of them helped me feel like I retained some small measure of influence over my life and the world around me. I couldn't tell whether the herbs were thriving or just barely holding on, but they were alive, and that was something. Maybe it would be enough for Tev to speak to me again.

That, and convincing my sister to willingly help Marre.

Twelve hours away from Spin, Nova sat in my quarters and plucked more strands of light from nowhere, adding them to her growing project. Tev's plants sat like a couple of children before her, soaking up a pale glow pouring through the crevices of her fingers.

"I'm curious," I said, eyeing her tedious work. "If you don't want to help us, why haven't you tried harder to get them to drop you off somewhere?"

"Maybe I was planning to disembark along with you when they drop *you* off." Another strand, plucked. The light played with contours of her face. "You've clearly outstayed your welcome."

"You don't know that."

"Even so, *you* don't have to be here. I do." Knit, purl. "My contract obligates me to stay on board, even if you are running from the enforcers. I'm not about to jeopardize my reputation by reneging, even if I do think you're making a mistake by throwing your life on Orpim away." She paused and looked thoughtfully toward the ceiling. "Although maybe there's a loophole in the SAG regulations that would allow me to get out of a contract with known fugitives. Are you sure they're not planning to drop you off somewhere?"

"I'm not sure of anything, Nova. And where exactly would I go, anyway? I'm better off on the *Axon* than I am out there on my own." Assuming Nova wasn't right about me overstaying my welcome.

She shrugged. "Oh well. So what's this about helping 'us'? Are you one of them now?"

Damn it, Nova. Where's your grief? Where are you hiding it?

"So if you're fulfilling your contract," I said, "that means you're willing to convince Birke to find cures for me and Marre? And for Aunt Lai."

She shrugged. One sleeve of her gown slouched off her thin shoulder. "Depends on whether I'm still here."

"You just said you can't leave."

Her eyes flicked at me over her work. Knit, purl. "Alana. Don't be naïve. You know that's not what I'm talking about."

"Huh?"

She sighed. "Don't you ever listen to anything I say about my work? I'm referring to transmutation. Ascension. Shedding the flesh."

"I'd rather talk about Birke—"

"You're preoccupied with things that aren't going to matter, in the end."

"So you think resenting life is the answer?" I don't know why I asked. I knew it was true; I hadn't seen her eat much since she came on board. A handful of nuts here, an injection there. All that unsated hunger carved a hollow path across her cheeks.

"Do you really think starving yourself—"

"Yes, I do!" She said with frustration. "We've been over this."

"I don't like it."

"Your approval is irrelevant. This is what it means to be a spirit guide."

"To starve yourself. Great."

"To thin oneself until catching a ride on death's back is as easy as taking a breath. A gasp, and the body is gone. Death waits for no one, so spirit guides turn to it with grace."

"For crying out loud, Nova, stop being so melodramatic. You're not even forty years old! Just because Mom and Dad died doesn't mean you need to!"

A hurt expression flashed across her face. "You don't understand. I can already feel my body browning at the edges, curling in on itself. Others won't see it for years, for decades, but it's happening all the same. Can't you feel it too? Don't you feel yourself dying, every day? Spirit guides would choose our own paths out of the body rather than wait to be ripped from it in a bloody shriek. Or fall victim to some—"

She caught herself, but I knew what she was going to say. *Fall victim to some disease. Sickness. Illness.* Something like that. She'd spent a lifetime tiptoeing around my perceived fragility, not realizing I was stronger because of my disease, not weaker.

"No." I placed my hand on her thin, cold fingers, and they relaxed—barely. "I feel myself living, Nova. Not dying."

"But you're dying all the same. I'm not some piece of trash to be taken by an ebb tide. Most of us feel this way, you know that. I tried preparing you for it. Mom and Dad knew—"

"I'm not Mom and Dad."

"Well, either way, most guides are working toward ascension. Just because we soothe dying clients and help them cross over doesn't mean we're so easily taken ourselves. Even the worst guides prepare their bodies; even they will feel death's breath upon their necks and dematerialize before she can take them. We'll all of us hide from her grasp, ride her skirts to the next plane. By choice, not by demand."

I shook my head and drew the rosemary plant toward me, touching its leaves. "You're too young to be talking like this."

"One day, you'll feel it too." Knit, purl. Her voice softened so much I had to lean in to hear her. "Only you'll feel it when it's too late. Your eyes will weaken. Your legs will start to hurt when you climb stairs. The space behind your knees will ache, like growing pains all over again, but this time you'll know the feeling is your body stretching and reshaping, pulling itself apart to make room for death. You'll fight it with medication like you always do, but she'll still come for you. Memories will lose definition around the edges, smoothing over in places that were once sharp and precise. Your skin will seem to expand and deflate, wrinkling in places that were once like silk. You'll feel as if you're shrinking inside your skin, disappearing. You'll get implants and upgrades, you'll fill your body with scaffolding to hold it together, to buy time, but the truth will remain: you're dying. You've always been dying. Life is a thin film, a veil between deaths."

Her words came from a kind of healthy privilege I couldn't begin to process.

"You're being morbid," I said. Antagonizing her was easier than trying to get her to see how much her beliefs hurt me. "Stop performing for me. I hate it."

She just kept knitting. "It's not morbid to admit the truth."

"Why fixate on it?"

"Because you can't overcome what you don't understand. If you understand that the moment you're born, you're already dying, then you can learn how to make yourself slight enough to take control of the process. You can relax the surface tension of your flesh enough that your soul can spiral out like vapor. You can *control* your passing into the next realm. You can *choose* your path instead of waiting for death to chew away at your body. That's all you're doing by chasing after medication and cures: buying time."

"So instead of 'letting death chew away at your body,' you starve your body so it chews away at itself?"

Finally, she looked directly at me. "I don't think you've heard me at all. I'm not doing anything *to* myself; this is *for* myself. I've tried creating a world of beauty to tuck myself inside, but that hasn't done anything but hide me from the truth. Beauty just softens the blow of embodiment."

She smiled sadly, then resumed her work. Knit, purl. "I would think you'd know how it feels to be stuck inside flesh that doesn't feel real, doesn't show the world who you really are. At least you've had the chance to do something about it by living one of your dreams. You're out here, aren't you? Isn't this what you always wanted, to be an engineer in the black? You're luckier than you think. Some of us aren't so fortunate as to find happiness in small things. Ascension is my ship to stow away on."

I'd wanted to see her grieve for our shared loss, but this was far worse. She wanted to run from it, straight into the afterlife.

"Nova . . ." I reached for her hand, but she pulled them both out of my reach, not missing a single purl.

"I'd like to work on my knitting now."

"That's really your answer, isn't it?" I said, standing, staring down at her. I felt sick with everything she'd said. "To just sit here and knit some frilly thing for you to wear for your clients. You're useless, Nova Quick, and you have no heart. You squander all your gifts. I'm ashamed we're related. Go back to your own quarters."

I didn't bother letting her reply or make a grand exit. I just left myself, the dull ache of guilt pinching at the pit of my stomach, competing with all my self-righteous indignation. Guilt that I'd lashed out at Nova because of my pent-up sadness. Guilt over my pride in the cargo bay that destroyed Tev's room. Guilt that I wasn't woman enough to talk to Tev myself, to bandage the wound I'd caused. Guilt about my parents.

Guilt that I'd left Aunt Lai to fend for herself in a hostile city while I chased down Transliminal so I could beg for help from the same people who had killed her sister and brother-in-law.

I didn't know where I was going; I just stormed down the corridor, out of the crew dormitory and around the corner until I passed the kitchen, glanced at the bridge, and headed down a short stairwell to the lower deck. I bumped Ovie when I passed him and didn't bother apologizing, not even when he growled and glared at me with those wolfish blue eyes.

All that talk about death. My muscles itched. I needed to feel alive.

Tev kept a small gym behind the cargo hold, and that's where I ended up at the end of my furious wanderings around the *Tangled Axon*. I changed into a pair of clean gym shorts that were too small for me by half a size, but I didn't care. I filled a canteen with water, threw myself onto the bench press, demagnetized the weights, and started lifting. I didn't care that I didn't have a spotter, didn't care that I was already feeling Mel's pinch at my nerves at the back of my calves, didn't care about anything except getting to Spin and getting rid of that damned device and crossing the breach. I wouldn't give Birke a chance to get to my sister. I'd get what Marre and I needed, and I'd take Transliminal down. Didn't matter that I didn't know how yet. I'd figure something out. Right now, I just needed to feel alive.

I did as many reps as I could, waited sixty seconds, and then started again.

I didn't keep track of the number. I just lost myself in the feeling of being embodied, of burning my flesh into submission with every movement. The heat in my body rose as blood rushed in to supply my muscles with oxygen. Alive, alive, alive.

A constant death was Nova's reality, not mine. That wasn't my truth.

Sweat trickled down between my shoulder blades as I sat up. Muscles burned under my skin. Tight, twisting, real. Burning away the grief of my parents' deaths, of losing Adul. Burning away the constant fear that haloed this ship. I climbed onto the floor and pressed my stomach onto the mat, palms flat, elbows bent. I waited, letting myself feel the texture of the material under my hands. The give of the foam beneath my weight. The smell of plastic and metal and old sweat. The salt of my own body on my lips.

I pressed, feeling every muscle in my body engage as I ran through a set of push-ups. Lost in my workout, I didn't hear Tev come in until the clicking and footsteps were right next to me. Her shadow fell over me and I scrambled, sat up, and grabbed a towel.

She was wearing shorts too, exposing her legs. Silver metal, laced with some kind of dark blue plastic, comprised her left leg. Whoever had made it fashioned it after the shape of her other limb, so you couldn't visually recognize that she had a prosthetic limb when she was wearing pants. Decent craftsmanship.

"Hey." I wiped my face, then sat back against the bench and leaned my elbows on my knees. "You want the equipment? I just need a second to cool off."

She looked at me, eyes flicking to my own exposed legs. It was quick, but enough to make me feel more flushed than I already was. She shrugged one shoulder. "It's fine. Take your time."

Standing on the other side of the bench, she faced away from me as she started her stretches. I couldn't help watching her move. Muscles twisted beneath her skin, and as she raised her arms to stretch each side, she exposed a band of skin around her stomach that set me on fire.

Twisting to stretch further, she caught me looking at her. I turned away and took a swig of water.

"It was an industrial accident." She glanced at me again, then twisted the other way.

"What was?" I said, as if I hadn't noticed all the sound she made when she walked.

"Oh please. My leg."

"Oh. I wasn't looking at your—"

She stood and did a few toe-touches. "Don't lie. Everyone looks. I hate when people act like that part of me doesn't exist when they know it does."

Stop being a coward, Alana. Reach out to her.

I gnawed at my lip for a second. Gathered my tied-back locs, tossed them over my shoulder. Agonized over what to say and ultimately tried to decide which would be worse: to say nothing and prolong our forced silence, or to ask.

Finally, I just went with it. "What happened?"

She stood up straight and looked down at me. I held her gaze and gave her a little smile. *What do you think of me?* I wondered. *Could you ever care about me after what I've done?*

"Sorry, that was probably rude—"

"I'd rather you say what you're thinking. I can't stand insincerity." That accent glided over me so smoothly I couldn't stand it.

Tev rubbed the back of her neck and sat down on the bench press, facing away from me. Anticipation wound tight inside me. Honestly, she could have recited Woolera's prime ministers in alphabetical order and I would have been eager to listen at this point.

"Okay. What happened?"

"I worked on a mining and refinery vessel for a while right out of high school, about eighteen years ago." She ran a hand through her hair. "I traveled half-way around Orpim before I found a crew that needed a deck hand. The captain told me, point blank, that every year they see more injuries on their ship than most cargo vessels see in ten. Only wanted me if I could stomach the work. I knew the risks when I signed up. But it was a way out and just about everyone thinks they're invincible at that age, so you know how it goes. I took the job. Just did whatever they'd let me do to stay on the ship while I tried saving money to move up, maybe transfer. Dirty, dangerous work. Not as bad as albacite mining, but bad."

She looked down at her fidgeting hands. "Sometimes I still wake up in the middle of the night because I can hear the machinery grinding in my head."

She paused in her storytelling, just sitting there. It wasn't in my nature to let a tense silence simmer in the middle of a conversation like that, but I forced myself to be patient. I felt lucky to be hearing her voice at all after enduring so much silence.

Eventually, she continued.

"I cleaned the off-rotation machinery, among other things. Whatever grunt work they threw at bottom-feeders like me. Anything to stay valuable. Keep a paycheck coming. It was going well at first. But yeah, some of that machinery? Death traps. You had to climb inside these big mineral processors to clean them, get all the grime and buildup off to prevent parts from breaking down." She described the machines and the tasks with her hands, shaping them as she talked. "You turned it off and your spotter stayed at the control panel to make sure it *stayed* off while you shimmied down into the funnel of the thing. That's where the processing screws grind the mineral to powder for distribution."

Sickness twisted inside my stomach. I didn't want to listen to what was coming, but had to. I needed to know her, even if it meant hearing something awful.

"There was an explosion at the other end of the ship." She sniffed nervously. "I found out later someone had brought othersider tech on board and tried hiring a spirit guide to jailbreak it to mod his own implant. Caused a chain reaction."

She shook her head. "We lost ten crew members the instant it happened, but I didn't know at the time. I was inside that processor. When the ship rocked from the explosion, my spotter lost his balance, fell into the control panel, and turned on the machine."

My stomach felt queasy just thinking about it. While she spoke, Tev's eyes were closed, fingers clenching the edge of the bench, jaw tight. "I can still remember the sound of my foot, my ankle, my femur . . . they cracked as my leg fed into the machine. Couldn't have taken more than a few seconds to eat up past my knee."

I must have looked distressed, because she glanced at me from under her bangs and then gave me her lop-sided half-smile and huffed a sarcastic laugh. "It's okay. Don't pity me. I hate that."

"No! I don't, I promise. Just. I don't know . . . "

She laughed in earnest this time. "Yeah. I know. Ouch, right?" She rubbed the back of her neck. "With an injury like that, your body goes into shock. I felt hot and cold. Almost started laughing. At some point, they turned off the machine and pulled me out. I don't really remember. I knew I was losing a lot of blood, and I didn't want to see it. I didn't want to look down and know only half of my leg was there, and the other half was more meat than limb. It's not something the mind wants to deal with all at once like that. Or at least mine didn't."

She shook her head and looked down at her prosthesis. "I thought maybe if I just didn't look at it, it wouldn't be true. I wouldn't be lying there, bleeding out. I thought if I just kept my eyes focused on the hands tight around mine, on the faces hovering above me, the moment would pass and I'd be whole again. If you don't see it, it's not really happening, right? If you don't look at it, there are a million potential legs that could exist other than the mutilated one you know is really there. It's only when you look at it that it becomes real."

I didn't tell her that something about what she was saying reminded me of the way my sister talked about death, and that it frightened me. No matter how awful it was, I didn't want her to stop talking.

"You'll do some pretty amazing mental gymnastics to convince yourself everything is going to be okay in a situation like that."

She stretched to the side, one arm over her head as she bent at the waist, obviously collecting her thoughts. All I could think about was how scared she must have been after the accident.

After stretching both her sides, she finished her story.

174 | Jacqueline Koyanagi

"At some point I knew I couldn't pretend to be whole anymore. I don't know how much time had passed, but there was a moment when I accepted I was really in trouble. The medical shuttle wasn't going to bust its ass to get there in time for a junior crew member on a mining vessel. So I started thinking about all the things I'd never do without a leg. It didn't even occur to me at first that I'd still be able to have a leg, just not the one I was born with. I didn't think of that while I was bleeding out on the floor of that damned mining ship. Honestly, I thought I wasn't going to make it. I'm still surprised I survived."

An ice-cold fist clenched my heart. Tev could have died. We could have ended up in a reality in which Tev didn't exist anymore. In which we never would have met. She'd managed to insinuate herself into a space inside me reserved for my work and family and my own continued sense of self. Now it felt like I'd spent the past three silent weeks squandering something precious.

"All I could think about was if I didn't bleed to death, I'd never do much of anything, let alone captain a vessel. And that's the only thing I wanted to do with my life. My family never set foot in the sky. Dirtheels, the lot of them, as much as I love them. They never had big dreams, never looked past Woolera. It was all burt droving for them. That's all they wanted, so that's all they'd planned for me."

"Maybe that *was* their dream," I said, cautious.

"Yeah." She sighed. "Maybe, but it wasn't mine. Living on the cattle station was like looking through dirty glass. I went out of my mind trying to feel connected to the station, trying to feel *alive*, but nothing worked. I loved the land and I miss it, but there was so much damned routine. Some of us weren't made to live planetside."

I wondered if she'd been droving cattle the same time I was busy causing trouble in Heliodor.

"I know what you mean," I said.

She was looking at me now, those green eyes clear and confident even when talking about something so terrible. Her chain necklace caught the light.

"We're not so different," she admitted. "When the Big Quiet is in you, I reckon nothing is going to stop you from seeking it out, even if it means stowing away."

"You just did it legally."

She gave me half a smile. "Says you."

I wanted to ask her why she was confiding so much in me. She didn't have to tell me about her drover parents or her dream of becoming a captain for me to understand what happened to her leg. I wanted to read into it, to think she'd forgiven me, to believe she might even feel some sliver of affection for me.

Breathless, I waited for her next words.

"It did take too long," she said. "For the medical shuttle, I mean. I don't remember them arriving, I was barely holding onto consciousness. I saw faces, lights, shadows. By that point I didn't feel much, but it hurt when they jostled me. And I remembered one of the women on the medical crew wore too much perfume or something; it made me sick, and I kept thinking, 'Do they allow that? Do they let medical folks wear perfume?' It's funny, the things you remember and the things you don't. To this day I can't smell that perfume, or anything close to it, without flashing back."

She rubbed her thigh just above the prosthetic leg, as if the memory pained her. "They couldn't save it. Obviously. They said if we'd gotten to hospital faster . . . So now I have this leg and a mountain of debt. I'm still paying it off, eighteen years later."

"That's ridiculous."

"What, love?" She raised her eyebrows and pulled that half-smile out on me again. "You mean engineers get five-star medical treatment in Heliodor? You surgeons have good health insurance there? It's all board-approved medication for blue-collar workers?"

"Well, no—"

"Exactly. I'm lucky I got what I did. My captain pulled some strings and got me a leg that wouldn't hinder my work. I got right back to it once I healed up. I was just more careful." She flexed her ankle, extending the leg. *Click.* "I've had to get it repaired and upgraded a few times, but it works. It's shaped well enough that, metal aside, it feels like it's mine. Makes people uncomfortable when I don't wear long pants but whatever. I didn't care about that sort of thing before I lost my leg and I don't care now. So don't feel sorry for me."

"I don't." I looked at her hard, willing her to believe me, because it was true. I couldn't imagine ever pitying Tev Helix. She was gorgeous and strong and maddeningly sexy, neither in spite of her leg nor because of it. At least now I understood why she was so upset about the accident in the cargo bay, even beyond the damage I'd caused. It wasn't really about the plants. Or at least not for the most part. I'd triggered her worst memories.

She stared back at me, eyes darting over my face. I wanted to kiss her more than ever, sitting on opposite sides of that bench. I didn't even care that I smelled like sweat and probably tasted like it too, or that Slip was on the other side of the *Axon*, unsuspecting. My hands ached to feel Tev's skin, a type of longing I usually reserved for metal women with plasma hearts. More than that, I wanted to know the rest of her. All of her. I felt like I could live a lifetime listening to her talk and still have so much left to learn.

I wanted to tell her that. To admit to my craving for her, my words coming in short gasps between tasting her mouth and burying my face into her hair, and I really did think about it. I thought about closing the gap between us, even if only with a small gesture—a pinky over hers, a thigh brushed with light fingertips. Something, anything to initiate contact.

But thoughts of Slip held me back. I did nothing, and Tev resumed stretching. The tenuous thread between us snapped once again, winding back inside my chest.

"I think it's your shift in engineering," she said, then picked up one of the free weights and started her bicep curls.

When I realized I was staring at her arm, at the way her muscles flexed down the side of her body, I colored and grabbed my towel.

"Right. Of course."

On my way out, I almost turned back around to look at her, to see if her eyes followed me. I decided it would be too disappointing if they didn't. So I let all those possibilities linger between us, and made for engineering without sparing her a glance.

For the rest of the afternoon, the *Tangled Axon* and her captain competed for my attention. While the ship's plasma pulsed above my head and Mel's crept in along my muscle fibers with tiny claws, I thought of the childhood Tev had described. A young version of her, radiant in the sun, dirt dusting her cheeks and boots. I wondered how many times she'd looked heavenward, how much of her youth she'd spent craving the sky, how often she imagined Orpim was an enormous ship instead of a planet, just to feel closer to her dream.

Those were *my* memories, my childhood, but I'd heard the same yearning in her voice that I'd felt all my life. Every time Tev spoke to me, she plunged roots into my core and split open the rock she found there. She was inside me, growing, and I cradled that seedling as if it were the only green left in the universe.

Chapter Eleven

Thanks to our collective criminal status, we couldn't dock at one of Spin's legal ports. Marre kept the ship a safe distance from the planet until we located an abandoned orbital shipyard just far enough away to avoid being detected.

Tev decided to leave Marre, Ovie, Nova, and the powered-down *Tangled Axon* to drift in the shipyard in silence, safely hidden by the surrounding dead vessels; a Gartik would have been flagged for screening immediately. The rest of us would take a shuttle and, we hoped, not be noticed in the usual heavy incoming traffic. At least the device wouldn't give us away for another hour, hour and a half tops at Marre's best guess.

"Bell Fisher," Tev said to me as we were on our way to the surface with Slip. "That's the name you want to pass around. You're looking for a Heliodoran woman, average in height—well, maybe a little on the tall side, but just barely—darker than you, short hair, definitely carrying some kind of sidearm."

Spin glittered beneath us, as if the lust and ecstatic release of so many bodies had ignited a million tiny fires across its twisting coastlines. Even at night, the albacite roofs and domes seemed naturally illuminated, pale and bright as white flames.

"How did you meet her?" I asked. "Bell, I mean."

Tev pressed the activation button on her biter a couple of times, testing its charge. Snaps of electricity arced across its teeth as she quirked her mouth in a half-smile. "You really want to know?"

The shuttle actually made me motion sick, bringing on more Mel's pain than I'd expected. *Shit. This could complicate things.* I did my best to hide my discomfort and just hoped I hadn't added a tinge of green to my usual brown.

"People are allowed to have weapons on Spin?" I said, trying to distract myself.

"No." She smiled fully this time. "Anyway, finding Bell is going to be tough, so even though I want you two to keep your eyes peeled just in case you happen to see her in passing, you're just going to have to ask around. Problem is, with system enforcers looking for us, you can't mention me or the *Tangled Axon.* If anyone asks who's looking for Bell, tell them 'Alia.' Should be enough."

"Alia?"

"My middle name."

Tev landed the shuttle in an abandoned lot near a repair shop that had long since closed, hiding it between two tall mounds of scrap. We'd have to hope scavengers wouldn't find the shuttle and pick it clean while we were gone. There were no other whole ships there. Just skeletons that once knew the sky, probably replaced by othersider vessels issued from Transliminal. Parts rusted over, useless to all but the most desperate machinists and copper-mongers. Pilot seats torn apart by rain and rodents. Engines with coil and wire pouring from their bellies like spilled entrails. As we left the lot, sticking to shadows and unlit paths, the emptiness of all those lost ships tugged at my chest.

"Come on," Slip said, urging me forward with her hands. "We need to get to the crowds."

I struggled to match the quick pace of the others, my feet unsteady beneath me as the every-growing symptoms of Mel's Disorder threw off my equilibrium. The shuttle ride seemed to have accelerated my symptoms. *Please don't let this get in the way of our mission.*

"Why is this here?" I said.

"What?" Tev looked irritated as she concentrated on choosing the best path through the rubble.

"The shop. The yard. I thought this was a resort planet."

Slip shrugged. "People live here. Someone has to run the place. Patrons travel in ships. So there you go."

"But these are all dead ships."

"Yeah, and we'll add our own to the lot if we don't hurry up," Tev said. "You two, cover the west block. I'll go east and we'll meet back here, at this corner, in an hour."

Okay. An hour. I should be good to go for that long before the Mel's gets bad enough to interfere, at least.

"What if they find us?" I said.

"Don't let it happen."

"But what if—"

"One hour." Tev touched Slip's waist and briefly pressed her forehead against hers. I forced myself not to look away. Maybe my guilt, attraction, and envy would burn off if I pushed myself hard enough.

Tev let go and started to leave, then hesitated as she passed me. Her posture was stiff and awkward, but she touched my shoulder and smiled a little. "I know this is your first ground assignment, but try not to worry. You can only do your best. We'll find her and we'll leave. Got it?"

"Okay." I swallowed. "Yes, Captain."

She patted my arm. "Good. Remember: one hour."

On our way into the first of the clubs—the name of which immediately escaped me, considering they all sounded the same—Slip linked her arm with mine. Guilt over my feelings for Tev made her every gesture of friendship unbearable.

"We already look a little out of place because of our clothes," she said, leaning close, "and we sure as hell don't have any money or time to buy new outfits. Act like we stopped in at the last minute. A tired crew who had to let off some steam. Happens enough not to throw folks off too badly if we just look like we're trying to relax."

As the door swung open, I squinted at the flickering lights. "Right."

Bass throbbed in my chest, amplifying the Mel's pain. We weren't even five steps into the place before the press of bodies crushed us, carrying us along like a human river. I fought every instinct to shove people back and tell them to get the hell off of me.

Nails glittered in moving lights, brushing delicately across the painted skin of titillated dance partners. A few high-end body mods stood out from the crowd—fresh fangs and tentacle-limbs caught the light, reminding me of my conversation with Dr. Shrike a lifetime ago. Bestial bodies pulsed with the music. Vast membranous wings brushed my arms. Arachnid legs sprouted from backs and bumped the shimmering décor. When we passed a woman with an actual third eye, blinking with her originals, part of me shuddered to think of the time it must have taken to recover from the neurological upgrades involved with a new sensory organ. What happened to people whose bodies rejected the upgrades? We never heard about them. Unless othersider tech didn't make mistakes. I wished I knew how it worked, how Transliminal could so effortlessly bend matter and space to their will. Seeing what they'd done to the bodies around us, I felt conflicted between my desire for them to help Marre, and my desire for revenge. What would Nova think of this place?

Part of me shivered under the thrill of their abilities. Flesh was almost limitless now. And here I was, falling apart, trying not to bend over in agony as pain radiated out in invisible spirals from my hands and back, louder than any bassline. The first stage of the disease came on so quickly.

Most of the patrons crushing in on us probably weren't wealthy enough for othersider mods, and they already enjoyed more luxury in a day than I'd know in a lifetime. Surely some of these people had been stuck with blood and meat upgrades from our side of the breach—grown, grafted, and integrated the old-fashioned way. Everyone knew that wasn't how the othersiders accomplished their body mods. How did it work? How did they manipulate reality so easily?

Either way, I'd have loved for my biggest problem to be whether my suit matched my tentacles or not.

Pain shot into my left palm and I grabbed it, pushing at a trigger point that was supposed to ease the agony some when the Mel's flared up. A trick I'd learned from Dr. Shrike that helped a little.

Slip glanced at me and gave me an exaggerated smile, and an encouraging expression that said, *Look happy.*

Right. *Look excited, Alana. Drunk. High. Look anything but pained and anxious.*

I ground my teeth to steel myself against the ache in my hand and smiled appreciatively at the other patrons as we wove our way through the thronging monsterfolk of Spin.

We identified people who seemed moderately sober and asked about "Bell Fisher," but most were either intoxicated or annoyed by the question. So we left and tried the next bar, the next club. And the next. Every new establishment was another assault on my senses, grinding against the Mel's symptoms, digging those familiar claws deep into my nerves and muscles.

Every place looked and sounded the same to me. Different color schemes, different overproduced music, but the same nevertheless. Forty-five minutes later, we still hadn't found Bell. For a moment we'd thought we'd found a lead when a man seemed to recognize the name, and although it turned out he did know Bell, he hadn't talked to her in two months.

We were in the fifth club of the night when the end of the hour loomed over us.

Slip turned away from a woman with live fish in her anemone-hair and leaned on the bar. "This is hopeless."

"What do we do if we can't find her?"

She shrugged, then slammed back a shot she'd been cradling. "No idea. Maybe your sister can figure something out."

"She has contacts in a lot of places, but not the kind we need. She hates Transliminal, remember?"

"Tev!" Slip looked past my shoulder and waved, her voice carried away by the rhymes coming in over the speakers.

I turned to see Tev hurrying toward us, tossing irritated glances at people who bumped her, tried to dance with her, spilled their drinks on her. We didn't have time to talk before she shouted: "We need to go!"

Slip's eyes widened at something behind me. I couldn't hear her, but I could read her lips: "Too late."

Three system enforcers entered the building, holding their palms up to random patrons to scan their eyes.

They knew we were here.

"Go," Tev hissed into my ear, pressing her hand into the small of my back to urge me forward. "Now."

Slip was already on the move, dodging dancers as she wove her way toward the back of the building. Every time Tev and I tried to make progress behind her, we were cut off by couples, triads, groups, drinks, arms, wings that could have been real or faux—it was hard to distinguish my own limbs from anyone else's, between the music and chaos and increasing pain, and the solicitors tossing advertising microchips at us like confetti.

I grabbed Tev's shoulder and pulled her down a couple of inches so I could reach her ear. "People are looking at us. They can see our anxiety."

"Shit." She ran a hand through her hair, then covered her mouth and nose with her hands while she thought.

"What about the *Tangled Axon*?" I said. "What if they've found it?"

"Marre knows what she's doing. I trust her."

The song switched and the crowd roared. More people

poured onto the dance floor from booths and bar seats, dancing against each other and us, bobbing their heads and hands, pumping fists, and popping their limbs in time with the occasionally-shuffling rhythm. Neon drinks spilled, splashing onto chests and shoes, painting folks with luminescent liquid. Bass thundered inside me, wobbling, whomping, and grinding against my organs. It was the kind of music Aunt Lai said sounded like "a robot frog with indigestion."

"We have to get out of here," Tev said next to my ear, pulling me back, but I immediately panicked a little. Slip was nowhere in sight, and we were still so far away from the door.

"Tev." My voice shook as I watched the enforcers scan their way through the room. "They're getting closer."

An officer scanned a green-haired woman with shining, quicksilver eyes. The scanner light flashed and the green-haired woman laughed, grabbing at the enforcer's reflective black body armor. He took the woman by the wrist and shoved her aside, into another dancer, who caught her. They collapsed into a pile of drunk laughter as the enforcer shook out his own wrist and moved on.

Sweat poured down my neck under the heat and movement and growing stress. "Fuck, Tev. What are we going to do?"

The crowd jumped in time with a particularly intense part of the song, hair and limbs thrashing around their heads. After a few nervous glances around the room, Tev grabbed my hand and lifted it a few times to show me—we needed to jump, to blend in, to appear to be having a good time. I felt ridiculous and I could tell Tev did too, but we followed the crowd's lead, each of us looking past the other to keep our eyes surreptitiously on the enforcers winding their way toward us.

The song ended, twisting into the next bone-grinding beat, so we stopped jumping. "They're not scanning everyone," Tev said, pulling me to her and dancing against me, encouraging me to do the same to stay blended with the crowd. "Maybe they won't pick us."

"Look at us. We can dance all we want, but we stick out no matter what. No offense, but you look as uncomfortable as me. And our clothes! There's no way. We have to get out of here." I tried nudging her toward the back door, but then I saw we were just a handful of bodies away from one of the enforcers in that direction, and another one blocked us in from the other side.

"We're trapped," she said. "We have to try harder to fit in and pray luck is on our side." She stopped dancing but kept her hand on my waist as she guided me back over to the bar, then slid onto the edge of a seat and pulled me toward her so that I stood between her legs.

"Tev—"

"Shh. Don't say my name." She leaned close and spoke quietly. "They have amplifiers."

Heat bloomed beneath her hands on my waist. I couldn't look her in the eye; I focused on anything else. Her neck. Her arms. Her thighs, on either side of me. I had to put my hands somewhere, so I placed them on her knees. Instantly, a fire flared in my chest and I slid them higher, moving closer to her. Half of me tried to forget about Slip, while the other half fought to keep her at the forefront of my mind.

Tev's eyes flicked to mine, her stare so fixed and intense it almost hurt. I didn't want this to end. I reveled in it, hanging onto her gaze, letting it work on me until I felt weak. Our hands grew heavier on each other as we lingered there, hiding from the authorities in a bubble of desire. In that moment, I didn't have to try to blend in. I was as lust-ridden as the rest of them.

"What are we doing?" Her voice rolled into me like the music, deep and rich. Real. I was full with the sound of her. The smell of her. Sweat and heat, and a touch of alcohol from her attempts at getting information at the bar. To say nothing of the sight of her—the tight lines of her waist, the curve of her neck. Trailing my eyes over her skin and body, over the hair plastered against her forehead by her sweat, over the lips that breathed so close to me, I felt my need for her unfurling.

"Alana." There was urgency in Tev's voice. "I want—"

My hands tightened. "They're right behind you."

I could almost feel the electromagnetic pull of the enforcers' bodies. Tev placed her hand on my cheek, bringing my mouth close to hers, pulling me against her. Her breath lingered over my lips, hot and sweet.

"We just have to hide," I said, voice shaking with desire. "Just don't make eye contact with them."

"Stop talking."

My breath came heavy, as did hers, her chest rising and falling against mine. Fear and need collided between us, making me so dizzy I was afraid I'd pass out. I licked my lips and grazed her thigh with my thumb, unable to help myself.

Her breath caught. She slid a hand toward the back of my neck and entwined her hands in my locs, almost possessively. Just as I was about to kiss her, Tev's eyes flicked to the left and she released me.

"Go."

Her voice jerked me out of my haze. I pulled back to look at her. "What?"

She slid off the seat, pushing me a little to make room for herself. "We have an opening. Go!"

She grabbed my hand and we were dodging between arms and legs, heading for the back door. Our palms were slick and hot, but we held on. Sweat dripped down my lower back while my mind cycled around a series of thoughts, over and over again, like a mantra: *Please let the shuttle be there. Please let Slip be safe. Please let us get out of here. Please let the* Axon *and* Marre *be okay.* Anger writhed in my stomach at the thought of the enforcers boarding the *Tangled Axon*, violating her.

Nova, I thought, nudging her with my mind. The first time in my life I'd ever deigned to empathically pray to my sister. *I sure could use some borrowed strength right about now.*

A woman with antlers turned to me, laughing, biolu-minescent moss glittering on the brachiating velvet bone. Red-flecked eyes gleamed as she grabbed at me, danced against me, breathed into my ear. I shrugged away easily, her limbs weak with intoxication.

Tev seized the woman's arm and turned the stranger toward her. "Who do you think you are, grabbing people like that?"

I touched her shoulder. "Don't call attention to us." One of the enforcers was about five people to the left, scanning eyes and glancing around the room. I looked away before we could make eye contact.

Tev released the antlered woman with a shove. The stranger just rolled her eyes. "Whatever."

"Touching my crew," Tev mumbled, face sour. "Fucking othersider groupies."

We maneuvered away from the nearby enforcer as incon-spicuously as we could, dancing our way through the crowd and several songs. Tev turned to me to say something when she stopped, looking surprised and confused at something behind me.

"Why, Captain, I'd never have expected to see you in such a loathsome establishment," my sister's elegant voice drawled over my shoulder .

I turned around.

"Nova?" I couldn't keep my voice down, enforcer amplifiers or no. Where had she come from? "What are you doing here?"

"Did you follow us?" Tev growled, sounding more like Ovie than herself and looking like she wanted to punch my sister. "Did you take my other shuttle? If Birke finds out you're here—"

"Yes, I took your other shuttle and parked in another lot. It wasn't that hard. Marre didn't protest and your wolfman was too busy in the engine room to notice. You think I'm just going to let you drag Alana around without keeping an eye on her? When she prayed to me for strength, I could feel her fear.

I'm not about to let my sister get arrested. Enough damage has been done to my family." She pushed her gold sleeve back to the elbow. "We're getting you two out of here in one piece."

Before either of us could respond, Nova flicked a few fingers at me and Tev. A cold pocket of air formed around me; my blood felt frozen in an instant. A million pinpricks shot across my skin, but it was nothing compared to the chronic ache I was used to. Not to mention, I was more preoccupied with what was happening to Tev.

We looked at each other in dazed astonishment. Tev's hair clumped together, darkened, and sprouted leaves, replacing the blond fall I'd spent so much time imagining draped over my body. She became a woman with ivy tresses, and the green of her eyes grew more vibrant—near-neon in the dark. My skin tingled all the while, my eyes aching as if sleep-deprived.

"Nova," I said, struggling to speak. It was the only word I managed to get out. How was she doing this? What *was* this? Why was Tev's body changing? Why did I feel so strange?

Suddenly, my veins seemed filled with light, I floated with such mindless happiness. I knew the cloud of content that had settled over me was artificial, but I didn't care. Pain had receded from my limbs and my nerves felt perfectly at ease despite the unnatural process taking place right in front of me. Moment by moment, my captain was replaced by a plant-woman who blended seamlessly into the body-modified crowd.

I laughed a little, drunk on whatever fog had clotted up my mind. Bliss and pleasure muted my incredulity over the bizarre abilities I hadn't realized my sister possessed. My skin was hypersensitive to every centimeter of fabric. I touched my stomach, reveling in the softness that sheathed me, then let my hands drift up to my face. Again, laughter drifted out of me, so distinct I could almost *see* the sound. A gold sound. Gold like my sister, gold like Adul. Gold sound that drifted up to mingle with the moving lights above . . .

I realized then my hands trailed over my scaled cheeks.

Scaled—so textured! Nova had transformed me into something *other*, too. Something reptilian. A distant part of me kept thinking, *How is this possible?*

When I opened my mouth and tickled the air with my forked tongue, the cold sensation made me laugh yet again. All of existence was right here, right in this room with all these beautiful people, right here with me and Tev and Nova . . .

Something heavy pulled at my tailbone. A thick, muscular tail slammed into a nearby patron when I turned around to look at my new appendage, but he just laughed and tugged on it playfully before moving on.

Most incredible was the utter lack of pain. My fuzzy mind was incapable of processing this. No ache, no twinge, no sharp biting sensations. No exhaustion or weariness. Just endless beauty and a feeling like I was connected to everything that had ever existed, ever would exist . . .

"Your eyes," Tev slurred. "They're yellow slits now."

I just laughed and touched her ivy-hair. "You're leafy. Tev, you're *so* beautiful."

Nova took both of our hands, guiding us through the crowd as we stumbled along in our new, haze-filled bodies. I tried petting my sister and telling her how much I loved her, how beautiful she was too—*all these beautiful women in my life, see how lucky I am?*—but the gold-sound just fell out of my mouth in a slur. I wanted to find Marre and Ovie and Slip and the *Tangled Axon* and see how beautiful they looked through my new eyes.

Was this how Dr. Shrike had felt right after her mods? The thought made me laugh. Everything made me want to laugh.

We passed by two different enforcers, the second of whom seemed like she might scan us. The black-armored woman turned toward me and raised her hand to my eyes. My body slowed. Every muscle, every pulse, lasted a lifetime. I watched worlds live and die in those moments, in the palm of her outstretched hand.

Nova stepped between me and the enforcer, a gold sheen flashing over my sister's eyes. Calm descended over the enforcer's face. The woman slowly turned her palm toward her own face, staring at the glow emanating from her implant as if it were the most remarkable thing she had ever seen. Tendrils of light escaped from its center, similar to my sister's knitting. Each thread of light split into several more, winding around her hand and detonating at her fingertips in little supernovae. A sleepy smile transformed her into a wonder-charmed child.

I want that, I thought, my whole consciousness having become a series of wants and sensations. I reached out in the hope of taking the enforcer's hand so that I could take a closer look at the lights, but Nova guided me away.

"This way, little sister." Her voice echoed.

I watched ivy-Tev as we bumped our way through the crowd, her vines swaying along her. A lock of ivy draped over her chest, where she stroked it over and over again, marveling at each patron she passed. I wondered what she was feeling, thinking. More than that, I wanted to touch her, to feel the vibrations of her voice along my skin, to smell the leaves in her hair.

Tev and I stepped through the back door, and as fresh air rushed toward me, the world hit me in the face.

There is an entire universe out here, a world that exists outside the building, I thought, and in my haze, nothing had ever seemed so incredible. I looked up to a darkened sky. The clouds above us were heavy with unshed rain; the smell of it was a living thing, crawling inside me. I touched Tev's arm and pointed upward. Her gaze followed the line of my finger as I leaned over and whispered, "Think about it. She's up there. The *Tangled Axon*. She's up there, *alive*, while we're down here. Everything always exists, all at the same time. Isn't that amazing?"

Tears welled in Tev's eyes. She took my hand and pulled it away from the sky. "And we're *here*," she said. "That's amazing too."

"Okay, girls," Nova said. "Let's keep moving."

Her voice brought me back just enough to make me wonder why my sister had never told me she could do this. Then my consciousness drifted away again, lost in wonder. When Tev and I started to wander away, Nova reoriented us, directed us, herded us. All was pure sensation—sounds and steps and sky and touch, infinite touch. Bass beat at our chests as we passed clubs. Buildings glittered along the street like a chain of jewels. My pulse throbbed in my head, neck, chest, feet, hands, but there was no pain. No pain! Mel's Disorder no longer mattered. It was gone, long gone, replaced by sheer physical existence stripped of pretense and baggage and culture. I existed at the exact intersection of my body and the outside world. Why had my sister never given me this gift before?

Each footstep hit the pavement like a small miracle. I bounced into every step just to feel the enormity of my own movements, to feel the realness of my weight as my tail lent me a new sense of balance. Were people all over the system experiencing things like this at the hands of the spirit guides? How had I missed out on something so transcendent? How had I never known about these abilities?

Nova's hand clamped tight around mine as she moved us along the densely populated sidewalk. Time's passage had no meaning while so much of me was tucked away inside a pocket of surreality, a wrinkle in my consciousness. I had no idea how far we'd moved from the previous club, or which building we'd entered when we finally peeled away from the outdoor crowd. I tucked my tail around my waist to prevent the door from slamming shut on it, and I laughed at the sight of the scaled, muscular thing that was somehow me and not-me at the same time. This seemed very funny, so I laughed, and the sensation of the laugh in my chest just amused me all the more.

Once inside, the music's gut-wrenchingly loud bass rattled my bones, and it occurred to me that if Nova hadn't transported my mind like this, I'd be in tremendous pain by now. More than half a day without Dexitek, with symptoms accelerated by the shuttle ride.

Eh, but who cared? Mel's no longer existed for me in that moment, so it didn't matter. Nothing existed or mattered except each step, each breath.

Nova paid our entry into the club, guided the two of us around a corner just inside the doorway, and ducked behind a stairwell partition. The longer I stayed in this consciousness-bubble, the more my perceptions were stirred into a froth. Meaningless, confusing. I couldn't have cared less about where we were, or the fact that several people had spilled their drinks on me, or that the weight of my tail made me feel entirely too large, because the only things that mattered were touch and smell and light and . . .

Awareness came and went, each moment a mere dust mote passing me by.

Without warning, Nova touched my chest and Tev's, dissolving our bodies back into their original shapes. Scales receded into my skin, prickling my nerves like a million tiny insects. My tail simply disappeared, tip-to-tailbone, and my eyes ached as I assumed their color shifted back to my usual dark brown. Meanwhile, the leaves fell from Tev's hair as if autumn had come upon her, and the vines transformed back into the soft, blond hair I was so used to admiring on the ship. Her eyes returned to their normal vivid green in lieu of the false neon emerald.

A sense of time and space reasserted itself as Nova released her hold on our minds. Reality anchored me, snapping back into place like a rubber band.

My calm was short-lived. Instantly, a nerve-lacerating shock of pain snaked down my arms, crippling my hands. I think I might have cried out, but it was lost in the music. My neck felt as if it were made of solid stone instead of flesh. A stabbing migraine throbbed on both sides of my head. My body seemed fragile as spun glass.

Tev was suddenly there, hands on my arms, holding me up. Her voice came from behind a wall of liquid, muffled and distant; I couldn't make out what she was saying.

Then, the sensation receded to a dull ache and I gathered my strength enough to stand up straight. "I'm okay," I said, though the worry on Tev's face told me she didn't believe me. "Really. I think whatever she did to us just hit me pretty hard."

"A side effect of the rapid transformation when you have a chronic pain disorder," Nova said, glancing around the corner as if watching for someone.

"How dare you change our bodies without our permission?" Tev let go of me and raged at her, stabbing her chest with a finger. "Our *minds*! That's assault!"

"I helped you get out of there, didn't I, Captain?" Nova said. "I thought you said you wanted my help getting a treatment for Marre. We can't do that if you can't find Bell."

I did my best to fight off the swells of vertigo and the stabbing sensation that cascaded through my limbs with each heartbeat. "Nova, what the hell *was* that?" I said.

"You wanted me to lend you strength." Nova took my face into her hands and examined my eyes. "How are you feeling?"

"Awful!" I batted her away. "What did you do? How did you do that?"

"You should have asked before you changed us," Tev added. "We didn't consent to *that*." In her distress, Tev kept running her hand through her hair, stopping at the top of her head, then letting the strands fall haphazardly. Every few sentences or so: hand, hair, mess. It made me want to kiss her, even while hurting, even while overwhelmed and confused by what my sister had done.

Tev continued ranting. "You couldn't be bothered to ask, could you? 'Hey, mind if I completely remake your body? Mind if I turn you into a shrub? Mind if I drug you and—'"

"There was no time," Nova said. "There still isn't. Bell is

upstairs, on the roof, in captivity. We should go to her now if you want her help with the device. Or would you prefer to debate consent?"

Tev stiffened. "How do you know she's there?"

"You're the one who hired me. I'm a spirit guide; it's my job to help my clients obtain what they desire."

"Wait a minute." Tev crossed her arms. "You mean to tell me you knew all this time exactly where Bell is? You let us run around this fucking sinkhole with the enforcers after us when you could have 'helped your client obtain what they desire?'" She quoted Nova with a mocking tone. "I could throttle you."

"I didn't know where she was until I came in here and was close enough to pick up on it. I've had nearly a lifetime to learn the subtleties of Alana's energetic signature. Bell is a stranger; it's not as easy."

"You lied to us."

Tev advanced on Nova as if she really were going to hit her, but I grabbed her arm. "Captain. Not now."

"I don't get you," Tev said to Nova, jerking her arm away from me. "I'm starting to regret bringing you on board."

"Oh, really? I'd like to see you fix your strange little pilot without me."

"Stop," I said as I doubled-over under the pressure in my joints. Fatigue clouded my head, my coherence slipping away in wisps.

Tev placed her hand on my back, voice melting into me. "Are you okay?"

I nodded, doing my best to ignore the growing knot of pain twisting up my body. "Fine."

"Then let's go." She gestured at Nova to lead the way. "The enforcers could find the ship any time now. When we get back, we're having a talk about what else you haven't told us."

Nova sighed dramatically.

"Don't ever change me like that again without asking first," Tev added.

"Okay, cattlegirl."

Tev turned toward her. "What did you call me? You'd better show respect—"

"Calm down, Captain." A wry smile curled Nova's lips. "It's a pet name. Besides, shouldn't you pride yourself on your heritage?"

"Just go," I said, clenching my teeth against the ache. Tev was in the right here, but I couldn't stand listening to them argue like children.

We wound our way up the stairs, careful not to slip on puddles of spilled luminescent drinks or shards of glass from dropped beer bottles. Just as we reached the top, Tev pulled out her biter and held it to the side, away from me, but I flinched at the sight of it. Nova paused, hand on the door, and whispered.

"Put that away."

"You've lost your head if you think I'm going out there unarmed."

"No, she's right," I said, rallying enough strength to speak clearly. "If they see us burst out there guns blazing, it's over."

I'd never seen her so eager, so vulnerable to her impulses. She seemed to fight against herself for a moment, working her jaw.

"Damn," she said, then put the biter away.

"Act confused," I said. "If we go out there and they see us, just act like a group of drunk patrons who got lost looking for a place to fool around."

Tev tossed an irritated look at Nova, shook her head, and gestured at the door. "Let's get this over with."

Nova waved her wrist over the door and something *snicked* into place, unlocking it. She pushed it open and the night air billowed over us, below an expansive, cloud-filled sky.

We briefly scanned our surroundings: an empty roof with one stone structure near the far end, and no other people. Wind swept over the building, making it difficult to hear anything. We glanced each other and hurried quietly across.

Tev pulled out her biter again, holding it at the ready. Our feet were feather-quiet, but my heart thundered as I struggled against the illness.

As we neared the structure, voices drifted toward us.

"—about our shipment." Male. Older.

"I'm just interested. You can't tell me you haven't researched your competitors." This voice was smooth and female, with the near-perfect enunciation common for system bureaucrats despite her obviously Heliodoran accent. Judging by the way Tev tensed when she heard that voice, I assumed it was Bell. I raised my eyebrows at her in question and she nodded.

Nova pointed at her eyes, then pointed toward the voices. She raised one finger, then two more. Her empathy helped her detect distinct minds; I trusted her judgment. So there were three people, including Bell.

Cramps plucked at my stomach, turning it to a ball of iron. The sharp stabbing sensation running along my neck and head made it difficult to see straight. *Please don't let this damned disease get in the way.*

"I find it hard to believe you're just feeling out your competitors," the man said, voice nasal and ragged.

"You don't have to," Bell said. Casual and confident. "You can go on about running your business and I'll go about mine. No harm done."

"How about I hold you here and let the enforcers decide what to do with you?"

Tev guided us to the far end of the stone structure, where we crouched down to whisper, barely audible.

"We have to go," she said. "We have no time."

I nodded, hoping she didn't see the sweat forming on my brow, or that I clutched my hands against my stomach to hide their tremors. Nova, however, gave me a long, disconcerting look—she saw straight into my body and glimpsed all the white-hot pain that made it so hard to concentrate.

"You take the third person, since you know where everyone

is positioned," Tev said to Nova. "I'll take the man. Alana, you free Bell. How is she being held?"

"I can't believe I'm being ordered to participate in criminal activity," Nova muttered. "Don't you think Alana and I have done enough for your little quest? I'd like to take her back to the *Axon* now."

"You were willing to be involved in this when you changed us." Tev said. "It's a little late to claim neutrality now."

"That doesn't mean I'm at your beck and call." She took my hand. "Being a guide does not entail freeing criminals from the grasp of other criminals at the behest of a criminal."

I took her hand off mine, squeezing it before letting go. "Let's just get through this. The more help Tev has, the faster we'll leave Spin."

"Most sensible thing anyone has said in awhile," Tev said, testing her biter. "So what kind of restraints do they have on Bell?"

Nova sighed. "Transliminal security-binds. You two can't do anything with them. I can, but it'll take some time. I'll use my empathy on her guard. Fear and panic to make it harder to fight."

"We'll have to take the other two down and get Bell to the ship. We won't have time to do our business here. Worry about the restraints later," Tev said.

"Your target's back is toward us," Nova said. "He has a weapon but I couldn't see what. Emotionally, he feels clear. Focused. I'd have to be touching him to get anything more specific from his mind."

Tev gripped the biter with renewed determination.

"Help the captain," I said, struggling against the pain. Tev looked alarmed now, but I ignored her and focused on addressing Nova. "I don't know how much I can do. Please."

She nodded. Tev's eyebrows knitted together as she took in my labored breathing, the sweat on my face and neck, the gnarled shape of my fingers.

I just nodded in the direction of Bell. "Go. Worry about it later."

Her anxious eyes lingered on me a moment longer before she and Nova led the way. I struggled to keep up, balancing myself against the stone. Nova peeled off in the other direction, approaching the third person from the side, while Tev crept forward, quietly releasing the safety on the biter. I caught myself holding my breath as she maneuvered as silently as possible to the edge of the wall, then sprinted toward the man. She wasted no time negotiating—Tev shoved the biter into the man's neck, who jerked and screamed through tightly clenched teeth as Tev released shocking impulses into his spinal column.

Well, that was one way to do it.

Bell watched from the ground, shocked. Her wrists were tied behind her back. She had dark Heliodoran skin like mine and Ovie's, and a natural attractiveness I'd always wished I had. Sleek and stylish in nothing more than an ordinary tunic, tights, and boots, she wouldn't have been out of place in a fashion ad.

I hurried to her as best I could, helping her stand. She said something but I couldn't hear it above the noise; I just smiled awkwardly and swallowed my nausea, guiding her back toward the structure where she'd be out of the line of fire.

I caught a glimpse of Nova and the other woman—an enormous, thickly built woman so muscular she was a wall unto herself—engaged in a struggle of their own. The sight of my sister engaged in a physical confrontation shocked me into stillness. Nova twisted the woman's arm behind her back, but she contorted out of Nova's grip and punched her in the gut.

"Nova!"

My sister barely reacted. Curses and shouts flew like spittle. Mostly the other woman's, though the longer it went on, the more Nova struggled to maintain control. Her opponent must have had a strong will to be able to fight through Nova's emotional projections. Nova dodged in a flutter of gold just as the woman detonated some kind of weapon I'd never seen before, firing what looked like a ripple of light into the stone wall. Debris tumbled down around us just as Bell and I made it back. One chunk hit me in the shoulder. White-hot pain raced through my entire body and I shouted, cursing. Cold dizziness disoriented me for a good ten seconds.

Bell's curses joined the noise as she kicked away some of the debris.

"Are you okay?" I said from my pile on the ground. Blood trickled down the side of her head and one of her sleeves was torn, her exposed skin ripped and covered in crimson.

"Grab my other arm," she said, crouching down and offering it to me, struggling to maintain her balance with bound wrists. I wanted to argue but had so little strength left, I just did as she said and she helped me stand. Blood coated my mouth. I tried my best not to dry heave.

Chaos raged around me while I struggled to hang onto my concentration. Tev crouched over the immobile body of the man who had interrogated Bell, looking between us and Nova. Several meters away, Nova struggled with the other person, the woman's limbs and hair and face and flesh shifting, morphing, raging its own battle, as Nova transformed the woman's body against her will, keeping her off-balance. Scales, feathers, useless extra limbs, horns. At one point my sister blinded her by growing skin over her eyes, and she wailed in horror.

Roaring thrusters howled over us, heat buffeting the roof. The snap and sizzle of plasma scorched the air as the most beautiful sight in the Big Quiet eclipsed the clouds: the *Tangled Axon*, her cargo bay open, hovering just above the building.

"That's a nice ship," Bell said, grunting through her speech. "How much would you be willing to sell it for?"

"Not now," I said. Slip and Ovie gestured wildly at us from the cargo bay with their free hands, pointing standard-issue military rifles at the electrocuted man and the woman still fighting Nova. The cargo bay door formed an unstable ramp while Marre held the ship as steady as possible, manually operating the thrusters. She might have been unsettling, but damn, she was an amazing pilot.

Tev hurried to us and took my arm. Shouts exploded behind us, plasma arcs from their weapons narrowly missing us, scorching the roof and sending shards of debris flying in our direction. Three enforcers poured out of the stairwell from the club below. Tev's strong arms helped me up, and I tried not to cry out as we stumbled along behind Bell. I prayed we wouldn't be killed when we were this close to escape. The voices behind us grew ever nearer. More debris sliced through the air with each shot.

Tev bellowed and slapped a hand against her neck, blood pouring from between her fingers.

"Tev!" I held her in return as we hurried, stumbling, desperate to get to the ship before we were captured or killed. Hot blood poured down the side of her neck, shoulder, and arm, our clothes and bodies sticky with it. One foot after another, we stepped onto the ramp and helped each other stay balanced enough not to fall off as the *Tangled Axon* swayed, hovering. Losing blood and obviously burned across most of the left side of her neck, Tev swayed on her feet and started to slip backward, knocking into Bell, but I grabbed them both. Heat spread beneath my hand on Bell's torso.

More blood.

Slip caught us and together we all struggled to climb onto the ship. Our unsteady footing was a mixed blessing; at least we were moving targets.

Nova returned the large woman's sight to her and backed away from the enforcers, palms forward. She picked up her skirts like a noblewoman and hopped elegantly onto the ramp as the cargo bay door closed, her golden fabrics whipping in the wind.

Marre wasted no time in ferrying us into the sky.

Chapter Twelve

Nova immediately went to work on freeing Bell's wrists from the othersider restraints, but Bell was halfway to unconscious, coughing up blood.

"Some way to say 'hey' to an old friend," she sputtered, eyes rolling back in her head.

"We are being pursued by an enforcer vessel," Marre said over the intercom. "Brace yourselves."

Everyone in the cargo bay held onto something or someone as the *Tangled Axon* banked. Tev and I grabbed hands and crouched down to lower our mutual center of gravity. Blood continued spilling from the wound on her neck, soaking the left side of her shirt in red. She looked pale and her eyes were unfocused. I ripped the bottom of my shirt off and pressed it against her wound. Blood soaked my clothes, and only some of it was mine.

"Tev," I said, placing my hands on her face. Cold fear filled my chest. "Tev, look at me—"

An explosion hit the ship, rocking us all. Some of the crates demagnetized and fell, one of them barely missing Ovie. Nova held Bell up as she continued plucking at the bands around the nearly unconscious criminal's wrists. Finally, a tangle of bright filaments fluttered to the floor and dissolved into the metal. She gently lay Bell down and brushed her hand over her forehead, pressing the other against her wound. "She's not well."

"Damage to the port thruster," Marre said. "Functionality at seventy percent."

The *Tangled Axon*'s suffering lanced me with every heartbeat.

"Help Tev!" I shouted at Nova, hot tears pooling in my eyes. "Fix her! She's hurt!"

She held up her hands. "I can't, Alana."

"What the hell do you mean? I had a fucking tail! You can obviously do a lot more than we thought."

"Sweetheart, that's all guide work—magic. Illusions. Not science. The most I can do is help ease their pain, which I've done already. They feel very little. We should get them to a facility."

Rage split me apart. If she could help them feel better, what about me? All these years Mel's ripped through me, and she could have done something to help?

"Them?" Tev said, trying to see who else was hurt, and shouting in frustration when she realized it was Bell. "Slip!" she bellowed, voice echoing in the cargo bay. "Help Bell! We need her!"

I set aside Nova's betrayal for a moment and touched Tev's face, turning it toward me. "We've got to get you to a facility—"

"No," Tev said, then coughed, grimacing. "I'm not going to hospital. We can't. Enforcers."

"Get the captain over here, now!" Slip shouted from across the hold, where she was unpacking medical supplies from an emergency kit. Immediately Ovie hurried to us and collected her from me, replacing my hand with his on the cloth.

"Lots of pressure," I said as I relinquished Tev, pushing my hand on top of his to demonstrate. He nodded, kind enough not to tell me I was pointing out the obvious. Fear gripped my stomach at the thought of losing her before I could tell her how much she meant to me.

No, stop. She'll be okay.

"Bell," Tev muttered. "We need Bell. Help her."

Heat and exhaustion and bone-deep pain threatened to render me unconscious, but I held on, fighting against the heaviness pulling at every part of me. Again the ship banked and I fell over, straight into Nova, narrowly missing Bell. My sister looked at me, blood-covered hands on my arms.

"You need help too," she said. "You don't have any left, do you?"

"Too busy being lied to by my sister, I guess."

"You are so stupid!" A trickle of blood ran down the side of her face where debris had nicked her. "Why didn't you tell us you needed more medication!"

"Why didn't you tell me you could take away my symptoms! Why don't you take it away now? Please! I need your help!"

"If I did that you'd be as mindless as you were on Spin. They need you right now."

"I can't believe you lied to me!"

Slip glanced up when she heard our shouting, but quickly returned to flushing and sealing Tev's wound. Tev sat on the floor, leaning upright against Ovie. Tev said something to Slip, pushing her away and sitting up, but Slip eased Tev back down and shook her head, replying with a stern expression. Tev pointed in our direction, then shouted in pain. She looked pale, but they continued arguing as Tev winced against the strain her muscles put on the wound.

"No!" Slip shouted at her, then looked at me and called out loudly enough for us to make out what she was saying. "Bell! You have to help Bell—I'm busy with the captain!"

That jerked me into action. I tied back my locs and turned to Bell's limp, blood-soaked form sprawled next to us, near a stack of strapped-in crates. White spots crowded my eyesight, blurring her face.

"Bell's dying," I said, unable to think of anything else to say or do. Mel's-induced brain fog clouded my mind just as badly as the knives in my head had obscured my vision.

Nova ripped the sleeves off her gown. "She's the only person who knows how to get the enforcers off our asses."

Despite everything, I laughed at her profanity, then groaned and grabbed my head. Every time I made a sound, all the pain in my body flared.

"Alana, look at you!" she said, pressing the fabric against Bell's chest. The dealer was a mess of ripped clothing and blood. She coughed and smiled up at Nova, saying something unintelligible.

"You're bleeding." I said, touching the wound on Nova's head.

"I don't care!" she swatted my hand away while trying to work. Gold fabric soon turned red, seeping up through Nova's fingers. "You'll die without your medication. How could you do that? I *knew* you weren't telling us! I always know when you're lying, Alana Quick!"

We banked again, knocking us into the crates. Instinctively, I looked toward Tev. Ovie and Slip worked to prevent Tev's wound from banging into anything; he held her steady while Slip covered Tev with her own body until we leveled out. Ovie shifted his weight and whined a little, letting it roll off into a growl.

While the captain and Bell bled out in the cargo bay, the *Tangled Axon*'s discordant sounds rolled through the corridors and into her belly. She was shaken and hurting, like a nightmare-plagued child, twisting my insides into a mess again.

When we leveled out, Nova continued putting pressure on Bell's stomach. I placed my hands over hers to help.

"Hey," I said to Bell, trying to summon a convincing smile. "Sorry we had to grab you and run."

"You—" Bell coughed up a mixture of spittle and blood, but my sister soothed her suffering. Nova's fabric had gotten lost in all the blood, our bloody hands still pressing down on her. She smiled, teeth coated in red. She strained to speak. "Help me live, I'll help. Device."

"I told her why we were looking for her," Nova said. "While taking away her pain."

I placed one of my hands on Bell's, uncertain whether she could feel it. "Please. How do we disable it?"

"Have to see."

The device was on the other side of the hold.

"You can't," I said. "It's too far. We can't move you. What if—"

She broke into another series of coughs, her whole body convulsing. The blood under our hands grew hotter.

"Slip!" I shouted. "We're losing her!"

"Wait." Nova held a hand up to me and Slip, shaking her head, eyes fixed on Bell's, Bell's fixed on hers.

Though only a few seconds passed, it felt like hours.

Peace melted across Bell's face as her eyes closed and her head rolled to the side, arms limp.

Nova released her and wiped her hands on her clothes, which did nothing to rid her of the blood. "She's gone."

"Shit! What do we do now!"

"I helped her cross over, but not before she told me what to do."

I grabbed Nova. "What? Tell me!"

Sadness filled her eyes. "It's what I've always known, Alana. Transliminal Solutions doesn't use technology. It's just energy. Baryonic manipulation that holds what they're calling 'programs' inside physical matter. But they're not programs, they're just . . . intention. Human intention. It's nothing different than what I do."

"I don't understand. What does that mean for the device?"

She sighed. "The only way you can get rid of it is to let it detonate."

"There has to be another way—"

She waved me off. "No, Alana. There's nothing else we can do. Don't you understand what I'm telling you? Transliminal Solutions. Birke. The othersiders. They're like spirit guides.

That's why we have to tell the crew about you running out of your medication. You need more of the Dexitek, not whatever they're offering."

I forced myself to look at her instead of fixating on Bell's blood-covered body. My mind raced between her words, trying to understand them. The othersiders were some sort of powerful spirit guides? I didn't understand.

The only thing I could muster was, "What did you say?"

"We have to find medicine for you. Steal it if we have to. You can't die, Alana."

"I'm not dying."

"Why do you say things like that when you know they're not true? Yes, you are!"

I laughed a little, trying to force some levity into the situation to get her to calm down. "Mind over matter, right? Isn't that what you're always going on about?"

"For spirit's sake! Stop joking!" Her eyes filled with tears. "We have to get you more medication. Screw the rest of them. I'm taking this vessel to a hospital."

"No!" I grabbed her. The movement sent shockwaves through the joints in my fingers, which were trying to cramp up again. "Don't you dare jeopardize this crew."

"I don't care about them!" Every word was sharp. "I care about *you*. I'm not letting their crusade to save Marre kill my own sister."

"Why should they feel differently than you?" I said, releasing her with a shove, probably a little too roughly. "Letting my well-being take precedence over everyone else would be the same thing. Besides, I don't see why you care so much when you lied to me. You could have helped me ages ago. You could've helped our aunt."

"Alana, listen to me. I didn't lie; I couldn't have helped you."

"Concealing information with the intent to deceive is the same thing."

I could tell she was trying to stay calm. "The only time I disclose my ability to relieve pain is when I'm helping a terminally ill client. What happened on Spin was a last resort; they would have arrested you otherwise. And you saw what happens when we manipulate the body! I can take away the pain, but it removes all capacity to function along with it. I don't agree with handing that out to just anyone."

"I'm your sister! Lai is your aunt. We're *family.*"

This time, she was the one who grabbed me and held on. "Yes, Alana. You're family. That's more than enough reason not to do it. I care too much about your humanity. I may not get all this engineering stuff but I know you look like the person you were meant to be when you're helping ships fly."

Her words stunned me. I felt like I was listening to a different version of my sister. "Where is this coming from? You always hated my work."

"I don't get you, and sometimes you embarrass me, but that doesn't mean I don't want you to be happy. How fulfilled would you be if you were pain-free but mindless, incapable of working? I can't take away your functionality; don't believe in doing that to people. Most guides don't, as a matter of fact, which is why the SAG keeps those abilities quiet and advises us to do the same. I especially won't do that to my own sister. I didn't tell you I could take away your physical suffering because I knew it would break your heart if you understood what the tradeoff would be. It's a horrible choice to have to make, Alana. Physical suffering and the ability to pursue your passion, or relief and mental chaos."

"But shouldn't that be my choice to make? You just made it for me by keeping it from me."

"What do you want me to do? Be sorry for not giving you the option of destroying what's left of your life? Well, I'm not sorry. You have the right to make choices for yourself, but so do I. I have the right to decide what I'm willing to do with my skills as a guide, and I'm not willing to do that to you."

My head hurt. I could barely think straight, let alone integrate all this new information about Nova and her abilities. I dug my knuckles into the back of my neck, trying to relieve some of the tension.

"You need your medication," she said again. "I'll *make* them get it to you if I have to."

"We don't have to raze the whole system just to get my prescription filled. I have something that gives me more time."

"This?" She reached into her own pocket and pulled out my Panacea sample.

"Give me that." I reached for it, and she put up no resistance when I snatched it away, crunching the wrapper. The small purple capsule looked more enticing than ever. At this point, dependency on the drug was the least of my concerns. "Doctor Shrike gave this to me. It can help me last until we get to the breach."

"Alana. You heard what I said about the othersiders' technology."

"Yeah, you said we have to blow a hole into the side of the *Tangled Axon*."

"You know that's not what I'm talking about here."

Her words echoed inside me: *They don't use technology. It's just energy. They're like spirit guides.*

She gestured at the Panacea sample in my hand. "Their technology is a lie."

"But this is medication—"

"It's not going to do anything more than what I did to you on Spin. I sensed that pill the minute I set foot on the *Tangled Axon*. I know exactly what it is, because we use something similar to help us become accustomed to energy manipulation during guide training, and to help us understand what it's like for our clients who want to experience temporary transcendence, like you did on Spin. It's very much what it's like to be led on a mystic journey. That pill is a contained unit of intention. Guide work. Very advanced work beyond anything I've seen on our side of the breach, but the result is basically the same."

"I don't understand . . . " I looked at the pill. This wasn't possible. I felt as if I'd been walking on a glass surface that had just broken beneath my feet, and I was falling. If this sample wasn't real medicine, neither was the treatment I'd been saving for. Transliminal wouldn't be able to help me or Lai. Nothing could.

"That pill isn't science, Alana. I knew it as soon as I sensed it in your pocket. That's why they refuse to talk about their technology. It's all an illusion."

I pinched the bridge of my nose, trying to push back the white spots. "That doesn't make sense. Transliminal prescribes medication all the time—"

"That so-called medication just warps your reality like I did, Alana. It shuts down the ego, alleviates pain, and stimulates serotonin production so that you don't notice you're suffering anymore. It doesn't cure anyone; it just makes illness and trauma more tolerable. If you'd taken the treatment—that one or anything else from Transliminal—you'd just wither away from Mel's Disorder without noticing."

My breathing became shallow. Denial crept up on me. What she was saying *couldn't* be true. "Then why don't we hear about it?" I said, grasping desperately at the lie I'd believed could save me.

"Don't you remember how you felt on Spin? Why would we hear about their lies if the end result is bliss? Why would you ever complain? You wouldn't even realize your illness had progressed until you lost consciousness. Why do you think I've refused contracts with anyone from our side of the breach who works for Transliminal Solutions? No one will prosecute them for their fraud because they don't want to lose the mindless joy Transliminal can provide. Not to mention they have some of our system's most powerful lobbyists passing legislation that makes it almost impossible to report on their activities. Even the SAG was silenced a long time ago. Why do you think no guides have said anything? I'm risking a lot just by telling you, but I have to."

"I don't understand," I said. "If the othersiders are like you . . . if they're basically spirit guides, for lack of a better name, then why does Birke need you?"

"I have no idea."

"Shit." I rested my arm on my knee, and my forehead on my arm. The panic had receded, leaving my limbs weak and shaking. I'd lost so much already, and now I'd lost hope as well. There I sat, with my disease digging its fingers into my flesh. "They're not going to be able to do anything to help me, are they?"

"We have to get your Dexitek filled. I'm taking you to a hospital."

"No," I said. "I'll tell the captain. They'll find a way to get my scrip."

"Alana!" Ovie shouted. Tev leaned against the wall. "She's asking for you."

I looked at Nova hard. She just gestured and sighed. "Go. I'll wait. But they'd better help you get your Dexitek, or I'm ending this and we're getting you to a medical facility."

"They'll help."

"We'll see."

I lingered for a moment longer, but she wouldn't look at me. She tore a clean piece of her dress away and placed it over Bell's face, then prayed.

I quickly crossed the cargo bay and knelt down next to Tev, collecting her hand into both of mine. She smiled, and though I could tell it was hard for her to muster the expression, it was sweet.

"Alana," she croaked. A thick bandage covered the left side of her neck, and blood had matted most of her hair.

"Does she need a transfusion?" I said to Slip as she returned to apply salve to a small wound on Ovie's arm. He smiled a little at me, wincing as she worked.

"No," Slip said. "I don't think so. It bled a lot but the debris only grazed her. We don't have the means to do a transfusion even if she needed one. She went into an acute stress reaction, but I think she's okay. I have a burn treatment patch on her. I was more worried about cardiac issues after getting hit with the plasma weapon but so far, she's doing well."

"She's also right here," Tev said, quietly. "How is the ship?"

Before anyone could respond, Tev shifted her weight and started to get up. Slip, Ovie, and I made various sounds of protest while I put my hands on her shoulders to keep her in place.

"You're staying here," Slip said.

"Marre." Tev winced as she tried to get comfortable against the metal bulkhead. "Report."

The pilot's young voice echoed through the hold. "We are currently fifty-six million kilometers away from Spin, in a geostationary orbit around Valen. No enforcers are currently detected."

"Engineering report?"

"Our port thruster needs repair," Marre said. "They used weapons I've never seen before. Maybe othersider tech. I've done what I can for now to stabilize our navigation system and we should be okay temporarily, but we need repairs to bring us back to full functionality. There's some minor damage to the starboard hull that requires attention."

"Good girl, *Axon*," Tev whispered, closing her eyes and resting her head against the bulkhead.

More tremors and a new wave of sickness crashed into me without warning. I pressed my palms against the floor to steady myself. Referred pain throbbed across the back of my head and into my temples, radiating out to just above my eyes.

"Alana." Tev did her best to relax and looked at me. "Are you okay? Your shoulder . . ."

"I'm fine—" I stopped and glanced back at Nova, who had climbed up onto one of the crates and stared straight at me. She would know if I lied.

"Actually, Tev . . . Captain." I reached into my pocket, where the empty Dexitek bottle was still safely tucked away, a false comfort. I withdrew it, took her hand, and gave it to her, wrapping her fingers around the pitiful plastic.

Her eyes flicked up to mine.

I bit my lip, not wanting to give her the litany of bad news that waited on my lips.

"I need help." I paused. "I'm out of medication."

She sighed. "I see."

"I'm sorry, Captain. I tried to hold out as long as I could."

"You should have said something sooner. What else?"

"What?"

"You looked at the ceiling when you said you're out of medication. We'll get you your pills one way or another, but there's something you're not telling me."

I looked at Nova, then at Bell's body, trying to figure out the best way to tell her that we'd have to inflict further damage on her ship by destroying the device. When I returned my attention to Tev, she was giving me a hard look, her will inviolable.

"What did Bell say to you before she died?"

"Captain, there aren't many options—"

"I just got shot in the neck. I'm not in the mood for obtuse answers."

Grabbing my locs and twisting them, I tossed them over my shoulder. I bit my lip, then sighed. "We have to detonate the device."

Chapter Thirteen

With Ovie's help, Slip had moved a protesting Tev away from the cargo bay and into the infirmary so I could get to work on the device. Ovie returned and stood at the top of the stairwell, supervising my work from a safe distance in the event that something went wrong. Marre remained on the bridge, maintaining an extra containment field around the cargo bay to prevent me and Nova from getting more intimately familiar with the Big Quiet than we were ready for. At least if we lost the cargo hold, we wouldn't have to lose everything in it.

"I still don't think you should be in here," I said to Nova, whose crossed arms indicated my arguments were futile.

"Don't you need to take the top of it off?" she said, waving a gold-wreathed hand in the general direction of the device, the blood on her clothes powerless to undermine her elegance. "Maybe you should worry about that instead of what I'm doing."

"What's gotten into you?" I crouched down and started unfastening the bolts holding the device's top panel to the body.

"You." She sat down in one smooth series of motions, folding her arms over her fabric-draped knees. "The fact that my baby sister isn't taking care of herself."

"Not now, Nova."

"You asked."

"My mistake."

She clucked her tongue and complained some more, but I couldn't listen to it. I knew better than she did my body was giving out on me. Staccato bursts of pain hammered at my temples while the muscles along my spine felt like twisted rope. Now wasn't the time to think about it, or about the fact that I'd been placing all my bets on a treatment that wasn't even real medicine.

I pulled the top panel off the device with a metallic scrape, then reached into the center of the glowing mass of strings and grabbed a nest of copper coils beneath it.

"Nova," I said, interrupting her speech about the importance of a stable income for securing proper medical care. "Go."

"What—"

"Ovie," I called out over my shoulder, barely able to see him from this angle. "Take my sister. It's time."

She started to get up, but hesitated. "That fast? Just like that? What if it—"

"Just go. There's time before it detonates. I'll be right behind you."

"Go straight to the infirmary," she said. "I'll be waiting for you there."

"Fine!" My arm ached from holding the position. "Just go, Nova! This hurts!"

One more moment of hesitation, and then she clanged up the stairs to join Ovie, who escorted her away. Before he disappeared, he nodded to me.

I almost yanked out the nest of wires, but first reached into my pocket with my free hand, drew out the Panacea sample from Dr. Shrike, and dropped it into the device.

"So much for magical solutions."

I tightened my fist around the wires, and with one quick, hard motion, I pulled, imagining I was breaking the leash the enforcers had on us.

Sparks flew from the center of the device. Bolts of electricity shot out and started destroying the remaining empty crates, searing the metal skin of the *Tangled Axon*. I shouted through her bone-shattering pain, feeling as if someone had thrown me into a meat grinder. The writhing mass of light grew twice, three times its original size, distorting the air around it like a heat shimmer as it rose above the object. Loud bangs and sizzles and crashes reverberated from the device, into the room, into me. The bigger the light grew, the more energy it released in bolts of power that split bulkheads. I didn't have the heart to look at Tev's room; it would be in the line of fire like everything else, burning like my body burned with the *Axon*'s pain. At least the two surviving plants were tucked safely in my quarters.

Hull plating warped in the growing heat. The smell of hot metal and scorched plastic stung my nose and eyes, blurring my vision. Already I was on my feet and running toward the stairs, skipping steps. One of the plasma arcs snaked out and struck the metal just behind me, warping the stairs in a flash. It felt like my left arm snapped in half. Metal groaned beneath me, dropped away. I shouted as I slipped with it, but held onto the railings with aching hands and lifted myself up to the next step, and the next, grunting with effort when my hips failed to cooperate. Hefting myself up onto the last step, I didn't bother taking a last look.

Good thing, too. Just as I turned the corner and ran for the infirmary, an explosion rocked the *Tangled Axon*, slamming me into the nearest bulkhead.

My head felt filled with pulsars, each one repetitively beaming electromagnetic radiation through my brain, until finally, I passed out right there in the corridor.

Head trauma, second-degree burns, and one third-degree burn to the leg that was too close to the plasma burst that had finally destroyed the cargo bay stairwell. Oh, and relentless throbbing in my hands, legs, and back.

My whole reality had narrowed to these sensations until I felt like that's all there was to life: pain and burns, and the chill of the regenerative goo that Slip applied to the burn sites every few hours. She also kept me supplied with intravenous anti-inflammatories and opioids that would help tide me over until we could get more Dexitek.

Mercifully, I spent most of the next few days unconscious.

When I woke up and felt half-lucid for the first time in half a week, it was to that weird plastic smell that permeated the infirmary. Not just plastic—charred plastic, like the cargo bay explosion was following me around the *Tangled Axon* just to make me feel bad.

Laughter, somewhere to my left. I turned my foggy head. It was Slip, laughing and patting Tev's leg, sharing some private joke. I couldn't make out their soft murmurs. I just saw Tev's mouth moving, and I noticed how her nose crinkled when she laughed, looking at Slip. It was the first time I'd seen her so unencumbered. Her face was sweet and, despite her injury, her laugh came from a deep place in her belly that I'd not heard until now. Yearning swelled in me.

You'd think with some serious injuries and a disease nipping at my heels I'd have more pressing matters to worry about than unrequited affections, but then you'd be wrong. I ruminated on it like a teenager, chastising myself for falling for someone unavailable. Easier than thinking about everything Nova had said, anyway.

The intimacy I'd felt on the observation deck, the tilt of her mouth toward mine in that club on Spin, the way she sometimes looked at me . . . none of it meant anything. Reading into small gestures would only drive me crazy. Raw jealousy and resentment boiled in me for the rest of the day, but I just imagined it was my feelings for Tev finally burning off like I'd hoped they would.

When Slip noticed my mood, I blamed it on the pain. At least it was half-true. Despite the drugs, a dull ache still radiated through my body and sleep barely took the edge off my fatigue. I knew some of what I was feeling were the echoes of the *Tangled Axon*'s own agony, her cargo bay shattered.

As badly as I needed my meds, I was starting to second-guess my decision to tell Tev about the Dexitek. Everyone knew just how bad I was hurting, now. They knew my body was breaking down by the minute. They knew I was useless. I didn't want Tev to look at me like an invalid, with pity in her eyes. Or worse, see me as a burden.

"Hey," Slip said, appearing at my side, immediately taking my vitals. Her stormcloud-hair and kind, broad smile warmed me in spite of everything. I tried sitting up, but quickly relented in favor of my pillow.

"Take it easy."

"How is she?" I said, careful to keep my voice down.

"Pretty pissed off about your sister keeping so much from everyone."

"What about her neck?"

"Tev will be fine. How do *you* feel?"

"Like ass."

She laughed. "Tev said something similar before I made her go to sleep last night."

Before I made her go to sleep last night. An off-hand comment, but indicative of their intimacy. If my feelings had gotten bad enough to crowd my mind like this, it really was time to push them to the side. Stop while I still could. Besides, the more I thought about her, the angrier I became. She had to have deliberately misled me. There was no way anyone would have believed her intentions with me on the observation deck had been entirely platonic, and I *knew* she had to have felt the tension between us on Spin. I remembered the way her breath caught when we were close enough to taste each other if we'd wanted. How could that be platonic?

I pretended to be asleep whenever Tev tried talking to me from across the room, determined to steep myself in bitterness for a while. As much as I longed for her, I didn't want to be in contact with her unless it was necessary. I did everything I could to nourish my frustration until I sat firmly in an emotional nadir of my own crafting.

By evening, I'd spent enough time torturing myself that I was grateful when Tev ordered everyone to the bridge to discuss our next move. Slip agreed that walking around the ship—albeit carefully—would be good for both of us.

Tev tried to rouse me.

"Alana." She shook my shoulder, but I kept my eyes closed and rolled over. "Hey, love. Walk with me."

I ignored her. I'm sure the whole thing was utterly ridiculous and transparent, considering she practically shoved me. I didn't care. I'd have pretended to be asleep for another hour if I had to. I knew I was being childish, but I couldn't stand the thought of walking down the corridor with her. Instead, I tried shocking my heart into submission with the truth, throwing it at myself like a splash of acid: *She doesn't feel the same way about you.*

After she gave up and left, I sat up and spent a few minutes steadying my body and mind, then made my disoriented way to the bridge. Slip was right—despite all the lingering pain, the instant I left the infirmary, I started feeling a little better. Stale starship air felt as good as fresh sky to this surgeon's lungs.

The crew was all hushed voices and solemn faces on the bridge, including Nova. When Tev saw me, she started to smile. I forced myself to demonstrate no emotion, determined not to give her the satisfaction of my unrequited affection. She gave me an inquisitive look that said, *"What's wrong?"* but I turned away and listened to what Ovie was saying, doing my best to keep my eyes from two people: the woman I didn't want to want, and the pilot whose forearm was currently nothing but bone below the honeycomb half-sleeve.

We still had to help Marre. Even if Transliminal couldn't do anything for me, maybe they could still do something for her. After all, whatever had happened to her had something to do with her SAG training. If the othersiders were nothing more than glorified spirit guides, they may be the very people she needed.

As soon as the thought flitted across my mind, Marre snapped her attention to me and a loud, swarming buzz swelled in my head. The buzzing briefly grew louder, then ceased in an instant. Honeyed scents surrounded me, replacing the torrent of noise, but no one else seemed to notice. She smiled, and turned back to her work.

" . . . two weeks," Ovie said as I finally looked away from Marre and focused.

"What's in two weeks?" I said, ignoring Tev's eyes burning into my skull. I sat down on the floor near Ovie, who patted my uninjured shoulder.

"That's how long Marre thinks she has before she destabilizes permanently. Maybe a little more, maybe a little less."

Tev placed a hand on her bandaged neck, wincing. "We need to get to the breach. Nova, are you going to help us, or not?"

"Only if you help my sister first."

"Marre is *dying*," Ovie growled, baring fangs. Just behind him, I saw the impression of raised hackles and a tail. Fleeting and insubstantial, like a shadow.

"Ovie," Marre said quietly, half her face a gruesome portrait of human anatomy. I watched each muscle around her mouth work as she spoke. "She's not our enemy."

"Contract or no, my loyalty is to my family," Nova said. "I think we should be discussing my sister's medical needs, or you'll lose the only leverage you think you have."

Nova straightened her spine. No one spoke. She held back the vitriol I could see simmering in her eyes, wrapped in a veil of grace and poise. Dangerous.

"We're taking care of it," Tev snapped. "I said we would, and we will."

"Oh really? And where exactly do you intend to obtain this medication?"

"We'll deal with the details after we secure your cooperation."

"No, Captain Helix. Once we have the medication, then we can talk about what I'll do to help you."

"No, we're talking about it now!" Tev slammed her hand against the navigation console, then winced again. "My ship is in desperate need of repair, my pilot is dying, my dealer is dead, and if you don't cooperate, all of it is meaningless. And Marre will die."

Nova shrugged one shoulder and looked around, as if the notion didn't bother her. I knew it did. "I'm not working with Transliminal until after we've gotten Alana's medication. No Dexitek, no deal."

"Get over yourself and help us," Tev said, then turned to me. "Alana, a little help, here!"

"We have to repair the ship," Ovie said, pacing. A tail and hackles flickered in and out of existence behind him. Canine ears shadowed his head, and one of them was turned toward our conversation, twitching. "We won't make it through the breach in this condition. Not even if we're towed."

"Ah." Nova folded her arms and smiled. "Well, I see a perfect opportunity, then. We'll obtain the necessary parts to repair this ship at the same time we secure Dexitek for my baby sister. Valen has plenty of colonies that can provide both."

"Between fuel and food—even if we cut rations—we just don't have the money." Tev talked more vigorously with her hands the more frustrated she became. "Marre and I have gone over the numbers and we're hurting as it is with the Quicks taking up additional resources. We just can't afford it. And we're already making a stop to barter for medication. There's no way we can afford supplies."

"We wouldn't be here if it weren't for *the Quicks*," I said, not bothering to conceal my anger as I stood and challenged her with as much dignity as I could muster. Probably a poor job with my increasingly crippled muscles contracting in pain, but it was the best I could do.

"That's right," Tev said. "We wouldn't be here in this shit situation, half my crew shredded and my ship limping along through the black."

"And my family wouldn't be dead if you hadn't been at Ouyang Outpost. You'd be nowhere without my sister, and without me that tracking device would still be stuck to the side of the *Axon*. You'd have nothing."

Tev took in a sharp breath and set her jaw.

"Okay," Slip said, stepping between us, holding her hands out to either side. She addressed Tev in particular. "Don't say things you can't take back."

"A little late for that," Nova said.

"You're the one pushing so hard for Alana's medication," Tev said. "Maybe you want to do a little spirit guide magic and help us get the supplies? Disguise us or something? Keep them from detecting us?"

Nova sighed. "Disguising you on Spin was different; at least there, you're expected to be intoxicated. Doing that on Valen would make it tremendously difficult for you to concentrate well enough to break into a medical facility and escape."

"Just make it hard for them to detect us."

"It's not that simple. Preventing one person from detecting you, sure. One person's mind can be clouded easily enough. But manipulating the perceptions of an entire facility so they fail to notice you? I can't do that, not even if I had your pilot's help. Not to mention the security systems I'd have to undermine. I'm just one spirit guide."

"So come with us and do whatever you can. It might not be perfect, but it'll help."

"I'm not breaking the law when I know they'll detect us. It's one thing to help you evade the enforcers when they want to arrest you for a genocide you didn't commit. It's another matter to throw my entire career away just to give you a false sense of security. It's not a matter of whether I would fail to conceal you adequately—I would. I know this." She sighed again. "I'm tired of defending myself here. I would happily pay to obtain the Dexitek legally if I could do so without giving away our presence, but all I have are my own credits; they'd trace them immediately. I'll do my part when we contact Birke—remember, you're not even paying me properly for any of this. You're the ones who need to help Alana."

"You're selfish." Slip looked at my sister, disgust dripping from every word. "Don't you have something to knit? Some client's vibrations you need to raise? Money you need to vibrate out of someone's pocket?"

"Enough," Tev said. She sounded weary.

No matter how badly Tev had played me, I still believed in what she was trying to accomplish. My woes weren't Marre's fault; emotions would have to wait. I took a deep breath and refocused. "I know we can't afford to repair the ship *and* get my meds. That's why we have to steal them."

Slip snapped her head toward me with an incredulous look, saw I was serious, and threw her hands up while pacing away from us. "You're crazy. We'll be arrested the second we set foot in a distribution center."

"Right," I said. "That's why we're not going to steal from a manufacturer."

Shadowed by his dark canine ghost, Ovie grunted. "Shit."

I nodded. "We have to find a repair lot. We have to steal from someone who wouldn't have the resources to come after us. And we'll just have to haul ass to make sure we can cross the breach in time to save Marre."

"Tev," Slip said. "I hate to be the cynic here, but how can we be sure Birke's not going to throw us back through the breach once she has Nova? Nothing says she'll adhere to any agreement she makes with us. How can we be sure she'll help Marre?"

"She has a point," Nova said.

"I had a lot of time to think today," I said, looking directly up at Nova from my hunched-over position, nervous. Stiffness crept into my hands. I folded them, not wanting the others to see them shake and interpret it as a lack of confidence. "I have an idea, but I don't know if you'll like it."

She raised her eyebrows at me. "Oh?"

I took a deep breath and refused to look at anyone, certain that if I did, I'd no longer have the nerve to speak. "When the time comes to bring Nova to Birke, my sister will transform me just like she did on Spin, only this time, Nova will make me look like herself. I'll take Nova's place when we go to meet Birke, and if Marre and Nova help disguise our intentions, Birke shouldn't be able to detect the lie. That might buy us a chance to bargain for a cure for Marre. If we keep the real Nova hidden, Birke won't be able to kidnap her or something and send us away. She'll have to help Marre if she wants access to the real Nova."

"Absolutely not," Nova said. "I'm not letting you risk yourself like this."

"We need to do *something* and like Slip said, we can't just send you to her when we don't know what she'll do. Does anyone have a better idea?"

"I like it."

My breath caught. Marre stood near her pilot seat, feet skinless and red, eyes full of electricity that sparked and sizzled in haloes around her head. I had to be hallucinating from Mel's or the drugs Slip had given me or both. Marre stepped closer to us. Buzzing erupted in my mind, an entire swarm of sounds. "I want to do it."

Tev rubbed her forehead. "Marre, if we do this Alana is risking—"

"I think she can succeed." Marre smiled. "I want to do it."

She walked up to me, took my hand into her cold one, and placed it onto her heart. Translucence rippled out from my palm, exposing her ribs in a shimmer. The ship's hum collided with the buzzing in my head, creating a dissonant sound; I felt like my blood ignited in explosions down my arm. Ripping sensations shot through my hand, like nothing I had ever felt. Energy pulsed through my limbs, my neck, my head.

As quickly as they had begun, the sensations ebbed away.

Slowly, my eyes refocused and took in a changed crew: An enormous black wolf, all solid muscle over a thick frame, still wearing Ovie's necklace. Slip's physical appearance remained the same, but fresh-faced and free of all that exhaustion she wore like a shroud. Her arms wrapped around wolf-Ovie, fingers entwined in his fur. Tev had become a young girl with a light dusting of freckles across her sun-kissed cheeks, eyes unburdened. I could smell the outdoors on her even from where I stood, all dust and—yes, rosemary, even as a child. Marre was just . . . gone. Above them all, an electric storm raged along the ceiling of the bridge, in and out of the walls, into the control panels. I was completely pain free but my mind maintained its integrity—it was a kind of freedom I'd never known. Only Nova seemed the same, although there was an aura around her bright enough to blind.

"You see it, don't you?" Nova said, moving toward me while the rest of them remained frozen in place mid-conversation, a moment out of time. Something worked inside me, twining together connections, ideas, *feelings* I couldn't name, but it was too nebulous to grasp.

"What am I looking at?" Both our voices echoed; I heard them within me and without, at once.

"Who they really are."

"What do you mean?"

"It's the ship's song, Alana. You've felt it, I know you have. The *Tangled Axon* changes you when you live inside her. Can't you sense it? Can't you feel yourself beginning to see people as they truly are? The ship is lending you her eyes."

"I don't understand . . . "

"You'll see." My sister smiled and clapped her hands in

front of my face once. The sound rang through me like a plasma bolt, breaking the spell. Instantly, the crew returned to normal, resuming their conversation as if nothing had happened, as if Marre had never approached me, as if they had remained as I'd seen them all along. All human, all present, all fully-grown. Part of me registered their words as they laid out our plan to take a shuttle down to Valen. I heard them discuss which medical facility to infiltrate for the Dexitek, which family-owned repair lot to target for spare parts to repair the *Tangled Axon*'s thrusters and cargo hold.

I grasped at delicate strands of understanding and failed, falling over the edge into an uncanny valley where I couldn't trust my own eyes. That frozen image of the crew haunted me, seared into my brain. What were Nova and Marre trying to say to me? Was I losing my mind?

My sister's voice still echoed through me, resonating with the part of me that knew things my conscious mind didn't.

The ship is lending you her eyes.

Chapter Fourteen

The next day, I was on a shuttle on my way to Valen's surface along with Tev, Ovie, and Slip. Concerned I'd overexert myself, Slip tried insisting I stay behind, but I had to get off the ship. As much as I loved being on the *Tangled Axon*, I needed to clear my mind more than I needed rest. I'd deal with the pain, with my cramping limbs and fingers, with the incandescent migraines.

Moving around would be better than picking at the strange images still kicking around in my head, or worse—letting grief or self-pity seep in. Maybe focusing on ship doctoring would set my mind straight about Tev and keep memories of Adul far away from my conscious thoughts.

The only problem was, how could I bring myself to steal from people who may as well have been me and Lai? I tried reminding myself that we were committing the lesser of two evils. We'd take from this family because we had no choice but to fly as far under the radar as possible. The *Tangled Axon* desperately needed repairs, and Marre's life depended on us getting to the breach in one piece. I tried not to think about the financial hit this family would be forced to endure. I tried not to imagine them closing shop and being forced to take whatever low-paying, eighty-hour-a-week job they could find. Or chew the scraps of part-time work, unable to make ends meet.

The shuttle banked and I held on, trying not to lean into

Tev, though my locs hit her in the arm. Couldn't help it if I had big hair. To make things worse, I felt Slip staring at me from across the small shuttle.

Could she tell how I felt about Tev?

I looked out the window to distract myself. A scrap-strewn shipyard loomed larger as we circled the lot. It could have been any yard on the Heliodoran fringe. Could have been ours. Looking at this repair lot, I couldn't keep my aunt from nudging her way into the forefront of my mind. I didn't even want to consider the possibility she'd been taken into custody. Barring that, was she keeping it together? With such a heinous crime pinned to our family name, I had no doubt she'd have run out of work by now, even if system enforcers hadn't detained her for questioning. If she'd gone out of business, was she making enough with her job at the call center to survive? Would she be able to afford her Dexitek refills?

We might be doing the very same thing to the family who owned this repair lot. Maybe they'd file a theft report with the enforcers, but who would investigate it? Fringe crime was expected. They'd do a few cursory sweeps of the property out of obligation and then declare it unsolved.

Could I do this? Could I really steal from my own kind, from people just like me and Lai?

"Alana?" Ovie was halfway out the door. I hadn't even noticed we landed, I'd been so lost in my thoughts. Tev and Slip were already gone, headed toward the medical facility around the corner. "You coming?"

I draped a large canvas bag across my body and hopped out, kicking up a cloud of dust.

Even on different planets, the shops were always the same. Dirt-caked and thick with grease. It smelled like home.

"You know what we're looking for?" I asked. The loss of my implant was hitting me harder than ever. Accessing ship schematics via neural interface would have been so much simpler.

He tapped his head, shifting his weight to adjust his own bag. "Got 'em memorized, just like you. One hour, no longer."

I nodded, and we headed in opposite directions through the shadows, through the aisles of parts, scavenged ships, and abandoned engines. I was almost distracted by a few extra fuel cell locks, but I knew we couldn't spare the weight or the space on the shuttle. It would just be nice to have some backups.

Truth was, it actually felt damned good just being in a yard again. I had to control myself or Slip was right—I'd overexert my body with the excitement and strain. Shopping for things I could make use of on the *Tangled Axon*, however remote the need, made me feel a little like a kid, which just made me feel guiltier. *I shouldn't be excited about stealing from these folks.*

Piles of waveguide filaments, loss cones, radiation filters, reflectors, magnetic mirrors, and miscellaneous battered, rusted engine parts formed small mountains between old cockpit seats and empty shuttle skins. Piece by piece, I plucked through the shipyard bones to find what was necessary for our repairs, keeping an eye out for random useful objects, getting my hands dirty. Felt good to be elbow-deep in a repair lot again—

A noise.

What was it? I hid and steadied my breath, cradling several parts in my arms. Sharp metal edges cut into my skin, but I kept quiet, not wanting to drop anything and give myself away. I listened.

Another noise. But it didn't sound like it was moving any closer. No footsteps. Just a quiet rattling of metal and . . . a voice? A little girl's voice. Babbling occasionally, quietly. Melodic.

I peeked around the corner, careful not to fall under any yard lights.

I was right. It was a little girl—eight, maybe nine years old. Hunched over a pile of parts and oh . . . my heart ached at the sight. Her hair fell across her shoulders in tiny braids, the symbol of an aspiring sky surgeon, an engineer-to-be.

She worked on a miniature Red Niv III. Memories of my

own tiny Series II Greenbelt flooded in: the sweat on my lips as I baked in the sun, watching the baby vessel become a dot in the sky.

I hurt for this child. Things were already looking grim for sky surgeons when I was a kid, but this girl barely stood a chance. It would be so much easier for her if she wanted to be a spirit guide or a net media consultant. Maybe I should have wanted that for her as I stood there, watching her from the shadows. Maybe I should have intercepted her before she made the same choices I did, before she fell so desperately in love with engines and flight that she'd sacrifice financial security just to get a taste of it. Before she fell in love with a starship captain who loved her medical officer instead.

Ultimately, I couldn't warn her away. She deserved the chance to make her choices, to carve out whatever life she wanted, even if it meant that life was threaded with struggle. I didn't realize I was walking until I was already halfway to her, cradling part of a magnetic mirror in my arms. Gravel popped beneath my boots.

The child's head whipped around.

"Hey!" She stood. "Who are you?"

"Shh!" I tilted my chin at her project. "What are you working on?"

"That's our stuff!" Her voice echoed through the lot as she pointed at me.

"Oh. Here." I handed her the part; I still had some of what we needed in my bag. "What are you working on?"

She took it, but I could tell she still debated calling out for someone. "Nothing."

"Oh, I don't know about that." I crouched down, knees popping, and pointed to the ship's small engine. I kept my voice low to encourage her to do the same. "That looks like a Lifeliner engine to me, so that couldn't be anything other than a Red Niv III. Red-Net retired those 'liners when they debuted the Niv IV."

Her eyes darted over my locs, and they widened in a moment of excitement before she forced a layer of nonchalance over it. "Are you a sky surgeon?"

"Mm-hmm. And you are too, I see."

She shrugged and sat back down, crossing her legs, knees embedded with gravel and dirt. "I want to be."

"Then you will."

"I don't know. Mom says it's not smart."

"With all due respect to your mother, that just isn't true." I gestured at her ship. "It takes quite a bit of intelligence to put together something like that."

"No, I mean . . . you know." She shrugged again to give herself an extra beat to think. "They want me to do something else. Go to college."

"They have degrees for folks like us. You can apprentice, too."

She lighted up. "That's what I want to do!" Her voice echoed, and I resisted the urge to check to see whether she was grabbing anyone's attention. I didn't want her to pick up on my anxiety. "I want to do that when I'm done with school. It would be a lot more fun than classes." She wrinkled her nose. "And I'm definitely not working in an office. Bo-ring."

I laughed. "I agree. That's what I did, you know. Apprentice." I leaned closer, ignoring the throbbing in my muscles and the bright flash of pain cascading through my head, hands, feet. "And you know what I do now?"

"What?" she whispered, then bit her lip and leaned in conspiratorially, as if my answer would determine the outcome of her own life.

I matched her quiet tone. "I'm not just a sky surgeon. I'm a sky surgeon *on a starship.*"

"Really?" She actually clapped a few times, she was so excited. Again I resisted the urge to glance around and make sure no one was coming. "I thought there weren't flying jobs anymore! That's what Mom says. She says they should drop the 'sky surgeon' part and just call you engineers."

"There's still room for us if you look in the right places. Someone has to make sure all those ships are healthy." I took a risk by touching her back, but still kept a respectful distance. "I won't lie. It's not easy when people tell you your dream is a bad idea. I heard it when I was your age too. But if this is what you really want, then don't ever, ever give up. We need you. All of us need you. If you love this—" I gestured to the Niv. "—then don't give up. Those ships want you to do your best. They can't fly without you."

A creaking sound came from somewhere far behind me as a door opened.

"Toren?" came a voice from the shop. "Who are you talking to? Who's there?"

I couldn't keep the fear from my face. I looked at the little girl and barely shook my head, discreetly putting a finger to my lips. I held her eyes. She tilted her head in confusion and said nothing, only stared.

"Please," I whispered.

Her eyes flicked to my bag, then back to me, and to the woman who called for her. I think she began to understand her new friend from the stars was probably in some kind of trouble, but would she suspect more?

I held my breath while the girl decided my fate. The pain increased the longer I maintained my position.

"Hang on, Mom! The lady just got lost!"

"Let me talk to her," the woman said, closer now. She wore jeans and a loose work polo, wiping her hands on a cloth.

Anxiety pinched at the migraine raging in my temples, shattering it into jagged shards of glass. Putting up a front was so much harder when half my attention was stolen by Mel's. I could try running and immediately give myself away, or I could talk my way out of this. That was Nova's skill, not mine, but with the girl's mother right in front of me, expectant eyes scanning me for any hint of deception, I knew it was the only viable option. Couldn't blame her, anyway. I'd be suspicious too.

I didn't even have time to breathe and collect myself, calm my nerves, soothe my angry body. Time to perform.

"Hi," I said, standing and brushing the dirt from my shirt. I hoped my hands wouldn't betray me by shaking. "Sorry to bother you so late at night. Your daughter was just giving me directions."

"Where to, hon? What got you lost in an old lot like this?" She glanced at my hair, then my bag. "You looking for parts?"

"Oh." I shifted my bag on my shoulder and winced at another stone-solid knot forming in my neck. How much time had passed since Ovie and I parted ways? Was he waiting for me by now? Were Slip and Tev okay? "No, I just . . . I knew I could turn to a family like this for directions. You know how people can be these days. So hard to trust strangers in unfamiliar cities, not until we've got ties. No kin here on Valen. I'm from Orpim. Heliodor. But I trust other folks who work with ship parts."

I smiled, as if there could be no question of our implicit connection.

The girl grabbed her mother's hand and tugged. "Momma. She flies on a starship."

The woman searched my face for a long time, but must have liked what she found there—her uncertainty eventually melted into a smile. "Well, of course, sweetheart. Come on inside and we'll set you up with a glass of water and I'll give you directions to wherever you need to go. Lived here for thirty years now; there's nothing in this city I don't know about."

"Oh that won't be necessary—thank you, really, I just . . . I have to get going—"

"Mirla?" a male voice called from the house. "Who's there?"

"We've got ourselves someone fresh from the Big Quiet!" She turned to the man and gestured for him to join us, as if I were an old friend of the family. Their kindness hurt my heart.

"Lights alive. We don't get a lot of business these—" The smile that had started to bloom on his face died the moment he stepped close enough to get a good look at my face.

Shit.

"Mirla, Toren, you two get inside." His voice shook. "Right now."

The girl's mother looked genuinely confused. "What are you talking about—"

"This is that Quick woman. She's one of the terrorists what massacred Adul."

Mirla cried out and grabbed Toren, dragging her toward the building. I heard the girl protesting, shouting something about flying, while the man lunged for me. I dodged him at the last second and wasted no time: I broke into a run, heavy bag pummeling my lower back. My legs hurt from crouching to talk to the girl and the muscles in my neck had twisted into a mess of pain and stiffness. One wrong step and I'd tumble; who knows if I'd be able to get up again. The migraine split open my head, strobes of light flashing in front of me with every footfall, but I had to push on, to make it to the shuttle. I'd collapse then if I could, but I had to make it. Had to get these parts to the crew.

"Hello?" the man shouted while he chased me, but I could tell from the tone of his voice he wasn't talking to me. He was shouting to be heard over his own panting, the thunder of his boots. "I've seen the terrorists! They're at my coordinates right now!"

By talking to the child, I'd condemned us all.

"Ovie!" I shouted. He was rounding the corner at a bolt, the black shadow-wolf echoing his body's movements as he struggled with his now-heavy bag. He must have heard the commotion. Barely giving me a glance, he threw himself into the shuttle and started the engine. I was running so hard my legs seemed to split apart and erupt into flames. If this man stopped me, that was it. I'd be done. If the *Tangled Axon* left me behind, I was fucked. If they stayed to help, we all were.

"Wait!" the man shouted entirely too close for comfort, and before I could get my bearings I was on the ground with a mouth full of dirt and indescribable, blinding pain in my neck and head, lights flashing, and everything was spinning, spinning, spinning.

Until the ground slammed into me and the spinning stopped. It took me a second to realize the man had caught up to me, knocked me over, and pinned me down. My head. Pain. My head, my head, my head. And my ribs. There were knives in my ribs. No air. The shuttle was *right there*. I could see its hull. Could almost touch it.

A low growl emanated from somewhere behind me. The weight lifted from my body, but now it was hard to breathe. I tried turning my head to look, but even that was too difficult. Unwelcome whiteness clouded my vision; it happened too often these days.

The man from the repair lot screamed under Ovie's barks and vicious snarls. His voice eventually tore in half, and he was quiet.

No stabbing in my ribs. No pain in my head.

Just sleep.

Chapter Fifteen

Opening my eyes was a mistake. Light instantly blinded me and the pain in my back and neck returned, accompanied by that familiar stabbing in the side of my head. Every time I took a breath, the pain was so intense it shouldn't have been possible to be both conscious and in that much agony. Yet somehow, there I was. And, oh joy, there was that charred plastic smell I loved so much. Must be in the infirmary.

"Heeeey," Slip drawled lovingly, appearing above me. She was little more than a blurred shadow with dark hair, so I tried to sit up, but my body had other ideas. I shouted and grabbed my throbbing side, but that movement hurt just as badly, so I collapsed again, which just made me dizzy. Definitely not my best day.

"Take it easy," she said. "He beat you up and you've got two broken ribs, but it could've been worse. You need to stop spending so much time in my bed."

"What?" As soon as the hoarse word was out of my mouth, I remembered. The shipyard. The little girl. Her father, chasing me. Ovie in the shuttle. The ground. The screaming.

"When did you get back?" I said. "The shuttle . . . "

"Tev used the hospital comm system to contact Marre when you two didn't show. Nova picked us up in the second shuttle."

Ovie had to have told them what I'd done, how I'd gotten distracted and ruined everything, how I'd forced him to do whatever it was he'd done to the man who had broken my ribs. I'd brought the enforcers down on us again. Wait, *were* the enforcers after us? I wanted to ask but somehow I couldn't get my mouth to work.

"Here." Slip tilted my head up, forcing me to endure the pain when I winced and cried out. There was a glass of water at my lips, and I was soon drinking, gulping, soaking the sheet over my chest.

"You've been out for a while," she said. "These painkillers are brutal."

"Dexitek?" I managed.

She winked. "Should be pumping through your body as we speak."

I grabbed her hand. "Thank you."

"Don't thank me, thank Tev. She's the one who held off security when they figured out we weren't the doctors we claimed to be. Girlfriend is vicious with those plasma channel weapons. She stole one from the chief security officer at the medical facility and stunned half their force when we fought our way out. Of course now we look exactly like the criminals they think we are, so maybe she should've taken a more judicious route. You too, clearly." She laughed and shook her head. "You're crazy, girl."

I finished my glass of water and wiped my mouth. "I didn't mean to."

She smirked. "Yeah, I don't think many people mean to get their ass beat."

"No, I mean I didn't mean to—"

Footsteps near the infirmary doorway.

"You're awake."

Tev. My heart jumped as fear trickled in. She'd kick me off the crew for my foolishness, to say nothing of what her opinion of me would be now. Not that it mattered much anymore. Between this and my earlier stunt with the device, I'd proven my irresponsibility several times over.

Doused as I was in all that shame, Tev was the last person I wanted to see right now. I turned my head to look at Slip, wincing against the pain, but she just smiled and excused herself. I heard the door slide shut behind her, and then Tev's footsteps drawing closer, leg clicking.

My mind raced as I tried to formulate a way to apologize that would make any difference, but I couldn't think of how to atone for being so careless, for screwing up the only chance we had to secure the parts to repair the *Tangled Axon*. Even with my own body throbbing in pain, I could still feel her broken, beaten hull, her damaged thrusters. Now what would we do? Every shop in the system would be on high alert, waiting for the chance to turn us in if we showed our faces.

Tev stood next to the bed. Instead of berating me, she turned my hand over and held it with both of hers, lightly rubbing a thumb over my exposed wrist. Her expression was soft, and that gorgeous golden hair fell around her, harsh infirmary light filtering through it like the sun.

"Ovie told me what you did."

I swallowed. Her words sounded tinny through my haze of pain and drugs. "Oh."

"Thanks."

"You're not angry?"

Confusion flashed across her face. "For what?"

"The girl—" I couldn't meet her eyes. "The enforcers. The man. He called the enforcers, and—"

"Not your fault. We knew the risks, and I had my own small army coming after me." She laughed, and her metal necklace caught the light, glinting. I loved the way the blue stripe through the center of the rings looked against the aluminum and her white skin. She was beautiful, especially now.

Damn it.

"I'm just glad we made it out," she said. "We're okay for now."

"Did we get the parts?"

"Not all of them. Ovie's been reviewing what we have to see if we can still manage the repairs. He probably needs your help, but—"

I struggled against the pain and sat up. "How is Marre? Is she holding on?"

"Whoa there, lady!" Tev placed her hand on my chest and gently pushed me back down. I resisted at first.

"I need to help Ovie and see Marre."

"You need to recover. You're no good to me all broken in half like this."

I couldn't help laughing a little sarcastically. "No good to you, huh?"

"That's right. I need both my engineers in one piece."

My engineers. Tears threatened to well up in my eyes but I held them back. I just nodded and smiled, but I could tell she saw my attempt to keep myself under control.

"Did I say something wrong?"

"No!" I laughed a little. "Absolutely not. I just never thought I'd make it here. To being someone's engineer. And until you said that just now, I hadn't realized how badly I needed to hear something good."

"You never thought you'd be someone's engineer? I find that a little hard to believe coming from someone who tucked herself inside a crate in my cargo bay."

My face grew hot, but luckily I didn't blush easily. I wonder whether she knew it was Slip who'd encouraged me to stow away. "I guess I always thought my dreams were a little foolish."

"Then so are mine."

I shook my head and looked at her no matter how much it twisted my heart. "Tev."

"You don't have to think that way any more. You're part of my crew."

I closed my eyes and fought more tears. My heart bled out before her and there was nothing I could do to mend it. "You don't understand. Good daughters are the ones who grow up to achieve something respectable. Good daughters don't grow up to be sky surgeons. Good daughters go to universities and pinch at their souls until they become spirit guides. They don't skip classes to work in their aunt's repair shop. They don't fail out of school because their fingers are too slippery with grease to tap out the answers to an exam."

I fell quiet, thinking of my family, of how Lai spent all that time with me while my parents were on the research station and Nova was away at guild training. Lai, who gave me a chance to do something with my passion for science and engineering. I never heard the end of it from Nova, who assured me that good, respectable daughters didn't come home smelling like ozone and metal. Good daughters embodied wisdom, trailing their hands over the hunched backs of the hungry masses, promising them a better life through prayer and manifestation. They guided souls through mystic journeys, beckoning them toward enlightenment with delicate fingers, bones like spun sugar.

Good daughters certainly didn't take on blue-collar jobs tinkering with plasma coils, and they didn't live on the dust-covered fringe of Heliodor. Good daughters bathed in coils of incense and lived in albacite-lacquered high-rise buildings.

Maybe these experiences had changed all that. Maybe Nova saw me for who I was, now. Instead of who I wasn't.

"What you've achieved means something," Tev finally said after a prolonged silence. "It means something to me, anyway. Look at what you've done for us."

"Caused a fire in your cargo bay before destroying it? Or almost getting us arrested? Or do you mean that I stole from a poor family just so we could take a stab at repairing all the damage I've caused—"

"Stop it." She didn't meet my eyes. "Alana, you were right about what you said before, on the bridge. If it weren't for you we wouldn't have Nova, we wouldn't have gotten that device off the hull, and you didn't destroy my cargo bay even if you're the one who detonated the device. If you hadn't done it, Ovie would have; we had no other choice. You're the one who's convinced Nova to cooperate for Marre. We'd be lost if it weren't for you. That's the thing about a crew: it doesn't work without all its parts."

Again a lump grew in my throat that I had to choke back before speaking. "You know, at age three, Nova could already project her consciousness two streets over, where her aetheric body had tea with one of our elderly neighbors and her cockatoo. She'd said Nova's presence manifested as 'the loveliest shade of lavender.'" I huffed a laugh at the memory. "The most I did as a child was wreck half my street with one of my experiments. By the time Nova was twenty, she was coaxing entire colonies into giving up gluten and meditating for the poor. I never understood how meditating would help bring food and medicine to the lower classes, but don't tell her I said that."

"Have you ever thought that making your own life about Nova might be taking something away from yourself?"

I clenched my jaw. She was right, but I couldn't talk about the real reason I had such a hard time with Nova. I couldn't talk about all the privilege she so ignorantly possessed, and how much I hated how flippantly she threw that away when she talked about wanting to vacate her body. She'd won the genetic lottery, and I hadn't, yet she was the one who squandered that health by starving herself. She was born healthy, I was born sick, and that was the end of it. Not that I'd have given her my Mel's Disorder if I could have, no matter what her faith entailed.

"You are my engineer," Tev said, her warm hand still firm on mine. "You've found a second family here."

I laughed sarcastically. "You sure you want a family member like me? I seem to cause a lot of problems—"

"I wouldn't take back the moment we met for anything."

Before I could respond, she leaned over, pressing her warm mouth against mine, shocking me into silence. Even in my drugged state, I felt desire rising in me as she pressed her palm against mine and entwined our fingers, her mouth hot and full of sweetness, as if she'd been sucking on candy. She tasted as wonderful as I had imagined.

Slip's face kept creeping into my mind, her kind voice echoing over and over again. But my passion for Tev collided with the parts of me that protested, overriding them, desperate for this small moment of release. I slipped a hand beneath her shirt and slid it along the curve of her waist, pulling her to me. She felt good, so good I didn't care how badly my ribs hurt. Even that pain was sweet under the weight of her.

She resisted and pulled back, biting her lip. She shook her head with a small grin and ran a hand through her hair. "I have to stop or you'll never heal."

"I don't mind."

She laughed. "I'm sure. Alana, about Slip—"

I reached up and entangled my fingers in the hair at the back of her neck, pulling her down onto me, kissing her deeply. It was wrong of me, but I didn't want to know. Not yet. I just wanted this moment. I could hear the *Tangled Axon* between us, charging every touch, humming and singing in the space between molecules, between atoms, between electrons and quarks. She sang with us as our need for each other spun out and in, deep and abiding. The pain from the pressure of Tev's body was excruciating, but when the sharp stabbing sensation throbbed in my chest with each pulse of my blood, tingling beneath the *Tangled Axon*'s hum, it only ignited me further. There was no way a partnered woman would kiss me like this, not someone as honor-bound and loyal as Tev. Maybe she'd been about to tell me she and Slip weren't together anymore.

I knew it was an empty justification. I couldn't bring myself to care.

Again she pulled away, this time gently extracting herself

from my grasp. "We have to wait," she breathed, flushed with desire. "I'd be angry at myself if I hurt you, and I need to talk to Ovie and Marre about the repairs. We don't have a lot of time."

"Tev." I kept my hand on hers. I thought of the plants I'd rescued from her charred room. "I need to give you something. It's in my quarters."

"Later." She squeezed my hand and started to get up, but then paused, leaned over and kissed my cheek, letting her lips linger before pulling away. I wanted to grab her and pull her down onto me, ribs be damned.

"Thank you for your devotion to this ship," she said.

I needed to ask about Slip. My brain circled in on itself, debating over what was right and what was easy. Instead, I said, "I'm really sorry about the man on Valen—"

"It's not your fault. The guy would have gotten us arrested if you hadn't stopped him. We'd be halfway to a penal colony by now. Ovie said the damage looked awful, but he took care of it. The shuttle's fine. I'm just glad you two could make it back."

The shuttle? What was she talking about?

"Focus on feeling better," she said. "We have just under two weeks until we get to the breach, and we're cutting it close. Marre calculates we'll be there with half a day to spare before she really starts struggling to hang onto herself." She ran her thumb over my palm. "Get some rest. We'll talk later, I promise."

On her way out, I heard her speak to someone. I couldn't hear what he said in response, but I could tell from the voice it was Ovie. They laughed, then I heard their footsteps heading in opposite directions—hers down the corridor, his toward me.

He folded the bedside chair out from the wall and sat, resting his elbows on his knees, surgeon locs draping over his shoulders. That wolfish face gave me an appraising stare. I felt diminished in his presence. Exposed.

Before he could speak, I asked, "What did you tell her about Valen?"

"I told her what happened."

I stared at him, but he didn't blink. "And what happened?"

He opened his hands as if to say the answer was self-evident, then leaned back in his chair. "You tackled the owner of that shop when you caught him sabotaging the shuttle. Banging it up, messing with the engine. Then I defended you when he started banging on your head instead."

"Why?" I whispered. "Why would you cover for me? I was stupid, and—"

"Yeah." He leaned forward again. A beat later, his wolf-shadow leaned with him. "You were stupid. But just like you were that kid once, I was *you* once. I've been in those Heliodor streets, collecting old parts for metal or money. I lived on the fringe. I've stared down the barrel of going back there after getting a taste of the Big Quiet."

"But that's not why you helped me."

He smiled, fangs and all. "No."

I rubbed the spot on my wrist where Tev had touched me, but I said nothing.

"Tev deserves to be happy," he said. "She doesn't need to know about you talking to that girl. She's had a hard time of it, with Marre's condition. You having a moment of weakness shouldn't get in the way of what she's found in you."

"And what's that?"

"Potential, I think." He scratched behind his ear, locs bouncing over his hand as he looked thoughtfully to the side. "For a fresh perspective in this family. For new life. Everything's been all fighting to stay somewhere, fighting to keep something, fighting to withstand some pressure. She deserves to have something worth adding to her life instead of just struggling not to lose everything."

"Ovie? That man . . . "

"He'll be okay. I just scared him and knocked him out."

I exhaled. "Good."

I wanted to ask him about Slip and Tev, but I knew if I did, I wouldn't be able to look him in the eye. I could barely look at him now, with the taste of Tev's lips still lingering on my tongue. *Say something. Tell him. Be honest with someone for once.*

"Thank you," I said instead, awash with guilt. "You didn't have to lie for me. About the repair lot."

"I didn't do it just for you."

"I know. Thank you anyway." I reached my hand out, and after staring at it for a moment, he took it.

"Ovie," I said. "I have to talk to Slip. I have to—"

"May I join you?"

Ovie and I looked toward the doorway, where Marre stood, small and barefoot as ever.

"I was just going," Ovie said, letting me go. Marre hadn't waited for a response—she just stepped quietly into the infirmary, holding a glass spoon and a small glass jar filled with golden honey. Her hair draped over her button-down shirt like silk.

"Thank you, Ovie," she said with very little intonation.

"Remember what I said." He looked at me, stern. "Don't waste your opportunities."

I nodded, and he left.

"It gets lonely on the bridge," Marre said quietly, sitting down in the chair in his place. Her bare legs were so thin I couldn't help thinking of my anorexic sister, and wondered what Nova thought of this time-frozen woman. Did she see Marre edging toward the veil between lives? Did she see something of herself in her? Why did she frighten Nova?

"I don't socialize," Marre said, barely above a whisper.

"Sometimes you come to see me, though."

The fingers of her left hand disappeared—first skin, then fat, muscle, bone—along with the flesh and hair on the right side of her head. The air around her rippled slightly, and the buzz returned, plaguing my tired head.

"You're staring again," Marre said.

"I'm looking, yes." No point in lying.

"You can't help staring at a woman whose body forgets to be." The rest of her face and hair flashed back into existence.

I tried speaking, but only managed something between a word and a grunt; I'd wanted to say, "I'm sorry," but knew it would be both inadequate and inaccurate.

"Don't worry. No one knows how to act around me. Except Tev. What can anyone say in response to the mad ravings of an eternal youth?" She smiled and looked down at her now-floating jar of honey, encased by one invisible hand. The other held the glass spoon like a child, fisted tight. She looked far more fragile than I think she really was.

"This is why I don't leave the bridge. I have forgotten how to talk to other humans if we aren't discussing navigation or ship operations."

I took a risk and reached out with my right hand, covering the cold, unseen fingers that held the jar. Translucence rippled up her arm as if she were made of water and my touch were a stone dropped into her. "I want to hear anything you have to say, Marre. I'd like to get to know you. You should come see me more often."

"The crew likes you." She offered the barest hint of a smile. "That is something. They're important to me. And you love this ship."

"Yes. I do, very much." It felt good to be close to her. Once I got past her appearance and eccentric demeanor, something about her made me feel at home. "How are you feeling? Are you going to be able to last until we get to the breach?"

She shrugged one shoulder, sucking on her spoon. Slowly, she took it out of her mouth, licked it a few times, and put it back into the jar. "It's difficult to say. Difficult to hold all the pieces together at once. May I eat my honey now?"

"Oh. Sure." I backed off and tried to think of something to say. "Did you want anything else with that? I think Slip has some bread."

"That isn't necessary." She dipped the spoon into the jar, retrieving a viscous ribbon of amber. "Ovie likes honey too. He's a good wolf."

Even having seen the shadow trailing Ovie, he still made no sense to me. The other crew members referred to him as a wolf, but they accommodated the *human* space he took up when he walked by. They watched him use his opposable thumbs when he worked on the engine, just as I did. He ate with silverware and spoke with his human tongue. The crew responded to these things, so they clearly perceived Ovie as human, just as I did.

Yet the wolf lingered, revealing itself to me in pieces.

The ship is lending you her eyes.

"You see parts of him, don't you?" Marre examined her jar, playing with the honey dripping from her spoon like thread. "You see the shadows but you still see the man."

I nodded slowly.

"The ship likes you too." Marre's dark eyes flicked toward me, locking their gaze on mine, that hollowness drawing me in like a gravity well. "She's letting you see the real world."

"It was really you who showed me, wasn't it? Not Nova."

She smiled. "Of course. I'm the pilot."

"I don't understand."

"Yes, you do."

I shivered at the sight of her. The jar was no longer full of honey, and her skin was no longer tattooed, no longer dappled with translucent patches. Buzzing swarmed my ears, sizzling and popping, melding with the song of the ship, weaving into a choral echo that swelled into me, aching. I watched the spoon dissolve around her hand, coating it, until her flesh was made of glass from finger to collarbone. In lieu of muscle and sinew, she was all wire and electricity beneath a crystalline surface. Tiny supernovae glowed where her eyes should have been— stars that lived and died in moments, lived and died . . .

The honey jar was now full of plasma, and it erupted into flares like a sun.

Chapter Sixteen

Marre haunted me night after night as I recovered from my broken ribs and near-relapse, sitting by my hospital bed with her jars of honey. Mostly she asked me questions about my childhood—she wanted to hear the story about the baby Greenbelt. I think she may have laughed, but it was too like a sigh to tell, and too drowned out by the buzzing and electricity. Such a strange way to pass a drug-laden couple of days.

During the day, Nova read to me from one of the books she had brought with her on a transparent imprint. Terrible story, really. Something about a spirit guide who fell in love with her instructor during guild training. Still, I was grateful for the gesture, and more than once Nova held my hand. My big sister, *being* my big sister, filling in the gaps in my heart that grief had carved. I wondered what Lai would say if she could see us like this.

Ovie interrupted us a few times to run through the schematics of the repairs and make adjustments with me. He even talked shop unrelated to the *Tangled Axon*, necklace circling his thick neck all the while, shaking when he laughed that heavy, wolfish laugh. I admired the craftsmanship of the jewelry and wondered if he'd teach me someday. If we made it through this.

By the time Slip had accelerated my healing far enough that I could leave the infirmary and we were halfway to the breach,

I'd thought a lot about what Tev had said about me making my life all about Nova. She was right; I did myself a disservice by looking at everything I did in the context of someone else. It was time to let go of childhood hurt and live my life without letting my sister throw it into sharp relief.

I knocked on the door of her quarters. She was draped across her bed, knitting in a supine position. The light from her project illuminated her as her fingers worked above her. I watched her for a moment, smiling; how rare it was to see her so relaxed.

Nova turned her head to look at me, still lying there with her arms above her, then resumed working. "Feeling better?"

"Oh. Yes, thank you. I, uh. Wanted to talk to you."

"So did I." She sat up, layers of emerald fabric spilling down her back as she made room for me on the bed, patting it. "Come sit with me. I want to show you something. Oh, did you bring your plants? I can light them for you."

I complied. "No, they're in my quarters. Look, Tev said something to me that—"

"See what I've made for you?" She lifted her knitting, letting it fall evenly in front of her, an opaque membrane of iridescence that kicked up her jasmine aura in a sweet breeze.

I sighed and rubbed my eyes with the heels of my palms. The movement hurt my ribs, but it wasn't anywhere near as intense as when I'd first come back from the repair lot. "Don't change the subject. I'm trying to talk to you about us, Nova. Me and you. I don't have time to look at your dresses or whatever—"

"Please." Her voice was firm. "It's not like that. Just look."

I sighed and gave the fabric a good once-over: a pool of pearl-white light in her lap. "Okay, it's pretty. What am I looking at?"

"Look harder."

I squinted to focus my eyes on the subtle movements inside the veil of light between us. Pale colors shivered across the surface. Knowing the way my sister loved to marry her guide work with everything she did, I assumed there were hidden dimensions to the fabric that my eyes struggled to grasp. Shapes and movements flickered in and out of my perception, here and then not.

"What is it?"

She floated it closer to me. "What do you see?"

"I don't know. Colors. Am I supposed to see something specific?"

She sighed, and the fabric fluttered. Her face was illuminated as if the knitting were made of water, dappled light flickering across her skin. "For non-guides, it works best in tandem with a comm link. I do wish you still had yours."

"Well I don't because I'd rather not be executed for genocide."

"Don't take everything I say personally. That wasn't a criticism, it was an attempt at connecting with you. I made this for you, you know."

"And I appreciate it—"

"No you don't." She was practically pouting now, half-hidden by the knitting she still held in the air between us. "But I'll tell you what it is anyway, because you need me just like you've always needed me, even if you are ungrateful."

"What are you—"

"Being a guide has taught me so many things about the way baryonic matter works, the way our presence in the universe distorts reality around events, like a flash that imprints—"

"Can we talk about your work some other time? My head is killing me. I can't think straight."

"Listen to what I'm saying!" She dropped her hands and the light crumpled into her lap. "I'm not as silly and vapid as you think, but you won't even give me half of your attention, or listen to me long enough to find out. You only hear what reinforces your opinion of me and you just ignore everything else."

The hurt on her face was sharp and raw, cutting through all my stubbornness until it fell to my feet in shreds. I'd been so wrapped up in myself and my own grief that I'd forgotten my sister's. She had lost just as much as me. Love for her gnawed at my heart, worrying away the steel chain and wire I'd wrapped around it for so long. "I'm sorry, Nova. I appreciate you being there for me the past few days. I don't think you're silly and—"

"Yes you do. But it's okay. Frankly I think you are too." She squeezed my hand. "I may not understand why you're so fascinated by things like this outdated old vessel, but I meant it when I said I want you to be happy. I'm not going to try anymore to convince you to live a life I understand. I've never seen you light up the way you do here; if tinkering with ships is what makes your heart sing, then that's what you should do."

"Nova . . ."

"Hush now, Alana. Your big sister is talking."

I let myself laugh, popping the bubble of anxiety that had grown around our conversation. I knew she was teasing me.

"You're good at what you do, but so am I. Remember Spin. Remember what I told you about Transliminal's so-called medication. It's all matter manipulation. Distorting perception and reality. Distorting the way we move through the world, the way the world intersects with us—our flesh, our nerves, our minds. There is more to matter than matter itself; it transforms when humans move through it. I know you don't like admitting that the way you feel a vessel's injuries is basic guide work, but it is. That's the same sort of magic I feel humming through everything, all the time."

I thought of the way the *Tangled Axon* had worked her song into my heart, about the inexplicable buzzing and honey-scent billowing in Marre's presence—not to mention her ghostly body. I thought about the canine shadow that followed Ovie around. The image of the crew that left a residue of uncertainty in my mind. All of it, a haunting inside my head.

"I think you'd be surprised about the way I've started seeing the world," I said.

"Well good, then!" She seemed genuinely pleased. "There's a lot more to reality than electromagnetism. Transliminal Solutions lives in my world—all illusions and handwavium." She laughed a little. "This isn't your electromagnetic, tech-based way of life we're talking about."

"They're passing it off as if it were."

"Yes, they are. Pernicious, isn't it? But I'm not talking about ethics right now. I'm talking about the mechanics of guide work."

I leaned back against the wall and gestured for her to continue.

"Surely you know about the pockets their ships create? About how they puncture our reality each time their ships are operational, each time they cross the breach from their universe into ours?"

"I've heard something to that effect, but it doesn't make much sense to me."

"Their ships' movement through our reality unravels the weft and warp of *over here* so *over there* can seep in. Does that make sense? They have to weave a pocket of their own world *inside* ours, or their ships won't work. All their supposed 'technology' functions that way. As I said, it's no different than guide work. As spirit guides, we shift and reconfigure reality for the purpose of manifesting our clients' intentions or helping them journey. It's what I did to dull your pain, for that matter. In Transliminal's case, their intentions are usually simple: exist in a universe different from their own."

Nova was using what I liked to call her "teacher voice," treating me as if I were a client.

"Okay," I said. "So they're, more or less, spirit guides. We established that."

"Right. And when they do their work, weaving those pockets inside our reality, it leaves an imprint. Think of how we used to record information on electromagnetic strips. So . . . " She tilted her head at me and raised her eyebrows.

"Guess what happens when someone uses Transliminal products or medication?"

"It leaves an imprint."

She snapped her fingers and pointed at me. "Exactly. Bits and pieces of data programmed into reality itself, like metaphysical flotsam. And guides like me are excellent at extracting that data. Easy as plucking strands of hair from my own head."

"Nova, can you please get to the point? What are you telling me here?"

She lifted the milky, cold veil. It shimmered like nacre. "Do you understand what happened at Adul?"

My heart raced. Even the mere mention of the name *Adul* was becoming a trigger for me. I was starting to realize my parents would be dying all the time, in my head. Over and over again, they would die, and Adul would fade, and I would never *not* see that when I closed my eyes, or when I heard their names, or when I heard certain sounds, saw certain colors, felt certain things. Everyday things, like the weight of the shoes I wore the day they died, or the feeling of the navigation console beneath my fingers. When I felt these things, I'd lose everything all over again. That was what it meant to grieve.

"Alana?"

I started, then remembered Nova had asked me a question about what had happened at Adul. I simply said: "What do you mean?"

"Tell me what you know about what happened."

I sighed and spoke quickly, to get it over with. "The planet was destroyed. Its inhabitants were killed. Our parents . . . " I paused to tamp down the grief. "We were framed. Something shot out from the *Tangled Axon* because of a Transliminal device on the hull—"

I stopped. Nova grinned.

"A device made from what?" she said.

"Transliminal tech," I said, my voice a near-whisper under the weight of what she was telling me she'd done. Now, when

I looked at her woven veil, I felt hopeful for the first time in weeks.

"I couldn't let my own flesh and blood be blamed for something so sinister. The moment I saw what had happened, I got to work extracting the imprint."

"You have proof." I grabbed her and knocked her over and kissed her cheeks several times. "Nova! You have proof!"

"Come on now, you're messing up my hair." She shoved me off her and patted the cloud of hair puffed up behind her head. "You are a heathen, Alana Quick. But yes. Everything that happened at Adul has been recorded here. The mere fact that this tapestry exists is proof Transliminal committed the massacre, not the crew of the *Tangled Axon*. It's proof that the attendant at Ouyang Outpost had been switched with a representative from their side of the breach, and proof that that ugly thing in the cargo bay was a ploy to get your crew out of the way."

"I can't believe this." I just gawked at my sister while she smiled. "We have to tell the others."

"I'm not so useless after all, now am I?"

Chapter Seventeen

I kissed my sister's cheeks several more times and laughed with her, pressing my forehead against hers. Joy exploded from my every pore and for a moment, I felt the ship tremble in celebration with us. After a lifetime of resentment, finally, *finally*, we were sisters in more than just blood and genes. I had been so wrong for assuming she didn't care.

"I'm sorry for doubting you," I said.

"Yeah, yeah." She gently pushed me off and waved her hand dismissively, though she couldn't hide her happiness, either. "I know, I'm fabulous. Now go tell your beloved captain."

Once more I kissed her, then ran toward the bridge. Between Tev's kiss, Nova's evidence, and the Dexitek relieving me of the worst of my Mel's symptoms, I felt galvanized. Forget broken ribs—even with the ache of injury splitting my side in half, how could I care? In the grand scheme, that was nothing. Life had promise again.

"I have to tell you—!" I said as I practically exploded onto the bridge, but stopped in my tracks, grabbing the entrance frame. All the joy drained out of me and seeped like acid into the floor.

While Marre sat at navigation and quietly guided us toward our destination, Tev and Slip were wrapped in each other near the other end of the bridge. Tev's hands at Slip's perfect, round hips. Slip's on her cheeks, fingers tangled in Tev's beautiful

260 | Jacqueline Koyanagi

hair. Intimacy in their eyes. It was a closeness she and I had shared only days prior. I shouldn't have been surprised—*she's her partner*—but I was. She'd kissed me while Slip remained ignorant of the truth.

Tev had played us both.

I couldn't stand it, couldn't linger there for a moment longer—not even to tell her about Nova's evidence.

Jealousy and embarrassment burned in my stomach, flames licking my shame raw. I hurried down the corridor to the crew dorms, thinking I was going to my quarters until I found myself opening Tev's door and running up the stairs to the observation deck. Anger spiraled out from me, scorching everything in my path. Roiling clouds of betrayal churned inside me like volcanic ash; I was all pyroclastics and lava, wild and ready to burn everything down.

One thought cycled through my mind: Tev led me on, and I was the fool. I blamed myself most of all for having let her do this to me and Slip. I should have known better. I was nothing more than her dirty secret—the neophyte engineer, the new plaything, the distraction. Something novel and insignificant to boost her ego.

I should have known! Women with swagger like that didn't develop feelings for women like me. Just like women like me didn't love women at all—we loved ships, stars, engines. *That* was the way it should have been, and I'd let myself wander too far from the values I'd held all my life. My mind had been clouded by the romance of all those stars, all that black creation outside the *Tangled Axon*.

Ships never lied to you. They loved sincerely, unabashedly. No games. Falling prey to human women invariably ended here, always like this, with a bellyful of fire-scorched shame.

"Marre, please open the observation deck window," I said, trying to keep my voice steady.

"Certainly."

The window flashed to transparency. I thought the view

would help calm me, but it did nothing. I still wanted to give my jealousy and rage room to lash out, to feed it enough oxygen to flare bright and fast, leaving nothing but a glass heart in its place. I wanted it to erupt and die out quickly so I could move past it and not care. But I thought of Slip's hand on Tev's waist, of her laughter, of their intimate embrace, and I knew I'd carry this with me no matter how much fire I filled myself with. This kind of embarrassment and loss of face was unlike anything I'd ever experienced, not even when Kugler left me because I couldn't meet her idea of what a marriage looked like. And even that still plucked at my heart.

Why was I surprised? This is what people did to each other. They took what they needed and gave only what they must. I should have been grateful I hadn't confessed anything stupid. People like her never apologized, never cared. They brushed their victims off as collateral damage and moved on to the next easy target.

The metal stairs shook from below as someone climbed. When the person reached the top, the slightly arrhythmic sound of the footsteps told me it was Tev.

"You disappeared," she said, her familiar accent tugging hard at my heart. "You said you wanted to tell me something—"

I turned around, hands in my pockets to keep from defensively crossing my arms. "You claim to love Slip."

Her head pulled back as if I'd slapped her. "You're upset."

I laughed and turned back around to look at the stars so she wouldn't see the sadness behind the rage.

"You were so excited on the bridge a few minutes ago. What were you going to tell me?"

"I'd rather not right now. Leave me alone. Just . . . " I waved her off without looking at her. "I'll tell you later."

"Yes, I love Slip. I won't lie about that."

Anger burned even hotter inside me but I didn't let it show. Did she want accolades? "Suddenly you're being frank?"

"I didn't say I wasn't in love with her. You knew about our relationship from the beginning. Slip said she told you."

Everything in me wanted to turn around and shout at her, but regardless of my feelings, she was my captain first, and I didn't want to lose any more face than I already had. I wouldn't give her the satisfaction, the *power*, of witnessing me fly off the handle. Even if I had control over nothing else in my life, I'd maintain control over my actions.

"You let me believe you wanted me. If seducing someone while your partner is just down the corridor isn't deception, I don't know what is."

"I haven't deceived you." Her voice wavered a bit. I heard her walk up to me. I just faced the silence, watching the stars, but I didn't have to look at her to feel her gaze sliding over me. "I do want you."

She took my wrist and stood right behind me, then nuzzled her face against the crook of my neck. Desire welled inside me again, as did all the resentment I'd held inside, but I choked back the bitter tears and collected myself as well as I could, stiffening under her touch. I didn't want to give her the satisfaction of either giving in or pushing her away. Finally, she pulled back slightly but remained close, still watching me.

"We agreed we weren't going to have kids," she said. "Me and Slip."

"Good for you."

"Please, just listen. Three years into the relationship, she changed her mind. Tried to get me to change mine, but I'd already told her I didn't want to be a parent. Kids are great, don't get me wrong, but parenthood isn't the life I want. I wanted her to respect that. To respect me and the terms of our relationship. Our family is the *Axon* and the crew, and I wanted her to want that life with me, the way she said she did when we first met."

Tev sighed, her breath brushing my shoulder. I could feel warmth radiating from her body. I fought my desire to collect her into my arms. "But people grow, they change. I can't fault her for that. If someone wants children, nothing should keep them from that. But asking a person to commit to parenthood when they don't want it . . . that's no different. Just like I couldn't fault her for changing her mind, she couldn't fault me for not changing with her, or for knowing myself. She's a good person and has a kind heart, and I still loved her. I do love her. We want to be together despite everything."

The high praise for her partner made my stomach turn with jealousy and envy and rage over how I'd been treated. My voice shook. "Then why did you kiss me if you love her so much?"

Tev trailed her fingertips along my arm, feather-light. "Because I want you. I care for you."

A shiver ran through me under her touch. "Kissing you back was a mistake. I don't help people hurt their loved ones. Or at least I didn't before I met you."

"Please look at me."

"I can't."

"Alana. Slip and I are together, but we're not monogamous. She's planning on starting a family with Ovie."

"What?" I couldn't help turning to look at her. "I don't understand."

When our eyes met, I could see she had been fighting against unshed tears of her own. "It works for us. I've been afraid to tell you. Afraid you'd stop looking at me the way you do once you found out, and I couldn't stand the thought. I know how traditional most Heliodorans are—"

"Don't make this about my culture."

She shook her head, pressing her lips together to hold back her emotions. Her fragility almost broke me, but I held my ground while she kept talking.

"I didn't expect this. I didn't ask to meet you, to feel anything for you. Slip has always told me I was free to pursue other relationships just like she is. I've just never been the type to spend much time thinking about romance or sex in the first place." She ran a hand through her hair, nervous. "I've never been bothered by her desire to have kids with Ovie, or any of the relationships she's developed over the years. I'm happy for her. Loving other people doesn't take away from her love for me, not even a little. I just never met anyone myself. I actually thought about asking Bell out when we made our first deal, but—"

"I really don't need to know."

"—but she's not into women, and I think I was just lonely anyway. So I poured all that untapped emotion into my ship. I've loved the *Tangled Axon* the way I guess most people love each other."

That pulled at me so hard I felt weak with it. She was speaking my truth.

"I'm so angry at you," I said, grabbing her arms and letting emotion take over. "You're impossible to read, then you seduce me, and then you drop this on me out of nowhere, just pouring it all out like the dam broke, and I'm just so angry at you. That's great for you and Slip, all that openness and trust, but come on, Tev! This is the kind of thing a person deserves to know ahead of time."

"Ahead of what?"

I felt myself flush and said nothing. I wasn't about to tell her that I'd fallen for her. Not like this.

"You know what?" Tev stepped into me so we were just a gasp apart, her voice low, insistent. "I'm angry at you too. This whole time, you've been a needle under my nail, this constant pinprick-pressure of a woman, while I'm trying to run a ship and do something about our pilot dying. And I can't stand it. I can't deal with having you on my bridge, in my engine room, getting close to my crew, letting my vessel change you the way she only does for the people she chooses, while just standing back and watching it happen without feeling something for you. And then you destroyed my room with that damned stunt of yours that could have killed someone! It could've killed *you*."

She was almost whispering now, breath hot on my lips. "I can't stand how much like my dreams you smell; it's torture. You are torture. You wear metal on your skin like you're made of it, and it bites at me every time you're around. No matter how many showers I take, I smell your scent on me, on this ship, while I'm trying to sleep. I don't understand it, and can't stand it. I can't stand how I want you so badly and don't at the same time, because you're what I've been looking for, and I don't know what it means to have found it."

Dizziness overtook me. I couldn't stand it, either.

I hooked my fingers into the waist of her pants and pulled her against me, kissing her hungrily, inviting her in, letting the sweet taste of her flood my mouth. She put her hands on my waist and pushed me until my back hit the concave dip at the front of the observation deck, where the window tapered off into the wall. Pain flashed through my body when the impact jarred my ribs, but it just made me feel even more alive. There was metal on one side of me and stars on the other, while she pressed against me and seared me from the inside out.

Her hand slipped beneath my shirt, palm flat against my skin, while her mouth explored mine, and mine hers. Everything I was—all my thoughts, all those roiling emotions—collapsed into this moment. Into each sensation. Into her.

I pulled her hips against me, craving her pressure on every piece of my body. The metal of her leg bit into me as she pressed it between my legs, like a challenge. My breath caught, but I just pressed harder into her, grinding my hips against hers, the pleasure and pain exquisite. Warm hands explored every centimeter of skin under my shirt, and then we became frantic. I pushed her away from me, lifted her shirt up and over her, and her hair fell in a gorgeous mess over her shoulders, her breasts. I removed mine, and we wasted no time devouring each other.

The warmth of her stomach and breasts pressing against mine just made me fiercer, the lingering pain of my broken ribs cutting into me in a way that heightened every sensation. When I pulled myself back to undo the buckle of her belt, she yanked my hands away roughly and turned me around, pressing me against the barrier, one hand on each of my wrists. The cold glass stole my heat while her body gave me hers.

I turned my head to the side while she pressed herself against me, her mouth close enough to kiss. Neither of us closed the gap. Her breath shuddered, then spooled out over my skin, soft and warm. Her muscles were taut against me, hands tight around my wrists.

We burned into each other.

She released my arms and touched my exposed waist, her mouth hovering near mine. I moved to kiss her but she barely pulled herself out of reach. I bit my lip in agony as she ran her fingertips slowly along my skin just inside the waistband of my pants, teasing me. Gradually, mercifully, she unbuttoned them and I kicked them off, resenting the inconvenience of clothes. Her lips grazed mine, but didn't give in. I shuddered with need.

Her hand was slow and torturous, pressing against my stomach, moving downward while she refused to kiss me, the energy inside me building with every pulse of my blood. Finally, her hand reached down and found me. I groaned and writhed under her touch, trying to kiss her, but she pulled back just enough not to let me, brushing her tongue along my bottom lip while she pressed her bare upper body against me.

She released me completely and I gasped a protest at even that small distance, but she grabbed my wrists again and turned me around, pressing my back against the window. All her ferocity unfurled into me, and I loved it, loved every moment, every touch.

"Say it," she said in that throaty, velvety voice, coaxing all my feelings for her out from under my self-control. Her hand slid along my inner thigh, suggesting but not fulfilling, and the ship's engine sizzled deep inside the vessel, coursing through us both. She teased me and I groaned under the ecstasy of it, wanting her now but not wanting this to end.

"Tell me." She brought one of my wrists to her mouth and bit it, then kissed it gently, every sensation perfect and terrible and agonizing. Her lips returned to mine, brushing my mouth as she spoke, her hand still teasing me relentlessly. "Tell me how you feel."

I tried breaking my trapped wrist free, but she held it firm. I tried again and succeeded, then held her face with both hands and forced her to look directly at me, still shivering beneath her touch. "I'm in love with you. I love you."

"Alana." She wrapped her free arm around the back of my waist and pulled me into her, short nails breaking into the skin of my hip. Finally she kissed me, deep and slow, and as I felt her slide inside me, my mouth broke free of her lips and I cried out, grabbing her, moving with her, desperate to touch her, to taste her, to learn every piece of her in excruciating detail, to luxuriate in everything she was. Electricity seemed to scorch our skins, the ship pulsing between us as she lifted me up against the glass, my legs around her waist, my heart bare, our spirits touching the soul of the *Tangled Axon*. The stars behind us watched and waited, holding their breaths, while the three of us twisted inside each other and burned, burned, burned.

Chapter Eighteen

During the next few days, Tev and I took the opportunity that slow, interplanetary travel afforded us and tore at each other with the urgency of younger women. I wanted to be ever beneath Tev, within and around her, in the same way I had fantasized about plunging my hands into the *Tangled Axon*'s engines. Never had I dreamed of feeling this way, of craving someone whose skin wasn't a metal hull, whose heart didn't pulse with plasma. Now I had both, and the moment-to-moment ecstasy of it threatened to burst through my skin.

Like the mother of the universe, I thought one afternoon as I shuddered beneath Tev in her quarters and grasped her, held her as tightly as I could. She pressed her forehead against mine and stayed there, body deliciously heavy, as we slowly spiraled back out into reality, my body melting into nothing under her lingering touch. Like this, I could believe I'd live forever. Created, destroyed, and recreated, over and over again.

"Alana," she said eventually, breath still shaking as she rolled to the side of me but remained close, head resting on her hand. I looked at her and touched her cheek. She turned to kiss my palm, lethargic under the weight of spent pleasure.

Then, eyes flicking toward mine: "I'm hungry."

I laughed, pushing her away. "So romantic."

She raised an eyebrow and grabbed me, nipping at my shoulder with that terrible, wonderful lop-sided smile that rendered me so useless around her. "Well as delicious as you are, I do need other nutrients."

Hunger bit at my empty stomach too. I couldn't deny it. "I want to eat everything."

"Everything, huh?"

I kissed her shoulder. "Blackberries." Her neck; she closed her eyes and arched her head back against the pillow. "Wine." Her jaw.

"You can't *eat* wine—"

Her neck again. "Cheese and bread with olive oil and honey." Her clavicle, my tongue tasting the sweetness of her skin. "Rosemary-baked pheasant . . . " I traveled to her chest, exploring every centimeter of her skin with my mouth.

A throaty laugh, her hands in my locs. "Do you think you'll find it there?"

"I've found something better."

It took another hour for us to climb out of bed, at which point we both felt on the edge of starving. Evidently, loving a starship captain takes a lot out of you.

"Caramel or vanilla?" Tev said, buttoning her cargo pants, her messy hair falling over her shoulders.

I groaned, lacing up my boots. Nutrient bars—all that dense muck—seemed inadequate now, thrown into sharp relief by the luxury of the past few days. I craved real food, to feed and be fed, to be nourished in every way instead of just sustained. Pre-packaged nutrition stole some of the magic out from under me, reminding me of why we were out here, of all we still had to lose.

"Surprise me," I said in a flat tone, following her out to the corridor and into the kitchen.

Tev stopped and kissed me in front of a wall of ration boxes. "When this is all over, I'll treat the crew to a real meal as soon as we have the money."

"Well, when *lunch* is over, remind me to show you something."

She raised an eyebrow at me and tilted her head, but I just

unwrapped my "food." As we ate our bars—vanilla, it turned out, which tasted more like toothpaste—Slip walked into the room with Ovie.

"Family dinner!" Slip joked, grabbing a box of jerky from high atop one of the shelves, fishing out a few packaged strips for her and Ovie, whose canine tail shadowed him, his hands dirty from working on cargo bay repairs. They laughed and talked and pulled up a couple of chairs to join Tev and me, setting off detonations of conflict inside my heart. Here was this beautiful crew, accepting me as one of their own, and yet Slip's presence reminded me of the reality of my situation: I was not the only object of Tev's affection. I tried to endure it, but the thought of them together threatened me in a way I couldn't explain. They had so much shared history.

Slip scooted closer to me, doing a lewd little dance in her chair with pursed lips before elbowing me and taking a bite out of her jerky. I tried to play along and hold onto the happiness of the past few days. She seemed genuinely thrilled for us. Everyone did. Even Marre, when she passed through to grab a new jar of honey with a skinless hand, nudged Tev's arm and winked at her.

Ugh, stop it, Alana. I wanted to just accept things for what they were and enjoy the moment, but my own simmering thoughts undermined me at every turn. Everyone else seemed so at ease, happy. Why couldn't I just let go and let these relationships be what they were? What was I afraid of?

That she will tire of you and return to her real life, with her real partner.

"Hey." Slip's hand on my shoulder interrupted my oh-so-helpful ruminations. "Can I talk to you?"

A flutter in my stomach.

"Yeah. Sure. Of course." I stood and almost kissed Tev's head, but didn't want to in front of Slip. How would we manage this if I couldn't even offer her such a small gesture of affection while Slip was in the room?

272 | Jacqueline Koyanagi

"I'll be right back," I said.

Tev gave Slip a questioning look but just smiled, returning to a conversation with Ovie in which she ran through our plans to cross the breach and get Birke's attention, organizing her thoughts. She'd done the same with me three or four times already in the past couple of days, interspersed with pillow talk. I found her determination irresistibly attractive. Here was someone with more to offer than mere domestic bliss.

So why did I blanch at the thought of a non-monogamous life with her on this ship?

Slip led me out into the corridor and away from the kitchen, where we wouldn't be heard.

"You're uncomfortable," she said.

"Oh!" I scrambled for an excuse. "No, just worried about Marre, and nervous about crossing the breach—"

"Don't lie."

For a moment I felt anxious, like a child caught making up a story to cover for her bad behavior, but she smiled at me. I bolstered myself. "Okay. Yes, I'm uncomfortable. This is weird."

"How?"

The question threw me. How was it not? "The whole . . . sharing thing. I don't know. I've just never done this before. I don't know how to be okay with her going off to be with you some nights. How to be okay with knowing you came first and mean more—"

"Did she say I mean more?"

"Well, no—"

"Girl, don't make things up just to torture yourself." She shrugged one shoulder. "It's not any different than your parents loving you and your sister at the same time. You think they loved her more because she came first? You think she took priority just because she happened to pop into the world ahead of you?"

"No . . ."

"Well, there you go."

"I feel guilty."

"About what? You're not doing anything wrong."

"I know you're okay with it, but I don't know if I am." I couldn't look at her.

"What are you afraid of?"

There was that question again, this time in that warm voice of hers, all comfort and confidence. I could see what she saw in Slip.

"Love is like sunlight," she said when I didn't respond. "You can give all of yourself to someone and still have all of yourself left to give to others, and to yourself. To your work. To anything or anyone you choose. Love isn't like food; you won't starve anyone by giving it freely. It's not a finite resource."

I swallowed, feeling irrational in the face of what she was saying. I knew my jealousy came from a place of possessiveness, and it bothered me. Slip held up a mirror with her words, and I wasn't liking what I saw.

"Is that how you can plan another family?" I asked. "By believing love is limitless?"

"It's not faith, it's my truth. My plans with Ovie only heighten my love for Tev. And vice versa. Happiness begets happiness."

"Doesn't it bother Ovie? That you're already in love with Tev."

"Psh." She laughed. "Have you seen how devoted he is to our captain? Besides, does it bother Tev that you're already in love with the *Tangled Axon*?"

The thought hit me like a splash of cold water, and something snapped into place. I had believed if you loved someone or something enough to be consumed by it, it simply wasn't possible to love anyone else. There wouldn't be space for them in a heart so full. Devotion was a single-file line. My work or a relationship. Not both.

But with Slip's words bouncing around in my head—*you're*

already in love with the Tangled Axon—something tectonic shifted in me. The magnetic pull of the ship pulsed around us, her hum vibrating beneath my soles—a reminder. The song of every ship that had come before her sang in harmony with her in a perfect choral swell.

My work was my first love. No matter how many humans I did or didn't fall for in my life, Tev would forever have to share me with my vocation, and I would have to share her with hers. We'd never give up the things that made us who we were.

And I'd have it no other way. Was sharing her love with other people so different?

Tev wanted me. She actively chose me each time her hand reached for mine, each time she found me with her eyes, her mouth, her heart. She chose me because she wanted me, not because she was lonely, or unfulfilled, or seeking completion. She already had a partner; she wasn't looking for me to rescue her from a future lived alone. She chose me for who I was, not for what I could give her. Wouldn't I rather be a constant choice than a default option? Wouldn't I rather choose her, choose the *Axon*, choose my life, again and again?

My heart played tug-of-war between clinging to familiarity and letting myself fall into a seductive, glittering unknown.

"Hey," Tev said, startling us. I hadn't heard her approach. Her eyes darted between us, tinged with curiosity. "Didn't you want to show me something?"

"Right." I looked at Slip once more. "Thanks. I have some thinking to do."

She casually saluted me with a couple of fingers and wandered away to the bridge.

"What was that all about?" Tev said as I took her hand and led her toward my quarters.

"You."

She raised an eyebrow. "I'm going to regret having you two on board at the same time, aren't I?"

I shrugged and smiled, letting her wonder.

How strange to be thinking about Slip and me sharing Tev's affection, crossing paths on the ship. *Happiness begets happiness.* She really did want Tev to be happy with me. Witnessing such a genuine, easygoing approach to human connection, seeing how they behaved with each other and with me, made this all seem more feasible. The space Slip had created in my heart for this new paradigm cracked open a little wider.

"Okay," I said as we stepped into my quarters. "Close your eyes."

"I'd rather not."

"You're no fun." I placed my hand over her eyes and she batted it away, closing them on her own as she muttered something under her breath about doing it herself. "Keep them closed."

"I will, I will."

Taking her hands in mine, I pulled them out in front of her and positioned them palm-up, to await one of the reclaimed plants. I collected the rosemary from under my bed where it was hiding, and though it probably wasn't as lush and healthy as it had been under Tev's care, with Nova's help, I hadn't done such a terrible job. Herbs must be hardy to withstand my black thumb.

Tev tilted her head and knitted her brows together as the scent of rosemary overpowered us. Before she could open her eyes and spoil it, I placed the bowl in her hands. "Okay."

She didn't look entirely surprised, but then I supposed a smell like that would give it away.

"You saved one."

"Two, actually. And I had to." I guided her to the bed and sat with her. "I know I was irresponsible and overeager, and my foolishness took your garden from you. I know it can't replace the old one—"

She shook her head and brushed the plant with delicate fingers. "This is one of the most thoughtful things anyone's done for me in a long time. Even if you did blow it up in the first place."

"Really, I'm sorry—"

"I'm teasing."

"You were just so mad, Tev. Honestly, I thought you were going to get rid of me, and I wouldn't have blamed you."

She set the bowl down on the floor, away from our feet, and placed my hand on her prosthetic leg. "You know why I was upset."

"I didn't know about your accident."

"That isn't the point. We could have lost the ship. Lost you."

I was quiet for a moment. "Why the garden?"

"Pardon?"

"What did it mean to you?"

She shrugged. "Just a reminder of where I came from. I'll be an old woman before I give up the sky, but sometimes I miss the cattle station. I needed a place that was for me, a pocket of home kept in secret. I don't know, sounds silly I guess."

I thought of Lai and the repair shop, of my parents on the research station. As much as I'd rather be out here than on Orpim or even in orbit around Adul, part of me missed my old life. All of me missed my family. "I think I get it."

"Thank you," she said. "For the rosemary. And for trying with me. For giving me a chance even though I'm not what you expected."

A small laugh bubbled up in me. "How could I not? Look at you. Look at who you are. You make the sky more glamorous than it already was. I'd be a fool not to at least try to open my mind for you."

A hearty laugh escaped her throat. "Glamorous. Not the word I'd use to describe myself, love." She leaned in close to me, touching my jaw and whispering against my ear. "Thank you for stowing away, sky surgeon."

Need for her suffused me, like sunlight. She *was* sunlight to me, she and the *Tangled Axon*, all brightness and hope.

I wanted to tell her that. To spill every truth from my lips like a prayer, everything I felt, and to tell her again and again: *I love you, I love you, I love you, Tev Helix.* But as I parted my lips to speak, I held back my words and kissed her instead, hoping she felt what I couldn't bring myself to say again.

Because I realized then, despite all we'd shared and our days spent wrapped in the exquisite warmth of each other, she hadn't yet said she loved me too.

Chapter Nineteen

At the breach, an armada awaited us.

More othersider ships than we could count blocked our path to the slice in the sky. From far away, they looked like a grid of lights in a net in front of the breach, pulsing in time with each other. Maneuvering past without Nova's help was out of the question. After much jaw clenching on Tev's part, she agreed to allow our safe passage to rest solely in my sister's hands.

Nova stood next to Marre at the helm, eyes closed, hands on the console.

Tev, Ovie, Slip, and I left them to their task while we watched our approach from the observation deck.

"Please let this work," Tev said under her breath.

Ovie whined in the back of his throat, shadow-tail tucked between his legs. It might have been funny to see a grown human whine like a puppy if he hadn't had such a good reason to be afraid. Slip placed her hand on his back and rubbed in slow circles, fingers disappearing into the umbra of his canine-self.

Tev nervously toyed with her necklace, sighing and shifting her weight.

My sister had explained it to me: she would channel her consciousness along the smallest filaments of reality's matrix, making minute adjustments around the *Tangled Axon* until she wove a space around us much like the ones Transliminal

280 | Jacqueline Koyanagi

used to maneuver through our universe. Reality rolled between her fingers, conforming to her intention to hide us from the Transliminal armada. An illusion of invisibility. From their perspective, we would be nothing more than a faint shimmer in the black, if they saw anything at all. All the *Tangled Axon*'s fiery brilliance would be contained behind a veil.

Marre angled us between the othersider ships and powered the engine down to its lowest cycle, letting the *Axon*'s inertia ferry us forward.

A single breach in concentration would collapse the entire illusion.

Two Transliminal ships crested the horizon of the observation deck as we drifted past, rising like strange suns. Bright blue tangles of light ringed each vessel, pulsing and fluctuating over a core of metal that glinted from the illumination. A single tendril-ring would have engulfed us ten times over; we were insignificant compared to these enormous ghosts. Shadows raged and roiled between the rings of light and the metal ships inside. Storms of nothingness shivered in dark clouds, darker than the black.

I could feel the *Tangled Axon* and her crew hold its collective breath.

Almost there.

Just as we prepared to clear the armada and cross through the breach, one of the light-tendrils snaked out toward us, slicing through the *Axon* without warning.

Lightning exploded in my head when the ship cried out in fear, the sound of a hundred storms raging inside my skull. The five of us on the observation deck stepped backward, trying to avoid the wall of blue light slowly cutting through the observation deck. Humidity saturated the air like a cold, wet morning. The smell of salt. Of beach.

Time seemed to freeze. Tev grasped my hand and Slip's as we continued backing up until our backs hit the far wall. Endless white-blue light stretched before us, permeating the

Tangled Axon, stopping just centimeters from our faces. Cold wind whipped our hair, our clothes.

Shapes flickered beyond the light. Movement in the form of winged and horned humans, shifting buildings along an alien coastline, enormous creatures I couldn't recognize. Mere shadows dancing just on the edge of perception.

Then, a shift—like changing a net channel. Soft whispers and distant glissandos. Machines. Scents—sweet, acrid, tart, musky. Salt. So much salt-air. A flicker, and the scene changed again. Humidity tinged with a mossy, green smell. Human shadows holding objects I couldn't recognize. Somehow, I knew: we glimpsed other worlds. Realities in which the othersiders had established a presence.

Energy gathered around us, like an intake of breath. Static ignited small sparks between strands of hair, fibers of fabric, even the air, humid as it was. The hair on my arms stood on end. Chills worked their way down my back. Something inside that Transliminal light beckoned me forward, calling me to it. Inviting.

The *Tangled Axon* tensed against our backs, desperate to expel the unfamiliar world gnawing at her hull.

Reality became nothing more than silence and held breath, coiled into a sharp point.

And then it detonated. All that power around us pulsed outward, ejecting the invading light. A strong gust of wind sucked us forward as the othersider ship snapped its tendril back into the light-tangle around the core body.

Just like that, we cleared the armada. We were *over there*.

Five people exhaled at once. I tried not to collapse and cry in sheer relief; I hadn't fully realized how terrified I'd been.

"What was that?" Slip said, voice shaking.

"Other worlds," Tev said. "I've seen them before, in experience booths on Spin. They're some of the realities where Transliminal Solutions already established itself. We're just one of many."

• • •

The strangest thing about crossing the breach between realities? How utterly unremarkable it was to be on the other side. Other than the need for Nova to sustain the bubble around our ship in order for it to continue working, there wasn't any appreciable difference. Not out in the black, anyway. Stars and dust were the same wherever you went, it seemed.

It was a good five minutes before we collected ourselves and left the observation deck, still haunted by what we'd seen. By the time we made it to the bridge, Marre was establishing an orbit around the nearest planet—home of the Transliminal Solutions capital city—while Nova concentrated on maintaining the ship's invisibility at the same time that she wove my disguise around me. As before, my mind slipped away from me, only this time I knew what was happening. It gave me just enough wherewithal to try to at least *look* like I wasn't high.

Nova couldn't break her focus to say goodbye; I knew she was with me as she manipulated my body, my voice, my energetic signature. Just like on Spin. Except this time I was transformed into my sister, not a bipedal lizard. I wanted to get a little reassurance from her, but all I could do now was trust.

"Do anything you have to do to help Nova maintain her concentration," Tev said as she boarded the shuttle behind me. "We can't risk them detecting the *Tangled Axon*, or her."

"Or me," I said, twisting a band of shimmering fabric between my hands, trying not to make a face at the sound of Nova's voice coming from my mouth. Even if this had been my idea, everything about it unsettled me. More than anything, I missed the soft fullness of my own body, the weight of my locs.

"I guess that means I can't hit on her?" Slip said, hand on her hip. "Damn. I thought this was the perfect opportunity."

"Funny."

I laughed harder than the conversation warranted, then

stuffed down the amusement. *Behave like Nova*, I coached myself.

"Be careful, Captain." Slip pinched Tev's chin, then looked past her and winked at me. "You too, surgeon."

I gave her a thumbs-up with my new hand and tried focusing on Slip's face, but the mist covering my mind made it difficult. The disorientation was tempered enough that I didn't feel as far away as I did during our transformation on Spin, but the world seemed a little more difficult to process than usual, and I was slower to respond. I hadn't even realized Tev had parked herself in the pilot's seat next to me until she touched my hand.

"You okay in there?"

I smiled and almost pinched her chin the way Slip did because the idea amused me, but thought better of it. "Yeah. I just feel . . . weird." My voice echoed in my head.

She laughed and cycled up the engine, beginning her pre-flight checks. "I have to admit, you *look* weird. Tell me if the effects start to get to be too much for you. We'll turn right back around and figure something else out."

"No." I gripped the seat and moved my new clothes around to try to get comfortable in them, but it was a bit like using a broom to sweep up all the sand on a beach. "I'll manage. I just have to get used to it for a minute. We have to do this."

Tev tilted her head in a skeptical half-nod and prepared to launch. "Whatever you say, love." She pushed the throttle forward and we departed from the shuttle bay, maneuvering across empty space over their bright blue planet until we met the stream of traffic heading into the atmosphere, one vessel at a time. Once parked behind an enormous luxury rental, Tev kicked her boots up onto the console.

"Might as well get comfortable. We'll probably move five centimeters in ten minutes."

I groaned. "Marre can't wait that long. We're going to be here forev—"

A male voice hopped onto our comm link. "Attention shuttle 431A-Red from Universe 58. This is Transliminal Traffic Control. Please respond."

Tev sat up and pressed the transmit button. "I read you, Traffic Control."

"You've been cleared for priority landing."

Fear raked its fingers through me. Had they detected our lie?

"Fantastic!" Tev said. "May I ask why?"

"Birke wishes to personally welcome Nova Quick to the surface. Proceed to Transliminal Solutions headquarters." He clicked off.

"Okay," Tev said, adjusting our flight path and maneuvering the shuttle away from the queue. "Let's go convince her to help our pilot."

I looked down at my thin hands, the silver fabric draped over my legs, the perfectly silver-tipped toes peeking out from my sandals. "I can't believe it worked."

"Looks like being good at what you do runs in the family. Nova's mind really is strong enough to convince them you're her." Tev gave me the lop-sided smile I loved so much. "Maybe too strong. I have to admit I don't really like the smell of jasmine."

I sniffed at my arm, the fabric of my dress. "I don't smell anything."

"That's because you're wearing it." She turned back to the view screen and adjusted more controls. "Hang on." The shuttle quaked for about fifteen seconds. "Compensating for atmosphere."

As the shuttle stilled, I relaxed my death grip on the arm rests, and leaned forward just in time to see Transliminal's capital city cutting across huge swaths of land in a complex geometry of light. Each bright band connected to several others, clustering in nests and nodes that shone like miniature galaxies. Strange how we lived in the long shadow of a place so luminous. I wanted to open the shuttle hatch and fly over the landscape, becoming a node of light unto myself, blazing across the sky.

Alana, I thought to myself while looking for something else to focus on. *Don't get lost.*

A fabricated forest of metallic trees circled the TS headquarters, with a section cut out for priority landing. We made our descent.

"I'm just going to secure the shuttle," Tev said. "Go ahead and disembark. Get some fresh air; I'm sure you need it."

I kissed the top of her head, taking in the rosemary scent of her before stepping outside, grabbing all the extra fabric at the hem of my dress to avoid stepping on it. I couldn't understand why Nova liked wearing something so impractical.

The air smelled different on their side of the breach. Too perfect.

No—too *empty*. As if it had been scrubbed clean of any evidence humans had walked through it. Frenetic blue and white light illuminated the surrounding trees, pulsing from inside the branches like blood and trickling out along the burnished "bark." Each branch was more quicksilver than hard metal, swirling and changing in subtle movements. Transparent leaves glittered in the rising sunlight of an alien star. I touched a tree and the bark rippled out from my finger-tips like liquid, shivering from trunk to glassy leaves, which plinked against each other like chimes. Eerie—but beautiful.

Tev disembarked from the shuttle and paused for half a step when she took in the surroundings, clearly alarmed by the surreal landscaping. She just wiped her hands on her shirt and headed toward me, glancing surreptitiously at one of the trees.

"Seems like there's nothing organic on this planet except the humans," I said, closing the distance between us. I was starting to get the hang of speaking coherently despite a clouded mind.

She snorted. "I have my doubts about them, too."

"This is going to work," I said. "Right? We'll be fine."

"Of course we will."

Her smile was half-formed under the weight of the lie, but I didn't push it. I just reached out (out, instead of up—so strange) and put my hand on the back of her neck, pulling her toward me for a kiss. "We'll be okay," I repeated, wanting to hear myself say it like I meant it.

She smiled at me in her crooked way and exhaled deliberately, nodding. "Yes. Also . . . "

"Hm?"

"It's too weird kissing you like this."

I looked down at my thin silver-sheathed body. Pale white shimmer accented my hands and feet. Like this, I matched this place so seamlessly I looked like a flower dropped from the canopy. I turned my gaze to her again and smirked. "What, you're not into the whole sister thing?"

"I like you better in boots and grease."

"That makes two of us."

Transliminal's headquarters sliced into the sky, a glass scythe curving over another copse of shivering silver trees. Fireflies winked between crystal leaves. We approached the main entrance from the south, Tev walking with her hand around my upper arm.

"You there! Stop!"

Four black-suited enforcers marched toward us with plasma channel weapons at the ready. We turned and raised our hands, palms forward.

"You're being seized," one of them said as he stepped to the front. "Come with us."

Tev tilted her chin at him. "Sure, but I'm thinking Birke will have your ass if you wave those weapons at Nova Quick."

The enforcer narrowed his eyes. "That may be, but you're wanted for genocide on your side of the breach."

"I'm far less inclined to accept a contract with someone

who would treat me like a criminal," I said, doing my best impression of my sister. Maintaining flawless posture was not as easy as I thought it would be, but I managed. My back would just have to hate me later.

"Consider us escorts, then."

The enforcer who appeared to be in charge led the way toward the front of the building while the other three penned us in like cattle. Just then I noticed traces of grease on Tev's right cheek, left there when helping Ovie with the *Tangled Axon*, and I couldn't help smiling a little at this small rebellion against the pristine cleanliness of Transliminal's campus. Made me wish I had mud on my immaculate sandals.

Even the largest high-rise in Heliodor had nothing on Transliminal's headquarters, seamless and towering far beyond what should have been possible. One perfect, unbroken piece of crystal that refracted light with brilliant clarity—it made me dizzy just looking at it. Obscene, really. I couldn't imagine why it would be necessary to create something so enormous. The entryway comm panel was an aurora of swirling color that disappeared into the wall in a gradient. The enforcer waved her wrist over it to activate it.

"Security code four-three-eight-alpha-six," she said. "Contact: Birke."

"Voice recognition and security code acknowledged."

The aurora remained quiet for a moment, then a face flickered onto the screen.

"Nova," Birke said. "I knew you'd take my offer."

A cold hand reached into me and stole my breath. This wasn't possible.

I could actually feel my brain trying to make sense of what I was seeing and failing, like constructing a solid framework out of limp string, or trying to find a way out of a tangled blanket. I didn't know what the enforcer was saying now, or how Birke responded. Other voices joined the conversation, but I heard them as if through water.

My eyes remained locked on Birke's face—her awful, impossible face. Everything else was muted, dulled, slow. Unreal. All that existed was the woman on the screen, who appeared in sharp, vivid color. Familiar expressions played on her familiar features, each familiar movement stabbing me with impossible, horrifying recognition.

It was me.

Chapter Twenty

"Send them up to me," Birke said.

The enforcers nudged us forward, winding reality back up to speed.

Riotous thoughts spun my mind into a frenzy. Birke was Alana—she was me from another universe. A version of me who had become a spirit guide—or at least their version of a spirit guide. I couldn't comprehend a world in which I didn't live inside the hearts of machines, didn't map my life by the song of their reactors. But here she was, a parallel self that had come reaching through the thin film between worlds, fingers outstretched toward my sister.

Her sister.

Where was the Nova from Birke's universe? Had she never existed? Had something hap—

A dark realization hit me, and I fractured into a thousand pieces. In her pursuit of Nova, Birke killed my parents, the Adulans, my childhood. A version of me existed who could commit such atrocities. She was *me*, and she had done these things.

Every nerve ending felt exposed, assaulted by thick, textured air that had become hard to breathe. The world had turned pale and narrow. Why did Birke want my Nova so badly that she would kill? What made finding her worth destroying so much?

Tev didn't flinch or take her eyes off the CEO's face on the comm panel. My face. The same planes and contours I'd known all my life, framed in a cloud of natural hair in lieu of locs. Brown eyes like mine, only tinged with a ring of red. I don't know why, but before we'd come to Transliminal Solutions, I'd expected Birke's face to be composed of harsh features chiseled sharp by othersider mods. Instead, I'd found myself.

My mind continued trying to bend around this knowledge that I existed elsewhere, that in another life, I was ruthless and self-serving and valued nothing that I cherished now. Some part of me *was* this woman, because she *was me*.

Nightmares of countless alternate lives would invade my sleep for months to come—if I survived whatever lay ahead— horrible possibilities and probabilities tugging at my sleeve.

I felt Tev's eyes shift to my face, watching my reactions, teasing apart the strands of *Birke* versus *me*. I felt her silent question beating against me: Had I known? Had I possessed some inkling that this other-me had pierced our world to drag my sister out of it?

Blood pulsed loudly in my head. My heart drummed so quickly it felt on the edge of exploding. This wasn't possible. And yet clearly, it was.

At some point, I was aware we had stopped talking to the on-screen Birke and had begun moving. Enforcers escorted us inside the building, passing us through a wall of light. I had never seen so much brightness in one place; it was as if we'd wandered into a hollowed-out star.

The interior walls and floor were made of albacite, smooth and opalescent, while the exterior maintained its illusion of pure glass. Veins of light split the stone like cracked desert, illuminating every surface from the inside out. Sunlight poured in through the transparent ceiling and refracted through moving, prismatic sculptures that floated above us like miniature othersider ships. I could see no doors or windows other than the enormous curved ceiling, until a hole appeared in one wall—small at first, then expanding to the size of the human who walked through it. The wall sealed behind her as if it had never broken, rippling back into its original shape.

The enforcer opened a wall entrance near the back of the building. When we emerged on the other side, I felt the air tighten around us. Somehow, we had ended up at the apex of the building without climbing stairs or entering a lift of any kind. Through the glass, their vast city spread before us. White-blue filaments glittered across the landscape below like a luminescent neural network grafted onto the planet, punctuated by metallic trees, glass flora, and shimmering light-nodes dripping along the filaments like beads of water.

"You like it, then."

My voice. We turned to face Birke, who none of us had even noticed on the far end of this enormous, empty room. Only Birke occupied the space—Birke, and one floating platform that seemed to serve as a desk. She delicately ate a plumberry plucked from a crystal bowl, not a single drop of juice escaping her lips. Such extravagance at her fingertips. I couldn't imagine what it would have been like to possess that kind of wealth, and yet there I was, watching myself look completely at home in it.

A perfectly-tailored black suit hugged Birke's body, the collar of her white shirt popped suggestively, the V of the neckline open just enough to draw the eye downward. Three translucent screens floated in front of her, displaying words and moving images. Some sort of net?

Neither Tev nor I said a word, though it was torture to refrain from shouting the questions that swarmed in my head. Birke too remained silent, eating her fruit and scrolling through one of the screens. After a tense thirty seconds or so, she tossed the fruit away and swept her arm over the projections, moving them to the side, where they hovered near the wall. She walked to the front of her desk and half-sat, half-leaned on the edge, crossing her ankles and resting her hands on its surface. Rings of light rotated up her forearms, almost as distracting as her jet-black lipstick.

"Come here," she said, crisp. There was no mistaking that she addressed me—Nova.

I complied, stepping forward with Nova-esque dignity, hoping it was convincing enough at close range. Even if she didn't buy this for long, it was enough to give us a chance to hold our real leverage over Birke's head. Then, at least Marre might be able to be whole again.

We stared at each other for a while, but it was hard. Seeing my face like this while I wore my sister's made me feel slightly unhinged. I didn't want to look at her for more than a few seconds, preferring to glimpse her out of the corner of my eye, like a ghost. Still, I tried to look confident as her gaze swept over my face.

Sweat trickled down my temple. Labored breathing betrayed my anxiety and disorientation. Would she see through me?

"Nova," she said. "I want you to come home."

"Home?"

She swallowed. "There's a space in this world meant for you."

What did that mean?

I barely smiled, dabbing my forehead with the back of my hand. "I'm not sure the Spiritual Advisory Guild will allow me to work for a criminal."

She laughed and opened her hands to me. "I'm no criminal, I'm your sister. That crew, on the other hand—"

"The System Office of Finance and Exchange might disagree with your assessment of this crew's character," I said, still attempting to mimic the rhythm of Nova's melodic voice. Before she could say anything else, I produced Nova's proof of our innocence, pinching the corners of the glimmering knitted veil with trembling fingers.

Faint light shimmered over Birke's eyes as her neural implant translated and transmitted the veil's content to her lenses. Tev and I remained silent as Birke watched it loop several times. I hoped the evidence of her role in the Adul massacre became branded onto her retinas.

"Don't bother trying to steal it or destroy it," I said. "I can make as many copies as it takes and you know it."

"You want me to exonerate your friends?"

"That's a given," I said, resisting the urge to clutch at my queasy stomach. "But what I want from you is help for a friend. She's hurt. Dying. Transliminal might be able to save her. If you help her, I'll sign any contract you want. But if you don't, I'm not signing anything, and I'll give this—" I lifted the veil "—to the authorities. You'll be a fugitive on our side of the breach."

Birke folded her arms and regarded me with what seemed like new eyes. Perfect fingernails tipped perfect fingers, not a speck of dirt to be found. "A friend, hm?"

"Yes. Our pilot. There was an accident at the SAG, and she—"

"You mean this one?"

Four enforcers entered the room with Marre and Nova—the real Nova—in wrist binds. I heard myself cry out in Nova's voice, felt the panic crawling up my throat, but the enforcer held me tight. Several patches of translucence rippled over Marre's face and arms, more persistent and frenetic than ever. Her buzzing sounded distant and muted, like color gone gray. Immediately my mind went to the *Tangled Axon*. Had they hurt her? Where were Ovie and Slip?

"Your engineer and medic are fine," Birke said, reading my thoughts. "They're confined to your ship."

Nova looked at me, releasing her hold on my body. Light and matter shifted—skin relaxing, bones shortening with a deep ache—until I was my loc-draped self again, scruffy outfit and all. Now, Birke and I looked almost identical, save for our hairstyles and clothing.

No, I thought, grateful for a fully-functional mind. *We don't just look identical. We are identical. We are each other.*

Birke quietly cleared her throat and smoothed her slacks, then clasped her hands in her lap. Every movement she made in *my* body was sharp and horrible, like blade against bone.

"Clever disguise, but pointless. And you can wave that thing around all you like," she said, gesturing at my hand, the veil hanging limp from my own plump fingers. "I have what I came for."

"You asshole." Tev lunged forward, but one of the enforcers grabbed her. She struggled as she spoke, a hard edge scraping against every word. Her eyes found Marre and lingered on her, helplessly. "Can't you see what's happening to my pilot?"

"Yes, I can." Birke took a few steps toward Marre, heeled footfalls echoing in the empty space along with Tev's hard breaths. My doppelganger watched Marre's shoulder disappear, followed by half of her neck. Velvet-red muscle shifted as Marre breathed.

"I can see you, you know," Birke said to her, eyes following the patterns of her fading flesh. Still watching Marre, she then addressed Nova: "And you can see her too, can't you? Did you tell them what she is? Do they know?"

"Know what?" I said. I looked at Tev, who seemed unsurprised, lips turned downward in frustration. Sweat plastered her bangs to her forehead. She wouldn't look at me, wouldn't respond.

I looked at everyone in turn and raised my voice. "Do we know what? What's she talking about?"

Birke let out a single amused huff as she examined Marre. "Well, it's a good thing we towed your ship into the hangar. This girl wouldn't last ten seconds more than a kilometer away from the thing." She touched Marre's skinless jaw, and a static discharge snapped at her hand. She pulled it back and shook it out, unperturbed. "Give or take."

Fire erupted in Marre's eyes.

"Marre, what's she talking about?" I said. "Tev?"

"Alana . . ." Nova said, sadness in her eyes. Sadness, and guilt.

My voice grew more frantic. "Why am I the only person who's confused here?"

"I'm sorry I didn't tell you before," Tev said, speaking to me but staying targeted on Birke, as if she'd disappear if she didn't keep her eye on her.

"Alana," Nova said again. She folded her hands over each other, looking down at them. "I'm sorry. I knew as soon as I saw her. I didn't tell you."

"What!" I nearly shouted. "What didn't you tell me?"

"Marre is the *Tangled Axon*."

Chapter Twenty-one

Birke rolled her eyes. "Now that's a little on the dramatic side. I wouldn't say she *is* the *Tangled Axon*."

"She's inside it," Nova said. "Bleeding out into the hull."

Understanding crashed into me. Marre's hollow eyes, her frozen age. The power and clarity of my connection to the *Tangled Axon*. The way Marre would follow me through the corridors, watch me work, visit me at night. Her uncanny connection to the ship and its crew.

The truth scored my heart, over and over, until I felt faint with the inevitability of it.

"You're a miracle," Birke said to Marre, lifting a lock of her black hair, careful not to brush finger against skin again. "Spirit bleeding out of one body and being suffused into another. Only there was no human body available to replace yours, so you bled into the nearest thing you could find. Your soul seeped into the metal of that bird out there. Your flesh disappeared with less and less to hold it together. Fascinating."

"Can you help her?" Tev said. "Please."

Birke considered this for a moment. "Yes. I believe I can."

"No!" Nova shouted, jerking her shoulder away from the enforcer who held it. Birke held up a hand to prevent the enforcer from recapturing her, letting her approach Tev. "You can't hear her mind the way I can. She's not going to help Marre, she's—"

"You're not seeing the big picture," Birke said. "I absolutely am going to help her."

"You're lying," Nova spat, eyes wide with terror. "Tev, she wants to use Marre. And me. Oh, spirit, she wants to use us both—"

"What's she talking about?" Tev said.

Nova grabbed Tev's arms. "She wants to take me out of my body and put me in a corpse!"

"That's a little hyperbolic." Birke sighed. "She's not a corpse, she's my sister. My 'Nova.' All her vital organs are essentially functioning in stasis—"

"She's dead," Nova said. "Listen to the way you're talking! Her brain is dead. Her spirit is gone."

Birke walked up to Nova and placed a hand on her cheek. With her back turned to me, I was tempted to attack her, but I knew the enforcers would be on me in a second.

"And yours isn't," Birke said. "You know I can see your heart just as you can see mine. It's what every guide was born to do, so do it: see into my intentions and know I'm telling you the truth. At first I just wanted to find you so I could see some version of my sister again, find some way to convince you to stay with me. But now that I've seen Marre? Oh, stars. So much is possible!"

Tears welled in Nova's eyes and her knees grew weak, but Birke held her up. "I want to help you, help my sister, help Marre. You've wanted to ascend to something greater, serve some greater purpose, your whole life. That much I can see on your face. You've made room for this." She gestured at Nova's frail body.

"My Nova didn't feel the way you do. My sister was vibrant and alive and healthy until the same disease that's ravaging your Alana stole my Nova from me. She wanted to be alive in a way you never have. She loved her body, her flesh. She loved everything about embodiment."

Birke's eyes searched Nova's face, as if she might find the sister she'd lost. In spite of everything, my heart ached for her. I knew that look. I knew what it meant to long for the things I've lost and look for them in living ghosts.

"Nova." The name came out of Birke in a near-gasp as her self-control broke. "Please hear me out. I'll use Marre's energy signature, her condition, to extract your spirit from this body, just as you've always wanted. I'll suffuse my Nova with your light, and Marre's. She'll be born anew. Marre will be free of her timid flesh. You'll be free of yours. And my sister will *live*. There is a place for everyone in this world; no one needs to die. In a way, the three of you will ascend together. You'll all become my sister."

Nova's eyes widened. "That won't be your sister."

"Maybe not in the same way she was before, but it's enough."

Hearing my own voice say these things drove me over the edge. I wanted to grab Birke and shake her and demand to know what had happened to her to make her grow into . . . this. If my Nova had died, surely grief would not have corrupted me into someone like Birke. How could someone who shared my body be so alien? Was it the difference of a single synapse? One twist in the timeline, and this is what I would have been?

"This is murder," Tev whispered. "You're going to murder them, just like you murdered the Adulans."

"I *had* to do that." Urgency continued pushing Birke's voice out of her body in desperate gasps, but then she paused, tugged on her suit jacket to straighten it. She wiped her hand across her desk, removing non-existent dust. "I couldn't risk letting you hurt the Nova from your side. I need her. I would do anything for her."

"Then please don't go through with this," Nova said. "I don't want to live in another body. And do you think Marre wants to be the catalyst in some gruesome transformation?"

"She already is a gruesome transformation."

"Don't say that." I hissed. "If she's gruesome, then we all are, in our own ways. She has a right to live."

Wild passion blazed on Birke's face, devoid of doubt. "That's the point! I'm going to give her that opportunity. She can't stay the way she is. You said it yourselves: she's dying. At least this way, she'll have the chance to be part of something bigger than herself. I do care, and I'm trying to help everyone!"

"Why don't we let Marre speak for herself?" Tev said. "She's standing right here."

Birke smiled, a terrible thing that spread across her face— *my face*—as if melting in the sun. Dread seeped in to my gut. "Yes, let's do that. Tell them, Marre. Tell them what you've already told me."

Marre looked at Tev, and then me. Honey-scent surrounded us, melding with the song of the *Tangled Axon*. Marre's buzzing heartbeat filled me in ways I still couldn't explain. I felt her speaking into the deepest part of me with mute intention: *It will be okay.*

My heart thundered. I almost wanted her to not answer Birke, to never move. If she never spoke, their lives would be like Tev's leg when she was injured on the mining ship: full of potential to be whole or destroyed. If we just didn't look at them, we wouldn't disturb those possibilities. We wouldn't shake one reality into existence, eliminating all others. We could just hold our breaths and live inside that moment, letting endless possibility eddy around us. All that potential would go on and on, and one day the glass leaves outside would fall, shattering around us like stars, but we would persist, frozen in time.

But Marre did speak, deciding which reality would crystallize and which would fall away. She snapped all that possibility into one clean line that pointed inexorably forward.

"I will do it."

"Nova," I said immediately. My sister didn't move her gaze from the floor. "Nova, don't do this."

"Nova," Marre said over me, though her voice was barely above a whisper. "It will be okay."

My sister took my sweat-slick hand and squeezed. "You've always been braver than me. More willing to take risks. I've always looked at you a little like a toddler stumbling toward a glass case, and now I'm doing to you what you've always done to me, running blindly forward while you watch on and pray. There's no joy in scaring you, Alana, but you have to trust me."

I shook my head and felt like I was losing my mind. How could this be happening? "Why are you doing this? Why would you agree to something so horrible?"

"Trust me," she whispered, resting her forehead against mine. Jasmine circled us. Grief cracked open inside me, surging like an ocean swell, so she was right: I prayed to drown it out. Prayed to no one in particular—maybe to Nova. Prayed the way a dying woman does, with pure need and desperation. Those prayers shattered when she drew me into her thin arms and held me. Her warmth radiated out, ported into me—a transfusion of peace that warred with my fear, leaving me as confused as ever.

"Don't take Tev for granted," she whispered. "There's magic in recognizing a kindred spirit, and an even greater power in letting yourself love them. When it scares you, let it—that's your ego letting go."

"I don't understand why you're doing this." I was vaguely aware that, somewhere behind Nova, Birke impatiently shifted her weight. Fear coiled around my heart like a serpent, squeezing the life and breath out of me. How could this be happening? I was about to lose my sister, just as I'd lost my parents. Relentless images of Adul drowned out everything else in my head, all those bands of atmosphere fading into nothing.

"Please don't."

"Trust me. I love you."

"Where will we do it?" Marre said. Invisibility pockmarked her honeycomb tattoo, her cheeks, her bare arms. One of her eyes.

"In the hangar." Birke hurried to us and gestured at the enforcers to follow. She placed hands at the small of Nova's back, my back, ushering us toward the wall. It was all I could do to not recoil under the touch of that woman who was both me and not-me—a me-come-undone. I wanted to put as much distance between us as possible, but I was trapped in this building with her, in this alien universe, where she would unravel the new life I'd found.

Marre didn't wait for Birke. She pointed a finger at the wall, tapped it once. The metal rippled, making a sound like something between a tear and the crack of a whip. She moved through the wall, slick and quiet, and for a moment her body seemed so slight that I was afraid she wouldn't make it to the other side in one piece. I could *feel* her struggle to hold onto herself as she seeped further into the *Tangled Axon*.

But when she stepped through, Marre remained whole. Or as whole as I'd ever seen her, anyway, with patches of skin and hair gone missing, fingernails flickering.

As we joined her, feet stepping onto a slick, flawless quartz floor, I let my eyes chase the albacite walls of the hangar upward. They disappeared into what looked like an endless white nothing, until my eyes adjusted to the brightness enough to see luminous clouds swirling at the hangar's apex. At the center of the hangar was our graceful old ship, the *Tangled Axon*, her engine cycled down completely, her dark, mottled hull more beautiful to me than ever while contrasted against this fake construct of a corporation. In front of her, three examination tables awaited us, topped by transparent casket-like enclosures. Two were empty, and one . . .

Neither the enforcers nor Birke stopped me as I approached the farthest enclosure, cold and afraid of what I'd find, but unable to stop moving.

Pale light illuminated the dead woman's perfect, dark face, her long locs draped over either side of her still body.

My sister.

No—Birke's sister. This version of Nova, who shared her face and body, but had become an engineer instead of a spirit guide, who had loved machines as I had, and suffered and died from Mel's—or some version of it. Most of her was hidden by a sheet, but I could see that she'd been much thicker in life than my Nova. More inclined to hold onto her body, to live in it and nourish it and *feel* its presence. Like me. Had she worked as hard as me to anchor herself to the world? To eat and sweat and work and *live*? Did the Big Quiet know the shape of her desire as intimately as it knew mine?

"Alana." Tev touched my waist, startling me. I looked at her, saw how her expression froze momentarily when she took in the other Nova's locs, her body, her eerily familiar face. Tev's next words came slowly; her eyes never left the dead woman. "We have to go inside the ship."

I grabbed her arms and spoke quietly and quickly. "We can't let them do this. There's got to be some way to get Birke to understand how wrong this is, how . . . " There was no word that could capture the horror of what she wanted to do.

"It's going to be okay."

"Don't give me that." I let go of her. "Don't tell me it's going to be okay when my sister is about to be killed, and what's left of her is going to be shoved into a corpse. How is that okay?"

"She's going to murder my pilot, too. She's turning her into some kind of fucking spirit glue. I have every reason to be furious." She lowered her voice until I could barely hear her. "Which is why we're not going to let her do this. Marre and Nova are shielding our thoughts right now so Birke can't detect our intentions, just like Nova hid the *Axon* through the breach and disguised you on your way to the surface. You and I are going to make sure this spirit transfer doesn't work, even if we have to destroy half the ship to prevent it. We'll cycle up her engines for maximum speed, but keep her anchored. It should give Marre enough power to overload the system."

"What about Marre?" I said. "What about what we came here for?"

"We'll have to find another way—" Her eyes flicked up at something behind me.

"All right, inside the ship," an enforcer said, voice close enough to me that I could feel her breath. She jabbed her weapon into the small of my back. "Go."

I wiped my damp hands against my shirt and let the enforcer herd us toward the *Tangled Axon*'s repaired cargo hold. When we passed my sister, I stopped, grabbed her sweet-smelling, fragile body, and hugged her tightly. She all but disappeared inside my softer frame. "Be safe."

I felt her smile against me, cheek-to-cheek. "You too."

Just then, I noticed Marre holding Tev's hand and watching us, eyes enveloping us like night. Her entire body rippled with translucence. The sight tugged at me: the woman I'd fallen in love with, hand-in-hand with the ship-human who had given me the sky. I opened one arm to Marre and beckoned her forward.

I had so loved the *Tangled Axon*. I'd stumbled upon a found family inside her hull, created a life for myself there. Marre's own red heart beat in time with that of the ship's plasma engine, driven by the same haunting spirit. I wanted to know what had done this to her, where she had met Tev, and what she saw when she looked at me. The possibility that I could lose Marre now, just when I was beginning to understand her, was too awful to believe.

A few moments passed with my arm lingering in the air. Just as I started feeling foolish, Marre disappeared and rematerialized with her arms around me and Nova, scarcely making a sound. Her touch was cold and light, like autumn. I cupped my palm around the back of her head and held her to me, feeling an electric charge between our skins. The *Tangled Axon* embraced me through Marre's fading body. I pressed my face to the top of her head and breathed in her honey scent that mingled with my sister's jasmine.

I heard her voice inside me, layered beneath and above and within the song of the *Axon: You have nothing to fear.*

But I was afraid.

The enforcer nudged me with the barrel of her weapon. "Let's go."

We marched toward the open cargo hold. Tev touched the small of my back as if to remind me that I wasn't alone, while I looked back over my shoulder at Nova and Marre. Each were helped onto the two tables—the vitreous containers now floating above—by Birke and an enforcer, respectively. Marre seemed shockingly small from this distance, with the clear enclosure descending over her pale body.

Before my sister lay down, Birke stopped her and placed her hands on her cheeks. Her lips moved as earnestly as if in prayer. What she said, I'll never know.

Chapter Twenty-two

Walking into the *Tangled Axon* now felt like becoming intimate with Marre. Each step was a step inside part of her. Each time my fingers brushed the ship's bulkheads, I touched some piece of her. Moving deeper into the center of her, the closer I felt to her heart. Now that I knew the truth, it seemed impossible I could have missed it. Every corner, every centimeter of this vessel was Marre; I felt it with every breath. The ship's pain, her song, her voice—they had all been Marre's. This ship was part of her body as much as her own hands or eyes.

We met Slip and Ovie in the mess hall, where the enforcer stood guard by the doorway and we took seats around the table. As I was about to sit next to Tev, she shook her head almost imperceptibly, then flicked her eyes toward the bench on the other side, near the entryway to the corridor that led to engineering. Next to Ovie.

I watched Tev's face as I moved into position, and she barely nodded. Then, slightly tilting her head toward the entryway, she glanced at Ovie and me in turn. It was the corridor leading toward engineering.

She wanted us to find a way to get to the ship's engine.

"Sit down," the enforcer said. "Don't try anything funny."

Slip rolled her eyes and grabbed a nutrient bar. "Oh, we're *hilarious*, can't you tell?"

She glared at Slip from under her black helmet. "Just be quiet."

"Status report," Tev said, voice low as she leaned over the table.

"Our lady is waiting," Ovie growled quietly.

"What are you talking about?" the enforcer said. "Stop it. Sit back, stop leaning over the table."

We each complied. Tev continued staring at me and Ovie, flicking her eyes toward the entryway again.

I reached into my pocket.

"Hey," the enforcer said, stepping toward me. "Hands on the table."

"I have to take my medication."

"Hands on the table."

"Please." I held one hand up, plaintively, while the other pulled out the Dexitek bottle. As I did so, the enforcer rushed me, but I quickly sat it on the table and put my other hand in the air as well. She stopped, surprised to see I was telling the truth.

"See? It's medicine. Please. I'm sick and I have to take it twice a day. Or do you want to have to deal with explaining why I'm passed out under the table from pain? You can even take the pill out for me if you want. But I have to take it."

She let out a sound of frustration, then gestured at the bottle with her weapon. "Hurry up."

"I have to take it with water."

"For spirit's sake—"

"Sorry my illness is so inconvenient for you," I snapped, moving toward the water pump on the other side of the mess hall.

"Stop. You there." The enforcer gestured at Slip, who was closer to the water. "You get it for her."

As Slip stood and turned toward the pump, I reached for my bottle and knocked it over, pretending it was an accident. It rolled off under the table. I muttered something profane and bent down to pick it up, exchanging surreptitious glances with Ovie.

"I'll get it," he said, standing and bending over, wolf-shadow hunting for the Dexitek with me.

"Get up," the enforcer said. "All of you, sit back down—"

While the enforcer's back was to her, Tev quickly stood, leapt up onto the table, and pulled an unopened crate of nutrient bars down off the shelf with an involuntary groan. As the enforcer turned away from us and toward Tev, she aimed her weapon.

Too late. I quickly stood and pressed the three release buttons at the base of her helmet's skull, removing it before she could turn around or understand what was happening. Tev shouted with the effort of lifting the box high enough to bring it down onto the enforcer's head at an angle. At the moment of impact, the enforcer's weapon fired in a plasma arc, barely missing Tev's face, singeing her hair instead.

The enforcer slumped to the ground. Tev plucked the weapon from her hands and got to work tying her up with electrical wire like a burt calf. She stirred a little and made a small sound. Slip pulled an injector out of her pocket, rolled up the enforcer's sleeve, and administered a dose of something.

"A hypnotic," she said. "Should keep her out cold for a while."

"You two, go," Tev said to me and Ovie. "Overload the *Axon*'s engines. Give Marre what she needs to fight back. We'll do our part on the bridge."

I started to leave, but Tev caught my wrist. "Hey. I'm sorry I didn't tell you about Marre."

"That's the last thing I'm concerned about right now." I gently removed her hand from my wrist, then kissed the inside of hers. "I'm sure we'll have a lot to talk about if we make it through this. Don't worry about it."

"Okay." She nodded. "Go. Be safe."

"We have to put her in full cycle," Ovie said as I left the mess hall and ran with him. We hurried through corridors and swung into engineering. His shadow-tail seemed so real to me now that I dodged it when he turned the corner. "I need you to remove the waveguide modulator while I reconfigure the thrusters."

"Removing the modulator could completely overload the engines. Destroy her from the inside out."

"Don't you think I know that? These are Captain Helix's orders, surgeon."

"It's just—"

"You want to be part of a crew?" He gestured at the waveguide system panel with a bundle of wire, black fur running up the length of his arm. "Now's your chance to prove you can take orders."

I looked up at the plasma heart beating above us, illuminating the space with a riot of flickering light. If we did this, the ship's heart would become so engorged and angry it could eat away at the bulkheads. She'd be like a beast gone mad, terrible and wild. How would it affect Marre?

I grabbed the extra toolkit from a wall compartment and got to work uncoupling the waveguide modulator coils from the waveguides. It was tedious, grueling work that coaxed out the symptoms of my disease. Muscles tightened along my neck, turning me into more statue than woman, but I just cracked my neck to release some of the tension and pushed through the pain. I worked to the rhythm of the *Tangled Axon*'s plasma heart crackling above us, and the sounds of Ovie's effort. Metal against metal as his tools made music alongside mine. The sighs and grunts of hard labor. Occasional profanity when his finger slipped or a wire snapped backward, cutting into flesh.

Sweat dripped from my forehead and into the ship's engine—a part of me becoming part of her. Never had my locs felt so heavy and hot, even tied back. Frustration coiled at the base of my neck. What if we didn't get this done in time? What was happening outside the ship?

Don't think about it.

The final modulator coil slipped free of its home and clattered to the floor.

"Here it comes," Ovie muttered, and stood.

Energy pulsed in the center of the *Tangled Axon*'s heart, the white-hot plasma above us rippling with power. Then, it expanded in an instant, exploding outward into the corridors and rocking the ship in a great crash, sending me toppling over backwards before I could grab anything.

Tev's voice boomed over the comm. "Everyone out! Now!"

I scrambled to my feet and followed Ovie out of engineering at a run, occasionally bracing myself. Every crevice of the *Axon* was illuminated with the plasma that bled out of the engine and into the rest of the ship. As we cut through the mess area, Ovie stopped, bent down, and linked the enforcer's limp arms with his, lifting her top half. He tilted his chin at her feet and spoke quickly. "Grab that end."

I picked up her legs and helped him carry her through the corridors toward the cargo bay, falling into bulkheads each time the ship quaked. As the *Tangled Axon* broke free of her restraints and rose in the hangar like an uncaged beast, we jumped out of her mouth and fell where we landed, crashing into equipment and tables and enforcers. The woman we'd carried groaned beneath me, but didn't wake.

Gloved hands grabbed my arms and lifted me up onto weak legs. Birke appeared in my line of vision and waved away the enforcer who held me. She left to help her unconscious comrade.

"What did you do?" she shouted. No matter how many ways Birke tried blocking my view, I kept the ship in my line of sight.

"Answer me!" Finally, she grabbed my chin and squeezed, turning my face toward hers. "What did you do!"

"Gave the *Tangled Axon* room to sing."

A wail of frustration rose out of Birke as she let me go and left to find Nova's containment unit.

Arcs of electricity haloed the *Tangled Axon* in three, four, ten rings of white-hot flame, her discharges multiplying the longer she remained trapped there in full cycle without the modulator to soothe her. I wanted to go to Nova and Marre and release them from their coffins, but I couldn't tear myself away from the spectacle. Wonder and fear warred within me.

My eyes saw the *Axon*, but my mind flickered between reality and flashbacks of the Adul massacre. Wild power burst from the ship's engines, flashing into flame and clouds of spark. Color shimmered in the air between each arc and reflected against the white walls—a storm of ribbons blazing in bright hues. We were awash in light, and it was coming from the *Tangled Axon*—our vessel, our home.

Marre.

Reality itself seemed to thin in the space around the ship. For a breath, silence. Not even the sound of my own heartbeat. The air puckered around the containment units and Birke.

I took a deep breath, hearing nothing.

In an instant, a piercing metallic shriek broke the stillness, and the *Axon*'s engines unleashed her rage into the space around us. Reality folded in upon itself, and then collapsed around us, a singularity of Birke's macabre intentions channeled through Marre. Plasma arcs broke free from the rings around the ship and snaked into the sky, sizzling and popping with white-hot fury. Sparks rained down on us in a firestorm. I could see no one else; there was only me and the ship in a vast sea of white, though I could feel the collective presence of the others around me.

Buzzing, snapping, and popping punctuated the *Tangled Axon*'s screams. Marre's screams. Fear suffocated me for an instant, but then—as a monstrous branch of lightning reached out for me—I glimpsed a vision of Marre's night-black eyes and felt the hum of the ship inside me like a balm.

• • •

White, everywhere.

Pure electrical current consumed me. Cold static charged my flesh, connecting me to every other soul in the hangar in a cacophony of memory and experience and life. Inside that glow, our individualities blurred at the edges, siphoning each other. At the center of everyone, Marre. The *Tangled Axon*.

Together we sizzled, froze, illuminated, and ignited at once, unfurling ourselves into an endless procession of alternate realities, each one with limitless possibility. In one reality, I was Birke, and I wasn't. Elsewhere, I was myself, and I wasn't. There were universes where I was a mother, a murderer, a spirit guide, a grandmother, a child dead at ten. I was a man, a woman, both, neither. I was a thousand, a million different versions of myself, each one true, because no possibility failed to manifest *somewhere* in the folds of existence. Birke, myself—we were just two possible outcomes of an unfathomably complex set of parameters that contribute to a human life.

I knew in that white nothingness (*everythingness*) that everyone else—from Tev to Nova to the enforcers—experienced the same thing, each one gazing into the infinite regress of their own lives.

We were alive and on fire, all of us, glowing from the inside out. I felt Lai, my parents, Nova, me. I felt Birke within me, part of me—one self of many that I could have become. I felt the sorrow of her loss, saw her own sister dead at twenty-eight from their version of Mel's. I watched as Birke's grief crystallized into feral determination just after her Nova had died. I watched her transform from a woman broken by loss, to the warped person I then knew.

Never again. Birke's voice echoed in my thoughts. *I will never lose her again. I will build a new universe where bodies aren't fragile, where the soul is limitless, where medicine is pure magic. And I will tunnel through a thousand realities to find my sister again.*

Her grief resonated with mine. I knew its bitter taste, its

color. I knew how it felt to see the empty space they once occupied. To resent even happy memories for the flaying pain they brought to the surface. I understood then that it was true: given the right set of circumstances, I could have become Birke. Any version of me from any reality could have become her.

My Nova touched my shoulder in the midst of the chaos, and had I found my voice, I would have cried out. No longer trapped inside the containment unit, her body looked more like Marre's than her own, with patches of translucence dappling her empty skin. No blood or bone. Only light, endless light, bursting from her thinning flesh in rays. She held her hand out to me, electricity arcing from her fingertips. Our palms touched, intensifying the current between us.

"It's happening," she said. Her eyes were spheres of blinding white. "I told you we would be okay."

I couldn't speak. Neither could Nova, I realized; her voice echoed in my mind. Wisps of light peeled away from her, and I knew I was witnessing her spirit spiral out of her body. The *Tangled Axon* dissolved her, cell by cell. Blood and muscle vaporized. Bone turned to dust and disintegrated inside the white fire I saw in Nova's eyes. Combusting into pure spirit.

She was dying.

I reached out to her, tears vaporizing before they could touch my cheeks.

Her hands went first. Fingertips, palms, wrists. Plasma arc and flame licked them away, leaving nothing but light and empty space behind. No matter how many times I tried to touch her, I couldn't. Her body just dissolved where my hands met her skin. My heart split open as I watched my sister burn.

Nova smiled with what remained of her face, but the rest of her was everywhere. She was within me, outside me. She had seeped out of herself and become something more.

I'm at peace with my place in this world, Nova thought to me. *Are you?*

A memory nibbled at the edge of my consciousness,

burrowing through me on its way into the present, and somehow I knew it was Nova who gave it to me. A memory of us.

Sunlight poured into our childhood kitchen in Heliodor. We sat at a table near the window, waiting for our mother to come home from a biosynth mission on the outskirts of the system. I laid my head on the metal surface of the table, leaning on my arm. Nova ate a plumberry dipped in caramel and talked about the boys and girls she liked in school. A tree outside our kitchen swayed, sunlight turning its leaves into emerald, its veins into intricate shadow-canals. I knew when my mother looked at those leaves, she saw possibility. Worlds of it—empty, distant planets like bone waiting for flesh. She filled them with green and watched them take their first breaths.

When I looked through the green and into the light beyond, I saw energy waiting to be harnessed. My mind glided over slipstreams of possibility. I saw sun and sky, and beyond it, the black. Silence and stars.

Nova-of-my-memory leaned over me and giggled, breath sweet with fruit. "I say there's two."

"Huh?" I lifted my head, and Nova playfully shoved me with sticky hands.

"You're not listening, are you? Where'd you go? I said there's two reasons to have a soul."

"I don't want to practice for your entrance exams anymore. Can we play?"

"Two reasons," she said, holding up her two index fingers next to each other. "One—" she moved one finger away from me, toward the window. "—is to feel the all world inside you, from *now* to *then* and back again. To breathe the breath of every ancestor, to know where you've been and anchor you to the physical world—to your body and everything it touches."

I grabbed Nova's finger and pretended to bite it. She laughed and shook it out, but didn't break her stride. "The other," she said, moving the other finger toward me, leaf-shadows shivering across her skin, "is so that one day, you can look into the eye of the universe and burn away that which separates us from God."

She paused for dramatic effect, practicing for her oral exam, but she needn't have. Her words sank into me like teeth as she continued. "Burn all the excess away until you've remade the world and there's no difference between matter and soul anymore."

Her eyes were distant, as if she were seeing reality transform right there in our kitchen.

I shrugged and sucked my teeth, looking back out the window. "What does that even mean?"

When she spoke again, her voice was close to my ear, sweet breath wafting like breeze across my neck. "It means one day, it won't matter what you believe in. When the time comes, your soul will leap out of you and give you no choice but to be what you really are."

My mind jerked back to the present, but as the memory faded, so too had Nova.

The *Tangled Axon* still hovered in the hangar, her electrical arcs sizzling and popping around the ship. The rest was silence.

Where was Tev?

The instant I thought of her, I saw her in my mind's eye. Another memory took shape, one that was neither mine nor my sister's, but Tev's.

I saw the girl she had been. Small, but strong. Skin a touch darker than it was now, from a childhood spent in the sun. Freckles dark across her cheekbones and nose—a dense galaxy compared to the light dusting she bore now. Muscles already developed from hard labor. Clothes pale with dust and wear.

She had a way with the burt cattle that bordered on the mystic; her parents had high hopes for her taking over the property. But the sky tugged at her like a promise. Hot wind blew across the Wooleran desert, throwing her bright hair around a smiling, upturned face. Days full of riding and herding could do nothing to shake the Big Quiet from her eyes.

Instantly, the memory shifted like blown sand. A small Heliodoran boy crouched beneath a table, adult legs a dark forest of pants and skin around him. Plastic canines jutted out of his mouth in a caricature of fangs. He held a bird leg between his hands and gnawed on it there on the floor, knocking one of the fake teeth out of his mouth, and when a woman re-crossed her legs near him, she accidentally tapped him with her toe.

Immediately she bent down. "Ovie Porter, get out from under there! I told you to come right back from the bathroom and sit in your chair like a human boy."

Little Ovie growled and bared his plastic fangs. "I'm not a human boy."

"That's enough!" the woman hissed. "You're embarrassing me. Get back on your chair or we're not going camping this weekend."

She sat back up and apologized to the other adults, while Ovie climbed back onto his own empty chair.

In the present, another bolt struck one of the equipment tables, scorching and ripping the metal with a crash. I could barely see anything through the blinding light except vague outlines of human bodies, and the ship like a giant, fiery eye.

"We're alive," Marre whispered inside my head. "It's okay."

A flash, and another memory. A sprawling estate on one of Spin's moons, bathed in spring sunlight. A young woman with long, black hair and a honeycomb tattoo peeking out from beneath a T-shirt that hung off one shoulder. She stood, bare arms outstretched, at the center of an apiary.

Thousands of honeybees swarmed around her in a winged cloud. Her unprotected physical form flickered, a small smile playing on her face. She said nothing, but I knew her memories in the same way that I'd known Birke and Tev and Ovie—I knew her heart and mind, just as she reached up through time and knew mine.

Marre.

Behind her, a Gartik transport ship descended into the open field behind the hives. The vessel's plasma arcs rotated around the engine with aching familiarity. Her name was not yet *Tangled Axon*, but *Chrysalis*, the letters emblazoned along the port rear hull in black script.

Marre's face tightened in concentration, her body still blending in with the swarm. I could feel her mind, her memories, her intentions. Her beekeeper family hovered in the background of her awareness, proud of their spirit guide daughter. Other pieces of her mind floated to the surface: Her forthcoming admission interview for the guild graduate program. Her father's recent acquisition of a ship to ferry their beeswax and honey products to the farthest reaches of the system.

And the ship inspector who approved the sale of the *Chrysalis* with only a cursory glance at engine stability.

The ship landed.

Marre's body flickered as she prepared to temporarily project her consciousness into the swarm, rehearsing for her Spiritual Advisory Guild interview. Advanced degrees in guide work were rare, but manage to impress the SAG, and admission would be guaranteed.

The unstable engine snapped. Marre opened her eyes, but it was too late.

An explosion discharged energy and fire in all directions, killing Marre's father instantly, absorbing her fluid consciousness into the *Chrysalis*, and knocking me back into the present. It happened so fast, I barely had time to process what I'd been shown. All my senses condensed into Marre's grief and rage over losing her father and the life she'd known. All that loss because one person couldn't be bothered to inspect an engine properly.

The omnipresent hum of the vessel collided with the buzzing of Marre's swarm, coalescing into one harmonic note, ringing in my ears. She was inside me—a vast cloud full of *mind* and *thought* and *knowledge.* Palpable intellect pulsed around me, the same intellect that had been leaking into the ship since the day of her accident with the *Chrysalis,* suffusing the ship with all the experience and love and soul that Marre once possessed. It leaked out of her in thin strands, day by day, hollowing her out, until she could no longer leave the ship without suffering. Even her body struggled to hold onto its form in the absence of so much of her vital essence—of that which made Marre herself. It was Marre who fueled the ship's heart, who had breathed life into the *Tangled Axon.* It was Marre who had called for me in my aunt's shipyard, coaxing me into the mouth of the vessel.

Just as I had fallen for Tev, I had fallen for the *Axon* . . . and now I knew, by extension I had fallen for Marre, in a way. It was Marre who I felt humming to me at night. Marre who reached out to me before anyone else, that first night in my quarters. Marre whose bulkheads I brushed with my fingertips when I needed grounding in something familiar and real.

A gust of heat blew outward, buffeting my locs and licking my face with flames like a thousand long fingers reaching out from the heart of the *Tangled Axon.*

All of us, every person—we were spread out before each other, exposed and raw. Our fears and dreams. Our lives. A vast, endless lake of experience spooled out through the aether and threaded us together. Where we emptied out into the universe, countless others from countless realities surged forward to fill us in. Somewhere in the mélange of souls were Nova and Tev and Marre and even Birke, each of them pulsing like a star.

And then, like coming to the end of a song, the mass of souls peeled apart, each distinct entity coiling back into its body.

But not Nova, I thought. *She's gone.*

My heart ached, at once bursting with love and sorrow.

• • •

Perfect silence. Only an occasional buzz and pop dotted the quiet as the *Tangled Axon* continued hovering inside the hangar, thrusters stabilizing her position. Marre stood in the mouth of the ship, channeling the excess electricity through herself. She seemed stronger now. In control.

Tev hurried to me, followed closely by Slip and Ovie. Warm hands cupped my cheeks, tethering me back inside my body.

"Tev," I said, taking her hands from my face, holding them. "She's gone."

"She's changed, love. Not gone."

Ovie placed a furred hand on my shoulder, shadow-ears pressed back against his locs. Slip gave me a sad smile. "We felt her too."

"I know." I reached into my pocket and pulled out Nova's knitted veil, pooling it in my hands like liquid. One last gift.

"What did you do?" Birke said slowly, somewhere behind me. Part of me still felt her echo inside me. In *Axon*'s storm, we had become part of each other, linked. How cruel it was that, out of necessity and momentum, the world threw her back into a body that was alone.

"What did you do?" Birke said again, gathering her wits. The ship continued hovering over us, but Marre had pulled back the plasma, corralling it closer to the engine and thrusters, as normal.

"Where is Nova?" Alarm crept into Birke's voice, her eyes darting around in search of the sister she'd tried to claim. "Where is she?"

I felt the clutch of grief threatening to choke my words. "She's not here, Birke."

Sadness and rage twisted her features, tightened her muscles. Tears welled in her eyes. The one person I needed to hate was the only one who understood my sorrow. How many times had she gone looking for her sister, only to lose her again? How many realities had she breached to find a version of my sister she believed could repair her family, make it whole? My chest ached for all the grief Birke was holding back; I could see it in her posture, her controlled movements. We'd lost my sister. Our sister.

"The *Tangled Axon* let Nova choose what to become," I finally said, unconsciously touching my chest where the lightning—or whatever it was—first pierced my body. I felt bereft of all those other souls that had touched mine, like hanging onto the edge of a dream.

Birke hurried from containment unit to containment unit, searching for Nova, though neither her sister nor mine were there. The only sounds were her heeled footfalls and the *Tangled Axon*'s calmed engine. Even the enforcers remained quiet, watching denial propel Birke back and forth, as if checking each chamber one last time would pull Nova out of the aether. Eventually, she slumped down and leaned against the charred metal. She rubbed her face, as if that's where grief lived and she could be scrubbed clean of its presence if she just tried hard enough.

Pity tugged me forward. I let go of Tev's hands and motioned for the crew to stay where they were, then walked to Birke and sat down next to her. A cramped muscle throbbed along my back, reminding me of the disease I still had to deal with.

Birke didn't look at me, but didn't tell me to leave, either. "Everywhere I go, she dies."

I leaned my head against the unit and looked up at the hangar's strange aurora-ceiling. Like Dr. Shrike's eyes. "My parents died at Adul. Now my sister is gone too."

Birke's breath caught. I didn't look at her. I hated crying in front of people; maybe she did, too. Out of the corner of my eye, I noticed Tev and the others talking to Marre, who disentangled herself from the *Tangled Axon*'s plasma. Her engines slowly powered the rest of the way down. Hitching, quiet sobs shook Birke's shoulders.

"We need you to exonerate us of the massacre," I said. "Come clean about passing guide work and illusions as medicine. We have the recording."

She huffed sardonically, then rubbed her nose. "Guess I'm done on your side of the breach."

I shrugged, thinking about the Transliminal mods on Spin, and the ecstatic transformation I'd experienced there. "Maybe not. People forgive pretty easily when you have something they want."

"Not after Adul."

Anger flared, but I suppressed it.

"Go home," I said. "Find something to live for instead of chasing death."

"I can't. I have to find her."

"Your sister is gone, Birke."

"My name is Alana. Not Birke. I use a pseudonym—"

"Yeah, I know."

"I have to find her."

I turned to her and looked into my own eyes. The same ones I'd had since childhood, staring back at me as if from a mirror. Eyes that had watched her Nova wither and die from my own disease, and then lost her again in countless otherworlds. I wondered how long it would take before she'd tunnel through reality again and look for Nova elsewhere. Nothing I could say now would teach her how to let someone go.

"Contact the authorities from my side," I said, then stood and extended a hand to her. My skin crawled when she took it and I helped her up. No matter what we'd shared, this was still the woman who'd destroyed one of our planets and killed my mother and father. I couldn't touch her without feeling violated.

"Tell them we're innocent," I continued. "Tell them what you did, or we will."

"I'll transmit my report within the hour."

"You know we have proof."

"I'll do it, don't worry. I have nothing left over there."

I lingered a moment longer, taking in the face that would plague me for years to come, when just something would trigger flashbacks of Adul or my sister's ascension. I gave myself that moment to memorize her, then turned around and didn't look back.

Tev and the *Tangled Axon* were waiting. And beyond that, the sky.

Chapter Twenty-three

The space Adul once occupied had been designated a no-fly zone. A vast field of beacons glowed inside a ring of buoys—tokens of communal mourning deposited by mining ships, transports, medical shuttles, private vessels, industrial shippers, and even a few othersiders.

By the time we arrived, Ovie and I had taken the mangled shell of the dead Transliminal tracking device to engineering, where we modified it to add to the memorial. We ripped out the copper nest at its center, leaving only a hull of magnetic mirroring inside. We installed one of our own beacons—a light that erupted from an opening at the top of the device, flickering like candles.

When we finished crafting our tribute to Adul, Ovie wiped his hands and stood. His bones shifted; muscle stretched. Fur sprouted from his skin. Claws clipped the floor where once heavy bootfalls echoed through engineering. Bright, ice-blue eyes stared up at me from a fierce, intelligent face. Wolf-Ovie shook himself off and trotted down the corridor to fetch his captain, leaving a pile of grease-stained clothes behind. No longer trailed by shadows of his true self, he was a canine in earnest when he willed it so. Ovie wasn't a man who was like a wolf, but a wolf who had tried to be a man in a world that wanted him to choose between one or the other.

But he didn't have to, now. The *Tangled Axon* had transformed us all, bringing our true selves to the surface.

I collected his clothes, folded them, and placed them in the nook at the back of engineering next to his box of pliers and rings. Atop the box was the smaller metal container in which we often kept small supplies like rivets, but Ovie's unmistakable handwriting was scrawled across it in silver marker:

Alana.

I picked up the box, opened it, poured its contents into my hand. A chain of linked metal rings pooled in my palm. Small purple niobium rings dotted a chain of aluminum, just long enough to fall at the bottom of my neck when I clasped it on.

My fingertips grazed the metal at my throat, cool to the touch. Joy unfurled in my chest. Nova would have loved it. She always said purple was my best color, and that I never wore enough of it. Grief shuddered through me as I realized she may have been the one to tell Ovie which color to use. She wasn't exactly shy about giving her opinion. Her ghost lingered everywhere, even between the rings of this necklace.

No, not ghost. I laughed through a few tears and gripped the chain, steadying myself. Nova was where she'd always longed to be. She wasn't dead, just . . . elsewhere. I had to believe it. In a reality where Ovie could be both a man and a wolf, where a woman could become a ship, where a person could experience every possible life across an infinite number of realities . . . it had to be possible for my sister to have moved to a higher plane, and for her to live on without flesh to bind her. I felt her in every breath, sensed her in every piece of metal I touched, saw her in all that black, silent creation outside in the Big Quiet. She was everything, as she'd always wanted. Maybe she'd been right about her place in the universe.

Maybe all of us were right, always. We chose who we were to become.

The necklace felt at home against my skin. I wiped my tears and stood, running a thumb over Ovie's handwriting. I may have lost my sister, but she hadn't left me alone. I had gained a family who valued me, trusted me, cherished me as one of their own. A crew who collected broken folks scattered throughout the system and called them sister, brother. People who not only chased their dreams, but became them.

In return for our devotion, Marre and the *Tangled Axon* lifted all our brilliance to the surface and let us be who we really believed we were. Out here, we lived in the flush and ecstasy of being exactly where we were meant to be, unafraid to open the door to our souls to reveal our highest truths.

There is no greater love than that.

"Launch," Tev said, hand pressed to the glass.

Everyone but Marre stood on the observation deck, watching as the *Axon* dropped our modified device into the field of beacons. Just one more firefly glittering in the black, a small thing by which to remember a species we'd barely begun to understand.

More than that, it was my memorial for my parents, for Nova. For all those who had lost something precious in the massacre. It wasn't enough. Nothing would be.

But it was beautiful. All that metal and coil fashioned into a shimmering reliquary in the dark.

We watched as the device became lost in the cloud of lights that grew day by day. In a matter of months, there would be so much glowing debris that the Nulan government would have to quarantine the area to prevent it from drifting and becoming a flying hazard.

Our silent crew stood in silent awe, remembering Adul and the beings she'd cradled in her atmosphere, wondering just how much we'd really lost. What thoughts and dreams the Adulans had that we couldn't translate. What their unique perspective had taught them about our collective place in the universe. We'd never know.

"I've got to get to Gira," Slip said, fingers idly running through the fur on Ovie's back. With her own name cleared, she'd gotten the Giran medical board to hear her out and ultimately reinstate her. In exchange, she offered to head a research and development team working on a cure for Mel's. "With your permission, Captain, we talked about taking the shuttle."

Tev flinched. "Do you really have to go all the way to Gira?"

"Just for a month here and there. I need to work with them on protocol and get the ball rolling."

"Maybe we could use the time to take some shore leave," Tev said.

"Tev." Slip raised her eyebrows, then turned to me and touched my arm. "Go. Be with your aunt."

Thank goodness for Slip's sensitivity.

Tev rubbed her forehead. "Both shuttles are low on fuel—"

I touched Tev's arm. "Please."

She looked at me, ready to argue, but I stared right back at her without relenting, pleading with her with my eyes. "Slip will be fine. She'll be back to us in no time, and she's doing important work. Please. I have to see Lai."

"I know, I want you to see her." Tev exhaled and rubbed a hand over her face, cocking her hip. "Okay, fine. Just bring my medic back to me in one piece, Slip."

Slip patted her arm. "You'll figure out the ladies eventually."

Tev swatted at her, then laughed and kissed her, sending her on her way. The whole thing was still so strange to me, seeing the woman I love kissing someone else, but I forced myself not to look away. This was part of Tev's reality. She loved Slip, and that was enough for me to want to accept their love as part of my life.

What I felt when their lips met surprised me: it wasn't jealousy, but warmth. Joy.

Happiness begets happiness.

As my brain struggled to process what was still so new to me, my heart took the helm, and I found it wasn't so strange after all. Eventually, my brain would catch up with my heart.

Ultimately, there's nothing to understand—love just *is*, in whatever form it takes. Like people.

Slip left Tev standing on the observation deck in a field of stars. I went to her and touched my forehead to hers, imagining all that starlight collecting in her cells, powering that fierce heart I'd fallen in love with so easily. "You look beautiful," I said. "You belong out here."

She pulled back a little and her eyes moved to my neck. Fingertips brushed the metal they found there, then traced a line to the hollow of my throat. "Ovie gave you a necklace, huh? He must think you're one of us now."

I smiled playfully. "Am I?"

"I don't know, love." She took a step closer, her lips brushing mine. "Think you can handle working on a living ship?"

"About as well as you can handle a stowaway."

"Then welcome aboard, surgeon."

I kissed her, finding her body with my hands just as she found mine. A riot of happiness fluttered inside me, almost too much to endure. We barely had any money and little more than a thin thread of hope to cling to, but it didn't matter. Nova's veil was tucked in my back pocket, insurance against Birke changing her mind. And somehow, with Tev wrapped around me like a balm, that was more than enough.

I explored her beautiful mouth, tracing my tongue along her lip, wanting to taste every part of her in slow-motion and savor all I'd found in her. But she then kissed her way across my jaw, my neck, my shoulder, lips trailing with the barest hint of pressure, breath traveling my skin, fracturing my self-control. Every nerve ending burst into flame. Her hands slipped beneath my shirt and pulled me close, palms heating me until I melted against her. As she slid them up and over, peeling my clothes away, I looked at her with bare love, unafraid.

She took my face into her hands and looked back. I felt in the deepest part of me that she could *see* me. She saw who I really was.

Every version of me, scattered across infinite star systems, birthed infinite others with each choice—each moment of love or hate or splendor split into every subsequent possibility, fathomable and unfathomable alike. And it was in *this* reality, with *this* version of me, that I had found the *Tangled Axon* and the people who lived inside her. It was here that I had unsheathed my heart and found Tev, found Marre, found my sister, found a family.

Found myself.

The people I loved were stitched together inside the *Axon*, all of us unraveling at the edges under the friction of a changing world. But we would be okay; we grabbed each other's loose ends, trimmed them, and tied them off, tucked them under. Together, we buffed our lives to a blinding brilliance and suffused the *Tangled Axon* with a will of her own. Together, we were incandescent.

We were *alive*.

Heliodoran dust kicked up in small tornadoes as the *Tangled Axon* landed.

Memories flooded in like past lives. Another version of me had stowed away here, a lifetime ago, on a then-unfamiliar Gartik transport. It was a version of me I barely recognized. A version of me who had yet to know what it means to fly, to break apart and mend, to fall in love, to wipe the grease from her hands and touch the face of God.

Sadness crested inside me, like a wave. My parents would never know this changed version of me. It would be a long time before every fleeting thought of them didn't suffocate me in loss.

Sparks rained down as Tev and I disembarked, the *Axon*'s plasma discharges stinging the yard's dissipator rods above us. Ovie curled up in the mouth of the cargo bay, tail tucked around his body, ears perked forward while he watched us.

Lai shielded her eyes, jogging out to meet us in one of the cheap suits she wore to work at the call center, hair still falling in long locs down her back. Our ship's song electrified the entire block, reverberating off the side of a nearby building and echoing back. In it, I heard Marre's voice. The faint scent of honey surrounded us in wisps.

When Lai saw who we were, she slowed, stopped. Dropped her hand. Disbelief shook her voice.

"Alana?"

I stopped a few steps away, smiling, while Tev lingered a few paces behind to give us space.

My heart swelled. "Auntie Lai."

For a heartbeat, we only stared. Her face looked worn by weeks of anxiety and fear.

"Thank goodness," she breathed, collecting me in her trembling arms. There was so much I wanted to say, so many things I wanted to thank her for, but I couldn't find the words. I just held her, choking on my gratitude, vowing to make everything up to her by showing her the stars.

"I didn't know if I'd ever see you again," she said against my hair. Words spilled out of her in sobs. "I heard about Birke's confession, but they wouldn't tell me where you were—"

"I'm okay," I assured her. "Everything's okay. I'll tell you the whole story, but I want you to meet someone."

As Lai reluctantly let me go, patting my cheek a few times and wiping the tears from her face, Tev joined us. She extended a hand to my aunt, resting the other at the small of my back.

"Tev Helix, captain of the *Tangled Axon*." They shook hands while my aunt gave me a knowing look, all too pleased to see her niece with a beautiful Wooleran starship captain. "Seems I caught a sky surgeon in my cargo hold somewhere along the way. Funny how that happens."

"She's a beautiful Gartik," Lai said. "There's a fire in her."

My heart skipped a beat. "You have no idea."

"So, Ms. Lai." Tev raised her eyebrow, smiling. "I understand you're looking for a job."

The End

Acknowledgements

Thank you to my editor, Paula Guran, for her insightful suggestions that turned this novel into the book it wanted to be. Thank you to the rest of the team at Masque Books for their work on *Ascension* at various stages, including Sean Wallace, Sherin Nicole, Natalie Luhrs, and Neil Clarke. Special thanks goes to Sherin for lending her likeness to Alana on the cover—you're the spitting image of my favorite sky surgeon—and to Scott Grimando for his beautiful artwork.

Thank you to my fantastic agent, Rachel Kory, for believing in the crew of the *Tangled Axon* when she plucked the manuscript out of the slush pile, and for the guidance that helped this book shine. To those who read early drafts of *Ascension* and offered their feedback, I give my heartfelt thanks: Dan Koyanagi, Christina Simon, Shveta Thakrar, Ty Barbary, Pia Van Ravestein, Stephanie Gunn, and Ash Autumn. Your comments were invaluable.

Thank you to my friends and family who lifted me up along the way with their kindness and faith in me, in particular Laura Vasilion, Emily Joy Walker, and of course, my wonderful mother and brother.

Lastly, I must thank three people whose influence on this book can't be overstated. Christina Simon has been my enthusiastic cheerleader for almost two decades, providing light and encouragement when I couldn't see the path ahead.

You are Family and you are in my heart, always. My partner Dan Koyanagi has never failed to believe in me, or to create a space in which I can babble my way through plotting. I love you and wouldn't be the person I am without your support. And finally, my partner Dani Higgins has kept me motivated with hir unwavering love and dedication. Sie lit my entire world on fire when sie came into my life, and in turn, ignited my writing. Calling you "muse" would never suffice; you are so much more than that. You are my firebird, my Companion. I love you beyond measure. The three of you are my found family, and you have transformed my life. I love you, I love you, I love you.

About the Author

Jacqueline Koyanagi was born in Ohio to a Japanese-Southern-American family, eventually moved to Georgia, and earned a degree in anthropology with a minor in religion. Her stories feature queer women of color, folks with disabilities, neuroatypical characters, and diverse relationship styles, because she grew tired of not seeing enough of herself and the people she loves reflected in genre fiction. She now resides in Colorado where she weaves all manner of things, including stories, chainmaille jewelry, and a life with her partners and dog. *Ascension* is her first novel.